IN THE COUNSEL OF THE WICKED

Richard L. Armstrong

LexWorld Universal Thrillers

To My Wife Mary

LexWorld Universal Thrillers
Dallas, Texas

Library of Congress Control Number: 2016912078

ISBN-13: 978-0997039306
ISBN-10: 0997039302

Printed in the United States of America

ACKNOWLEDGMENTS

Writing a book, I've found, is not an easy thing. I wish to thank all those who put up with my absence, whether physical or mental, as I pursued this solitary craft. Thanks most especially to my Mary, who both allowed and supported this.

First, I acknowledge my special thanks to my sister-in-law, Rose Zaccaria, for her tireless, devoted and exacting work of editing my manuscript. This is a thankless job which she happily accepted, while also encouraging my work. To my brother-in-law George Siddons and my sister Terri Siddons, I give my heartfelt thanks for their devoted job of copy-editing and substantive proof-reading under time pressure.

Next, I wish to extend my deep gratitude to my son Christopher Armstrong for his inspiration for the cover design.

Finally, thank you to my many colleagues, friends and clients over the years who have provided the ample material for the story within these pages.

*"Blessed is the man who walks not in
the counsel of the wicked, nor stands in the
way of sinners, nor sits in the seat of scoffers..."*

— THE BIBLE, PSALM 1:1

CHAPTER ONE

It happened, it seemed, at the speed of light. One moment the young woman stood at the crosswalk, watching the traffic signal, her toddler at her side. The next, she was writhing on the concrete gulping for air, hands clutching at her throat in vain. For Bradley Jones, his instinct and Army Rangers training took over. In an instant, he covered the several hundred feet separating them and found himself kneeling over her, staring into the contorted face. All around him he could hear the alarmed voices of the gathering crowd.

"You!" He pointed with authority at a middle-aged woman standing nearby. "Watch this boy for me, will you?" The woman nodded nervously, grabbed the toddler's hand, and led him away from the busy intersection. Jones placed his palm ever-so-gently on the young woman's abdomen, then switched to her chest. Good...she was breathing, albeit with very rapid, shallow gasps. Her heartbeat was fast, too, but strong against the heel of his hand.

"Ma'am, are you epileptic?" whispered Jones in her ear. "N-n-n-o-oh!" came the feeble reply in a course whisper, from between gritted teeth. "Do you need medicine...pills, or anything?"

"Al...r-ready..." she managed to wheeze.

"Already what, Ma'am?" echoed Jones.

"Already....t-took s-s-some."

The woman, still writhing, clutching, motioned with her head in the direction of her hand bag. At this point, Jones was dialing 9-1-1 with his thumb on his cell phone. With his other hand, he rummaged through the lady's bag to see what he could find. In seconds, it grasped a pill bottle, which he extracted and held up to the sun. The bottle read: **"Trial Study Sample: Not for public sale."**

"Ma'am, did you take this...drug?"

She nodded her head up and down furiously, still clutching at her throat.

Suddenly, a blood-chilling shriek pierced the afternoon air. As the milling crowd recoiled at the sound, the woman raised her head and fixed her gaze directly at Jones. The foam now dripping from her mouth and the dime-sized pupils made him catch his breath. Without warning, the woman's head dropped to the concrete with a thud. Her mouth let out a long, tired breath, then transmitted a final shudder the full length of her body. Then, she lay eerily still. On reflex, Jones put his ear to her chest and confirmed his worst fears. He began CPR. Between chest pumps, he fetched a wallet from her purse and found a driver's license. It identified the woman as a Kate Johansson. He then called one of his buddies down at the station house.

"Jim? Jonesy here."

"Hey man, what's goin' on?" Jones paused to push the heel of his hand hard on Kate's sternum.

"I got a lady down on the pavement at the Johnson and Latimer cross walk. You got someone dispatched?"

"Hold on....Yeah, I think the call just came in. Hey, what's wrong with the lady?"

"Well, I think she's gone... drugs or something.' I'll try to bring her back, but hustle, will you? There's something awfully funny about this."

"I'm on it, bro." Jones could already hear the sirens in the distance.

* * * *

Near Oruro, Bolivia, South America

The gnarled, veiny hands of Ol' Farmer ached dully as he continued to rake the solution of leaves and brine back and forth in unending rhythm. He paused a moment to rub the spot where a muscle pain nagged his lower back. The sun beat down without mercy on him this September day, making him grateful for the broad brimmed hat shielding his sweat-soaked forehead. He nudged it upwards an inch so that it exposed a line of course gray hair, and turned his face into the gentle breeze. The rush of air mingled with his fresh sweat, cooling his wrinkle-etched cheeks momentarily before he returned to his work. In the distance, bathed in the azure shadow of the jagged Andes, through squinting eyes, Paulo saw them. Hundreds of laborers busily harvesting the leaves over which Paulo and his companions toiled. He turned and glanced over his shoulder to the southeast, about the length of two soccer fields. There the Factory erupted five stories out of the earth. Paulo wondered fleetingly what went on inside the Factory, what was the end result of his labors.

"You, Old Farmer!" The gruff voice shattered the stillness, making Paulo's heart skip a beat. "Yeah, I'm talking to you. Quit looking at the scenery and get your lazy ass back to work! There's plenty of others 'would like your job." The hulking foreman displayed an ugly whip and an even uglier Uzi carbine hung from his waist.

Paulo hastily returned to a half-stooped position and began raking double-time, face toward the ground. Through his sweat and the pain of his aching back, Paulo knew the foreman was right. Leaving his tiny farm to become a common laborer had not been easy, but it had provided a steady flow of *dinero.* This job was his, and he would let no one take it away from him. Better than working in the tin mines. Still, he couldn't help but wonder what in the world anyone wanted with the leaves of the common Queñua tree...."

Inside the factory, in a cavernous office surrounded by a panoramic view of Queñua groves, sat Jack Harte, the rotund chief executive of Rowalter Enterprises, S.A. His neck taut from the twin emotions of dread and worry, he slowly rubbed thumb and fingers over deep furrows etched above bushy eyebrows. Perspiration had gathered on his forehead and saturated one hand as he cradled the phone on his shoulder and scribbled furiously with his free hand on the pad in front of him. "Fix air conditioning," declared the pad.

"Gary," Harte growled, "I've spoken with every laboratory from Spokane to Tallahassee, and I can't shake out a single one who is set up to do the kind of testing we're going to need to make this fly. I'm sitting on three tons of marketable product down here that will rot—do you hear me—*rot* in the warehouse if we can't get this past the feds in Washington. It's the hottest pharmaceutical phenom since Viagra, and I can't—I *won't*—wait three years for FDA approval!"

"I know," responded a meek voice, "But we've got to have at least one successful clinical trial before I can justify—well, you know—introducing it." There followed an awkward pause, as if the man on the other end was trying to decide how best to deflect Harte's anger. "We've got people working on it around the clock, Mr. Harte, Sir. I've spread a couple of million around this town. 'Been schmoozing congressmen on the right committees, some influential staffers, and even a couple of senators. I've been discreet, of course, you needn't worry about that. With a little luck, we might just be able to bypass the FDA altogether and place this at certain strategic hospitals. You know—to patients who otherwise have no options. I feel like we're close; I really do, Sir."

Harte felt the blood rush to his face, popped a pill in his mouth and slammed a gulp of water after it. "Well, damn it all, see if you can get someone on the Hill to cut us some slack and push this thing through. I don't want to lose $500 million over this!"

After another extended pause came the reply, "I-I'll see what I can do. If you could just give me another couple of days Mr. Harte, please Sir."

"We've covered this several times before, haven't we? You've got twenty-four hours, Gary. Not a minute more. Understood?"

There followed a long silence. "Understood."

With a click the line fell silent. A hint of a smile crossed Harte's lips. He'd made his point. He swiveled his chair around, heaved his ample body upward to a standing position, and strode deliberately to his office window. There, thick eyebrows knitted together in thought, he stared worriedly out over the Andes slopes.

* * * *

First International Plaza, Dallas, Texas

Dane drummed his fingers distractedly on the long burnished mahogany table, then shifted uncomfortably in his seat. He'd been sitting so long, he vaguely wondered if his butt had fallen asleep. His eyes skimmed the room impatiently, flitting across the never-used ash tray, the glistening silver pitcher and glasses, then dwelling momentarily on the handsome display board encased in richly carved red oak. He was light-years away from the here and now, and only ever-so-vaguely aware of the monotone voice emanating from the other end of the room. The stacks of papers and expandable files, the computer projection system, the Mont Blanc pens nestled into starched white shirt pockets, the unmistakable smell of leather, all of them the accoutrements of the upscale metropolitan law firm of which he was a part, impinged but little on his consciousness. Dane was grateful for the skill he'd acquired somewhere between his second and third year of law school at Vanderbilt: that of listening just enough to be able to reply halfway intelligently if spoken to, without ever *really* concentrating on a lecture. This skill had served him very well through graduation: at the top of his class, in fact. It came in very handy in dull partnership planning meetings such as this one, permitting his mind to wander at will to far more interesting topics...such as Susan and the baby.

"I *said*, what's your assessment, Dane?" The words jolted him back to the conference in progress. Jerek Barbour, "Jerry" to his friends, shot him a look from the far end of the conference table to his left. Dane glimpsed the half-smirk on Jerry's face, then felt a line of sweat collect at the top of his forehead.

"I...er...Dane cleared his throat, "...I haven't fully considered the implications of the proposed merger," his mind now groped to remember where the conversation had left off a moment ago, "but the numbers seem sound, and they practice in the same general areas as Salacuse & Lockridge. Perhaps..." Dane fumbled momentarily but camouflaged it well, "a committee should be appointed to meet with their managing partner and explore this further."

"I wholeheartedly agree," replied Jerry, whose eyes swept the table with as if surveying a jury. He then riveted his glance on Dane, mouth curled into a patronizing smile. "And I think it only appropriate that you, as the youngest partner on the firm's

Management Committee, accompany Rob to such a meeting."

"Just what I need," Dane groaned to himself— *"another responsibility with no money to show for it."* He knew that up-and-coming associates and partners-in-waiting were expected to shoulder such chores with a smile. As though an aspiring young partner should be grateful for the opportunity to work *gratis*, sort of a rite of passage to be cheerfully endured before he could amass piles of money and delegate such onerous chores to underlings. Rob Jenkins was Dane's assigned partner and mentor, and Dane his protégé, so he was naturally expected to attend.

"I'll see what I can manage, but it will take a lot of doing with the *Bell* trial coming up. See if you can get Rob to send out feelers and set something up. Have him call Gina with a few dates."

"Fine, fine! You know, Dane, I have a good feeling about this merger. If it's successful, it will double Salacuse's size within twelve months, hold the line on overhead, and not dilute our client base. We would be the largest law firm west of Chicago, and the most profitable." Dane tried valiantly to work up some excitement, but his voice sounded unconvincing even to himself.

"Yeah, I see what you mean. Well, I've got to make a court appearance at 1:30. I'll leave it to y'all to work on details."

* * * *

1:25 P.M.: 195th District Court of Dallas County, Texas

The courthouse lobby was teaming with humanity today, even more than usual for the Tuesday following a three-day weekend. Whites, Blacks, Hispanics, Asians, both men and women: they were all here for their great day of justice: their Day In Court. At least sixty per cent would leave unhappy with the result, Dane mused. Fifty per cent because they lost, and the additional ten percent because even though they won they'd believe the system, their lawyer, or their opponent had cheated them out of a verdict better still than the one they'd received. Dane pushed brusquely through the crowd that huddled uneasily around the elevators, holding his briefcase ahead of him as if were a staff to part the waves. He thrust it between the closing elevator doors and they reversed, permitting him to wriggle through. He might still make it a few minutes ahead of his hearing, with a little luck. All he needed was a couple of minutes to check the court's file to see if Judge Hewett had received his summary judgment brief. But receiving wasn't reading. Dane didn't delude himself: few state court trial judges had the time, even if they had the inclination, to read briefs prior to their hearings. But he hoped to win this legal skirmish handily with the polished, concise argument that had become his trademark. Quickly, he rehearsed the strongest points in his mind, tying each to its own supporting facts as the floors ticked by. Six floors, six arguments. The elevator display flashed a green digital "6", jolting him as it lurched to an uneasy stop. He squeezed out, wondering as he did so whether Jewel, his law clerk, had attached a copy of the case the Supreme Court handed down just last Thursday—the one he believed would cinch the Court's ruling.

"Dane—Dane, is that you?"   A familiar, yet unknown voice caught him off guard.

"Yes, but who—" Dane whirled around in the melee, and found his face inches away from that of an attractive young woman. "Jenny Pemberton! How long has it been, ten...fifteen years?"

'Try seventeen, silly. You never were that good with numbers–guess that's why you went into law, huh?" Jenny's smile lit up the area.

"Tell me about it," retorted Dane, his mind flashing back to the inquisitive, attractive girl from his senior year at Madison High. "It's been a long time, Jenny. Whatcha' been up to?"

"Lots, actually. I'm working as a legal assistant with Hutchison Davis. I've been there now about six months, and they've assigned me to the litigation section. 'Suits me just fine...I think I'm going to like it. You?"

"Just the typical mix of big cases and big firm politics–not half as much glamour as you'd expect." Dane, in spite of himself, found himself strangely attracted to this girl whom he hadn't dated since his youth. Jenny's perfume heightened his awareness of this, with just a suggestion of some luscious scent— not the overpowering "I-bathed-in-it" smell characteristic of so many women. She sported a few wrinkles at the corners of her eyes, but otherwise seemed liked the years had treated her kindly. "'Sounds like you landed with a good firm and a better position," then, glancing suddenly at his watch Dane reluctantly added, "Say, Jen, I gotta' run to a hearing. 'Guess I'll see you around this place again?"

"You can count on it—I'm here lots." She smiled over her shoulder, then turned to dash into an elevator, long hair flying.

Dane vanished in the next instant behind the burnished oak door that separated the corridor from the 195th District courtroom. The massive door buffered the din from the courthouse traffic, as Dane's lanky frame strode to the front of the courtroom. A hearing was already in progress, with a battery of attorneys on each side. Grateful for the respite, Dane sat immediately behind the bar in the first row. He propped his attaché on his lap, extracted the Grundy file and a yellow pad, and waited.

CHAPTER TWO

Susan glanced at her nails, blew, held them up to the light, then blew again. Jackie would be getting off the school bus in a few minutes, and a few minutes later bursting through the front door. She gratefully seized the opportunity to pretty herself up as much as a woman eight and a half months pregnant can. Susan had thought that she was fairly secure in the self-esteem category, and had come through her last pregnancy unscathed and feeling good about her looks. This time it seemed different, though. She became nauseous more easily, put on weight with merciless ease and speed, and she had a certain uneasiness about the baby. It didn't move inside of her the way Jackie had. Granted, Jackie was a dynamo of compressed energy, even considering his age, but with this pregnancy whole days would sometimes go by without the baby moving. Susan made a conscious effort to dismiss her worries as groundless, telling herself that this was going to be the little girl Dane and she had waited for.

In no time, it seemed, Jackie sauntered into the living room, threw his books down and made for the refrigerator. "Mom," he managed between chomps, "Me and Jason wanna know if we can shoot some hoops down at Olsen Park. Okay?"

"Have you forgotten so soon, Jackie? I'm scheduled for my last visit to the doctor today, and you're coming along. You know I don't have a babysitter."

"Ah, shoot!" Jackie moaned, "I hope it doesn't take as long as last time. Suddenly he perked up. Are we going to listen to his—I mean her—heart again?" Jackie's eyes were bright and curious.

"Maybe," she answered, and we *still* don't know whether it's a he or a she. Maybe we'll find out today."

Jackie scrambled to find his basketball, and once he did, stuck it up his shirt. They proceeded to the car, backed out of the garage, and drove East on Latimer to the East Dallas Medical Center. As she drove, Susan again fought back the nagging uneasiness. She had not felt movement in two days. As she turned right from Cooper Drive into the Obstetrics Building parking lot, her confidence momentarily returned. She left the Jaguar convertible and walked toward the west entrance with Jackie dribbling the basketball behind her, counting aloud with each bounce.

First International Building, Dallas, Texas

Dane strode quickly down the hallway past the secretary cubicles, each with its own cache of laser printer, computer station and assorted stack of files. The hearing had gone very well, despite the judge's gruff demeanor throughout. Success had been his, Dane mused contentedly, because of his last-minute attention to detail. He trusted no one with the actual research–even his most accomplished legal assistant, who was well acquainted with his idiosyncrasies. That distrust, coupled with his acquired knack for crawling inside the judge's mind and anticipating his slant on the case, had achieved a very respectable winning record for Dane. Dane smiled wryly. Of course, there are no real-world Perry Masons, no Leland McKenzies, and there never were. It was tough enough winning a majority of your cases without having to fight the ridiculous public expectation–fostered by just such TV legends–that a "good" lawyer never, or very seldom, loses. You take your cases as you find them: warts, wrinkles and all–and if the facts are bad, well, you can't make a silk purse out of a sow's ear. *"Such is the eternal consolation of the trial lawyer who does his best, yet comes up short,"* Dane mused, half aloud.

He turned the corner, narrowly avoided running into a newly hired summer associate carrying a cup of coffee, and made it to his office. As a "senior" associate in a firm of over 200 attorneys, Dane enjoyed a spacious, if not opulent, office on the 43rd floor. From the south side of the building, he had a panoramic view of all of downtown Dallas, and could even catch a glimpse of some buildings in Arlington, home of the Texas Rangers. It would be at least 6 months, a year at worst, before he could hope for a corner office which came only with the coveted position of partner. He flung his overstuffed briefcase onto the leather side chair and sank into his large swivel, tufted executive chair behind the desk. Dane, still a young man, relaxed his six-foot three-inch frame by stretching his lanky legs to their full length underneath his desk. He let his blonde head go limp on his neck, rotating it three times, then sat upright. His blue-grey eyes were set close together, and gave off a misleading sleepy appearance. Nothing could be farther from the truth, however, and many an opponent had been lulled into a false sense of security by Dane's easy-going persona. Once that happened and the attorney's guard was down he would, with calm, surgical precision, slit his legal throat, resuming his seat at the counsel table. By the time his adversary realized the extent of the damage inflicted on his case, it was too late to do anything but to numbly admire Dane's prowess.

There were a few wrinkles on Dane's face—a couple of lines across his forehead and the bare beginnings of some on either side of his mouth from his ready and often-used grin. Though tall, Dane was not particularly large. Always the skinny kid, he had played basketball throughout high school. His body metabolism was such that he could eat often without gaining too much weight. As he sank into his chair, he frowned disapprovingly at his midsection, making a mental note to get back to the health club for his three-a-week work out.

Dane's gaze swept appreciatively around his office. He'd talked his decorator out of the bold, simple lines of the new contemporary look in office design. He preferred the muted tones of leather and fine woods, because of the more sobering tone they set for his clients. "Easier to quote fees in this environment," he mused, approvingly. Besides, with lawyer advertising cheapening the profession's image these days, he had a responsibility to take the high road, to hold onto some dignity. A stack of memos—he still preferred them printed—was piled neatly in the middle of his desk, and his voice message light was flashing. He decided to tackle the memos first.

He sorted through, making mental notes of what was most important, laying aside the others. Deposition, deposition, reschedule conference, meeting, and—his eyes suddenly halted. Gina had printed an email regarding a call from an old classmate and colleague. He hadn't seen Craig Johnson in quite some time, but whenever they spoke, something positive always seemed to come of it. Not infrequently it turned out to be a decent client referral. He picked up the phone and punched the buttons rapidly with his first two fingers. After a minute, he heard a familiar south Texas drawl.

"Dane Ingersoll! Well now, you returned my call in under 24 hours this time! That's gotta be a record for one of you big-firm-blue-bloods." Accustomed to this sort of coarse joshing from Craig, Dane played along.

"Tell me about it, you lazy side-winding ambulance chaser. If you were ever in your office for more than five minutes, I might stand half a chance of getting ahold of you. How'd you come out in that federal narcotics case?"

"Not bad. They dropped all charges on one fellow, another plead to 15 when he shoulda' gotten 50, and the third was acquitted. How 'bout them apples? But, forget about me. Have you got room for another case?"

"Oh, I think I might manage to squeeze one in. Whatcha got?"

"This one is just a bit unusual, not exactly up my alley, Dane."

"Well, let's have a listen, Craig."

"All right then. It seems there's this client corporation that wants a good liaison with the FDA in Washington. They deal in pharmaceuticals, exporting from South America, and have a decent developing market in Latin America. I gather they're pretty big, but they're not too street smart with the regulatory procedures here—you know, independent lab testing of new drugs, keeping the approval process moving, and so forth. I thought I remembered you doing something on an FDA approval case a couple years ago..."

"That would be the Szeroka matter. We wound up in federal court over that little deal, but eventually got it approved and released for market."

"Yeah...yeah, that's the one," Craig went on. "I gave them your name, and they should be contacting you by tomorrow. They seemed pretty hot to trot."

"Fees any problem?" queried Dane.

"Don't seem to be, but I'd get my money in good old American greenbacks if I were you—you know that devalued currency down there."

"Duly noted," said Dane appreciatively. His intercom broke in. The voice of Gina, his secretary, calling through, announced that Susan was holding on line 3. "Craig, I gotta take this call. But it sounds like something we could handle, and I'll update you when I hear from them. Let's grab some golf next week."

"You're on, fella. But you'd better practice that sorry drive off of the 10th tee."

"I'll be ready," Dane smirked. He switched lines without hanging up. "Hi, Susan. How you feeling today, Sweetheart?"

"Actually, pretty good, compared to last week," she replied. Then, somewhat more somberly, "The baby still hasn't moved, but the doctor says not to worry—the heartbeat's strong and the sonogram is normal. 'Guess I'm just over jittery."

"See–I told you the doctor would set things straight," Dane chided. "The baby is perfectly healthy, it's just that every baby's activity level is different."

"Did everything turn out to your liking in court?" she asked, mumbling something at Jackie.

"Absolutely," he said with more than a trace of self-satisfaction, "I gottem' dead to rights."

"'Atta boy, Tiger."

"Thanks, maybe the *real* tiger can show his stripes again once this little critter is born."

"I'll be waiting," teased Susan.

Dane hung up, musing on just how much he loved this little cheerleader-turned-mom that he had married. Abruptly, he decided lunch was in order. After that, he could give a little more attention to the merger proposed in the firm meeting this morning. With a little luck, he could pawn off some of the number crunching on a first-year associate, then get down to billing some hours before his afternoon gym workout. He ambled next door to see if Dwight Hector in the probate section was ready to grab something in the downtown restaurant district. He was, and off they went.

Food and Drug Administration, Washington, D.C.

The shabby little office was tucked away unpretentiously off of the elevator vestibule on the seventh floor. The F.D.A., primary occupant of the building, made incredibly far-reaching and powerful decisions from this unimposing edifice, decisions which the average American citizen was relatively powerless to change. The NDA receiving office on the seventh floor was modestly appointed, and performed a function roughly analogous to the function of an air traffic controller. All of the tens of thousands of New Drug Applications—or NDA's—received every year in this very office began their long trek through the seemingly endless bureaucratic maze known as the Food and Drug Administration. Here, all of the crazy, and all the legitimate applications for as-yet-unmarketed drugs, could be found in file after ponderous file. The typical application contained more than 100,000 pages. By law, the FDA was required to review each application within six months of receipt. In practice, however, this rarely ever happened, with the average application taking up to thirty months for approval. Here too, government clerks like Timothy Mire spent many hours each day on the phone, attempting to explain complex government regulations to both the intelligent and the sub-intelligent. Surrounded by stacks of documents, Tim focused for the moment on an application before him. It bore the stamped words "CLINICAL TRIAL III: SUSPENSION" in faded government-issue red ink. Paper clipped to the upper left-hand corner was a phone message slip depicting the name "Gary Thompson," with the notation, "Call Collect." Tim dialed the numbers and heard the telephone ring. The operator obligingly put him through, whereupon a man with a high, tense sounding voice answered.

"Timothy Mire, FDA, returning your call."

"Yes, yes Mr. Mire...uhm...I've certainly been awaiting your call. I'm Gary Thompson, for Rowalter Enterprises. I understand you are waiting for that supplemental clinical trial report, prior to giving us preliminary approval to market."

"That is correct, sir."

"Listen, uh, I'm sure there is some flexibility to that clinical trials requirement—you know, for those who have work-in-progress, and are holding product for shipment...(*long pause*)...isn't there?"

"I'm afraid not, sir. The federal regulations are quite clear: we must have full reports on all three phases of clinical trials to accept your New Drug Application. "And," he droned on, "your Phase III Clinical Trial Report does not meet the federal criteria."

"*This guy cannot be for real*," thought Gary. He had heard about bureaucrats like this, but never met up with one, especially one that rivaled a mainframe computer for personality. "Lookit, isn't there someone I can talk to, some extra money I can pay, to get this attended to? We have a lot riding on this." Gary knew the answer before he even heard it.

"I'm sorry, but regulations are regulations, sir..." The voice trailed off into a robotic drone that evoked in Gary's mind images of dank government libraries and army green government file cabinets.

Gary hung up with Mire in mid-sentence, suddenly enveloped in a mixture of fury at the bureaucracy and frustration at his own helplessness. He was unaccustomed to feeling powerless, and didn't like it at all. He sorted through how he was going to break this to Mr. Harte.

As he pondered the situation some more, his eyes darted nervously around the room in which he was seated. The jagged tips of the starkly beautiful Rocky Mountains through his window momentarily eased his sense of ennui, but only momentarily. He pensively mused on the antlers of the 10-point buck jutting out from the wall over the fireplace opposite him, as his mind whirred like a computer through the myriad of laboratories he had contacted over the last several weeks: first in Denver, then in Philadelphia. And the universities: Berkeley, Cornell...you name it, and he had dealt with them. It was difficult enough to get them to act on such short notice. But the real kicker was that all of them were reporting essentially the same thing: significant traces of an as-yet-unidentified substance in the sample vials of drug Rowalter had provided them. The beginnings of what would become blinding migraine began to ripple through his scalp, moving toward his temples. As he reached up to rub them, he lowered his head and his eyes fell on a scrap of paper sticking out of his portfolio. It said simply "Dane Ingersoll, (214) 555-9871." Through his pain, he groped for the phone.

CHAPTER THREE

Blip...blip...blip...Susan's eyes flitted sporadically from the screen of the odd-looking machine across the room, to her abdomen, where two wires dangled, and back to the screen again. Jackie was sitting in the other room, reading car magazines with a friend. Thank heaven for Jeanine, who had responded cheerfully when Susan called. It had been so unexpected–yet, somehow, in the depths of her female spirit, she had known. The doctor had run the monitor over the usual places, felt her tummy as always, making the usual sounds of approval. Then, like a cloud that obscures the sun at midday, his expression changed. At first, a look of confusion, then of worry stared back at her as she lay upon the examining table. "Just a routine check on the fetal heart monitor," he had said. "Nothing to worry about." But Susan was not fooled. Something was wrong and she knew it. She felt it inside of her. She'd faintly heard the doctor mutter "...irregular heartbeat" to a resident in the next room. He'd had her transferred to a bed in the adjacent hospital, smeared clear jelly on her huge abdomen, and taped on some electrodes. Now she studied the strip of graph paper slowly inching its way out of the machine, recording squiggly lines that looked like the Dow Jones ticker as it went. She wondered what it meant, and fought down her fear mightily. She would not call Dane, not yet. She wanted to be sure this time, so he couldn't pooh-pooh her feelings.

Doctor Weinberger reentered the room and picked up the five-foot length of paper, examining it. He peered up over the rim of his glasses, and said tersely, "Susan, I think we're going to have to take the baby."

Susan felt her heart skip a beat, as she stammered out, "Wh-wh-y? through dry lips.

"We're getting late decelerations on the fetal monitor. That means the baby could be in some distress, and your blood pressure is quite a bit higher than normal. I'd like to run an OCT."

"What will that tell you?" Susan willed her mouth to move

"Essentially," he explained, "it will put the baby through some false contractions to see how it does, and we'll be watching it very closely on the fetal heart monitor. We should know pretty conclusively by then." That all sounded very well and scientific, but it did nothing to assuage Susan's growing sense of alarm. What was going on inside of her? Why were things not the way they were supposed to be, the way they had been with Jackie? She studied the doctor's face with laser-like intensity, looking for even subtle signs of concern. *How, and when, would she know her baby was all right?* She asked the nurse wheeling her into the next room if she would take a message to Jeanine. It was, simply, "Call Dane and tell him I'm here." She decided against telling him anything more, until there was more to tell.

The intercom buzzed in Dane's office. He had just picked up a line from someone in Colorado when Gina sang out, "Somebody named Jeanine on line two." "What could she be calling for...," he muttered, instructing Gina to take a message on the Colorado call. He took the call on the speaker, "Yes, Jeanine, how's the neighborhood today!"

"Fine, so far as I know, but your wife's not so good. 'Sounds like the baby may come early, unless something changes."

"What are you talking about?" he half chuckled. "Susan just went in for a routine exam today. What could possibly have happened since this morning?"

"I'll tell you what's happened," she said, seeming irritated at Dane's nonchalance. "The baby might be in distress, and the doctor is doing some testing on her. She sounds pretty worried, Dane."

"Is she okay otherwise?" he asked, his tone suddenly more somber.

"Seems to be, but she needs you. I've arranged to take Jackie home with me and Bill and I will keep him as long as you need us to."

"Thanks, Jeanine, you're a champ. I'll be there in thirty minutes." Dane was through the door within seconds, yelling to Gina to hold his calls on the way.

"Tell Scott I won't be able to make our meeting this afternoon–can he reschedule?" Gina nodded her acknowledgment, and alerted the receptionist to Dane's absence as he lunged into the elevator.

* * * *

Another wave of pain hit Susan's stomach as she stifled a groan. A nurse who looked to be in her early fifties and grossly overweight had been stimulating her breasts manually, apparently in an attempt to induce labor. Although the pain was tough to bear, Susan managed to keep an eye on the fetal monitor strip to the right of her bed. Though she had no idea what she was looking for, or how to interpret what she saw, it gave her something to do, to occupy her thoughts, until Dane arrived. Jeanine had not been allowed to stay with her, and she wondered how Jackie was doing. In the space next to hers, separated from her movable bed by only a curtain, some young girl–or so she sounded–was talking with two or three people excitedly about her sonogram. The doctors had just identified her as-yet-unborn baby as a boy, and she was effusively chattering away. Susan was at once angry and jealous. Why her? All of her family members for three generations had been in perfect health. Was her baby's number up? Not a superstitious person, she was bright enough to know that such favorable odds don't continue unchanged forever. She quickly chased the thought from her mind, and was helped along by Dane virtually bursting through the door, and striding into her room.

"Hey, peaches," he feigned cheerfulness, "What gives?" Susan melted into tears instantly.

"I d-dunno," she stammered. The first crack was beginning to appear in Dane's facade of denial. He summoned his courage and managed a half-smile. The doctor appeared in the hallway outside the door, and Dane saw him. "Be right back," Dane muttered, walking backward, casting a glance over his left shoulder. He winked, smiling, "Don't go anywhere."

Alone with the doctor in the bustling hallway, Dane plied him with question upon question. Blood pressure: hers–high and rising, baby's–normal, but vacillating. Contractions: weak to normal, but baby not descending into the canal. Heartbeat: hers–normal, baby's–slowing down dangerously after each contraction. The test they were running should tell them something within two hours. TWO HOURS! Dane left the doctor, nervously reentered Susan's room, and as his eyes briefly flitted over the fetal heart monitor, sank into the chair at her bedside and groped for her hand.

* * * *

The man heard the phone ring crisply four times. From over a thousand miles away he heard a pause, then an inhumanly pleasant female voice intone, "Your call has been forwarded to the automated voice messaging system for Salacuse & Lockridge..." [*Pause, then in a male voice*:] "Dane Ingersoll" [*another pause, then the female voice resumed*] "is not in. If you wish to leave a voice mail message, press one; if you wish to speak with an operator, press two." The man's finger gingerly, impatiently stabbed the "1." "Hi...I'm Dane Ingersoll, and I'm sorry I'm unavailable. Leave your message and I should be back later this afternoon or in the morning." *B-e-e-p.*

"Mr. Ingersoll, I have an urgent need to speak with you concerning a pressing legal matter with the Food and Drug Administration. Please call me, collect, at (301) 555-9287. I must hear from you soon." He dropped the receiver roughly into the cradle, slammed his briefcase shut, and headed for the door. Gary Thompson was the genuine article: unpretentious, no-nonsense, strictly business. At age 43, he worked 20-hour days, six days a week, had two divorces behind him, and child support payments that rivaled the monthly payment on the high-priced condo he owned in upper Manhattan, NYC. His normally placid demeanor disguised a meteoric temper. Hypertension had landed him in the hospital briefly two years ago, after which his doctor practically arm wrestled him into cutting back to a mere 50 hours a week, and taking a vacation. That lasted all of two weeks, during which he had begun fuming and pacing like a caged tiger. In no time, he was back to the only thing he knew how to do: work. He slid into the charcoal gray Jaguar parked in front of the cabin. The cabin was Rowalter's, not his, and despite its breathtaking surroundings an hour northwest of Colorado Springs, he personally would have preferred Denver. Thompson was not a man given to solitude. Turning the ignition key, he grabbed and downed the coffee remaining in the cup in the shift console, clicked on the cellular, and entered the 2-key code which would forward phone calls that were placed to the cabin's landline, to the car. He pulled the car onto the gravel road, bearing east toward State Highway 18 heading toward Colorado Springs. He had an appointment with a sizeable laboratory to make by 1:30—the last on his list. With this one, he had a little different business than the others he had dealt with. Rowalter owned a 50% interest in this lab—enough to have a substantial impact on its business, but not "independent" enough to satisfy the nerds at the FDA. That's okay, he mused grimly, the right side of his mouth curling in the mere hint of a smile, they'll get theirs. He had a healthy bonus riding on this project going through, and nothing was going to spoil it. He made a sharp turn left onto the state highway, brought the powerful engine to 70 in seven seconds, set the cruise control, and set his satellite radio to Mozart. Classical music was his sole concession to relaxation. If he could just get this stuff to market and into the distribution chain before the other pharmaceutical giants who were on the same trail like bloodhounds, he could be $200,000.00 richer by next Christmas. Nice stocking stuffer.

The laboratory was invisible from the highway. About a quarter mile after the Air Force Academy exit was a barely noticeable dirt road, flanked by what looked like tumbleweeds clustered together. If you didn't know the road was there, you'd have already passed it before you realized it. The Jag swung deftly onto the road, fishtailing on the gravel, then righting itself as the rear wheels filled the air with billows of dust. He quickly brought the car to 45—he dared not go faster on the gravel—and in a few minutes dipped below the horizon of visibility from the highway as the road entered a steep downgrade. A couple of quick turns and he was there. He was not unexpected. Pulling around the rear of the stucco-clad building, he eased the dust-blanketed car under an overhead door which lurched open immediately at his approach. His eyes scanned the TV cameras protruding from ceilings and walls, then returned to the blackness which now enveloped him. He fought to adjust to the sudden complete darkness, which yielded to fluorescent lights in a few moments. He found a marked parking space and steered the Jag into it. Getting out, he strode briskly to a metal door with a thick, deeply recessed window. He placed his right hand on a glass plate to the immediate right of the door handle. A second later, he heard the latch click, and he swung the door open. He entered, suddenly aware of the overwhelmingly dank smell that had always characterized the place, but which he had never grown accustomed to. He was in a small room which led into a long narrow hallway. On the wall to his left was a speaker with a button. He punched the button sharply and barked, "Holloway, it's Gary." The speaker crackled back. Then, faintly, he heard "I know, I saw you on the monitor. I'm in 2-Z." The door at the end of the hallway disappeared into the wall as he approached, revealing an elevator behind. Gary punched in the appropriate floor. When he arrived, he turned right, went down a hallway, turned left, and halted at a room marked simply "2-Z". He pushed back the door to reveal the white-haired Dr. Holloway. Holloway's eyebrows nearly met in the center of his creased forehead, in a look of intense puzzlement. Flanked by two young male lab assistants, he hovered over the controls of some indiscernible electronic gadgetry, which might just as well have been NASA Mission Control, for all Gary knew.

"You got what I came for?" asked Thompson.

"Should be ready any minute now," muttered Holloway distractedly.

"It *should* have been ready six *months* ago," commented Thompson with ill-concealed sarcasm. "We've got money we can't lay our hands on—more money than you've ever seen—because we're waiting on *you*." In his trademark professorial manner (in fact, he had been dubbed "the Prof" by Thompson), Holloway proclaimed flatly, "You can't hurry science; this is a process that's never been attempted before." As the lab techs scurried over to some apparent measuring device at the opposite end of the room, Holloway's eyes scrolled through lines of data on a computer run sheet attached to his clip board. Suddenly, the Prof seemed to locate what he'd been searching for, and he emitted a satisfied grunt. "We have successfully completed the initial test trials. Whether or not you can get FDA approval is another story, but we have met your company's production standard, and the first batch is ready for them."

"Hallelujah!" shot back Thompson. "When will it be bulk-packaged and ready to pick up?"

"I would estimate by tomorrow at, say, 10:00 a.m."

"We'll have a truck here. Just make sure it doesn't waste the trip," he barked.

The Prof chose to ignore the remark from this insolent Rowalter flunky, and returned silently to his work.

CHAPTER FOUR

The room was deafeningly quiet in the grey half-light of predawn. The window opening onto the hospital courtyard belonged to the waiting area for the obstetrics unit, where Susan had been located before the complications had set in. Dane's right arm had fallen asleep under his head, and now prickled assertively as he stirred from his head-cocked position on the couch across from the coffee station reserved for expectant fathers. The charge nurse for obstetrics had finally banished him from the floor when the decision had been made to "take the baby" by emergency Caesarian section. When the last test showed the baby going into distress for the second time, a team of precision-trained doctors and nurses, led by Dr. Weinberger, had swiftly sprung into action. Dane had been somewhat lost in the midst of it all, and had developed a neck ache, the chief effect of which had been to render him terse, gruff, and a general pain-in-the-neck himself. He had silently wondered if the staff knew he was a lawyer, or, even worse, a trial lawyer. He decided they must, and, being unwilling to subject them to needless fear of a malpractice suit, had reluctantly acquiesced to leaving the area. After all, he had reasoned, did he want someone tending his wife and child who was more concerned about being the target of a law suit than about their well-being? If the roles were reversed, what would he be thinking about? "Enough said," he'd muttered to himself, as he took the elevator down to where he now lay awkwardly, in a rumpled heap. Sleep eluded him, as he drifted suspended in a half-conscious stupor. A blurred glance at his watch told him it was 5:10 a.m., and his heart lurched as he realized he had been here about two hours.

Rousing himself, Dane stumbled into the hallway just in time to nearly collide with Nurse Robbins, the RN assisting the surgical team.

"Excuse me, Mr. Ingersoll. The doctor would like to see you upstairs." Her matter-of-fact tone sounded a bit ominous to Dane.

"I-i-s everything all right?" he stammered uncharacteristically.

"You'll have to talk to Dr. Weinberger," she said, professionally. They entered the elevator around the corner, passing the infants' nursery on the way. The twenty second ride seemed like as many days, and the elevator stopped abruptly at the seventh floor. The doctor met them in the hallway before they reached the conference room. One look at his face told Dane instantly that something was gravely, gut-wrenchingly wrong. The doctor's face bespoke struggle, and more than a hint of fear.

"Mr. Ingersoll, he said without sitting. I have some bad news." *"Out with it!"* Dane erupted inwardly. Only society-imposed inhibitions restrained him from pinning the doctor to the wall and screaming at him, *"What is it, Doctor? What have you screwed up, and how bad??"*

"Mr. Ingersoll, the baby–a girl–appears healthy, but seems to have several, rather severe problems..." *"Severe?"....."Rather?"*...Dane's eyes stared straight ahead as his brain rapidly probed the possibilities.

"Of course, we can't know yet, but she may have severe brain damage, and possibly heart problems as well." ***"Severe brain damage!** You damned quack! You stinking excuse for a doctor...!"* Dane felt certain his heart had stopped beating within his chest. He felt an indefinable mixture of relief over Susan being okay, and sickness at his stomach about the baby—Natalie, they had decided, if it was a girl.

"She will have to stay at the hospital on a respirator for up to a month for us to observe her more closely and conduct some tests."

"What s-sort of tests, Doc?" Dane finally managed to mumble.

"There is a battery of neurological tests we run on newborns exhibiting her behaviors. Because she is a newborn, the data will take some time to interpret, and I want to get a specialist to look at her for that purpose. I've also called in our pediatric cardiologist."

"But, what do you think she has?"

"We don't know yet. I have several theories, but we have to run the tests to get a better idea."

"All right, doctor. Whatever it takes, you do. Just make sure she has the best—I mean the *very best possible*—care. When can I see my wife?"

"She's heavily sedated. It will be a couple of hours, at least."

Dane decided to grab a cup of coffee across the street; he was sick of the machine brew in the hospital cafeteria. Wearily, he extracted his cell phone from his rumpled coat pocket and called the office. "Gina," Dane croaked hoarsely into his voice mail, "Looks like I'll be awhile at the hospital." He paused, momentarily contemplating whether to tell her why, then decided against it. "Keep my schedule clear for this morning.

I'll update you later on whether—or when—I'll be coming in." He then touched a second button on the phone, pre-programmed to retrieve just voice mail messages from his office. Two were routine interoffice memos from other associates in the firm. A third was from a man he didn't recognize, a Larry—no, a Gary— Thompson, from somewhere in Colorado. Mr. Thompson wanted to set up a meeting with him, and mentioned Craig Johnson. Dane made a mental note to call him back this afternoon. He first sipped, then gulped the coffee, tossed two bucks on the table and headed out the door of the coffee shop searching for his jet-black BMW. The caffeine had begun to take hold, and his mind started to function after its normal manner. Deciding he might as well use the next couple of hours to get changed, he found his car, still parked between the emergency ward and maternity lot. He unlocked it with the key as he approached, slid into the seat, and began the half hour ride home.

As he rounded the corner onto Marlin Street, Dane caught a glimpse in his rearview mirror of a car that he thought he had seen a couple of miles back. "Probably nothing," he thought. Still, the bright blue Lexus was something he was sure he would have remembered, and it had dogged him now through three turns. In a split second, he decided to take a sharp right across two lanes at the next intersection, just in case. He heard a screech as the car attempted to follow suit, but he successfully shook his unwanted travel companion. He remembered what he had seen in the rearview mirror, though: a man in his mid-thirties with longish, black hair, slicked back. Startled, but too tired to be shaken, Dane mulled over the crazy scene as he parked the car, plodded into the house, and flung himself onto the bed. Before he realized it, he drifted into a fitful sleep, all the while mumbling to himself to check his health insurance later.

* * * *

James Patterson quickly downed the last gulp of coffee, wolfed his last bite of donut, and turned his attention to the urgency of the situation at hand. Depicted on a large screen at the front of the room was what the speaker described as a molecule—but, a molecule like none other ever known. As the technician in the back of the room manipulated a remote hand control, the multicolored figure on the screen jumped to life with animation. The red, blue and green spheres which had represented different elements of the chemical compound nimbly rearranged themselves into what looked like a crystalline formation. A few frames later, they again morphed into a completely new shape. In their reconfigured form, they looked—to James at least—like they had multiplied into hundreds of octagonal, crystal-like shapes.

"What you see here, gentlemen, is a mutated variant of a molecule commonly found in a certain variety of woody plant high in the Andes mountain range in certain portions of South America. We don't yet know what is responsible for the mutations which we have seen occur. All we *do* know is that certain traces of the substance have been turning up in the dung of llamas in the region, llamas that have turned to these plants to supplement their usual diets because of the record drought."

James fought to stifle a yawn, then surrendered to it. As a 15-year veteran of the Bureau, and of Army intelligence before that, he had sat through a lot of lectures from eggheads. He'd somehow managed to endure them all, provided someone could demonstrate to him a practical application of the high-sounding scientific theory. But, *llama dung...*?

"We first became aware of this mutated compound from tagged llamas under study by the Peruvian Horticultural Institute. Researchers there began to notice that llamas which had a higher percentage of Queñua leaves in their diet had more stamina and could pull larger loads over a longer period of time without tiring. Moreover, the compound seemed to have an addictive effect of sorts. The longer the llamas being studied had been consuming the Queñua leaves, the more their bodies seemed to crave the compound. They began to eat Queñua leaves to the exclusion of most other staples in their diet. Then, for no discernible reason, after about six months or so of this behavior, the llamas would suddenly, violently, die from hemorrhaging of the lungs which caused first, respiratory, then heart failure."

Dr. Quintain, the current speaker, casually flashed onto the screen several gruesome photographs of dying and dead llamas, together with inset frames containing cross sections of lung tissue. He then surrendered the podium to James' direct report at the Bureau, Philip Harless. Harless occupied the position one rung below the director of the FBI. Characteristically, the deputy director wasted no time in coming to the point. Dressed in a rumpled suit, his prepared talk was custom tailored to this group of only twelve of his most select agents. His gruff and no-nonsense manner conveyed what was unmistakably Harless: the man who had fought his way up from the bottom of the Bureau to be the next heir apparent to Henson Stockman, Director. His steel-grey eyes and steady gaze left no room for doubt concerning the seriousness of the matter at hand.

"Gentlemen," began Harless, "we have what we think is a brewing crisis on our hands. Medical experts, working in tandem with chemists and others in our department, have reason to think that shipments of this mutated compound are entering the United States in one form or another. The problem we have, at least for the present, is that there is nothing illegal about the compound. It's far too new to be a controlled substance. So far, we are not aware of Americans having ingested it directly or indirectly. We are concerned, however, because laboratory animals that have ingested this compound have exhibited the same characteristics as the llamas, and the doctors tell us there is no reason to expect humans would react any differently." Harless paused for dramatic effect, then added, "AND, there have been two deaths reported from native Peruvians who ate the meat of llamas who had ingested the material." Another pause followed, as his eyes scanned each of the agents'.

"Is the Bureau wanting us to interdict shipments, or what?" queried James. "Because if the stuff isn't illegal..."

"Quite correct, James," said Harless, as if he had expected that very question at just that moment. "But we cannot interdict any shipments found, just yet. This 'drug' in its non-mutated form has medicinal value.

Applications for FDA approval have recently been filed. We have taken jurisdiction without the FDA's knowledge at this point. The reason, quite simply, is that we don't have sufficient information to say that the drug always mutates, or under what conditions it does so. Our job at this point is to try to spot any shipments which make it across our borders, obtain samples and run tests to see what's in them. If we find the mutated form, we clap a lid on it and try to obtain a court order to interdict shipments. Meanwhile, we are pursuing special initiatives with selected committee chairmen of Congress, to try to classify it as a dangerous drug. But don't hold your breath—you know how long that can take. Oh, and one other thing ..." His eyes scanned the room, now boring deeply into first one agent's eyes, then another's. "This substance has addictive qualities to it that make cocaine and heroin seem like Kool Aid".

"What are we supposed to do while we wait for the FDA and the Congress?" continued James. "We can't very well station ourselves at thousand-mile intervals along the Mexican border with syringes and lab kits."

"No, James, we can't. That's where some of our intelligence comes in. Our investigations reveal that there is at least one, and maybe more, companies who are pursuing efforts to get this drug—we call it 'PZT'— onto the shelves with record speed. Most folks, even within the government, are blissfully ignorant of the dangers of the mutated form. And, for now, that's the way we want it to stay. It would cause mass hysteria that could spill over into all pharmaceuticals sales. Stock prices could plummet. People who need the non-mutated form of the drug would be deprived of it.

It could inspire a new wave of screwballs who start adulterating drugs on store shelves again."

"So our efforts have to remain *totally* under wraps?" The question came from Agent Wilkerson in the back of the room.

"Until we have something more substantial to take to Washington, this receives top security priority," Harless affirmed. "You are to discuss it with no one." Then, turning to Patterson, "But there is one person I'd like you to begin a watch on. Some of our guys under cover in Dallas think they have a line on some young, hot shot attorney who has done FDA litigation—a real sharpshooter—who might be taking on the FDA case on behalf of the leading PZT manufacturer and supplier. Put somebody on him. I've got his dossier in my office. Swing on by and pick it up before lunch."

"Roger that, Boss, but, if you don't mind my asking, mightn't we have a little problem with attorney-client privilege there?" "You have a law degree, James. You know how to steer clear of the privilege," Harless shot back.

"I'm glad you have so much confidence in me, boss," James said, tucking his notepad under his arm and heading for the door.

CHAPTER FIVE

The jarring clatter of the phone interrupted Dane's dreamy stupor. He groped in the dark till his hand found, then missed, then seized the receiver again. He propped himself up on one elbow and managed to croak out a "hello" just before the answering machine kicked in.

"Dane, this is Jeanine." Dane's mind, still groggy, struggled to call up the name. *Jeanine…neighbor…*it finally clicked and he was awake. "I'm with Susan at the hospital. She's finally shaking off the sedative." Dane's heart suddenly leapt; then, just as suddenly, sank like a rock into his stomach. He knew he would have to find the words to tell Susan about the—his mind recoiled from it— "illness." *"Does it even have a name?"* he wondered.

"Here she is, Dane."

"Hi, sleepy head," he managed, steeling himself and hoping she missed the worry in his voice. She didn't, of course, and read him like a book, as always. "Is everything all right?"

"Oh sure, everything's fine. Listen," he stuttered, "There's 'um, something I have to tell you. Only, I'm not sure I can do it over the phone. The baby…"

"Hush," she interrupted. Then, more softly, "I know about Natalie."

The name "Natalie" hit him between the eyes. He had been so preoccupied with his daughter's condition that he had completely forgotten the beautiful name they had chosen, should they be blessed with a daughter.

"You do?" Dane asked. Then, angrily, "Who told you?!"

"Please don't be upset. Dr. Weinberger didn't want to break the news without you there in the room, but I made him tell me. Remember—I knew something was wrong almost from the start." She uttered the words not so much as an 'I-told-you-so,' as with a disconsolate sense of resignation.

"Yeah, I guess you did, didn't you," said Dane reflectively, sadly. He was astounded at his wife's composure, which he attributed partly to the medication she was on. A groan of pain came over the phone. "Baby, we need to talk about this with the doctors soon; but only when you're feeling better. You'll have to let me know when that is."

"I think I can manage. But, right now, I'm not sure there's much we can talk about...I mean, the doctors are still looking at Natalie."

"Is the neurologist there yet?"

"I think so. I know there are two or three doctors besides Dr. Weinberger, and they all seem very interested in Natalie. It kind of scares me. I just want to *hold* her, Dane!" This was the first sound of strong emotion in Susan's voice, and Dane's heart melted.

"I know, Darlin', and you *will* hold her. In a few weeks, we'll bring Natalie home and everything will be just as it should." He spared no effort to convince himself, as well as Susan, of the truth of his statement.

"And I want to hold you too, Great Dane."

Dane smiled at the nickname that Susan only used when they were making love. Under other circumstances, he would have loved to do the things that had earned him the name. But right now, it was the farthest thing from his mind. "I can't wait to hold you Susan." I'll be back this afternoon right after a meeting I have. Maybe we can talk to the doctors then."

"Yeah, maybe then. I'll hold on till you get here," she said, sounding tired once more.

"You're a trooper, Susan. I love you." He hung up. Dane got off the bed, stepped in front of the bedroom mirror, and dragged a brush through his tousled hair. He glanced at this watch, which showed nearly 2:00 p.m. already. He'd cleared his calendar of court hearings yesterday when he got the first call from the hospital. Thank God there were no trials. He had left one appointment on his schedule though: that new client referral from Craig Johnson, by the name of...Gary Thompson. He checked his phone calendar. "Thompson/Rowalter Enterprises" appeared next to the 2:30 p.m. slot. Good. He'd have just enough time to make it to his meeting. The exercise in disciplined thinking that goes with a client interview might actually prove therapeutic, he thought. Then, he could be with Susan.

After a quick, uneventful drive during which he spotted no more blue Lexus automobiles, Dane breezed into his office with ten minutes to spare. His appointment was already waiting, a fact he knew from the completed client opening sheet placed neatly in the middle of his desk blotter by Gina, his super-efficient secretary. As usual, he entered by the side hallway door, purposely avoiding the client waiting area. This gave him an escape hatch, should he need to duck out without being seen for the more-than-occasional "emergency hearing." It also was a great way to elude insurance and copier salesmen and the myriad of other peddlers of goods and services that, according to them, every lawyer simply mustn't be without.

Dane picked up the interview sheet and scanned it. Gary Thompson, he read: Rowalter Enterprises...age 42...Vice President in Charge of Marketing Development. Dave went out to the reception area to greet Mr. Thompson. The man had dark features, a pronounced receding hairline, medium build and a goatee. He bore the look of a man who is stretched too thin–haggard and with a jumpy, nervous sort of energy, like a squirrel trying to beat the snow storm. They shook hands, remarked about the weather, then began the fifty-foot trek around the curved hallway to Dane's office. Once inside, Thompson plopped himself into a side chair and placed his slim burgundy attaché case on his lap, as a support for his bony elbows. His eyes darted quickly to the right, then swept left, doing a wide-angle assessment of the office. Then, they came to rest on Dane's eyes, just as Dane completed his standard opening phrase, "What can I do for you?" Thompson got right down to business.

"Mr. Ingersoll, I hear you are very good at what you do. A highly competent trial lawyer, and a respected government regulatory lawyer. That's why my company is interested in retaining you." The man already had Dane's interest. As a senior associate, it greatly enhanced Dane's chances of gaining a partnership berth if he could garner his own clients.

"We are a pharmaceutical company, primarily. Oh, we have some other interests through wholly owned subsidiaries: agribusiness, food additives, biomedical and so forth. But all these are subordinate to, and dependent on, our drug business. Americans are consuming more drugs than ever before—of the legal kind, I mean. Prescription drugs, over-the-counter, therapeutic...from aspirin and antacids to the latest in super-antibiotics and designer immunotherapy drugs, we are surpassed only by the food and tobacco industries, and about ready to overtake tobacco. By and large, we are successful in developing and getting our pharmaceuticals to the market. However, we have only one problem—the FDA. Usually, we have a very good rapport with them. But our application for approval has bogged down. Something to do with an independent lab study. Well, now we have such a study, which clearly shows that our product is perfectly safe and effective. Testing was supervised by none other than Dr. Norman Holloway, and—"

"*The* Norman Holloway?" Dane interjected. "The one who won the Nobel prize in biochemistry a few years back?"

"Bingo, the self-same one. And he don't come cheap; you can mark that down! In any event, we are poised to distribute this product on a widespread basis throughout the United States. We're already marketing it in certain South American countries as a wonder drug to help slow the aging process. 'Does things like improve memory function, energy level, libido, and endurance. But it also has been used as an experimental drug in treating certain neurological disorders in the aging. Personally, I think the uses of PZT are just beginning to be known."

"Not that I don't appreciate your thinking of us, but why come to a litigator like me? I did a federal trial a few years back in which there were approval issues involved, but that doesn't make me an FDA specialist."

"Mr. Ingersoll, Rowalter has—as is its habit—thoroughly and exhaustively researched your background. We know all about *United States Food & Drug Administration v. Szeroka.* We've read the court transcript, chapter and verse. Hell, *every* pharmaceutical company has. We know how long it took, the witnesses you called, the lab studies you culled through, the evidence you presented. We also know how you got the FDA injunction against product sales and distribution lifted, opening the way for a pharmaceutical company to make hundreds of millions of dollars on pent up demand. Your tenacity and skill have not gone unnoticed, I can assure you."

"But," Dane struggled to keep a sense of humility in the midst of the accolades, "Wouldn't I be correct that this is not a case where the FDA has issued a cease and desist order? That is, you have not even received preliminary approval, correct?"

"Quite so."

"Then what is the need for a lawsuit at all, at this stage of the game?"

"Quite simply, to break the log jam by seeking a declaratory judgment that the drug PZT is perfectly safe for human consumption based on the lab work we've already done. Of course, if we can also prove unreasonable delay by the FDA caused a loss of profits, I would like to seek damages on those grounds."

Dane stifled the urge to laugh aloud, knowing just how absurd the notion of collecting damages from a federal agency for delay really was. "Do you have actual results of double blind clinical studies involving humans, utilizing a control group?"

"Enough material to keep you busy for months–all independently verified. Mr. Ingersoll, please know that there will be no lack of evidence for you in this case."

Dane's memory momentarily flashed back to the five-week-long trial he had commandeered six years ago. It had taken literally dozens of witnesses, many doctors, still more users of the drug, and thousands upon thousands of documents. The witness interviews alone had taken over a year to complete. Things were different now, he mused. He had one case under his belt, and he felt good about his competence in the field, *but something—*

"Mr. Ingersoll, we would like to retain you—"

—Yes, something right-brained, indefinable, intangible caused him to hesitate—

"—immediately. I understand you are up for an equity partnership position with your firm. I am certain the garnering of Rowalter Industries as a client could only be an asset to you under such circumstances. After all, it *is* the third-largest pharmaceuticals company in the world."

Thompson was right. There were no guarantees on the outcome of one's first try at partner. Bringing in a new, large institutional client would give him a huge head start with the partnership committee as it scrutinized the five candidates vying for only two precious partnership positions. *Still, this hint of a gnawing sensation in his gut—surely it was just the worry over Natalie, or was it?* Instinct, more than anything else, took control of him now as Dane heard himself say, "I'd like to think about it. Do you have anything you can leave me?" *Are you out of your mind, Dane? Do you want him to shop his case down the street to the pharmaceuticals partner at Hughes & Jensen?*

"Sure, I understand perfectly. Here is our firm's annual report, statement of objectives, and a laboratory report on PZT. The lab report is confidential. But, don't take too long. Rowalter can't afford the wait. We *can*, on the other hand, afford to pay you handsomely for your expertise."

"Sure, sure...Give me forty-eight hours, all right?" *You idiot, don't let him get away!*

The men rose together. "Suit yourself. But I need to hear something by Friday." Dane held the ponderous office door open and offered his hand to Mr. Thompson. Thompson's was a little cold. Eyes darting, as if he had ten other places to be, he disappeared down the corridor to the plush waiting area.

Without hesitating, Dane strode to his credenza and hit the intercom button, "Gina, get me the Food and Drug Administration in Washington, D.C."

CHAPTER SIX

James Patterson knew how to tail someone. And he was an expert investigator, one that could vanish into the background, and whose keen powers of observation missed nothing. His eyes functioned not unlike an optical scanner, his mind like a solid-state computer hard drive. Among the elite agents of the Bureau, he was rumored to have a photographic memory. He didn't, but like many others in law enforcement who have reached the apex of their profession, he had mastered the ability to notice–and to mentally file away–details which were seemingly insignificant to others. Not to mention the fact that he was smart—very smart, gifted with a mind like a steel bear trap. Like many FBI agents, he had interviewed with the Bureau while in law school, then gone to work for it immediately following graduation. Just in case, he had taken the bar exam in his home state of Pennsylvania, something the job had not required, but he did it anyway. He had received a perfect score, the only one to do so that year. Bright and driven as he was, James knew his limits. He was where he wanted to be. The thought of working for some monolithic law firm on the 100th floor of a downtown office building turned him downright cold. He preferred to gather the evidence in a manner that the lawyers would appreciate, thank you very much; let them worry about how to get it admitted as evidence in a court of law.

Patterson began by surveying the map of downtown Dallas he had brought to the office this morning. Spreading the map across his desk, he began to mark with blue colored straight pins the buildings within a five-block radius of the First International Building, the domain of several large law firms including Salacuse & Lockridge. After ten minutes or so he had narrowed the field to three likely candidates: one directly across the street eastward, one two blocks to the north, and one on the street that bordered the building on the west, but a little closer to the infamous Dealy Plaza. Patterson was slightly partial to this last location, probably, it occurred to him, because he had always been so spellbound by the JFK assassination.

"Carla," he yelled out to the office next door, "get on the phone with our Dallas office and have them get me appointments with the owner's representatives of these three locations," handing her the map. "And I'll need a flight from Dulles International to DFW, arriving tomorrow afternoon. Get me a car, too–a plain color, solid black or white. The Dallas field office can arrange it–talk to Benji."

"Yes, sir." Carla, already thinking ahead as was her tendency, headed for the phone. She sensed the excitement of Jim's new assignment, but could only guess as to the big picture. "Shall I set up a meeting with surveillance before you leave?"

"Roger that."

"And what about living arrangements, Sir? I assume you'll want the usual house, fully furnished and outfitted?"

"Don't worry about that. I'm sure the advance team has already located one somewhere in the suburbs. I'll blend right in. Just find out where it is and get me directions from downtown before I leave."

"Have suitable security measures—?"

"—Yes, Carla, I'm sure Deputy Director Harless has seen to it."

* * * *

The room was smallish and starkly furnished. Six straight backed chairs were positioned around a table, with a window overlooking a hospital courtyard behind. The air in the room betrayed its location, as the vapor of alcohol mingled with the smell of various medicines. Two of the chairs were already occupied by doctors discussing something in hushed tones, the sterile, fluorescent light bouncing off the bald head of one of them. Though their conversation was sub audible, their faces suggested disagreement. A third doctor, dressed in a suit but jacketless, stood several feet away. He stared out the window, his glance darting every minute or so to the seated doctors. Mounted on one wall of the room was a flat screen television.

Two hallways away, Susan, still weak from complications of her delivery, stared into a video camera which had been attached to the television in the corner of the room above her bed. Her mind raced over a thousand pathways, each dead-ending in unanswered questions. Her stomach fluttered, whether from the medicine which had steadily dripped into her veins for three days, or from her haunting fears, she did not know.

Suddenly, Dane was in the doorway, the shadow of his lanky form cutting a hole from the fabric of the hallway light that entered her room. Without a word, he came to her bedside, pushed aside the IV apparatus, and gathered her in his arms. Her tears flowed silently, profusely, until he could feel their moist warmth through his shirt. "It's going to be all right...", he whispered.

"How do you know?" Susan finally managed after several minutes.

"I just know", Dane mustered his best courtroom confidence.

"But—"

Dane gently placed his index finger over her mouth, "Sh-h-h-h. I need to get back with the doctors. They're waiting for us. They'll answer our questions. I love you, Darlin'."

"I love you, too."

Dane rose, restoring the IV contraption to its rightful place, and left the room, retracing his steps to the "conference room" with the doctors. He briskly entered the room, a mock smile on his face. "Gentlemen, I'm Dane Ingersoll, Susan's husband." He extended his hand, and the doctors each shook it in turn.

"My pleasure," replied the suited man who had been standing apart from the others. He gestured toward one of the chairs. "I'm Dr. Woodbine, and this is Dr. Stapleton and Dr. Jaynes", nodding to each in turn. "If you'll excuse me, I believe we need to add your wife to our little conference." He ambled awkwardly toward camera, flipped a switch, and adjusted the lens. Then, after pausing a moment, he cleared his throat, and spoke to the camera. "Susan, are you with us?" he squinted.

"Y-yes," came Susan's voice weakly. Dane could see her face on the pillow, her eyes still moist with the tears of moments before.

"Good." Woodbine replied, businesslike. "Then, let's begin." His manner was of a man confident in his work, who'd had conferences just such as this hundreds, perhaps thousands, of times. "Dr. Weinberger, Susan's obstetrician, brought us in on this case because of complications in the delivery of—" he hesitated.

"Natalie," chimed Susan and Dane, exchanging glances through the monitor.

"Er yes, Natalie", continued the doctor. "You should know that the doctors on our team—those present here—are an integral team of specialists from Boston, where they are heads of their hospitals' respective specialty departments in neonatology. I specialize in diseases of the infant nervous system. Dr. Stapleton is a pediatric hematologist. And Dr. Jaynes is an immunologist specializing in rare diseases in the premature and newborn. Each of us has a special interest in your little girl." Dane supposed he should be impressed with the medical brain trust, but his heart only felt like lead inside of him. He wondered if he would be sick, right here and now.

"You see; your daughter has a heretofore unknown disorder. Her cells are manufacturing a chemical which essentially 'fools' her system into thinking that a foreign substance or tissue has entered her body. Therefore, her central nervous system commands her lymph and blood cells to manufacture substances, among them antibodies, that are not only unnecessary, but actually destructive of healthy cells."

His throat suddenly dry, Dane glanced up to the monitor, where Susan's eyes were riveted in a look of unspoken horror.

"Mr. and Mrs. Ingersoll, we are still trying to identify this disorder," he continued, businesslike. "And, we will need time. We would like for the patient—er, Natalie—to stay here a while longer for tests and observation."

"You mean to tell us that you don't even know what to *call* this problem?" Dane went into cross-examination mode.

"How long is 'a while'?" Susan asked, incredulous.

"I would anticipate needing at least sixty days." The other doctors nodded in solemn agreement.

"As for Dane's question, I'll let Dr. Jensen answer it. Ralph?"

Dr. Jensen shifted in his chair. Mustering the demeanor of a doctor who knows he doesn't know, he looked directly at Dane, and at the monitor over his left shoulder. "I'm afraid we don't know exactly what to call this dysfunction. It starts out mimicking some of the symptoms of cerebral palsy and similar central nervous system disorders. However, it doesn't appear to be entirely neurological. That is why Dr. Stapleton and I have been called in. There are numerous harmful agents that have been introduced into your child's blood stream, which may be being secreted through the glands, or from some other source. Frankly, we are not yet sure from where. These agents are warring with healthy blood cells, and compromising your daughter's ability to ward off infection and disease. This is why it is so important that we try to find some answers before we release her. At least here, we can keep her in a sterile environment until we can identify the nature of the problem."

Expressions like "nature of the problem" made Dane very unsettled. They had too much wiggle room in them. He far preferred things he could name, even if he didn't necessarily know what the next step was after the naming of them. This disease—or whatever it was that gripped his little girl—sounded insidious, and indefinable. He wasn't sure against what—or at whom—to direct his anger and frustration.

"Dane—" began Susan, her eyes pleading. He read her mind instantly.

"Look, doctors, as much as we want to take Natalie home, we want whatever this thing is, taken care of properly. For once and for all. Of course you'll have to keep her here—we know that. But..." Dane stumbled.

"Isn't there any way you can tell us what her chances are?" Susan picked up the slack.

The room fell still just long enough to leave no doubt of the answer. "I'm afraid not, Mrs. Ingersoll," said Woodbine, his tone apologetic. "This is uncharted water, and most of our work will have to be done by analogy to other, more familiar diseases. But Natalie's is a priority case for all of us, and you can be sure we will leave no stone unturned."

Dane recovered. His voice trembled with emotion. "Gentlemen, this little girl means more to me than anything else in the whole world. I want you to spare no procedure, no inquiry, no resource or expense, in finding a cure for this...**whatever** you call it." He handed Woodbine a business card drawn from his suit jacket. Call me any time, day or night." He scrawled their home and cell phone on the back, and thrust it into the doctor's palm. He stood, glanced again at Susan through the monitor, thanked them and left. Suddenly on a mission, he charged down the corridor and made the couple of turns back to Susan's room. She was sitting up in her bed.

"Dane, what are we going to do?" "I, Baby. I guess we'll just have to wait and pray. He huddled her close, and stroked her now-tangled hair. How's Jackie?" It occurred to Dane that, embarrassingly, he didn't know. He'd been so wrapped up.

"I'm sure he's doing fine with Jeanine."

"Have you told him about all this?"

He gulped at the thought. "No, but I'll find a way today." With that, he kissed her.

"I should be out tomorrow," she said flatly, vacantly.

"I know—they told me. I'll be here as soon as they're ready."

CHAPTER SEVEN

The Ellis County Courthouse was built in the southern style of the 1870's. Like countless other such edifices in Texas' 254 counties, it bore a stately, anchor-like presence in the downtown square. It was sort of a reference point for anything of importance: the post office was two blocks east and one block north. The First Baptist Church was ten blocks due west on Travis Street. The courthouse was surrounded on all sides by parking spaces, each with a meter that offered rates unheard of in Dallas to the north. A deputy cop with nothing better to do checked twice daily to see how many of the out of town lawyers he could ticket for exceeding the two hours allowed for a quarter. A mother and daughter loitered at the base of an imposing granite statue of William Tecumseh Sherman. The lawn was manicured, the shrubs well-trimmed, and islands of recently planted red pansies and bluebonnets, the Texas state flower, appeared at each of the corners. Though the pillared architecture was visually pleasing, upon closer inspection it was readily apparent that the building sorely needed restoration. Ellis County was not known for its large tax base, and old courthouses such as this were not inexpensive to maintain. The county boasted one district court and one statutory county court, compared to ten civil district courts and five county courts at law in Dallas, just an hour and a quarter to the north.

Inside, up the narrow stairways still built of their original material, Dane trudged to a trial he had this morning at 9:00. He had prepared for it for a solid week—just how, he didn't quite know—in the interstices between the developing crisis with Susan and the baby. As he rounded the corner at the top of the stairwell, he nearly collided with Stephanie, his trial paralegal.

"So you beat me, huh Steph? What's the lay of the land in there?" he said, nodding toward the ancient, weathered courtroom doors.

"Calm, so far. Only one advance member of the defense team. I've begun setting up our exhibits. We're just waiting on our computer operator now. John is here, set up, and an eager beaver, as usual."

John Rugs, who smiled and waved at Dane from a distant seat in the public gallery, was the best civil jury consultant in the business. Dane neither knew nor wanted to know what made people like Rugs tick. He only knew they all had double psychology degrees and charged gobs of money to read meaning into things like crossed legs, wrinkled brows or drumming fingers.

Dane had calculated—and predicted to the court at the pre-trial conference—that this trial would last only three to four days. He'd decided to streamline the prodigious trail of evidence he planned to introduce by digitizing it onto a USB flash drive. Each essential document, graphic or drawing could then be fed via his laptop or tablet onto a large LED screen placed in front of the jury. This electronic wizardry seemed wholly at odds with the 19th century surroundings of the courthouse, but this simply was not Dallas or Houston, where all the gadgetry was built into the courtroom. And, Dane found that juries appreciated the ease of viewing the exhibits.

"Dane, are you ready to go?" Dane, startled, lurched upward from the stooped position over his catalogue case. It was Harry Bell, one of his clients.

"Howdy, Mr. Bell. 'Couldn't be more so. 'You ready to kick some butt?" Dane spoke barely above a whisper, as defense counsel was seated less than ten feet away. "I sure am. Aren't we, Missy?" Harry's rotund wife had just waddled up beside him. "You've got that right." Dane had thoroughly prepared his clients for testimony, both direct and cross exam. They exuded the confidence that only comes with careful, incessant preparation, buoyed by the calm air of self-assurance that enveloped Dane, who practiced at the top of his craft.

Still, a nervous stillness hung in the air—the palpable feeling of "what-will-happen-next" that always precedes the opening gavel at a jury trial. As he continued to arrange his counsel table and Stephanie organized the Plaintiff's exhibits, the 45 members of the jury panel filed in, the shuffling of their feet echoing through the musty smelling courtroom. One by one the aging bailiff called their names, mispronouncing at least a third of them. From them would be selected the final pool of twelve jurors and two alternates who would have the power to decide the Bell's fate. Stephanie dutifully filled out the jury chart that was a standard part of any trial lawyer's toolbox, with names and occupations from the juror cards corresponding to the seat that each panelist was given.

Harry and Missie Bell were, as instructed, seated to the left of Dane, in full view of the jury. By design, their chairs were turned to face the jury panel, and they dutifully smiled at each prospective juror who made his or her way down the courtroom pews in front of them. This would not be a high publicity trial like the capital murder cases tried by some of Dane's friends in the criminal bar. But it mattered to Harry and Missie Bell as much as if it were. For the Bells had lost their entire life savings to the wiles of an investment advisor who had placed their hard-earned money in highly speculative investments, then "churned" their account—the practice of making extra commissions by trading too frequently in and out of those investments without his clients' knowledge or consent. Besides being up for criminal charges before the white-collar division of the D.A.'s office, Newcomer Burnwood, the Defendant, was being investigated by the Texas State Securities Board and the SEC for securities fraud on a grand scale. It seemed some of the investments he had put his clients into were his own private "deals" he had put together with neither the proper safeguards nor the required disclosure. Fortunately for the Bells, they had a negligent hiring case against the Wall Street brokerage house that hired Burnwood. Incredibly, the firm had failed to check out Burnwood's checkered background in the S & L industry and as an off-the-street broker prior to coming to work for them. And, also fortunately, Shelton Financial, the brokerage, had an errors and omissions insurance policy with a one-million-dollar cap, backed by reinsurance totaling ten million dollars.

Judge Eugene Fize has just entered the Courtroom, wearing the look he was known for: one that said, "I really don't want any part of this job but the status and salary; let's get this case over with as soon as possible so I can get back to the country club." He motioned to his bailiff, then leaned forward to mutter something to the court reporter who sat, hands poised, below the bench. As the bailiff placed both rather large court files in front of him, the judge motioned both counsel forward "Gentlemen, are there any matters remaining to be taken up by the Court by way of pretrial?" Although both Dane and lead defense counsel answered in unison, "No your Honor," it was a question that was always asked. Several critical motions of Dane's had been granted Thursday of last week, among them the Plaintiff's Motion In Limine. The Court's ruling had kept out several potentially damaging pieces of defense evidence until they could be evaluated outside the jury's presence.

"Fine, then gentlemen, you may begin your *voir dire* examination of the jury. The Plaintiff has requested three hours, and the Defendant one hour. Therefore, I have allotted two hours by way of compromise. You may have your seats at the counsel table."

As Dane and his opponent took their seats, the Judge launched into his monotone instructions to the jury, prefaced by greetings and pleasantries designed to break the ice. In small counties such as this one, this was one of the few chances a judge had to glad-hand with the voting public. True to form, Judge Fize didn't let the opportunity slip by. While he did so, Dane carefully studied the juror questionnaires. He placed them in three piles: "favorable", "unfavorable", and "not sure". The "favorable" category contained people who had answered that they had significant retirement savings, a strong interest in saving for retirement, or who simply liked to invest. It also contained married persons advancing in years, because Dane thought they would tend to identify with his clients. It was no accident that the jury panel had been presented with such specific questions. Dane, working with his jury consultant, had moved at pretrial that he be allowed to submit a customized questionnaire to the jury prior to *voir dire*, and his motion had been granted. The information the questionnaires provided was invaluable.

The "unfavorable" pile contained stockbrokers, investment bankers, or other professionals who might tend to side with the Defendant merely because of their line of work. Dane was careful not to pigeonhole too much, however. Sometimes fellow professionals were the hardest on their own—figuring a bad apple gave their entire profession a black eye. He would ferret that out when he questioned the panel, during *voir dire*.

The largest category—"not sure," was the one that he would whittle away at during the questioning, by a careful, methodical probing of the jurors' minds and prejudices. By doing so, Dane would flush out any unknowns and strike them from the panel if they would harm his case.

Judge Fize seemed to be drawing near the end of his canned speech. Abruptly, he paused, drew a long and deliberate breath, whispered something to his bailiff, then peered down at Dane. "We will begin with the Plaintiff. Mr. Ingersoll, you may proceed." "Thank you, Your Honor," replied Dane, who rose and strode slowly, confidently to the bar separating the spectator section from the counsel table. He began by introducing his clients to the panel. As he outlined the plaintiffs' case, every eye was fixed on this good-looking, youthful, wiry lawyer with the easy manner. His object—and the eyes of the panel members told him he was succeeding—was to wrap flesh and blood around this legal controversy. As Mr. and Mrs. Bell retook their seats next to Stephanie at counsel table, he outlined the basic facts, being careful not to get into the evidence and draw an objection. Then, he honed in on the first three rows. When he concluded two hours later Dane had, with disarming brilliance, managed to identify five potential jurors who thought they themselves had been bilked financially. Four of these readily admitted that people over sixty years of age should be treated with special deference in their retirement planning. Of more importance still, about eight panel members had dropped their guard enough to reveal that "over-active investing" would not bother them "so long as the investments produced a positive result" for the investor. Yet all conceded that the investor should at all times retain the full power to make investment decisions. Since the defendant had neither treated the elderly Mr. and Mrs. Bell with special deference, nor produced a positive result, Dane felt he had conditioned the panel very well for the evidence to come.

Next it was the defense's turn. The judge introduced the jury to the lead defense counsel, a 45-ish looking gentlemen from a Chicago firm with five offices nationwide. As his opponent rose to take his crack at the jury, Dane's mind wandered to Gary Thompson and Rowalter Industries. Something told him—he wasn't sure just why—that this was not your run-of-the-mill FDA approval case. Something wasn't quite right, but when he'd checked the company through his sources, no adverse reports had come back. His eyes flitted back to the jury panel, as his opponent droned on. He decided dismissively that this attorney probably wouldn't be too much of a challenge, then returned to his thoughts. A tightening began in his gut and moved slowly upward until it gripped his solar plexus. As he became consciously aware of this, the thought dawned on him that he was worried— about Susan, the baby, his finances, the guy who had followed him, and who knew what else. But there was no time to dwell on that now.

During the defense *voir dire,* Dane continued to wrestle with the creeping anxiety. As both sides examined their lists and made their jury strikes—the Defendant with his two attorneys and Dane, Stephanie and John with the Bells—he felt a tightening around his neck, like a pair of malevolent hands. Finally, both lawyers handed the judge their lists of names to be stricken from the panel, and the judge announced a five-minute recess at precisely 12 noon. Dane's team continued to huddle at counsel table while he forced himself to focus on the opening statement he would give right after lunch. Following the recess, his Honor officially seated the resulting jury of five men and seven women, row by row. He then swore them in, and promptly dismissed everyone for lunch, announcing that trial would begin at 1:30 p.m. Dane knew he could not last that long without doing something to break the brooding cloud that had overtaken him.

"I have some calls to make," he told his paralegal and consultant. Y'all go on ahead and grab a bite with Harry and Missie, and I'll meet you in a few."

"No problem," Stephanie said from halfway across the courtroom, John at her side. We'll stake out a booth at Shirley's Barbecue across the street. 'See you there."

Before she was out of the court room, Dane had exited and beat a hasty path to the antiquated wooden booth pay phone just around the corner from the rear courtroom exit. It was one of the few in the state that still worked. As he approached the phone, he reached into his coat pocket and pulled out a crumpled letter from First Fidelity, Ltd., his health insurance company. He again began reading the opening phrases of the letter, as he had this morning when he had found the letter absent-mindedly tucked inside his morning paper. "We regret to inform you that coverage of the claim on your wife has been declined. Our medical investigation reveals that she was a carrier of the disease in question for a period exceeding two years. Therefore, she is excluded from coverage under your policy." Dane's stomach lurched all over again as he continued reading. "Moreover, because your daughter's condition is a direct result of the preexisting condition of your wife, it is excluded from coverage to the extent that her treatment is related to such a condition." The letter concluded by saying that this particular condition was on some kind of "Rare Disease List" and for this reason, wouldn't have been covered in any event.

Dane, his stomach still churning, slammed the door shut and jabbed the numbers into the dial pad in staccato fashion. The phone rang twice, then answered with a gruff voice. "Jerek?" Dane barked.

"Dane? What's wrong?"

"I'll tell you what's wrong," he said, voice quavering. "I have a wife in the hospital and a baby with a deadly disease, and the insurance company is denying coverage!" A long pause followed.

"That's insane, Dane. I know some people at that company! They used to be a client of ours at the Stutman firm. You let me have a crack at 'em, and I'm sure we can get it covered. Besides, if they don't, we'll sue their asses."

"Yeah, yeah, I know" Dane mumbled dejectedly. "You forget that I was an insurance defense attorney, too. You know as well as I do they will tie it up in a Dallas court for three or four years without even batting an eye! Just what do you suggest I do in the meantime?" Hearing the words he'd just uttered, Dane suddenly hated himself for what he had done to deserving claimants and their attorneys all those years working for insurance companies.

"Look, Jerek, this thing could bankrupt us. The doctors are saying it's some on-the-fringe disease they never even heard of. The insurance company is blowing smoke—if it's *that* unknown, then it can't be on some "Rare Disease" list. But what scares the dickens out of me is, if they deny the claim nobody else is gonna pick up the insurance!"

"Calm down, Dane," soothed Jerek. "I'll make some phone calls and give you a buzz tonight. Just get that trial under your belt. Maybe the partners at the firm can come up with something to help out."

Dane relaxed, but only a little. "Thanks, buddy", he said. "Be in touch—soon." His next call was to the hospital. The phone rang twice on the third-floor nursing station, then the no-nonsense voice of the charge nurse told him it would be a little more time before Susan could come home. "Perhaps a day or two. Sorry, doctor's orders," she said, undoubtedly for the hundredth time today. "*What was going wrong*?" Dane chafed. He hung up, then called his son Jackie at Jeanine's house, and was caught off guard at how calmly Jackie had taken the news of his new baby sister's "illness". His shouts of "I'm doin' great, Dad!" were punctuated by sounds of splashing in the background mingled with yelling kids. Clearly a pool party. Jackie seemed more concerned with when Mom was coming home—he asked three times—but even the delay in her discharge didn't seem to faze him very much. After all, he had Jeanine's ten-year-old son Don to play basketball with. Dane had underestimated Jackie's resiliency, or perhaps his childish immaturity, in not yet grasping the issues grown-ups spent so much time worrying about. Musing some more, it occurred to him that maybe it was better Susan was coming home in a couple more days. At least by then this trial would be over and they could spend some time together.

He hung the phone up, wiped his dripping forehead, and headed out the door and across the street to meet his trial team for lunch.

CHAPTER EIGHT

The first day of trial ended promptly at 5:00. Dane had just completed an extensive direct examination of his first witness, Missy Bell. Dane hoped he had gambled correctly that the emotional Mrs. Bell would strike a sympathetic chord with the jury, a majority of which was composed of women. Without being maudlin, Missy had, indeed, evoked a sense of the innocent, elderly woman who had been done wrong. John Rugs confirmed that the jurors had received Missy's testimony well. Now the other side had Missy on cross. So far, she was bearing up well, and opposing counsel hadn't scored any measurable points.

Wearily, Dane packed up his briefcase, leaving the trial exhibits behind the witness stand, and headed for his car. As he slipped into the seat and put his key into the ignition, he didn't notice the grey Acura sedan parked a block and a half away on Travis street at a meter. As Dane pulled out of the courthouse space, the man behind the wheel of the Acura carefully placed the magazine he'd been pretending to read on the other side of the front seat, and pulled away from the curb. He pressed a button under the dashboard that activated a video camera. With his left thumb the driver lightly touched a recessed pad in the steering wheel, instantly accessing a secure channel on the built-in cell phone. Swiftly and silently, he glided into position behind Dane's sleek black Beemer, careful to interpose at least a couple of cars between him and Dane as the two cars began merging with the highway. Jim Patterson had not wasted the many years of experience, and was at the top of his game. "I have acquired the subject, who is now northbound on 287, about 60 miles outside of Dallas." He spoke the words in near monotone, and his hands never left the wheel as he spoke to the speaker mounted in the dashboard. "Roger, report at 15-minute intervals," a male voice crackled. The Acura stayed on Dane's tail with the precision of a cruise missile and the stealth of a feline, all the way into Dallas. Regular reports of the Beemer's position, complete with video images, were beamed to a satellite, amplified, then echoed back to an office in Washington D.C. Dane remained blissfully unaware of this as he turned into the parking garage just down the block from the towering edifice that enveloped his office.

Dane pulled into his reserved parking space, intending only to pick up his messages and check his desk for any urgent mail before heading home. The parking garage was virtually empty at 6:30 p.m., as was always the case downtown. He entered from the north side door to the garage elevator vestibule, and rapidly ascended to floor 43 without the elevator pausing for any stops in between. As he rounded the corner into his spacious office, he spied a note on his chair—the spot all secretaries were instructed to leave the most important matters, lest they be ignored. The note was from Jerek. It read:

> *"Dane, I called everyone I knew at First Fidelity.I reasoned, cajoled, and threatened, but they stood firm. They're not going to budge. The president is a jerk, and so is the legal department. I'll talk to some other partners and see what we might do.*
>
> *Sorry, Jerek"*

Dane collapsed in his chair.   Every fiber and ligament felt like it weighed a million pounds. His mood was every bit as dark as the deserted, cavernous office in which he now sat, alone. He knew in his gut that Jerek's offer to "talk to the partners", while a nice gesture and well intentioned, was equally futile. Short of a protracted lawsuit which could tie him and his family up for years with no guarantee of the outcome, there was nothing they could do.   Even if the firm represented him free of charge, the doctors and hospital would have to be paid in the meantime. Any loan the firm might advance would have to be paid back, and the amount that would be needed boggled his mind. He was not yet a partner, and did not make the mid-six figure salary characteristic of one. There simply was *no limit* to what it would cost to help Susan and Natalie, as bankruptcy hovered before him in an almost tangible visage.

Abruptly, Dane jerked himself up from his slouched position and began groping blindly around his desk. The moon had begun streaming into his window, and its eerie light illuminated a morass of papers and miscellany. Impatiently, he pushed aside first one pile, then another and another, finally standing up and rubbing his temples in frustration. After a momentary pause, he spied a lone business card on the far corner of the desk, and lunged for it. Pulling the chain on his desk light, he seized the card between two fingers and held it under the lamp. "Gary Thompson, Vice President, Rowalter Industries", it read.

He lurched for the phone, and frantically poked the numbers on the card into the keys. Three rings were followed by a clicking sound, as if the call was being forwarded, then more ringing.

"Hello, Gary Thompson here." He almost hung up, but restrained himself. "M-Mr. Thompson? Dane Ingersoll here." A brief pause, then "Oh, yes—Mr. Ingersoll! To what do I owe this late call?"

"I-I'd like to talk to you some more about your case, if you are still looking. When can we meet again.?"

"A-S-A-P! Are you free tomorrow?"

"I'm in trial in Ellis County, but you could meet me at the lunch break, say, at 12:15, at the coffee shop across from the courthouse?"

"That's a winner, sir. I think you'll be pleased to be on board with Rowalter. And I *know* Rowalter is pleased to have on its team a man of your many talents."

"See you then. Goodbye."

Dane flung the handset back into its cradle, stuffed the wad of phone messages into his coat pocket, and began the trek back to his car. Somehow, though, what should have provided at least some momentary relief only brought an uncanny sense of foreboding. The darkness enveloped him as he slid into the seat and drove silently home.

* * * *

The cross examination of Missy Bell was textbook. James Dougherty, lead defense attorney, had elected to do the work himself—something Dane had fully anticipated. Cross exam of a star witness was no assignment for a third-year associate, no matter how brilliant he might be. It represented the highest art and skill of the trial attorney, in and of itself. More to the point, the likes of Missy Bell posed some unique challenges on cross. The attorney's task was to identify glaring inconsistencies in her story, but without reducing her to tears or bullying her. To overstep that gossamer line even an inch would alienate the jury, creating a strategic advantage for Dane that Dougherty might never reclaim. John Rugs was on the edge of his seat for the entire two hours, carefully noting every glance, expression or gesture of the panel.

Dane had coached Missy well. She appeared forthright and truthful; mildly indignant, yet respectful. Her answers were terse, and she volunteered nothing gratuitously. Every answer was followed by "Sir"—not just to evoke the Southern custom still followed in parts of Texas and the South, but to buffer Missy's utter hatred and contempt for the defense. Her eyes remained riveted on her adversary's lawyer and did not waiver, just as Dane had coached her. Her tone conveyed the truth: she had lost her and her beloved husband's entire retirement at the hands of a greedy and unscrupulous broker. The jury must be brought to understand this, and each juror must become just as righteously angry as she was. At five past twelve an obviously tiring Judge Fize pulled off his glasses, rubbed his eyes, and dismissed the jury for lunch.

"Are you going to at least join us for lunch *today*, Boss?" Stephanie queried as Dane kicked his attaché back under the counsel table. "No, I think I'll run an errand. But don't worry; I'll be back by 1:30." Stephanie smiled suspiciously, as Dane hurried down the steps and out the south courthouse entrance to McDougal's, a local eatery which was this tiny town's answer to Denny's.

The coffee shop was filling up rapidly with the local regulars, as Dane slipped into a booth toward the back. As the waitress brought his iced tea, Gary Thompson, looking somewhat disheveled, ambled in the front door, scanning the crowd. Dane suppressed the impulse to raise his hand, simply fixing his gaze on Thompson until their eyes met. A half smile crossed Thompson's face, then he deliberately charged down the center aisle and extended his hand.

"Mr. Ingersoll, so glad to see you again! Charming little town they have here, isn't it?"

Dane noticed the tiny beads of sweat collecting on Thompson's forehead. "Yes, if you confine yourself the courthouse square." He half smiled, masking his own undulating emotions.

Thompson wasted no time in getting to the point. "Mr. Ingersol," he paused, riveting dark eyes on Dane's, "things have deteriorated rapidly even since we last met. There have been several developments. Two states: Maryland and Louisiana, have already begun inquiries into PZT. It is probable, we believe, that administrative hearings before the pharmaceuticals boards of those states could begin within ninety days or so. Of course," he paused for dramatic effect while a look of righteous anger gathered on his face, "this is all brought about by the incompetent fools up at Food and Drug. They have stonewalled approval of PZT for no reason at all, despite mounds of independent laboratory evidence that it's perfectly safe. Our sources believe the FDA may have been influenced by a few big players in the U.S. pharmaceuticals industry who feel threatened by our entry into the marketplace." He brought his face to within an inch of Dane's, as if sharing a secret between friends, "You know how political—and how powerful—*that* industry is." Dane recoiled from Thompson's foul breath, but nodded anyway, obligingly playing the straight man.

"Secondly, some big gun law firm has weighed in for several of the states down south—Texas, Georgia, Alabama. Exactly why they are intervening at this late stage, we don't know." He held up a brown envelope obviously full of papers. That firm has begun what looks like us as preparations for an injunction suit in the event we do gain FDA approval." Dane listened, taking it all in.

Thompson's hand slipped deftly inside his coat, and out came a business-sized brown envelope. Opening it gingerly, he slid a cashier's check, face downward, across the table until it rested in front of Dane's fingertips. Dane turned it over. His heart stopped momentarily as he read "One Hundred Thousand Dollars". It was a cashier's check made out to him personally, not to the firm. The memo slot on the check read simply, "Opening Retainer: FDA". Dane wavered, but only a moment, as an image of Susan, Jackie, and little Natalie appeared almost as vividly as if they were standing before him. A chill shot up his back, and he grasped the corner of the check, placing it in his inside coat pocket with an erratic jerk as if he were afraid he would change his mind. Next, Thompson handed Dane the brown over-stuffed envelope.

Thompson straightened up suddenly. "Mr. Ingersoll, we'll need you to go to work right away. There are several meetings in Washington scheduled this week. In preparation, I strongly suggest that you arm yourself with plenty of data. I'll have everything you need hand-delivered to your office tomorrow morning. We want you to spare no effort on our behalf. Simply call me with anything you need, and you'll have it."

Dane strove mightily to assume a business-as-usual demeanor which belied his real emotions at the moment. "Yes…that will be fine. I'll have my legal assistant begin a review of it while I wrap up this trial." Hoarse with excitement, yet relieved at the sudden reversal of his finances, he bid Thompson goodbye. As Thompson exited the restaurant, Dane finished the last bite of his sandwich, slapped a ten-dollar bill on the table and headed back to the courthouse south entrance. Twice on the way over, he fingered the long piece of paper now at the bottom of his coat pocket, smiling as he did. Only when he was inside the courthouse door and out of public view did he turn into the attorney's lounge on the first floor. It was vacant. Dane popped open his briefcase on a rickety table. With a lingering glance at the check, he placed it in an accordion pocket inside, grabbed the handle, and bounded upstairs to the courtroom.

As he rejoined the troops on his side of the counsel table, they instantly sensed his lifted mood. "What'd you do for lunch, go to Vegas?" Stephanie joked.

"Yeah, I broke the black jack table, against worse odds than we have with this jury", he smiled. Stephanie looked at him quizzically, but decided against any further questions. She was just happy her boss looked more like his old self than he had of late. Ours not to wonder why.... As the last juror settled into the box, Dane mentally readied himself for the passing of his star witness back to him. It happened quickly, and as expected, Dane did not disappoint. It took him only ten minutes to shore up the relatively minuscule damage that Dougherty had wrought on cross examination. When he was finished, Missie smiled confidently, first at the jury, then at her lawyer. Taking full advantage of the pause, Dane leveled his gaze confidently at his Honor.

"Pass the witness."

"No further questions," said Dougherty, with a look somewhere between resignation and pain.

John Rugs, with a side-long glance, passed a folded note across the railing to Stephanie, who in turn slid it down the table to Dane. Dane opened it and cast a quick downward glance. It read, "I give the jury 8 out of a possible 10 for finding Missie credible, and a 7-plus for identifying with her plight." Dane suppressed a smile. What John hadn't written was that the primary reason Missie didn't earn all A's was a man in the back row who seemed strangely given to staring at cracks in the ceiling and similar banalities.

The next witness was, as one would imagine, Harry Bell, who had been sitting raptly all morning watching his wife testify. If Dane was to build the trial to a crescendo, he needed to carry the momentum forward from this point without any breaks or gaps. That included, among other things, avoiding repetitive testimony at all costs.

For the rest of the afternoon, Dane presented Harry to the jury as the thoughtful, prudent, and financially responsible breadwinner that he was. The strategy was to so clearly establish Harry as someone that the average juror could identify with, that Dougherty would have tremendous difficulty going rough on him without raising the jury's ire. Not known for his superior intellect, Harry had to be led by Dane on several occasions, at least to the extent he could get away with it. But for the most part, Harry presented quite well as a stalwart, hardworking and protective husband — too honest to be fabricating or slanting his tale of financial ruin. When Dane passed him back to the defense at 5:00 p.m., he was satisfied. He knew that it would break Dougherty's concentration to start cross-examination of Harry in the morning rather than now. He was also certain that Dougherty knew that was precisely why he'd timed it thusly. He also knew that Dougherty would now be staying up till all hours tonight, in order to prepare that cross-examination.

As the day's testimony came to a close, Dane finally allowed himself to think about Susan, Jackie and Natalie. It felt like an eternity since he had seen them. Driving home on the busy freeway to Dallas, he could think of nothing else but the touch of his wife's face against his, the fragrance she usually wore, her deliciously supple body against his—it had been so very long. In a few days Susan would be home from the hospital, and he would tell her all about the new big case that was his and his alone. It made the bitter pill of the news about Natalie go down just a bit easier. He turned to exit onto Ibsen Boulevard. With a little luck, he thought, he would be able to afford Natalie's treatment and Susan's medical bills besides. But, first, he had something to do. Routing himself by the bank, which he caught just before the drive-through lanes closed, he pulled into one of the stations. From the glove compartment, he pulled a pre-printed deposit slip in his and Susan's name. Hesitating for a long moment, he suddenly sprang into action, feverishly making out the deposit slip for $100,000. He leaned over his briefcase and opened it, then reached down deep into the accordion pocket to feel for the cashier's check. It was there. Reverently, he extracted it and set it next to the deposit slip. He indorsed the back of the check, then on the "Cash withheld" line of the deposit slip he scrawled "$20,000." Slipping the deposit into the delivery tube, he closed the cover, heard the air suction begin, and watched the girl open it through the drive-through window. She smiled at him as she always did, then looked down and hesitated for a brief moment.

"Mr. Ingersoll, I'll have to get this amount of cash approved, excuse me a moment". Dane nodded back from a distance. The young lady was back in a moment, and a minute later he had $20,000 in large bills in his hand. He reached for his glove compartment, opened it and extracted an envelope into which he placed the money. He sealed it, and with a pen marked on it "Salacuse & Lockridge". He replaced the envelope in the glove compartment, inserted his key and locked it. Restarting his car, he wheeled out of the bank parking lot and drew a beeline to his house, where he would sleep alone yet another night.

CHAPTER NINE

The Bell trial concluded the following day. The case went to the jury about 2:00 p.m., and its members deliberated for four hours, before coming back with a unanimous verdict for the Bells. Just as Dane had planned, the jury became angry—even indignant, according to John Rugs—and awarded a total of $10,400,000 to Dane's clients, not counting attorney's fees. During the deliberations, Dane had called and arranged for a private nursing service to accompany Susan home, but still felt guilty he couldn't be there. "I'm just fine, Honey," she had assured him, "You stay with the jury and I'll be here when you get home."

Susan, as always, was selfless. But she was also brooding and morose, and understandably so, because little Natalie had had to stay behind in the neonatal unit at the hospital. Natalie's condition was guarded but holding steady at the moment. The sight of her hooked to a dozen tubes was heart-rending. The medical triumvirate of Woodbine, Stapleton and Jaynes cautioned against optimism as they continued to "search for the problem". They need not have worried, as Dane was anything but optimistic. What reason could there possibly be for optimism? The doctors, for all their degrees and pedigrees, didn't seem to know any more than Dane about what to do.

Dane took a much-needed day off. It was Wednesday. They left Jackie at the neighbor's till evening to give Susan a little rest. Dane felt utterly burned out from the stress of the trial and the worry over Susan and Natalie. He slept in like a bear in hibernation till ten, then lay in bed most of the day reveling in being with Susan again after so long. They held each other for hours, whispering softly of good times, and of Natalie. Dane yearned to make love, but Susan, though wanting to please him, still hurt too much. They prayed and wondered nervously what would happen with Natalie. Dane deliberately avoided any mention of the insurance situation. At dinner time, Jackie rejoined them, and Dane went out for some Chinese take-out. Susan lay in bed, trying valiantly to look like she felt better than she did.

After Susan was asleep for the night, Dane lay a long time staring at the ceiling, unable to sleep. Finally, as he heard the grandfather clock in the foyer sound 2:00, he swung his feet over the side of the bed and spotted the huge stuffed envelope under his briefcase in the corner. "Oh well," he thought, eyes squinting in the dimness, "at least it will lull me to sleep". Dane stumbled out of bed and fetched the envelope. Heading for the kitchen, he stopped by the cupboard, retrieved a mug and made himself some instant hot chocolate. He then propped his feet up on the coffee table, turned on the lamp and, sipping the hot drink, reached into the envelope.

The first thing he pulled out at random was a letter from one Lawrence Goggins, a chemist at the Food and Drug Administration in Washington D.C. In straightforward yet scientific jargon, it discussed what appeared to be test results of a spectrograph test run on a drug sample. The letter, directed to the CEO of Rowalter Industries, referred to the "B Trials"— apparently tests of various samples of the substance at varying temperatures. Enclosed with the letter were some graphs that had been machine drawn by spectrometer. Nothing particularly out of the ordinary so far. Trace elements were represented by different colors on a pie graph. The only thing which piqued Dane's curiosity was some handwriting scrawled in the lower left-hand corner of the second page in red ink. It read "Decay rate 2.7 times normal, at 75° F."

This letter was followed by a series of relatively innocuous form letters from the FDA to Rowalter Industries in Mexico, each asking for some additional information and test results. Next, Dane extracted some laboratory test results using rats, complete with color photographs. It was not immediately clear who performed the tests. As he quickly perused the photographs, his eyes suddenly froze on a blow up of a rat in a grotesque position. Its body was frozen rigid in an arched position, with the back curved into an excruciatingly contorted posture—even for a rat. The head, neck and back were arched up and back in a convex pattern that made its nose nearly touch its hindquarters. More arresting still was an unnervingly eerie look on the rat's face; a terrified, heart-stopping look of mixed agony and horror. The animal's tongue lolled out of its mouth and looked distended and bloody. At the bottom of the photograph appeared the caption: "Effects of administration after 7-day decay period." Dane took another sip of the hot chocolate, and forced himself to look away from the gruesome image.

Mixed in among the materials appeared a letter on Rowalter stationery from a Jerry Johnston. It was addressed to the director of the FDA Pre-Certification Division. The upshot of the letter was clearly to argue the point that Rowalter had demonstrated the safety of a drug known as "PZT" for administration to humans "numerous consistently applied independent laboratory trials". The letter was professionally done, and read like an article in a chemistry research journal, containing ample footnotes citing numerous supporting studies. It contained an extensive section subtitled "Resistance to Decay of PZT under a Variety of Environmental Conditions." The conclusion stated, "PZT has been conclusively shown to produce no statistically significant ill effects in humans when administered within one year of release." Dane felt his eyes began to grow heavy. He chugged the rest of the hot chocolate and returned the materials to the envelope. For some indiscernible reason, he felt confident in his client's findings and had a satisfied feeling as he went to bed. This would be an interesting and profitable case. Yet, as he drifted off to sleep, he couldn't quite rid himself of the rat's contorted visage.

Thursday morning, Dane made it to the office around ten. He had left Susan sleeping soundly. On his way to his office, he stopped by the 39th floor, and went directly to James Thompson's office. It was not often that Dane had dealings with the firm's billing partner, or with Jeannette, the partner's blonde, bubbly and beautiful secretary. On those few occasions where actual cash was given by a client, Jeannette also functioned as the collecting agent.

"Howdy, Jeannette!" Dane managed a cheerful greeting, belying his true feelings. "'Gotta' *swell* retainer, and they paid in cash!" he said, caricaturing mock-adolescent enthusiasm. Then, more seriously:

"Put it against *Rowalter v. United States Food and Drug Administration*—it's a new matter."

"Roger Sir," Jeannette beamed back, counting the cash and jotting a receipt which she slid across the desk.

"Yessirree, Jeannette, Sweetheart, I think we've gotta' big one here."

"It's hard to see how you trial types can get so frothy over such boring cases—I mean, approval of drugs and all. Haven't you ever tried a murder or rape or something?"

"As a matter of fact I did once, and the guy was as guilty as sin. But in a strange kind of way, these cases have as much riding on them as any murder. And a whole lot more money." He winked.

"Maybe so. But I don't see any glamour about them. What's the big thrill?"

"Stay tuned. You might just be surprised."

Dane practically jogged to the elevator on the other side of the double glass doors to Jeannette's right. He narrowly avoided colliding with Jerek Barbour as he did so.

"Whoa, boy—going to a fire? Say, did you get the note I left you?"

"No" and "Yes", Dane grinned. Jerek squinted, perplexed.

"Don't worry, Jerek, I know you tried hard to help, but I've got it handled. We may not need the insurance after all."

"Don't *need the*—!" Jerek echoed, but his words were cut off by the elevator door closing. Moments later, Dane reached his destination and bolted for this office. Rounding the corner by his secretary's desk, he came face to face with—

"Hello, again Dane."

"Jenny Pemberton! I thought you said you were with Hutchison Davis. Are you across from us on one of their cases?"

"Close," she smiled sweetly. "But no cigar. I've been hired by your litigation section. I understand that's your section, too."

"You could say that. But, I didn't even know you were looking."

"Neither did I, until they told us they were closing down the anti-trust section at H&D." Jenny wore an attractive but professional black dress with a slit up the calf. It showcased her still-girlish shape. She brightened suddenly, shifting the weight of the stack of files she carried. "Maybe you could show me the ropes, sort of introduce me around?"

"Sure," he hesitated for a millisecond, then said "Why not? I've got this new FDA case I'm working on. Let's meet for lunch tomorrow, and we'll talk about it. Then I'll show you around the firm."

"'Sounds like a plan," she smiled and continued in the direction of the library.

Back in his office, Dane spread out on his conference table which looked out over the skyline. He pulled out the stacks of paper Thompson had given him, and began placing them in piles. He pulled out a legal pad on which he had written in block lettering,

"WASHINGTON, D.C. Prep", and began scribbling cryptic notes. As he did so, the dead rat with the bloody tongue kept flashing across his mind. He abruptly laid down his pencil, rose and strode across the room to his credenza. He located Gary Thompson's number on his electronic Rolodex, and punched in the numbers on his speaker phone. Two rings and a click let Dane know the phone was being forwarded, and a moment later Thompson's now-familiar voice could be heard on the speaker. Some incidental hissing made Dane think he was on a cell phone. "Gary Thompson, Rowalter Enterprises."

"Yes, Gary, Dane here. I'll be ready for the hearing in Washington. But I wonder if you could field a couple of questions for me. In going through the materials you left for me, I couldn't help noticing the lab rat studies. Could you explain for me what the results were—and what happened to the specimen that looks...well...like it's been tortured?" Awkward hesitation on the other end of the line.

"Sure, Dane." Walter's voice was confident, almost flippant. "It seems that one of the batches of PZT that was used in one of those studies was—er—formulated without first running it through some pretest quality checks. Now, I'm no chemist, but my understanding from the lab is that some adulterant found its way into the mix—obviously, some slipshod quality control. They caught it on the next batch, though. I don't believe you'll find a repeat episode in the documentation. And, feel free to call Dr. Norman Holloway, our chemist in charge, if you need more technical backup on it." He rattled off the phone number, which Dane scribbled on the corner of his yellow pad. He made a mental note to call Holloway, knowing that any adversarial attack by the FDA would surely demand answers to precisely Dane's question.

Next, Dane buzzed the office of Dean, a first-year associate who had shown a talent for computer assisted research. "Alton Dean," droned the monotone, against classical music playing in the background. "Alton, 'gotta project for you with a short fuse. I will have an important hearing with the FDA on a drug approval case in Washington within the next several weeks. Can you drop what you're doing?"

"Sure, if Fenton Wells will yield to you. His deadline is two weeks off."

"Good. I want you to get everything you can find on a drug called PZT, made by a company named Rowalter Enterprises out of Bolivia. Start with tests on lab animals, then cover experiments with humans. Look at any medical journal articles, symposiums, clinical trials, that sort of thing. I want the bad as well as the good. If you have to translate foreign written articles of the internet, do it. And don't whitewash anything. This is for cross examination by the feds."

"I know enough Spanish that I shouldn't have to use a translation engine. You forget I minored in it in college. Do you want it briefed?"

"Yeah, give me a recommendation as to whether it's safe, based on a solid consensus of medical opinion."

"You got it", said Alton, letting his eagerness show. Most first-year associates looked at research as a necessary evil along the long path to the courtroom. Alton viewed it as an art form unto itself.

As the intercom fell silent, Dane mused about a medical expert. He would need a pharmacologist or research physician...an academic type...and preferably someone that had never accepted a dollar from Rowalter. Better still would be someone with a teaching position at a prestigious university. As he began flipping through his "Physicians" file, his intercom buzzed.

"Yes, Gina."

"Boss, there's a Dr. Zimmerman on your line one— something about some FDA hearings."

"Put him on." The speaker phone crackled to life.

"Hello, Dane here."

There was only silence; then, "Mr. Ingersoll? Dane Ingersoll?"

"This is he, go ahead," Dane answered, somewhat impatiently.

"I'm Dr. Richard Zimmerman. I am the head Chemist at the Center for Study of Experimental Drugs, Johns Hopkins University."

"And—" Dane knew he sounded rude, but he had no time for uninvited guests at the moment.

"And," repeated the Doctor, " Someone at Rowalter Industries suggested I get in touch with you regarding an experimental drug known as PZT. I believe you are working on a trial or a hearing dealing with the subject."

Dane halted, momentarily startled. He was at once pleasantly surprised and amazed at the diligence of Mr. Thompson. "They certainly don't leave much to chance, do they?"

"I beg your pardon?"

"Oh, nothing. Yes, Doctor, I'm glad you called. I wonder if we might get together in my office. Say, tomorrow afternoon?"

"I think that can be arranged. I am in British Columbia in the middle of a trial today, but they tell me they are finished with me for the week. What time do you need me there?"

"Three o' clock should be fine. I won't be ready for you till than then, anyway. I have more to do than I can say grace over". As he hung up, Dane's mind whirled with questions about just what Zimmerman's ties to Rowalter were.

* * * *

Federal Bureau of Investigation, Washington, D.C.

Jim Patterson was frustrated. He and his hand-picked special agents from the Dallas Field Office had tracked the Dallas trial lawyer for nearly two weeks, yet failed to produce anything of real value for Deputy Director Harless. He had been briefed that Rowalter Industries had retained the services of Dane Ingersoll, specifically through the acumen of Gary Thompson. Operatives working closely with Patterson had obtained recorded conversations of most of Ingersoll's and Thompson's discussions, and it was obvious that the attorney was now heading full bore for an FDA trial in Washington, which the Bureau believed could well determine the fate of PZT. Jim pulled into his specially designated parking space, marked "Senior Special Agent Patterson," at the J. Edgar Hoover Building, 935 Pennsylvania Avenue. Nearly sprinting from his car, he took the steps two at a time as he jogged to make the meeting with Deputy Director Harless by 1:00. Harless had mentioned that Fred Hue, Executive Director of the National Drug Intelligence Center (NDIC), would also be present. That fact alone told Jim that this meeting was serious business.

Jim arrived at Harless' massive office door just as Fred Hue was arriving. Hue's face, normally composed and business-like, looked as white as a ghost. He half-smiled a terse greeting to James, who quickly decided to reserve his questions till they were with the deputy director. Harless was hunched over his credenza in classic pose, half stooped, staring intently out of his window, favorite cigar between two left fingers. He heard both men enter at the other end of the cavernous office and turned, waiving them in. "Hello, Fred, Jim. Coffee?" Both declined. Jim was wired enough already, just from watching Hue. "Jim, I understand you're on that lawyer's trail in Dallas. You got anything to show for it yet?"

"I'm afraid not a lot I can sink my teeth into, yet. He's met with Thompson from Rowalter two or three times, and we have those conversations. And we have some video. We know he'll be in Washington next week to try to change the FDA's mind in a major hearing. I think it may be time to make contact."

"My thoughts, exactly. How, though? We need to carry it off without Ingersoll necessarily being aware it's us. He might get worried, and in the process alert his client. Fred, have you got any thoughts?"

"You could use a doctor or chemist posing as a forensic expert." Hue had some of his facial color back now. "It's a good bet that to be ready for the FDA hearing he'll be using an independent, or one of Rowalter's people. Find a way to get an expert we know in a position of influence before he hooks up with anyone else."

"There's only one problem with that, Mr. Harless," interrupted Jim. Expert witnesses are not in the habit of just calling up out of the blue and volunteering their services. It not only looks suspicious, it brands them as anxious to be hired, and therefore unreliable."

"I agree with you," mused Harless. "But haven't you unearthed anyone close to Ingersoll—someone he trusts, who we could gain access through?"

"Perhaps..." Jim seized on an idea. "There's this new legal assistant hired on by his firm. Our investigation reveals that they knew each other in high school, and even dated at one time. There appears to have been no rancor when they parted."

"That sounds like it could be just what we need." Both Harless and Hue nodded their heads as if on cue.

"Jim, I want you to engineer the contact. We need to move pretty fast with this one. We have a phenomenal increase just this past week of cases of mutating PZT. Our eastern bureau Chief has identified at least 12 cases. So far, there is no indication the FDA has put two and two together, but it's only a matter of time before their chemists connect the dots. This hot dog attorney has got to be brought into the loop.

"You'll have my full report by next week, Boss."

"Fine, but be careful. There's a lot riding on this for a helluva lot of people. Watch your back, Jim."

CHAPTER TEN

<u>First International Building, Dallas</u>

"Sweetheart, you've got to get down to the hospital right away." It was Susan. Gina had switched the call to him in the 47th floor conference room—the designated "War Room" for the Rowalter case—where Dane and Jenny were surrounded by stacks of paper. "Dr. Weinberger says there's been a serious development". Gina's voice faltered as she mouthed the words.

Dane's heart skipped a beat. Then, catching his breath, he gulped, "I'll be right there. Call me on the cell phone in three minutes." He yelled to Jenny over his shoulder as he bolted for the elevator—"Call Dr. Zimmerman. I don't know when I'll be back!"

"I hope everything's OK!", she shot back.

Downstairs in the car, Dane fumbled for the phone and dropped his car keys as he fiercely stabbed at the "Home" button.   As he did so, his thoughts raced. Just last night, they had stood at fragile little Natalie's bedside, and everything had seemed to be going well. What could have possibly gone wrong since then? Susan answered in the middle of the first ring. She was breathless, and obviously headed for the car herself.

"Dane," she said, her voice quavering, "I think it's serious"—*a long pause*—"they say she's in and out of consciousness!"

"Go straight to the hospital," Dane croaked back. "I'll meet you there."

With his very best attempt at composure, he talked to himself saying, "I'm sure she's fine," but disbelieving the words as soon as he'd spoken them. His tires laid scratch as he spun out of the lot and onto the freeway ramp. For the next eight miles and what seemed a lifetime, he and Susan spoke by cell phone, alternately wondering aloud, then each upbraiding the other. They pulled into the East Dallas Medical complex literally within seconds of each other. Without stopping to embrace, they bounded in unison up the steps of the old building and into an already open lobby elevator. Dane's heart pounded audibly in his head in the stillness of the elevator. He was sure the other people could hear it. Suddenly, they lurched to a stop on the 6th floor. Deciding not to wait for the doctor, they ran down the hallway to the NICU. The expansive unit was dimly lit, with nurses moving slowly and deliberately amongst the incubators. Each incubator contained the frame of a tiny little infant, sometimes barely visible beneath webs of tubing. As his eyes began adjusting to the low light, Dane spotted Natalie's name on the incubator in the far corner. There was a curtain drawn part way around her. She still had tubes hooked, it seemed, everywhere—including ones reaching into her tiny nose. Dane's eyes met Susan's, as they absorbed the pitiful, heart-wrenching sight. Natalie's eyelids were closed, and her color had changed since the night before to a more sallow hue. Dane slipped his arm around Susan's waist. They heard footsteps softly behind them, and turned together to see Dr. Weinberger staring somberly at them. He looked weary.

"Well, Doctor...what gives?", Dane heard himself ask.

"I'm afraid Natalie's condition has deteriorated rather significantly." His eyes alternated between the floor and the Ingersolls' intense gaze. Her breathing, even on the respirator, has become more erratic. Liver enzyme tests are not encouraging."

Dane locked gazes with Susan for a moment, and each suppressed a gasp. Susan broke the silence first. "Doctor, we're not giving up," she paused to catch her composure, to find the right words. "Surely there is something that can be done that you haven't tried yet. I know you've worked hard, but I just refuse to believe—" Her voice broke with raw emotion.

"Doctor Weinberger, shoot straight with us. What are our options?" Dane took over.

"Because so little is known of this malady, there are not very many. There is a treatment which is in the experimental stage. No long-term studies have been completed on the residual effects, though. There would be a significant level of risk involved. Besides, I'm not sure we can get the drug we need. For the time being, it's been black-listed by the FDA. Even if we could somehow acquire it, you'd have to release us and the hospital from any liability for negative effects of the drug before we could touch her. I'm sorry to be so direct, but—"

"What is the risk of doing nothing?" Dane interrupted, trying hard to ignore the ominous hissing of the respirator.

"In my opinion, near certain death; and potentially a quite painful one. Judging by the tests performed today, I don't see much reason for optimism. Of course, you're free to consult with Drs. Woodbine,

Stapleton and Jenson, and I would encourage you to do so to answer any questions. But I must tell you, my opinion reflects my consultation with them."

"I don't think we need to talk with them if they're going to say the same thing you just did, Doc. It doesn't seem as if we have much choice, does it, Hon?" Dane squeezed Susan closer to him. Susan had collected herself, but she couldn't speak without crying, so she just nodded.

"I assume you need a decision now?"

"There's not much time".

"Do what you can, Doctor. And for God's sake, do *everything* you can." Susan's eyes showed resigned agreement. "We'll sign what you need us to."

Weinberger left the room, promising to stay in touch, while Dane and Susan hovered over their daughter's incubator like doting guardian angels. They remained there into the night, breathing through the masks they'd been given to wear. Strict NICU visiting hours were long since up, but the charge nurse, who was an understanding sort, looked the other way. In the quiet of the night, broken only by the sound of the respirators and the low, eerie light coming from the medical equipment, the young couple huddled together. They asked themselves why, cried, comforted each other, then quietly but firmly resolved to go on. Not until this moment had Dane ever quite realized the love he had for his new daughter. Somewhere around 1:00 a.m., the charge nurse gently approached and whispered it was time to go.

* * * *

The Ingersolls finally reached home around 2:00 a.m. They retired to bed, where they got just about as much sleep if they had taken a cold shower. Fitfully, Dane drifted into half slumber with Susan's head resting on his right forearm. He could feel the moistness on her cheek from her tears. *"Somehow we'll get through this. Somehow things will be all right."* The amorphous thought filtered through his consciousness.

* * * *

About 9:35 a.m., Dane's mind-numbing slumber was shattered by the ringing of the telephone on the night table three inches away He sat bolt upright in bed, realized where he was, then lunged for the phone, knocking over the alarm clock in the process. It was Weinberger.

"Mr. Ingersoll, things have stabilized somewhat for Natalie. We began the experimental treatment at around 4:00 a.m. We still have a long way to come out of the woods, but I do feel like she's doing better. Her vital signs have stabilized and we are seeing some positive signs in the liver enzyme tests. For now, at least, your daughter is beginning to turn the corner a little bit." Dane's head was completely clear now. Susan had awakened, and had a quizzical look on her face, demanding information. Dane shared the receiver with her, crooking it under his chin, while silently mouthing the words, "Natalie's better!"

"We'll need to keep her on this treatment for quite some time, of course. The next couple of weeks should tell us whether her body's defenses can recover. But you need to be aware that we don't have a lot of data to go on at this point. We'll need to keep a close watch on her because of the experimental nature of this treatment."

Dane and Susan held each other a long time. Then, Dane did the one thing he always cautioned his clients not to do, but which they routinely did anyway— he permitted himself to hear only the good news, and blocked out all the rest. It seemed as if he saw the world through new eyes in the space of a few short hours. Susan was no different, and they chatted hopefully about Natalie's prospects as Susan got up to make coffee. Dane, despite the impending hearing in Washington, had slept in. But suddenly, he had a rush of energy, and had to get to work—for Natalie's sake as much as anything.

CHAPTER ELEVEN

The streets were busy as usual with the lunchtime crowd on Akard Street. Jenny had tried to chum up with some of the other litigation section paralegals, but they seemed to already have their clique, and had left early for a nearby eatery. So, she struck out on her own for lunch, negotiating her way through the hundreds of other girls who were also on lunch break. The men in the law firm, and the couple of women who were partners, never seemed to take lunch breaks, often ordering food in if they ate at all. Part of the lawyer macho image, she thought to herself. Jenny knew this part of downtown. She was only two blocks away from the Transamerica Building which housed her old job at Hutchison Davis. Gradually, she maneuvered her way to the intersection at Akard and Forester, where sat the venerable institution of Schneider's Deli. There, she thought, she would find some of her old Hutchison gang. The sun caressing her sleeveless shoulders felt good as she waited for the light to change. The famous Mercantile Bank clock and the trademark red Mobil flying horse were visible from her vantage point amongst the eight or ten people waiting to cross. The wind gusted suddenly and she reached down to hold her skirt in place.

Jenny did not see the man deftly approach her from behind. As the light changed, the man matched his gait to hers. Then, when they both mounted the curb on the other side, the man seamlessly interposed himself between Jenny and Schneider's. Simultaneously, he extracted a wallet from his coat, flipped it open to reveal a badge, and muttered the words, "Hello, Miss Pemberton. F.B.I." Jenny's heart leapt to her throat. She glanced around nervously to see who was watching. "I'd like a few moments with you. May we step inside?"

What was she going to say—"No?" Of course she'd step inside. The man escorted her to a booth in the back, in a separate room off of the main dining room. They sat, and the agent began to speak, in a voice that sounded like her father's—brisk and businesslike, but not entirely devoid of concern.

"My name is Agent Patterson."

"*Just like in the spy movies—no first name,*" thought Jenny, still disoriented.

"I understand you work with Dane Ingersoll at the law firm of Salacuse & Lockridge," he paused as Jenny nodded furtively, glancing around the deli. Mr. Ingersoll is working in an area that the Federal Bureau of Investigation is very interested in at the moment." Jenny's expression became quizzical. "We know that he has recently been engaged by a new client—a certain 'Rowalter Industries, S.A.' We also know the nature of the work he is doing for Rowalter, and about the upcoming hearing in Washington, D.C."

"Wh-why is the FBI interested in Dane Ingersoll or his w-w-work?" Jenny managed to stammer. "A fair question," Patterson responded with anchorman objectivity. "Our agency has reason to believe that Rowalter Industries may not be pursuing an entirely honorable enterprise."

"What reason?" Jenny's eyes had widened, and her curiosity had suddenly eclipsed her fear. "I can't divulge to you everything I know at this time, Miss Pemberton. You understand, of course." He uttered this last phrase in the same manner as if Jenny was a fellow agent he was taking into his confidence. "But", he paused and leaned forward on his elbows with hands folded under his chin "I can tell you that what Mr. Ingersoll thinks is just a normal pharmaceutical certification case, is really much more than that." Patterson's voice grew suddenly hushed. "The drug which Rowalter seeks to approve—though beneficial in many cases—has some very negative effects—very dangerous effects. It has the ability to alter its molecular structure, and becomes highly habit-forming when it does so. It also, in such form, can kill." He looked at Jenny, whose face had gone ashen.

"And you want Dane for ..." her voice trailed off, puzzled.

"We want Mr. Ingersoll to know just what the implications are of that drug getting FDA approval without this information coming out. Listen: I've got a law degree. I know Dane has to do the best job he can for his client. But I also believe he has a conscience, and that he would want to know what information we possess before he went before them on such a critical matter. We have some lab tests and reports we'd like to make available to him."

Regaining her composure, Jenny began plying Agent Patterson with questions.

"How do I know this is for real, and that this drug is what you say it is?"

"We've had our top chemists working on it for some time. To our knowledge, there has never been anything quite like this drug in all of pharmacology history: a drug that has legitimate medicinal uses, but which mutates completely at random in certain organisms to become a lethal substance. Controlled substances like heroin or cocaine don't alter their form, even though opiates have some medicinal uses. That makes this drug especially problematic, since all forms of it will not necessarily be dangerous, and some never will, at least in the short term."

"What you seem to be asking is for Dane to pull punches in representing his client. How can you expect him to do that?"

"Frankly," Patterson replied, "I don't. He's too good an attorney for that, has a good success record and a killer instinct. We've done a thorough background on him." Patterson motioned toward a bulging portfolio that Jenny assumed contained a dossier with much material. "Besides," he continued, "the FBI is not looking to get any attorney in trouble with their state bar association on ethical grounds—you know—not zealously representing his client and all."

"Where do I fit into all this?"

"That's a good question. We'd like you to help us plant some damaging evidence in Mr. Ingersoll's case. Not enough to raise unnecessary suspicions, but just enough to poison the well so that the drug isn't approved. That will buy us the time we need to marshal the proof we need to go after Rowalter."

"But I don't understand why you don't just release the information you apparently have, without going to all this trouble. Once the information got out, the product would be pulled, wouldn't it?"

"Not without a couple of things being triggered—very negative things. First, a public panic. This product has already found its way to lots of pharmaceutical warehouses, wholesalers, and doctors and hospitals. Someone within Rowalter, no one exactly knows who, managed to finagle sort of a "trial use period" with the FDA, after which independent lab tests were to be performed before sale could continue. This is somewhat unusual, and probably could not have happened without a bribe or some connection between a Rowalter higher-up and someone of corresponding position within the FDA. It's already working its way into the medical infrastructure, and to announce something for which we still don't have irrefutable evidence could cause a lot of people who are genuinely benefitting from the drug to get hurt."

"Second, we expose the government to massive liability if we act before we have proof positive—both from Rowalter, and from patients who are receiving apparent benefits from the drug." He paused for emphasis. "I say 'apparent' because it is still arguable that no significant benefit is received, at least when compared to the incredibly addictive power of this drug."

Jenny accepted this information bemusedly. To "poison the well"—to somehow plant harmful evidence into the case—went against every last instinct, and ethic, in her body. Yet, if true, she didn't want to expose people...innocent people...to a deadly risk that she had been told about by a reliable source. *Maybe he's not with the FBI. Maybe he works for a Rowalter competitor. No, this guy seemed too legit. And how could he have tracked her down so smoothly unless he were a Fed? If only this Patterson fellow hadn't found her and told her this; if only she hadn't bumped into Dane that day or come to work at Salacuse & Lockridge; if only..."*

Patterson abruptly interrupted her thoughts. "The FBI has access to experts in the field of experimental pharmacology. The best way—maybe the only way—to successfully influence the case without being detected is through one of these experts." He reached into the portfolio, pulling out a sealed brown envelope. "Look through these materials tonight. Everything you need to know is in here. Let no one, absolutely no one, see the contents.:

"But h-how do I know you are who you say you are?"

Instantly, Patterson pressed a card into her hand. Staring back up at her was the well-known blue and gold FBI logo with Patterson's name and the words "Special Agent" beneath.

"There, now may we count on your cooperation?" His unblinking eyes—half asking, half commanding—bored into hers.

"I—I suppose. But how will I know..."

"Don't worry," Patterson read her mind. "We know when and how to get ahold of you. We have a very close watch on everyone involved in this matter."

"What a comforting thought," mused Jenny, as Agent Patterson slid the envelope to her side of the table.

"We need to know tonight beyond any doubt whether you agree to cooperate with us. Review the contents of the envelope, then call me at the number on the card. It's answered 24 hours a day, wherever I am. And Miss Pemberton," his tone was firm and even, "I must know by this evening. Remember: let no one else see the materials", he glanced quickly at the envelope. "If you won't cooperate we will be retrieving them from you promptly. Show them to anyone else, and both their existence and their origin will be officially denied." Jenny only nodded, words failing her.

A waitress had appeared at the table, inquiring about lunch. Agent Patterson suddenly softened and seemed much less business-like. "Lunch?" he half smiled at Jenny, as if this were just another social visit. "No thanks," she replied blankly. I've lost my appetite." Jenny slid out from behind the booth table, clutching the brown envelope in one hand, and slinging her purse over her opposite shoulder. As she walked hurriedly away, Patterson commenced ordering his lunch as if this sort of thing occurred every day.

Jenny's walk back to the First International Building was performed on automatic pilot; she was not sure how or when she actually arrived back at War Room on the 47th floor. Her mind raced with the speed of a computer, darting here and there in a thousand directions. Even though she had to get ready for Dane's meeting with Dr. Zimmerman and arrange hundreds of exhibits for the hearing, her mind wouldn't let her concentrate. The envelope burned in her hand as if on fire. When the elevator doors opened on the 47th floor, she made a bee line for the lady's room, flung the door aside, and went into one of stalls. She locked the door, sat on the commode, and carefully removed the contents of the envelope with trembling hands.

She extracted three documents of eight to ten pages each. Each had a cover sheet declaring in large, bold relief letters: **"FEDERAL BUREAU OF INVESTIGATION: CONFIDENTIAL DOCUMENT. DISCLOSURE SUBJECT TO FEDERAL CRIMINAL PENALTIES."** Her eyes hovered, momentarily still, over the caption of the first document. Then, drawing a deep breath, she made herself turn the page. What she saw made her recoil in disgust. Underneath the title, "Mutative Effects of PZT in Long Term Study" by Dr. Lawrence Standig, in the inset, were three photographs of chimpanzees. Each one was quite obviously dead, and the face of each contorted into a grotesquely horrifying grimace. The eyes were bulging, the chests concaved inward, and the bodies stretched into pretzel-like postures. Blood appeared in large splotches at various places on the bodies.

On the following page were inset pictures of two adult men from Peru, also writhing in apparent pain, and also quite dead. The expressions on the faces were like nothing she had ever seen, with each man's tongue bloody and swollen, dangling out of his mouth. Printed in three even columns under the pictures were the doctor's observations, including the fact that the Peruvian men had been known to have a diet which included the chewing of leaves from the "Queñua tree" over many years. The author surmised that a physical dependency had set in, theorizing that when the intake of the chemical found in the leaves was halted the substance had mutated, or rapidly changed its molecular structure, to a deadly substance. The article also, in a footnote, stated that because no controlled studies had been done on humans, no firm conclusions could be drawn.

Jenny flipped hurriedly through the other articles, both of which had more pictures of the same gruesome subject matter. Some involved experiments on cats, dogs or guinea pigs. In every one, a seeming addiction and withdrawal were somehow connected with mutation of the substance, followed by swift and horrible death. All of the authors were heavily pedigreed, and two of them came from South America: one from Brazil, one from Argentina. One of the men had an Oxford Ph.D., and another, Yale. Jenny felt a wave of nausea grip her stomach, and for a minute thought she would vomit. She quickly slid the articles back into the envelope and exited the restroom. The palms of her hands bore a cold, clammy sweat.

Back in the War Room, there was a bustle of activity, with law clerks running everywhere. Dane was arriving just as Jenny got back. The world seemed brighter to Dane for the first time in weeks, and he actually found himself noticing Jenny's appearance. She was dressed in a red blazer and a navy-blue skirt with one of those slits up the side that invited attention to her slim, tanned legs. Her auburn hair was worn short, revealing an attractive neck, which swept classically downward into equally classic shoulders and ample breasts. A gold belt marked her slender waist. She had busied herself with the files, and appeared to him to be totally immersed.

"How is the baby?" she asked, partly hidden behind a stack on the conference room table.

"Better, but still being watched closely. The doctor says the next week or so is critical."

"If there's anything I can do to help, let me know, OK?"

"Sure thing. Thanks. What's going on with Dr. Zimmerman? Are we set to talk with him?"

"Er, yeah", stammered Jenny uncertainly. I set him up for a meeting with you today at three, hoping you would be back from the hospital. One of the law clerks will be picking him up at DFW, terminal 3.

"Good. I'll need Alton there with the brief he promised me on positive and negative effects of the drug. I'd like you, Jenny, to bring any case studies you can find, using actual subjects in drug trials—that's *medical*, not legal. Can you whip something up for me?"

Jenny gulped, averted her eyes, and waited what seemed to her an eon to respond. "Sure...sure thing." Then, more boldly, "Do you want me to stay within the United States, or to go worldwide?"

"If it's in English, I want it. Oh, and also—we may be working late hours for the next few nights, tabbing exhibits and planning strategy. Think you'll be up to it?"

"You know me, Dane. I'll do whatever is necessary." The words had a haunting ring, even as she uttered them. Normally, she would have been exhilarated to stay up and work a late night with Dane on anything whatever, but things seemed so different since lunch hour. "Dane, how much is this case worth to you in fees?" She tried mightily to make the query sound nonchalantly curious.

"Do you promise not to tell?" he half smiled, lowering his voice to half volume.

"Sure thing," Jenny played along.

"Easily two hundred thousand, perhaps much more, if any appeal work is involved."

Jenny suppressed her astonishment at the number. "I guess it's really a 'must win' situation for you, huh—I mean, with you being up for partner and all?"

"Let's just say I never allow myself to consider the possibility of defeat—either for the client's sake or my own. If I play, I play to win."

After half an hour of activity, mostly involving pulling materials together for the meeting with Rowalter's expert witness, Dane whisked out of the War Room and upstairs in search of Alton. Jenny took this occasion to dart out also, down the hallway that ran behind the reception area, and around the corner into a narrow vestibule. The vestibule contained a door which opened into a narrow room not much bigger than a phone booth and with the same purpose—to allow well-heeled clients to make calls while sitting at a tiny writing area out of earshot. It afforded just the privacy Jenny required. Shutting the door quietly, she entered, sat, and fumbled through her purse for James Patterson's business card. She retrieved it, stared at it a moment, and slowly began dialing the numbers into her cell phone. As she did so, her hands began perspiring noticeably again. The phone rang only twice before she heard the words, "FBI, Dallas Field Office." She asked for James Patterson, and waited for the phone to transfer.

"Patterson here."

"Mr. Patterson, this is Jennie Pemberton.

"How are things going, Miss Pemberton?"

"A-alright...I guess. I've looked at the materials you left with me, and they are very...um, informative."

"*We* thought so. What do you think should be done with that information, Miss Pemberton?"

"Well, is—is it reliable?"

"Miss Pemberton, we didn't run any tests ourselves. But our crime lab people say they don't see any fault with any of the testing methodologies used in the studies."

"Are people really dying from this drug?" Jenny had to force the word "dying" out with great effort.

"That's a tougher question. The theory hit on by these doctors, which has yet to be proven, is that the drug lies dormant in the human body for some time. It can be six months, or it can be years. Then, for some mysterious reason, it becomes active, changing its molecular structure. Two things then happen. One, the drug becomes addictive—strongly so. Two, after it has mutated several times, it becomes lethal."

Jenny paused a long time, then spoke. "I-I'd like to help, but I'm not sure how. Dane is having a meeting with Dr. Zimmerman, an expert suggested by Rowalter, within a few hours. I could share the information you've left with me then..."

"No, that won't do. If Zimmerman is really on Rowalter's payroll, he won't go along. We'll have to find a way to alert Dane through another expert. Someone we know and who is credible."

"How are we going to accomplish that in a couple of hours?"

"Just leave that to us. Do you have Zimmerman's flight information?"

"Um, yes. Why?"

"Never mind why. If you want to make sure Dane Ingersoll has the facts in this case, and keep innocent people from dying an unspeakable death, you'll get it for me now."

Jenny ran around the corner into the War Room clutching her phone, and retrieved a file, from which she extracted a small slip of paper. A moment later, she was back in the tiny room. "Okay," she reported breathlessly. "I've got it. Flight number 267, American Airlines, arriving at DFW from St. Louis at 1:55 p.m.— Gate 34."

"Good." Patterson seemed pleased. "Call me back in precisely 15 minutes. I'll be getting you some new flight information. For now, tell Ingersoll that there has been a delay of that flight getting out of the St. Louis airport, and it will probably be an hour to an hour and a half late. I'd postpone the meeting with Zimmerman until 4:30." The phone clicked abruptly, and Patterson was gone. Jenny, bewildered, shuffled back to the War Room. When she got back, Alton and Dane were having a spirited conversation about how to get some unknown report into evidence. Dane looked up as she entered. "Where have you been?"

"Oh, I just thought I'd call the airport to reconfirm Dr. Zimmerman's arrival time, since I'd heard there might be some bad weather in St. Louis this afternoon." *"Pretty smooth,"* she thought to herself.

"Yeah? Will he be here for his three o'clock appointment?"

"Unfortunately, no. The airline is saying his flight was late in getting off the ground. It looks like he may not be here until 4:15 to 4:30 p.m." Jenny's face was completely sincere. "I'll let the clerk know who is picking him up."

"Terrific," Dane muttered sarcastically. "It's all right with me," chortled Alton, his glasses askew on his face. "It gives me extra time to put my blockbuster report together for him. It'll be worth the wait."

"I certainly hope you're right. Time is running out fast for Friday."

"Mr. Ingersoll, I'm working on some stuff that makes PZT look like the miracle humanitarian drug of this century—on a par with Salk and Sabin."

"What about the rats?" Dane shot Alton a mildly worried look. "What rats?" Alton paused, "Oh...*those* rats. Not a problem. A couple of uncorroborated studies by a second-rate laboratory. We have ten times that many studies showing the overwhelmingly beneficial effects of the drug," he smiled confidently, gesturing to an eighteen-inch stack of papers on the conference table. "All I have to do is tab and index them, make some blow-ups and get them into a Power Point."

Dane looked pensive, and Jenny could tell he was working on an idea. "Say Jen, how's about the possibility of dredging up some people who have used the drug and could testify to its positive effects?"

Jenny's stomach dropped through the floor. She felt like such a traitor already. "I-I'll see what I can do...b-but it's awfully short notice to get people to Washington D.C. by Friday."

"So it is. I'll have an associate check with the FDA to see if they'll accept video testimony, with the opportunity for the government to cross examine each witness."

Jenny winced as she pondered the monumental task of getting names of such people—where would she begin? Web sites on hospitals, doctors, medical schools...the *phone book?* Her mind spun in circles. For now, she busied herself organizing exhibits, while Dane and Alton disappeared to separate ends of the office. Then, stealing a glance at her watch, she realized it had been sixteen minutes since she talked to Patterson. With electric-like energy, Jenny whisked out of the corner War Room door, turned the corner and was back in the tiny phone room. A moment later she heard the even toned voice of James Patterson.

"Did you tell them?"

"Yes. They expect his flight to arrive around 4:30."

"That's good—you're doing fine. Dr. Zimmerman— *our* Dr. Zimmerman—will be arriving on flight 37, American, at 4:25 p.m. He'll be wearing a charcoal grey pinstripe suit, glasses, moustache."

"What about the real Zimmerman?" The thought had only just now occurred to her.

"Don't worry. He's been taken care of."

Taken care of? Jenny cringed, and went silent.

As if sensing her thoughts, Patterson said, "We only work through legitimate channels and methods, Miss Pemberton. No harm has befallen or will befall Dr. Zimmerman."

"Can I ask another question?"

"Fire away."

"I've been asked to round up witnesses for the hearing who have had PZT successfully administered to them. I don't know whether I can do it, or do it in time. But if I could, what impact would that have on your efforts to get the drug disallowed?"

"Frankly, it doesn't help. But, you have a job to do, and so do I. I can't tell you how to do yours any more than you can tell me how to do mine. If we're able to do this right, the FDA will see how much of a problem this drug is even if you call ten witnesses who swear by it. Besides," he paused for emphasis, "I'd like to see you come up with any witnesses who will so testify— especially in a four-day period."

Patterson, of course, had an unarguable point. But it didn't change the fact that she was working for Salacuse & Lockridge, and for her ex-boyfriend-up-and-coming-partner, on a big case. He was right: she had a job to do. And as a certified legal assistant, she was required to "zealously advance" the interests of the client her supervising attorney represented.

"Grey pinstripe suit, glasses and moustache, huh? Okay, we'll have somebody there." She hung up the phone, then nervously intercommed the new information upstairs to the second-year law clerk who was to pick up the good Dr. Zimmerman. With that, having washed her hands of Patterson for the moment, Jenny proceeded to her computer. At least, she reasoned, she could find *some* users of this drug. After all—wasn't it the job of the *adversary*—the FDA lawyers—to mine information damaging to Rowalter's case? No traitor was she: Dane would be pleased with her when this was all over. She smiled at the thought.

CHAPTER TWELVE

St. Louis, Missouri

Dr. Elias Zimmerman drove down the Cardinals Turnpike in Saint Louis, cell phone mashed to his ear. He was fuming. His bearded face convulsed with anger as he thought of all the appointments he had cancelled a couple of days before, on impossibly short notice, to appease Gary Thompson. Rowalter had been a longstanding client, and he would do anything reasonably within his power to accommodate their demands. In some years, half of his income had come, either directly or indirectly, from Rowalter Industries. You didn't just ignore a client like that. But Zimmerman had a professional life apart from Rowalter and his forensic witness duties. He was a distinguished professor in charge of his own department at Johns Hopkins. He had two articles he was writing for the American Journal of Pharmacology. And, worst of all, he had a day of golf he had scratched for this suddenly oh-so-important meeting with Dane Ingersoll, Esquire, down in Big D! Thompson had better have a good explanation for this one. It was Thompson's assistant, though her voice seemed different than usual, who had placed the call to the professor as he was literally about to board his plane for another business commitment. What would they have done if he were airborne—turned the plane around and sent him back to the city by the river? "Well," he thought "If they want me again for this matter, they'll pay double—no, triple!"

Dallas, Texas

The preparations had all been made for the eminent professor. The conference room usually reserved for only the firm's best clients had been readied. Drinks and pastries were waiting. Leather-bound folios with fresh legal pads were set out expectantly at each of 4 places: one for Dane right next his computer tablet, one for Alton, Jenny, and of course the good Dr. Zimmerman. Alton also had his tablet computer humming, and was at the ready to call up articles, retrieve a website, or simply take notes as called upon. The LED demo monitor, normally hidden behind oak panels recessed into the conference room wall, was in plain sight, the panels fully retracted. A desktop computer sat on a rollaway stand nearby, fully equipped with presentation software in the event it was needed.

Frankly, Dane did not know what to expect from Zimmerman. All he knew was that Rowalter said he was a good man in his field, and that he needed just such a person desperately. Dane didn't like a client telling him what he needed, but he wasn't a chemist, and he wasn't writing the checks in this case. He drummed his fingers on his desk, inexplicably nervous as he awaited Zimmerman's arrival. He reviewed his notes, and as he did so, his eyes fell on a memorandum that had just arrived from Jenny. It listed six people living within a 1500-mile radius who had experience—in one way or another—with the substance known as "PZT." She was working furiously, it said, trying to run these people down. He stared at the memo, pondering the chances of actually talking to some of these people and, should he be so lucky, of finding one who'd actually had a positive experience he was willing to share. His thoughts were interrupted by the crackle of the intercom.

"Mr. Ingersoll, Dr. Zimmerman is here for you. He's being shown to the 34th floor conference room...and there's a Mr. Cajon who'd like to speak with you on line 2."

"I'll be down to meet Zimmerman right away. I don't know a Mr. Cajon; take a message."

"Got it."

Dane bolted out of his swivel chair and made his way briskly down the hallway to the elevator. Within minutes, he entered the conference room and warmly greeted Dr. Zimmerman, who had the look of a busy man who had just stepped off a plane. Dane had envisioned more of an academic, bushy-faced type. Zimmerman was clean shaven, except for a thin, well-trimmed moustache. He stood about six feet tall, medium build, and appeared forty-ish. He wore glasses, but did not use them as did the stereotypical college professor, and instead removed them when he read. His grey pinstripe suit was crisp and well-pressed, and he broke the absent-minded-Einstein mold with stylish shoes, button-down collar, matching tie and an overall attention to detail.

Zimmerman had already spoken with Jenny and Alton when Dane arrived, and was chatting amiably with them about some movie they had all seen. His deep, resonant voice was at once commanding and disarming, revealing a slight German accent.

"How was the flight, Doctor?" Dane queried.

"Oh, fine, fine" he said, removing his coat as if to get right down to business. He laid it over a conference room chair. "'Quite a delay in getting off the ground in St. Louis, but we made it."

"Well, let's get down to business, shall we?" said Dane, motioning Dr. Zimmerman to a chair. "Tell me a little bit about your background, and how you came to know my client."

Jenny fought hard the urge to exchange glances with the surrogate Zimmerman. While he launched into what promised to be a lengthy verbal resume, Jenny slipped silently out the conference room door and back to her office.   It was Dane's job to woodshed "Zimmerman", but hers to cull through and isolate all possible users of PZT. She retrieved her messages at the work station outside her cubbyhole office, which was on the same floor as the conference room. Jenny silently wondered what Zimmerman was saying now...how he was pulling it off, as she distractedly flipped through her telephone messages. Suddenly, her gaze froze on a crumpled slip she had almost missed. "Mrs. GL" was scrawled across the top. Underneath, the message, "*Had treatment—wants to talk*" appeared. Vickie, her secretary, must have taken the call after making the dozens of canvassing calls which Jenny had foisted upon her. Jenny's heart skipped a beat, then restarted, noticeably faster. She raced into her office, picked up the phone, and began hurriedly dialing the long-distance number. The area code, she guessed, was somewhere in Florida. In the middle of the fourth ring, a voice mail message kicked in. "Dammit", she muttered forcefully, hitting the desk in frustration. She drummed the desk with her fingers nervously while the message played out. She hit redial...same thing. This time she left her name and number, including her cell phone.

Jenny touched the red button on her phone and spoke toward it. "Vickie, bring me the list I gave you this afternoon on the PZT users."

"You got it. 'Be right there," came the reply.

Moments later, Vickie was at her side, placing in her hands a crisp 8 ½ X 11 sheet displaying ten names and phone numbers. Jenny did a double take, and looked up at Vickie, eyes flashing.

"What happened to the other fifty names I gave you? You had about three legal pages full of information!"

Vickie looked taken aback. "Why...I did as you wanted. I deleted all the names you told me to."

"What in the name of heaven are you talking about?" Jenny's mouth had dropped open.

"A staff member on the case called and said to delete all but these names because you had decided the others were a waste of time; so, these were the ones I contacted." Her voice was now plaintive.

Suddenly Jenny's face became stone, her voice somber. "*What* staff member?"

"H-he didn't give his name, but said you asked him to call. I figured it was one of the other attorneys on the team...or somebody. Did I do something wrong? You mean, it wasn't you who—?"

Jenny shook her head slowly, deliberately, her mouth a taught line. For the first time since this all began, she felt a shudder deep within her, starting in her gut and moving upward through her spine, neck and head. She forced herself to shake it off.

"What did the voice sound like?"

Vickie pondered this. "It was a man's voice. Um-m, no accent, kind of deep, even gravelly. I-I got the impression it was someone maybe forty or older, but not elderly."

"What *else* did he tell you?" Her voice had a desperate quality to it now.

"N-nothing—the-that was all," Vickie stumbled apologetically. "Thank you, Vickie, that'll be all for now." Vickie nodded, visibly flustered, and returned to her work station. As soon as the door closed, Jenny again picked up the phone, stared at the first remaining number on the list, and dialed it. Her fingers moved slowly and deliberately. The phone rang once, twice, three times.

"Hello." It was a man's voice.

"Um, yes. My name is Jennifer Pemberton, with the law firm of Salacuse & Lockridge in Dallas, Texas." Her hands were sweating again. "We are conducting research regarding the use of a rather new experimental drug called 'PZT'. Are you familiar with that product?"

"Yes," he said pleasantly.

"Are you Mr. Donald Swythe?"

"Yes, I am. How can I help you?" She was caught off guard by the unusual cooperativeness of the man.

"W-well, I have just a few questions, and this will only take a few minutes. We are conducting a survey among former and current users of PZT to compile data on its benefits, affects, and side effects, if any. How long were you using PZT?"

"My doctor prescribed it while I was in the hospital. I believe I was on it intravenously for a week or so."

It wasn't what Jenny had been hoping for, but it was a start. "Do you know the reasons your doctor elected to place you on the drug?"

"I haven't the slightest idea. But it was a miracle drug. I might not be alive today if he hadn't used it. Nothing else was working, and my blood pressure was dropping like a stone after I was in a severe automobile accident. PZT, I believe it's called, arrested the free fall and leveled off my blood pressure. My broken bones and bruises took as long to heal as anybody else's, but the PZT kept me from dying on the operating table." The man sounded like a pharmaceutical television commercial, for Pete's sake.

"Your doctor's name, if you don't mind?"

"Not at all. It's Glenn Stevenson. He's on staff at Dallas Lutheran."

"Thank you for your time and cooperation, Mr. Swythe."

"You're welcome—no problem at all. Any time I can be of help..."

"*Yeah, I'll bet.*" Jenny set the receiver down and placed her head in her hands. "*And what were you expecting?*" She braced herself, and with all the enthusiasm of someone rearranging chairs on the deck of the Titanic, plunged through the next ten or so persons listed. Of that number, a statistically incredible seven were at home and able to talk. Without exception, Jenny encountered the same, infomercial-like enthusiasm for PZT, and the same "miracle-drug" accolades. The predictability of it all was positively eerie, and she suppressed a shudder.

All the same, Jenny didn't know what she should be feeling: she was decidedly hitting pay dirt for Rowalter Industries. Yet she didn't feel good about her achievement. She could feel anger welling up inside of her—from where she was not exactly certain. She was, for one thing, angry with herself. She had not gotten her paralegal degree so that she could undermine her own boss's client, working against him. What was wrong with her, anyway? She began to feel an ominous sense of foreboding, a sense that an unbelievable powerful and malevolent group of people was toying with her.

Sternly, she admonished herself to be strong. Dane must know of this. She knew she had to tell him. She *would* tell him—soon. "When he's out of the meeting with Zimmerman. That's it," she thought. "That's when I'll tell him."

* * * *

Dane exited the conference room confused and more than a little bewildered. He had just spent two intensive hours with what was to have been his star expert witness. The good Dr. Zimmerman seemed to have peerless credentials and a wealth of experience. He was bright, poised and articulate. But there was a problem. PHENYLZANADIOXIDETETRACHLORAMINE, known as PZT, was, according to Zimmerman, a potentially dangerous—even lethal—drug. He had stopped short of calling it deadly in all cases. Dr. Zimmerman even thought it might have some narrow therapeutic uses in certain limited situations. "Something like medicinal marijuana," thought Dane. But the drug's uncanny ability to mutate after an extended period of use, opined Zimmerman, seemed to outweigh its potential for good. Dane scheduled a follow up meeting for tomorrow at 3:00, but he was already very skittish about calling Dr. Zimmerman as a witness. Why would Rowalter suggest a witness that opined that their precious new drug was dangerous? His mind flashed back briefly to his other FDA approval case—*U.S. Food & Drug Administration vs. Szeroka*. There were no gruesome deaths, no writhing lab mice in that case, just lab reports, independent university studies, and a few complaints from environmental groups who'd already been crusading against the big pharmaceutical companies anyway. Pretty plain vanilla, actually, compared to this case. Why in the world couldn't this case be simpler, like *Szeroka*?

Sullenly, he sank deep into his office chair, when there was a knock at his door. "Come in," he muttered, mildly irritated that whoever it was had made it to his door by sneaking past the receptionist. Jenny's face appeared in the crack between his door and the back wall. She looked cute in that posture, but the thought quickly succumbed to Dane's bad attitude. Her eyes searched his, immediately deduced that he was depressed, then hesitated. Perhaps this was not the time, she thought.... Her hesitation lingered, but Dane seemed not to notice. He waived her in and motioned her over to the leather couch against the opposite wall.

There was a long pause. "Whatcha got for me, Jenny?" It was obvious she needed a push.

"Dane, I think someone is tampering with our investigation." Dane allowed the words to sink in for the briefest of moments. "Specifically, with potential witnesses," she clarified.

"What are you talking about?"

"I had Alton assemble a list of PZT users from various data bases he was able to pull together. When I had my secretary bring me the list to start contacting them, it became obvious it had been tampered with by some unidentified male caller." Dane's eyes widened with interest, his gaze suddenly frozen.

"Dane, the caller told her I had authorized the deletion of more than half of the list. Not surprisingly, it turns out that the only people remaining on the list all love the stuff." She paused, studying the effect of the words on her boss. Dane hung on every one. But he surprised her with his next statement.

"Somehow, I'm not surprised. Funny, though, isn't it?"

"What do you mean? How could it possibly be funny?"

"Well, I just got out of a meeting with one of the world's most noted toxicologists, who also happens to be on Rowalter's payroll, and he's saying the drug is one of the most dangerous he's ever seen." A look of puzzlement like that of a lost child swept over his face. "Will someone please tell me what is going on here?"

"Dane, have you stopped to consider that this drug may *not* be worthy of FDA approval—that maybe it hasn't been tested by any truly independent labs, or worse, that a bunch of folks stand to make money by its approval, whether it's safe or not?" Jenny fought to hold back all that she knew.

"The thought never once crossed my mind," Dane said with a wry smile.

"Well, where do we go from here?"

"I'll tell you where: Home to regroup. I've had a heckuva day and I basically need to go somewhere, lick my wounds, and mull things over. I'll need those case studies you promised me by 1:30 tomorrow. "And," he glanced wearily at his watch to check the date, "it's T minus 2 and counting. We've got tomorrow and Thursday and then: 'D' day."

"Roger, Boss." She strove, and failed, to sound professional. Her discouragement was obvious.

Dane, oblivious to his assistant's struggle, grabbed the message his secretary had left for him on the way out and nearly sprinted for the elevator. He was tired and hungry, and just wanted to get home and vegetate. Dane took the garage elevator to the lowest level, shifting his mind to neutral as he located the Beemer. He was in such a hurry to get home to Susan that he didn't even bring the cordovan kidskin briefcase that was as much a part of his anatomy as his arms and hands. As he slid into the leather seat and flung his suit coat into the back he remembered the message still crumpled in his other hand. He glanced down at it. It said simply "Mr. Cajon", and checked the box, "Call back". As he wheeled out of the garage steering with his left hand, he dialed the phone in the console with his right, inputting the numbers. The phone rang once, then came a man's voice, "Hello, Mr. Ingersoll." Dane answered, "Hello, Mr. C—", then abruptly halted, realizing with a tinge of embarrassment that he was talking to a voice mail recorded message. He paused while the gravelly voice—half machine, half human—continued: "Mr. Ingersoll, we know that you are working on a big case for Rowalter." Dane's heart suddenly suspended any semblance of beating. "We know you, and are intimately familiar with your abilities. You must succeed. You *will* succeed. Do not be concerned with any information, evidence or witnesses being planted by others. You will be supplied with everything you need, as and when you need it. We will be in touch with you shortly." The phone clicked dead. Dane sat, the car idling at the parking lot exit, staring numbly, dumb-struck, at the cell phone. He slowly swallowed the lump in his throat, then with deliberate effort shook off his trance-like state. He dialed Susan with a quivering hand as he pulled out onto Clarington Boulevard.

"Hi, Baby" she answered. "When will you be home?"

"Oh, thirty minutes or so," Dane resolved to sound calm, and amazingly, pulled it off. "How's Natalie?"

"I was up there today, and she seemed to be doing fine, even better. For the first time they're talking about her maybe coming home in a couple of weeks. Isn't that fantastic?"

"Yeah, that's great news. Do you need me to pick up anything on the way home?"

She paused to think. "How about some Mandarin takeout? I'm kind of tired today, and running behind."

"Sure thing. I'll see you in about 45 minutes. Love you."

Dane pulled into the left turn lane about a mile down the road, at Moline. After a couple of quick zigs on smaller streets he found himself at Tai Wong and Son, a local but little-known favorite who served consistently good Mandarin Chinese. He reached for the glove compartment, where he kept his credit cards locked. As he released the latch and extracted his credit card holder, his glance fell upon a plain white envelope perched atop the grey binder that was his owner's manual. He pulled it out gingerly—probably an old letter or ad he had tossed in and forgotten to read. As he unsealed the flap, his eyes riveted on the grey-green of money. His mouth went dry. He searched his memory with flawless speed and accuracy. No, he had not put any money in his glove compartment; he never did. He slowly, disbelievingly pulled out a thick wad of bills, and counted them with trembling hands. Fifty crisp $1,000 bills. His hands began to tremble. Despite this, he forced himself to check the envelope for notes or other signs of identity. Just as he suspected, there were none.

He shook his head suddenly as if awakening from a bad dream, then resolutely replaced the money, slammed the door shut and locked the glove compartment. He quick-stepped into Tai Wong's, and absent mindedly placed the same order he'd placed a hundred times before. His mind was a million miles away, relentlessly probing the possibilities. The voice he had heard on the phone was not that of Gary Thompson of Rowalter. Anyway—if Thompson had wanted to lend him encouragement at this point in the case, why not just contact him personally like he had twice before? Alternative number two, he supposed, was that it could be a sizeable competitor trying to lure him into accepting "dirty" money as a fee. If he accepted it, besides compromising his professional integrity, the competing company's lawyer could anonymously reveal the matter to the newspapers, or even the state bar. This would compromise the case, or at the very least postpone it, while Rowalter sought out new counsel. In the meantime, the competitor would enter the market ahead of Rowalter, gaining an early foothold and a competitive advantage it might never forfeit. But if it was a competitor, why then place a phone call urging him to win at any cost, thus benefitting Rowalter? Alternative three: Perhaps it was a hireling representing a consortium of pharmaceutical companies, all of whom, like Rowalter, had a keen interest in legalizing this drug so they could all share in the obscene profits.

Dane paid for the order and a greasy bag of hot Chinese food was thrust into his hands. Suddenly, his mind homed in on a fourth, chilling possibility he hadn't considered: that the call was from a DEA agent, trying to entrap him into accepting money which was to be "laundered" ill-begotten gain with an arguably legal drug. They could contact him in a few days, ask him to place the money safely in his bank account, and see if he took the bait. If he did, they could try to pin the whole thing on Dane, and by implication on Rowalter. The FDA approval case would automatically crash and burn in the process. If he had entertained any possibility of keeping the money to handle the astronomical medical costs for Natalie, such thoughts had now vanished.

Dane pulled into the garage of his spacious split-level home in the fashionable Turtle Creek section of Dallas. Jackie met him at the car, and smothered him with hugs and chatter as soon as the door was open. Dane warmed to his greeting, which lifted his spirits ever so slightly. Once in the house, he deposited dinner in the kitchen, then groped his way to the recliner and collapsed into it.

"Rough day?" Susan asked innocently as she puttered around the kitchen, assembling dinner.

"Rough as they come."

"How's the FDA case coming...you know, what's-their-name..."

"Rowalter," he filled in the blank for her.

"Do you want to talk about it?"

"Only if you have ready answers," he sighed,

Her facial expression urged him on. Dane hesitated a moment, like one does when he is afraid a story is too long and complex to be worth the telling, then decided to take the plunge. "What would you do if you retained one of the world's leading drug experts, who just happened to be paid for by your client, and he told you that your client's drug was the most potentially dangerous drug he had ever seen?" She started to open her mouth, half in surprise, and half in utterance—but Dane held up his hand in a "Wait, but there's more" sort of gesture. "And suppose further that on the way home you got a phone call from an unidentified person who assured you would win your case no matter what. And suppose further that you opened your glove compartment and found fifty thousand dollars in new bills wadded in there, all within a couple of hours."

There was deafening silence. Finally, Dane turned around, craning to see Susan's face in the kitchen. She was as white as a sheet. "I-I would call the FBI," she said in a nearly sub audible whisper.

"That's what I figured you'd say." His face was half resignation, half irritation.

"Well, what are you going—er, I mean—what would *you* do?"

Dane raised his feet, which were propped on the recliner foot support, and leaned backward as far as it would let him. "I'm not sure, Babe. But one thing is for darn sure: I can't just do nothing. This thing has taken on a life all its own, and I can't just let myself get swept along at the mercy of the waves, so to speak."

Secretly, of course, Dane knew his wife was right. He hadn't even quite admitted it to himself, partly because he was mentally exhausted from the day, and partly because he didn't want to lose unilateral control of a case he had just begun to get excited about. But he would have to think about all that tomorrow. In a matter of a few minutes, without even realizing it, Dane drifted into an exhausted slumber.

CHAPTER THIRTEEN

Alton glanced nervously at his watch, then back at the computer screen which flickered in front of him. The remnants of a half-eaten sandwich were scattered on a napkin to his left. Papers, huge stacks of them, obscured every chair in the room, obviating any possible place to sit. But for a few not-so-obvious indicators, the room might as well have been a college dorm room, and Alton a panicked undergrad preparing for finals. He had been going like this now for several days without a break. For anyone else, it would have been a marathon, but not for Alton. He was one of a rare and vanishing breed. Alton loved to poke among obscure resources in dark recesses of old libraries, like a spelunker looking for long - forgotten antiquities. The principal difference between him and previous generations of kindred spirits was that he was born into the age of the internet, high speed computers, lightning-quick research databases, streaming data and flash drives. So Alton did nearly all of his treasure hunting without ever leaving his office.

Alton was bright: extremely so. The word genius was too rigid, too confining to properly convey his capabilities. A *summa cum laude* undergraduate in bioscience engineering at Stanford, he eschewed a career at NASA to attend Harvard Law, where he had entered law school with a perfect score on his LSAT exam. He then proceeded to become the first graduate in the last fifty years to matriculate with a perfect 4.0 average. He had been a college debater, and though not a particularly gifted speaker, coveted by many a debating squad because of his superlative research capabilities and facile mind. After graduating Harvard law, he had turned down many lucrative offers from top firms on the east and west coast for two reasons: he loved the Dallas Cowboys; and Salacuse & Lockridge had offered him a position that was perfectly tailored to his capabilities. You see, Alton didn't care whether he ever set foot in a court room, whether it was for a nationally publicized trial or to argue a landmark appeal. For him, the ultimate rush was retrieving and putting into award winning form the best of all possible briefing. Not only was his research impeccable, but his legal arguments carried with them the logical force of a steel trap. Whoever benefitted from his efforts found every point fully documented, including witness statements, newspaper articles, photos, and of course, irrefutable briefing on the law. Salacuse & Lockridge knew that they had snagged their own captive brain trust, and compensated him well for it.

In front of him lay a neatly bound draft, complete with excerpts from patients—mostly in other countries—who had been successfully treated with PZT. But something was bothering Alton as he began to wrap things up. He had studied the mortality rates in localities where PZT had been used experimentally for a sustained time period. In over 85% of those localities, mortality rates were sharply up beginning twelve to twenty-four months after the first use of the drug. Worse, it appeared that those rates then stayed up and plateaued. This in spite of the fact that all of his other research, particularly in the United States, gave the drug high marks for effectiveness and safety. Something was wrong with this picture; it just didn't fit. Alton made the decision, after some thought, to level with Dane Ingersoll about this apparent inconsistency. He believed the best approach was to emphasize the strongly supportive research which they relied on to win the FDA case, but to footnote and at least mention the problematic mortality rates. Better that Dane know about it and fashion an argument to deal with it in advance; rather than be caught unprepared and be torpedoed. It was with this thought in mind that Alton had launched a section of his brief devoted to the mortality rate increases. He could postulate no reason for the spike in deaths other than the use of PZT in a given area. The highest rates were found in the Andes mountains of Peru. He was halfway through the first paragraph of analysis when his computer, for no apparent reason, froze up. He attempted unsuccessfully to shut down the program, then rebooted. He was tired, and extremely agitated at the thought that he might have lost the huge portion of his document typed before the last automatic save interval. As he clicked the mouse to open up the last version of the document, he gasped, mouth gaping, at the monitor screen. It read simply, "NO FURTHER RESEARCH ON THIS SUBJECT WILL BE ALLOWED." He must be dreaming. He pinched himself, shook his head as if to clear it, then looked at the screen again. The same message appeared, virtually shouting at him from the screen. He rebooted, then tried entering another document. No problem: he was into it immediately. He navigated back to language on the mortality rate studies, and the stark message again appeared.

Alton was no techie, but he went and checked the network connection with the host server in the office. Nothing obvious appeared wrong. He ran back to his computer and rebooted again, only to get the same unnerving result. "This is surreal," thought Alton, mumbling to himself. He grudgingly shut things down completely, and decided to head home. It was 11:00

p.m. He scrawled a note to the computer guru the firm kept on staff, and practically chucked it onto his desk chair as he headed to the reception area elevator.

In the parking garage, he headed toward his unpretentious Fiat runabout, the only car left in the garage at 10:30 p.m. The jingle of his car keys echoed off of the concrete walls, floors and ceiling, alternating with the percussion of his steps. As he reached within ten feet of the car, something suddenly felt tangibly wrong. For the briefest of seconds, Alton could feel the hairs on the nape of his neck stand at attention. Several feet to his right he caught a flicker of movement in the shadow of one of the large pillars which supported the garage ceiling. Before he could even process what might be going on, something resembling a man's arm had slipped tightly around his throat and his arms were pinned to his side, immobile. A voice somewhere behind him—a man's voice— spoke in a low, even tone.

"Mr. Dean, don't be alarmed. Simply follow instructions, and everything will turn out fine." Alton's throat was pressed shut, and he had trouble breathing, let alone responding. "You won't be hurt, just listen and do as we tell you." The pressure had relaxed some around his throat, and Alton could now deduce that he was in a vehicle. He was afraid to move, as his body was being spread out on a back seat. He caught a quick glimpse of a couple of figures moving noisily about, then his eyes were enveloped in darkness as a blindfold was pulled roughly around his head. Amidst his fear, he could feel anger rising up into his throat, threatening to burst out in a wild yell: *"Don't you fools know what you are doing? You can't just go kidnapping lawyers from big downtown law firms!*" Then he abruptly realized how silly the unarticulated thought was. What was he going to do, *sue* them?

The anger had receded and the fear returned. There was a screeching of tires, as Alton felt his head pressed by centrifugal force against the side of the car. The last thing he remembered was the bumps in the road, the sound of the two guys mumbling low between themselves in the front seat, and a non-descript country western tune playing in the background. Alton felt something prick his arm, then overwhelming sleepiness, as he slipped into an ocean of pure blackness.

* * * *

When he awoke, Alton was not sure where he was. His neck was sore, and he instinctively reached for his arm—the one he wasn't lying on—to rub the painful spot where the hypodermic had been jabbed. A man and a woman sat on a couple of chairs across a smallish room, perhaps ten feet away. Still groggy, Alton couldn't make out their features; but they seemed partly obscured in shadow anyway.

"'So glad you dropped in for a visit, Mr. Dean."

"W-h-o-o are you, and why have you b-brought me here?" Alton rubbed furiously at his eyes.

"Let me address your second question first," the male voice continued. The voice was business-like in tone, devoid of emotion. "We have been observing you for some time now. You have information, lots of information, concerning something of great interest to us. Furthermore, you are unusually skilled and adept at assimilating the information you have gathered into a helpful body of research." He paused, remaining motionless while the woman shifted slightly in her chair. Then he leaned forward in the half darkness. In the mottled shadow which covered the room, Alton thought he detected a half smile cross the man's face. "The only problem is you are working for the wrong team."

"Who are you?" Alton repeated.

"For now, let's just say we both work for the same client."

"*Rowalter Industries?* Then why in the world are you doing all this to me? Is this how you treat people who are working for the same client?"

The woman now spoke. "Mr. Dean, allow me. You have only a small piece of a very large picture. For now, however, you will have to be satisfied with the following explanation. There are people out there who have deliberately tried to malign Rowalter—some by publishing contrived studies which are designed to mislead. Many millions of dollars, perhaps billions, are at stake. As a matter of fact, you have stumbled across some of those studies in your research and briefing."

The man chimed in again. "You need more, shall we say, 'balance' to your research. We are here to provide the other side of the story." Suddenly Alton felt like he was a journalist covering a presidential campaign. Strange, he mused sarcastically, that somehow the "fairness doctrine" as applied to the pharmaceuticals industry had utterly eluded him in law school. "We would like you to work for us until we obtain complete approval of our new drug, and it is released into the marketplace."

"But," Alton forced the words through his throbbing head and out his mouth, "most of the data out there is already on your side. The chances of PZT being approved for distribution are already quite high anyway."

"Oh, you are quite correct. But it is the very type of obscure case study you've stumbled across that was responsible for a six to ten-year delay in the entry to market of drugs like Prothoracyn, Alphacline, and even Viagra. A delay of that proportion can mean the difference between complete domination, and being squeezed out by a larger competitor. With tens of millions in investment capital and research on the line, it is a risk we would be foolish to take." The woman appeared to nod her agreement.

"You'll be allowed to stay in pleasant surroundings, very comfortable surroundings, really. And you'll have at your disposal all the latest computer research tools. Of course, you'll be expected to support the Rowalter position, and you've made clear you know what that is."

Alton inwardly recoiled in disgust at the thought of producing preordained research findings. His mind raced now, the grogginess gone. He fought through the tangible hatred of his captors, forcing himself to be levelheaded. There was a way out of this dilemma and he simply must find it. It started by learning exactly where he was, of which he currently was completely ignorant. Propelling him forward was the thought that, surely, when all this was over, he would not be allowed to live. In the event that this mystery drug gained full approval, his utility to these heavy-handed ruffians would soon expire, and what he knew would in fact become a huge liability.

"Soon, Mr. Dean, you will be transferred to your room, which, I think, you will find quite agreeable. The effects of the drug you have been given are already wearing off. You will then be oriented to the facility, and to what we expect from you. And, "he paused and locked gazes with Alton, "we expect great things."

Alton wondered precisely what "great things" were expected of him even as he pondered what he might have told his captors while under "the drug". His mind worked mightily to recall any sounds or sensations from the car ride that could provide a clue as to his whereabouts. He had no way of knowing that he was deep underground, far away from human eyes. The woman, who hadn't said much, loosened the bands which still tightly bound his wrists, while he asked to be allowed to visit the restroom. The request was granted gruffly, and someone appearing like a hybrid between a male hospital orderly and a prison guard escorted him through a meandering hallway. Everything was dimly lit. Alton, as a result of this and of the drug, had lost track of time. He was unsure whether it was now daytime or still dark; whether it was an hour or a day since his abduction. He scanned the walls for windows, seeing none. His expressionless escort stood, sentry-like, against the wall of the hallway as Alton turned the corner and entered the restroom. The room itself, swabbed with a pastel green paint that was badly peeling, provided no clues either. He looked for air vents, to no avail. Just then he thought of his cell phone and suddenly wished he had it with him.

* * * *

The sun rose in Dallas, flooding the crisp eastern January sky with hues of gold and crimson. Jim Patterson, with five hours of sleep behind him, munched a cheese Danish as he accelerated his teal blue Buick Riviera onto Stemmons Freeway, nosing between an eighteen-wheeler and VW Jetta. Jim hit some buttons on the center console with deft precision borne only of doing the same thing the same way for ten years. He entered his four-digit code which prompted a computer, via a secure satellite link from Washington, to upload, encrypt, then retransmit messages to the electronic brain in his car. There, the messages were instantly unencrypted by a computer algorithm which was changed automatically every day. There was virtually no chance of a message being intercepted, other than by a very smart agent gone bad—with lots of help. Such an agent wouldn't be able to unencrypt the message without the algorithm. The simulated human voice—female, which Jim preferred—recited to him his messages in the order they were emailed or phoned in. Most of it was standard office stuff: Deputy Director Harless had called a telephone conference for tomorrow at one EDT for all Field Office chiefs; his secretary in the Washington bureau said he had been accepted to teach summer classes in marksmanship at the FBI academy in Richmond; and on the list went. The velvety-yet- synthetic voice lilted on as Jim popped the last of the danish in his mouth. Then, with a jolt, he realized he had heard a name he knew. He nimbly hit the pause button, then sent a signal from the console ordering a playback of the last two messages. Then he had it. Dane Ingersoll, the litigator from Dallas, had left him a message. His face broke into a knowing, almost smirking half-smile, the one he was famous for with his colleagues at the Bureau. The long awaited, the fervently anticipated, had just happened. Ingersoll had responded; his plan was beginning to work. Jim hit "save", preserving the message in his own system, then entered the playback command.

"Uh, yes. I'm not sure if I have the correct office, but my name is Dane Ingersoll. I am an attorney with offices in Dallas, Texas, where I also live. I need to talk to an agent about some disturbing goings-on in connection with a case on which I am working. Please have someone give me a call at my office today, in confidence. My number is "5-5-5 - 4-9-3-8.""

"*Smart*," thought Patterson. He knew enough not to leave details—all of which Jim already knew, anyway—on an FBI answering system. He stopped the playback and hit speed dial for his office. He was about a mile away yet, sitting in bumper-to-bumper traffic.

"Newcombe, FBI." It was only 7:45 a.m., but Jon Newcombe, an ambitious assistant special agent in charge in the Dallas field office was, as usual, hard at it. "Jon, we've heard from Ingersoll". Patterson's words were terse and spoken in the staccato tone of Officer Joe Friday of *Dragnet* fame. "Line up an appointment for him today, wherever he wants, on my schedule. Block off at least two hours". Jim rattled off the phone number to Newcombe, who scribbled it down, pulled up a computer screen at his desk, and entered the information. "Done," he confirmed. "Anything else?"

"Yeah. Transcribe all of the wiretaps and have them in my office an hour before whatever appointment you set. Thanks."

* * * *

Dane had arrived at his office. He was a bundle of nerves, not only because of the impending trial just two days away, but because of the surreal feeling of being in the middle of a universe he didn't understand. Reality was pressing in on him inexorably, buffeting him with currents and eddies changing too rapidly for him to understand. But he had to work through it. He would survive it because he was the tough-minded trial attorney, the hard-working son of a west Texas rancher. He allowed himself only one thought, a thought which he clung to with all his strength: *Get through this case and win*. And that meant pulling the evidence together. *"But you're meeting with the FBI, today, for God's sake!"* the nearly audible thought impinged on his consciousness, and made his neck hairs stand on end. He had met with the FBI before, especially when he was on loan to the Dallas County District Attorney's office via a special litigation training program with his firm. But working with the Feds against a common enemy or a criminal suspect was light years apart from meeting with them on his *own* behalf. He went on a hunt for Alton, hoping to retrieve one of those peerless, fully annotated briefs of his. His ulterior motive, he admitted to himself, was to get his mind off his frayed nerves.

Alton's door was closed, as was his wont. Dane carefully cracked it open, the better not to disturb Alton's undoubtedly feverish pace. His computer monitor screen was not visible from this angle, surrounded as it was by stacks of papers, articles and books. "H-m-m," Dane mused aloud, "Pulled an all-nighter." Eagerly, he picked his way through the melee of work product, scanning all the while for his brief, until he stood facing the computer screen on the far end of the office. The monitor was black, yet the green light indicating the power was on shone steadily. *"Probably in sleep mode—like Alton right now,"* thought Dane. Instinctively, yet not knowing exactly why, Dane reached out and hit the "Enter" key. The monitor flickered to life as if shouting the brazen message: "NO FURTHER RESEARCH ON THIS SUBJECT IS ALLOWED". Startled, Dane hit the "Enter" key once again. A brief flicker, then the same words appeared, as though spoken by some stern employee in the Library of Congress. He was about to try rebooting the computer, but stopped himself short, lest he wipe out hours of unsaved work. He reached over and pressed the button on Alton's intercom. "Yes", answered Rebecca, Alton's legal assistant.

"Rebecca," have you heard from Alton yet this morning?"

"Come to think of it, no."

"Don't you find that odd?"

"Extremely. He's usually in at 7:30, and earlier lately with this big case you're on."

"Well, he may have worked all night, but", Dane glanced around the room again, then continued "I don't see his brief which was due on my desk this morning." "This isn't like him." He felt the beginnings of that panicky feeling he used to get in the pit of his stomach before law school exams. " Why don't you call over to his house and see what the story is?"

"You've got it."

Dane was off like a lightning bolt to the War Room, and nearly capsized Jenny as he rounded the corner of the hallway. "Morning Jenny!" Dane reached deep to sound cheerful, failing miserably. "Any sight of Alton yet?"

"No," her eyes flickered concern. "Anything wrong?"

"Well, no Alton in sight, no brief, and his computer is on the fritz with our hearing tomorrow morning— Yeah, you could say that."

Dane checked the War Room: No Alton. He paced quickly to the telephone and buzzed Rebecca on the intercom. " Is he in his office?" "I'm sorry Mr. Ingersoll, but he isn't." Dane fought the feeling of panic that had begun in his gut and was crawling higher. Grabbing his phone, he reached Jenny back in her office.

"Any luck?"

"I wish. I've tried his home four times—no answer. Same thing on his cell.

"Jen, do me a favor and grab some file boxes, go to Alton's office and pull everything he's done together; if we can't locate him I'll have to start cataloguing it and see what he's got."

"Consider it done."

Until now, Dane's distress had more to do with the fact that his top research specialist was unavailable the day before the FDA drug approval hearing. Suddenly and without warning though, the notion that something more ominous was in order began gnawing at him. The panic in his lower abdomen was now joined by sweaty palms. He thought of the phone message he had left last night, as if it were a distant dream, and as swiftly as the thought invaded his mind, his phone buzzed. "Mr. Ingersoll," came his secretary's halting voice, "It's—uhm, Mr. Newcombe, uhm—Special Agent for the Federal Bureau of Investigation." Dane took a deep breath, cleared his head, and reached his hand tentatively toward the intercom button. As his index finger came down, the voice he next heard was not his, but that of some person outside himself—someone very unsure of himself, yet striving mightily to maintain control.

"Dane Ingersoll here."

"Yes, Mr. Ingersoll. I'm Jon Newcombe, assistant special agent with the FBI field office in Dallas. We have your message from last evening." There was a slight pause while Dane took this in. Newcombe continued, "I've been instructed to block off two hours in Special Agent James Patterson's schedule today to meet with you. Would noon till 2:00 be all right?"

"Normally, yes." Dane forced himself to remain calm, using a business-as-usual tone. "But I've got a big administrative hearing in Washington, D.C. tomorrow, and I can't spare that much time. What about an hour over lunch?"

"All right, then," replied Newcombe agreeably. "We'll need privacy, though. I can have lunch brought into our office. We're at One Main Place, Suite 489.

Catty corner from the Federal Building on Commerce. Please be there at twelve sharp."

"Not a problem. I'll be there." As he killed the speaker phone, Dane was stricken with the realization that Newcombe already knew what he was going to say, just as surely as if he'd had a fully equipped FBI surveillance van parked down on the nearest street corner or had tapped his phone. "*You're starting to lose it, Dane,*" his mind retorted, as he wearily dismissed the thought. Money appearing in glove compartments, experts who did apparent about-faces when it came time to testify, and now associate attorneys who vanish—just plain *vanish*! You know, as if by magic. Something was horribly, terribly amiss; yet, Dane told himself over and over again, there *was* a logical solution. There had to be. Dane clung to the thought like no other. It gave his existence meaning at the moment.

Dane left a rambling voice mail on Alton's home landline, then called his cell phone one, two and three times. Each time it rolled to voice mail immediately. *Did he even have it with him*? He put out the equivalent of an APB to all three receptionists manning the phones to direct any word of, or from, Alton to him immediately. He managed to dredge up an older cell phone number he wasn't sure was still active and called it. Disconnected.

Dane culled his brain to think of family or friends he could contact. Alton, like many of his personality type, was principally a loner. Not that he was antisocial, but typical social conversation tended to lose his interest after more than several minutes. Once his eyes started to dart, one knew his mind was no longer in the conversation, if indeed it ever had been. Rather, it was off to his latest brainstorm, whether it be a certiorari brief he was preparing for the supreme court, or a new supercomputer he was working on in his garage. As a result, Alton had few, if any, close friends. In fact, Dane could think of none to call. Alton lived alone, and the only time he had heard him talk of family, he seemed to recall that they had lived in the Northeast: Rhode Island or somewhere, perhaps.

By 10:00 a.m., Dane, Jenny and another young associate who Dane had pressed into service were frenetically running through the exhibits, organizing notes and preparing argument. The War Room looked exactly like it did during all such times: a battle zone with no organization whatever that was apparent to the casual observer. And still no Alton. Dane resigned himself to parsing what he could of the hard copy of Alton's brief, since Alton's computer was useless, for the time being. The new associate, Dick Reynolds, called the FDA to verify the hearing setting had not moved. It had not. Twenty-three hours and counting.

CHAPTER FOURTEEN

It had been ten days now that Natalie had been holding even, but Susan didn't see it that way. *"Oh yes,"* she thought, *"She's not breathing by a ventilator, and she's out of the incubator, but she is still in the hospital with tubes stuck in her!"* Her days dragged surreally by with leaden speed. With Dane gone so much, her only diversions were Jackie's ball games and ladies' Bible study once a week. With Natalie on her mind, she had time for little else, anyway. She visited the hospital at least two hours each day, and yesterday had stayed even longer, plying the doctors with questions. She had had quite enough of doctors and hospitals—she just wanted her baby. And, she wanted her husband back.

Today, Susan sat patiently, all things considered, at Natalie's bedside in the NICU, watching her rhythmic breathing as the tiny chest moved up and down with that mysterious quality reserved for babies. Nurses and medical personnel whisked noiselessly past her, preoccupied with their assignments, and seemed totally oblivious to her and Natalie's existence. Susan felt her blood pressure beginning to rise. *How can you be so inhuman, so utterly complacent? Don't you see what's happening to my baby?* She could barely restrain herself from jumping up in the middle of the room and screaming at the staff. Susan pulled herself away from the nursery, stormed through the double doors into the hallway, and fished her cell phone from her purse. She'd had quite enough; she was going to get her little girl home.

But Dane was not to be reached, just at this moment. He had just parked his car in the Federal Building parking garage, and his phone was turned off.

He did not want to be disturbed during this most important of meetings. He had been in this place fifty—maybe a hundred—times before today, but never with a mission like this. To say he was nervous, like a young associate heading to his first trial, neither did justice to his emotions nor described the deep gnawing in this stomach. It was like the panic you fight down in the moment you lose control of your car or a boat or plane, and the realization caves in on you that the die has been cast: there is nothing you can do to stop it. So absorbed in his thoughts was he that Dane suddenly found himself at the door of the Regional FBI office without quite realizing how he got there. The chrome and glass door with the scales, shield, and the imposing words "Federal Bureau of Investigation" would not have impressed him on any other day. Today, though, was not "any other day," and his heart lurched in staccato beat as his eyes beheld it.

Dane handed his card to the receptionist sitting at the corner desk, and announced his presence. No sooner did he seat himself than James Patterson entered the room. "Mr. Ingersoll. I'm James Patterson, Senior Agent in Charge," he extended his hand and grasped Dane's. "Follow me." Dane accompanied him down a short hallway to an unpretentious, sparsely furnished office about the size of the most junior of associate's at Salacuse & Lockridge. The office was cluttered with no-nonsense, government issue furniture. A beat-up green leatherette couch sat in the corner with a coffee table. Patterson stood behind a well-used, executive size metal desk as he gestured for Dane to take a seat across from him.

"Coffee?" offered Patterson as he settled into his. "No, thanks, "*I'm wired enough already*" thought Dane. He took the measure of Patterson quickly: mid-forties, grey at the temples but otherwise with a head full of red hair, receding hair line, trim build, six feet tall, maybe 6'1". Probably worked out at the local FBI gymnasium—or whatever.

"I have some sandwiches being brought in—chicken salad, tuna and roast beef. I hope that is all right with you," Patterson started, settling easily into a swivel chair behind the desk.

"Fine, fine. I'm not really hungry for lunch."

Patterson leaned forward on his elbows, looking directly at Dane. "What can we do for you, Mr. Ingersoll?"

Dane's mind went momentarily blank. "*Where to begin?*" he groped. Hesitantly at first, then picking up steam, he launched into a description of the case he was involved in, taking scrupulous care to avoid too much detail about the legal case itself. Other than shielding his client's confidential communications though, he pretty much bared all, from the grotesque pictures of the PZT experiments right down to the place where Alton's computer went berserk. He didn't slow down until he got to the part where Alton inexplicably vanished. His eyes flitted sidelong to Patterson's at that point, to gauge his reaction. Patterson's gaze held steady with a look of pensive interest, but devoid of any hint of surprise. Dane guessed that he had seen and heard far too much in his career with the Bureau for that. It seemed as though several minutes passed before Patterson spoke. Dane observed him closely.

"Mr. Ingersoll, I can certainly see why you are worried. I would be, too. After all, you are representing an extremely large and powerful pharmaceutical concern. We know more than a little bit about them." Patterson's eyes now took on a quiet, knowing sense of confidence. "One thing is clear: they have a lot of money on the line in this thing, and they mean to protect their investment, *whatever* it may take."

So far, he had said nothing Dane didn't already know. Patterson sipped his coffee, then with studied deliberation set his mug, which bore the imposing F.B.I. insignia, down on the corner of his desk.

"You see, Mr. Ingersoll, you—by representing your client as you are paid to do—have stumbled onto some information which I and my colleagues have been gathering for several months. The results of our investigation are not particularly flattering for Rowalter Industries, and they are damning for their patented formulation commonly known as PZT." Dane purposely stifled the fear he felt in his gut, knowing that ultimately it could not be beaten down. The truth never can.

Patterson continued, "My superiors in the agency have documented 22 deaths worldwide that can definitely be traced to the use of Rowalter's miracle drug. Over 100 more deaths are questionable, but quite probably traceable to PZT's use. We can make available to you, should you desire it, all of the material corroborating these deaths. One possible theory explaining your friend Alton's sudden disappearance is that he was beginning to stumble into territory which

Rowalter didn't want explored: case histories or other evidence of these deaths." Patterson paused momentarily to observe his audience, and decided Dane was still with him. "But, more to the immediate point at hand: what to do about tomorrow's hearing. Just exactly how do you, as Rowalter's attorney, intend to present the 'attributes' of PZT to the one administrative body vested with the power to make this drug legal?"

Strangely, that thought had not even occurred to Dane until this very moment. Like legions of other experienced litigation attorneys, he was so focused on winning his case and finding the evidence necessary to do so, that he had developed tunnel vision. This was not a case of comparative drug effectiveness, undesirable side effects, nor even of insufficient peer review having been done. This was a case, if Patterson was shooting straight with him, in which a statistically staggering number of users of a drug had lost their very lives before the drug was even released in this country. Dane looked directly into Patterson's eyes, which still waited expectantly for an answer to his question. His answer was more knee-jerk than thoughtful.

"Easy. There are as many or more positive effects of PZT than bad; the utility to society greatly outweighs any incidental risk of harm." He knew the moment the words left his lips that he didn't really believe what he'd said. It was if he were back on the moot court team at law school all over again. "*Think like a lawyer,*" they had taught him, and taught him well.

"So you can ignore all of the evidence that we have accumulated, and even the pictures of the rodents you reviewed?"

Dane blinked away the startled look that momentarily crept into his eyes. "How did you know about that?"

"There's not much about PZT we don't know, Mr. Ingersoll". Patterson's voice took on a condescending tone. "You might also wish to check with your paralegal—a Miss Pemberton—on information that has been made available to her. It is of a far more graphic nature than the rodent studies you have seen."

Dane choked on a sudden surge of anger. What right did the Feds have to go poking around amongst his staff, messing with the details of his case? Surely this violated FBI ethical standards! On the other hand, he reasoned, if they have this much adverse information on PZT, there had to be something to it. The lab studies *had* been difficult to defend. And just how *would* Dane present anything approaching a convincing case with these shortcomings?

"Just what do you suggest I do? Abandon my client's case or turn 'state's evidence' and risk being pulled before the Texas bar on ethics charges? I can't be expected to sabotage my own client's case, no matter how I feel about the drug. And what about Alton Dean—where does he fit into all this mess?"

"We are very well acquainted with Alton's situation. As we speak, he is in the possession of operatives of Rowalter Industries."

Dane caught his breath and swallowed, as he processed the startling information. Noting that the revelation had had its desired effect but before Dane could ask questions, Patterson went on.

"As a matter of fact, you might be surprised to know that we anticipated Mr. Dean's suspicions, and allowed them to blossom—all the time under our careful scrutiny, of course. Alton is really quite a valuable asset to both us and Rowalter right now, whether he realizes it or not. Let's just say that he is not out of our sight for a minute."

"I–I don't understand. What would Rowalter Industries want with Alton Dean? And, where is he?"

Patterson gave a hint of a smile and one end of his mouth. "For a bright, accomplished trial attorney, you don't catch on too quickly, do you? Alton is a threat to Rowalter because he has unearthed several "negative" case studies that the higher ups thought they could suppress, or at least whitewash. They cannot allow that to get out at this time. And they naively think there is a possibility that they can convince Alton their drug is completely safe. As for Mr. Dean's location, we know where he is, but are not at liberty to disclose it, for security reasons."

"That is the dumbest notion I ever heard—why would Alton cooperate with people who took him by force, even if they had the most compelling case in the world?"

"Oh, I quite agree with you. Nonetheless, I would not underestimate the shrewdness of these people. They have been around the block a few times and are not small-time players, by any means."

"Then why did you allow them to take Alton, and put his life at risk?"

"I'm afraid you'll just have to trust us on that one; I assure you his life is not at risk."

"You guys really are amazing. You allow my friend and colleague to be kidnapped by an obviously malevolent company backed by big money, with their entire future profitability standing or falling on his cooperation. Why should I trust you? Do you remember a tiny little place called the Branch Davidian Compound in Waco, Texas? How many lives were lost there when someone listened to this kind of bull?"

Patterson blinked, and just for a nanosecond, Dane thought he saw anger and maybe an instant of fear flash across his eyes. It was not a comfortable subject for him, he observed. "What realistic options do you have, though, Mr. Ingersoll? If you are concerned for your friend's safe return, you will cooperate with us."

"What is that, some kind of veiled threat? If I cooperate with you and throw this case, how do I know Rowalter will not take its vengeance out on Alton and kill him?"

"Simple. Such an action would not only result in the non-approval of PZT, but also an international incident the likes of which have not been seen since the Iran hostage crisis. You don't kidnap and knock off an American lawyer and get away with it without a trace. Rowalter would cease to exist and its principals—those that could be found and tried—would be jailed or receive the death sentence. They simply won't risk it. And, mull this over: If they wanted to hold Alton hostage solely to affect your performance at the hearings, don't you think they would have contacted you by now? Instead, you had to find out from me, remember? Oh, incidentally, I'm not—nor will you ever hear me—asking you to 'throw' the case before the FDA. What I *am* asking is that you inject irrefutable evidence we have gathered into the hearing, and then stand back and let nature take its course. You could argue the case any way you wished. But, whatever you do, you must not let anyone think that there is any connection between Rowalter Industries and Alton's disappearance. Let folks think he has been randomly kidnapped just like any of several hundred other people each year."

Dane soberly took in what Patterson said. He knew that technically he was correct; that he could argue the case however he wished. But if he injected the damaging FBI evidence about the drug into the proceedings, and it was as bad as Patterson said, there was little doubt about the effect it would have. Yet, confronted as he was with an increasingly potent case against the drug and its inventor, how could he continue to defend it? He did, after all, have a conscience.

"I'll think about it," was the most he could manage.

"Please do, and do so quickly. We don't have a lot of time, you know."

"*Nothing like turning up the heat,*" thought Dane as he rose to leave and looked at his watch. Panic began to take hold as he did so. He and Patterson parted awkwardly, both of them acutely aware that nothing had been settled. But Dane, seeking some solace and help from the feds, had instead come away with nothing but a feeling of utter and complete foreboding. His stomach tight like a vise and his mind running a thousand directions, he trudged to the parking garage watching his breath billow into the cold air. He fingered the business card Patterson had pressed into his hand as he left, the one with a personal number scrawled in pencil on the back. Almost as if Patterson continued to plead with him telepathically through the medium of the business card, Dane had a growing sense of certainty. In an instant, he knew what he had to do, and his steps quickened with purpose. He headed back to the offices of Salacuse & Lockridge; back to Alton's office.

A block away, in a deserted alley behind an abandoned building off of Jackson Street, stood a man wearing a grey wool overcoat. His collar was pulled up high against the cutting cold of the January morning. His shoulders hunched over, he grasped a small walkie talkie in his right hand, and the stub of a cigarette in his left. The crackle of radio static was muted by the downtown traffic that was just beginning to pick up. The man stole a furtive look around the corner of the building. The old but infamous Texas school book depository was visible in the distance, as the man caught sight of trial attorney Dane Patterson heading for the Federal Building parking garage on Griffin Street. A look of alert expectation crossed the man's face as he muttered something into the walkie talkie.

Back at Salacuse & Lockridge, the War Room had become the setting for structured chaos. Those who were not direct participants in the melee would have discerned no order at all. Dane had called Jenny from his cell phone on the way back to the office, asking her to pull together the associates working on the case, and prepare a separate conference room. She knew something unusual was brewing from Dane's voice, but couldn't put her finger on just what.

Dane had never quit a case in his life; it just wasn't in his nature. But he saw no other way out of his dilemma as he took the elevator up to his office. If he stayed on and did what Patterson suggested, he would be violating the lawyer's most vaunted professional ethic: to zealously represent his client within the bounds of the law. He would also be throwing in the proverbial towel...fighting with one hand tied behind his back, something he could not abide. Still, if he purposely concealed the damning evidence against PZT, he wasn't sure he could live with himself. As he stepped out of the elevator into the reception area, the heaviness in his gut was almost unbearable. He marched down the east wing of offices, where Alton used to hole up to work his miracles. He took one more long look at his office, then turned on his heel and with an air of utter and total resignation, and walked directly to the conference room full of associates awaiting him.

As Dane entered the room, the eyes of no less than six of the firm's brightest young litigators trained in his direction. Those that didn't know Dane in person—that is, most of them—knew of him by reputation. There was not a one of them who did not feel a sense of privilege and honor to be working with such a top-notch attorney on this case. They were primed and ready, and expected to hear something not unlike the locker room speech given by the Dallas Cowboys coach just before leading his troops out onto the Super

Bowl gridiron. The video presenter was positioned where he had asked Jenny to have it, and some incredibly graphic pictures had been arranged in a folder just to its left. The projection screen was lowered and waiting. Each eager young attorney had either his yellow legal pad with pen poised and ready, or his laptop. Dane nodded a silent greeting to the group, and with no further preliminaries, began speaking.

"Gentlemen, thank you for being part of this team and this superlative effort. Our evidence is ready, and our case is thoroughly prepared. I want to get into some of the high points of the hearing, but before I do, you deserve an update on your colleague and my friend, Alton Dean." The associates exchanged nervous glances. "As you know, Mr. Dean was reported missing the day before yesterday. Besides being a fine human being and a friend, he was also very instrumental in pulling together the more difficult research and briefing in this rather unusual case." Dane paused and took a deep breath. "I have just returned from a meeting at the Federal Bureau of Investigation. While there is not much I can tell you at this point, I *can* tell you that they know where he is, and that he is all right." The associates gawked, bursting with a million questions spawned by the news. Dane continued: "Please let all of your efforts from this point on reflect and honor Alton's level of dedication."

"Now, you are all familiar with the issues in this case. It is not a complex case, from a legal standpoint. It is a challenge, however, because some of the research we have culled through—much of it Alton's— is, frankly, not supportive of our case for FDA acceptance of the new drug." Dane nodded at Jenny, who reached to lower the lights, then hesitated as a messenger appeared in the room. The young man whispered an apology for the interruption, placed a folded paper in Dane's hand, and vanished noiselessly through the door. Dane unfolded the paper on which was scrawled the words, "Rowalter Industries needs to speak with you immediately. Urgent." Dane handed the microphone to Jenny, motioning her to take over, then excused himself to a borrowed attorney's office across the hall. He had no particular reason to be nervous, but he felt his palms getting clammy. When he lifted the receiver, he heard a voice he was not familiar with: low, gruff, matter-of-fact. "Mr. Ingersoll, this is Rowalter. As I'm sure you know, we've been watching you. We know where you were this morning, and we know what you are contemplating doing. Don't do it. Don't show the photos to anyone in the firm, and you will not introduce them into evidence before the FDA."

At the only break in the unidentified man's voice, Dane drove a tank right through. "Just where do you get off telling me what to do, or gumshoeing around after me like Sherlock Holmes? Do you know what you can do with your case, Mister...what is your name, anyway...or do you have one?"

"Mr. Ingersoll, you may want to reconsider your position as representative of Rowalter."

"Damn right, I want to reconsider my position, I don't *want* the position, and you can..."

"That's not what I mean. I don't think you're in much of a bargaining position to terminate our relationship, or to alter our chosen strategy."

"Oh, is that so! And who, pray tell, is going to stop me from firing you as my client?"

"Nobody, I suppose, as long as you don't care about what becomes of Natalie."

The phone went silent, and Dane felt his breathing stop. Just the other side of the door, Jenny had jockeyed into position to hear what she could of the conversation. The other attorneys remained uneasily in the room across the hall, their curiosity piqued.

"What is that supposed to mean?" Dane growled through clenched teeth.

"Listen carefully my attorney friend. We have our eye on your little girl more closely than you know. You know that IV she's been hooked up to for weeks? Well, it's carrying a special brew of PZT into every cell of her body. And it's keeping her alive, even helping her. But if you obtain a ruling adverse to us—one which makes the drug illegal and pulls it off the market—you may notice just a slight deterioration in her condition. You see, Mr. Ingersoll, hospitals have a bit of a problem administering illegal drugs." The voice dripped with sarcasm. "What's more, if we don't have your total cooperation in our endeavors, the mutations that can occur, as I'm sure you are quite familiar, can produce some rather interesting and unpredictable results. You see, right now, we have a stabilizer being added to your daughter's solution to prevent or retard mutation. We need only to withhold it, and the PZT can mutate freely, randomly, at any time, up to a million times in a single twenty-four hour period."

The man had Dane's attention. His heart was beating again, at double its normal rate, his breathing shallow and erratic. "Listen you SOB. You come near my daughter, and I'll take you apart, limb from limb. And you keep your stinking drugs away from her!"

"Suit yourself. If we take our drugs away, she'll die within hours."

"No—wait...don't d-d-o that..." Dane needed time, time to think.

"Fine, then. I thought you'd begin to see reason. So, we may expect your full cooperation then, Mr. Ingersoll?"

"Y-Yes, I suppose so." Anger had yielded to fear.

"Oh, and just a couple of suggestions. Don't tell your wife about our secret. She would get too hysterical. Just keep it between us. It'd be a shame if something were to befall little Natalie because our confidentiality was breached. *You* understand: attorney's ethics and all." The voice let out a chuckle that made Dane certain he was capable of murder for the first time in his life. "And I wouldn't recommend contacting the FBI, the DOJ, or anyone else. We're watching your every move. By the time they got to the hospital, it just might be too late."

Dane slammed the receiver down with such force that Jenny recoiled from the door. He turned brusquely away from the phone, eyes moist with volcanic anger that had nowhere to go. Jenny had backed away, but now stuck her head in, a sympathetic expression on her face. She had only heard Dane's half of the conversation, but it wasn't hard to discern that something was horribly wrong. Dane beckoned her close, and hoarsely told her to go tell the waiting associates that there would be no presentation after all, that a family emergency had come up.

"W-What is it, Dane?" Jenny asked boldly, revealing her concern in her voice. His composure just beginning to return, Dane locked eyes with her. "I-I can't tell you. Let's just say my daughter is in grave danger." She had a sudden overwhelming desire to hold her old love, to cradle him in her arms, to caress and mother him. To combat the feeling, she scurried across the hallway to the still-waiting room of curious associates and made the announcement. As the meeting broke up amidst the cacophony of closing briefcases and laptops, rustling legal pads and whispered questions, she rushed back to the office where Dane paced the floor.

"Dane, why can't you tell me?"

"Jenny, if I tell you, you must take a blood oath not to tell anyone in the world, unless I tell you to. Telling you could also put you in some danger."

Jenny gulped, then plunged headlong, whispering in hushed tones. "Okay, I'm game. I won't tell a soul. What's going on?"

"What's going on is that Natalie has been given this godawful stuff, and she isn't even out of the hospital!" Dane's voice hesitated, then broke, as he refused to bring to his lips the word "addicted". Jenny felt a rush of empathy again, but those feelings gave way to confusion.

You don't mean...?"

"Yes, I *do* mean...PZT. Because I'm closing in on the truth about their prize concoction, they're apparently willing to try anything, including attacking my little girl. What do I do? The hearing's tomorrow and I *can't j*ump off the case now..." His voice trailed off, and Dane stood in the middle of the room, as lost as a child alone in the dark.

At that moment, a law clerk scurried into the room and handed Dane a fax message. The header said simply "Food & Drug Admin. Washington, D.C." He willed himself to concentrate as he scanned it. "It says they are postponing the hearing about two weeks, to February 20th. Something about the Administrative Law Judge being ill and a conflict with another hearing setting."

"That's good news, Dane! That gives you just the time you need to get off the case with these creeps."

"Yeah" he said feebly. Normally, he would have given her argument about all the reasons he should stay and fight. But Dane's fight was gone, drained out of him with the telephone call. Without warning, he snapped out of his trance-like state as adrenalin began surging back into his system. "*I've got to get ahold of Susan,*" his brain screamed as he staggered back to the elevators. Jenny watched, utterly at a loss for what to do next. She decided to call Patterson. He would surely know what to do.

CHAPTER FIFTEEN

Alton awoke in a room vastly different from the one in which he'd awakened earlier. Here there were no shadowy figures that he couldn't see, and no stench. A modern desk and chair were placed in the far corner of the room, with a computer, keyboard, monitor and mouse and printer adorning them. He was on a bed with starched white sheets, made up hospital style. The room was otherwise modestly furnished, but had some color from wallpaper on one wall and a small bouquet of flowers in a vase perched atop a shelf table under the solitary window. Noticeably absent was any view outside the room. The light streaming through the window suggested a clumsy attempt at creating faux sunlight, which in turn generated an oddly shaped rectangle of light on the floor near his bed. He felt suddenly hungry, and thought he smelled coffee drifting in from somewhere. A jutting out section of wall hid his view of any access to the room. He swung his legs over the side of the bed and, wincing at the pain that seized his neck and shoulders, stood up. He took a few steps toward the opposite wall and peered around the jut-out, to find a tray neatly arranged with scrambled eggs, bacon, toast, juice and coffee. Alton approached gingerly, to see whether it was as real as it appeared. Satisfied that it was, he reached for the tray, then suddenly stopped. It occurred to him that his "hosts" could have laced anything into this food. *"But,"* he reasoned, *"if they wanted to kill me, wouldn't they have done it by now? They're keeping me alive for a reason, whether they need me—like they said—or for some other reason. Why go to all this trouble otherwise?"* Satisfied that he had dealt with the issue logically, and driven by his hunger, he moved the tray carefully to his bedside, and began wolfing down the still-hot breakfast.

Ten minutes later, with his hunger satisfied and noticing no ill effects, Alton undertook a brief survey of his body. He had bruises on both wrists where his arms had been held to his side, perhaps with handcuffs after application of the hypodermic. His right upper arm was still sore to the touch from the needle. By far the worst was his neck, where he had been choked by a man whose hands had to have been the size of an orangutan. It hurt to swallow, and he felt like a whiplash victim when he tried to turn his head to either side. He performed a couple of neck rotation exercises to try to loosen up, while grimacing from the pain. That done, he again focused his attention on his surroundings. First, the door. He crossed the room and tried the knob, which didn't budge. Clearly, it was locked from the outside. Some diffuse light appeared underneath the door, suggesting a lighted corridor. He squatted, then slithered carefully down to his stomach, suppressing the urge to yell out from the pain as he peered through the half inch opening. No sign of human feet, although he thought he heard faint voices in the distance.

Raising himself to his feet, Alton turned his attention to the computer in the opposite corner. He quickly sized up the equipment: a CPU with both a platter and stationary hard drives, DVD ROM, cable internet hookup, and a cat6 cable which vanished into the wall to what he presumed was some remote file server. No wireless connection was apparent, but then, he could be underground or who-knows-where. This would be tricky, he knew, but he had to try. A keystroke on the ergonomic keyboard produced a pop up box which asked for a password. Alton spent the next five minutes trying all the standard password combinations he could muster, including ones a pharmaceutical company might use. No luck. Ignoring the pain, he dropped to his knees under the table and tipped back the CPU box, peering behind. Sure enough, he located a factory tag bearing a serial number. The number was an alphanumeric sequence containing nine characters. Having no pen or paper, he instantly memorized it, then crawled back into his seat. He tried every conceivable combination of the characters without success. Twenty minutes later, he hit upon the idea of converting each letter to the corresponding number of the alphabet, with "B" becoming "2", "D" becoming "3", and so forth. He did the same in reverse with the single digit numbers, converting them to their corresponding letters. He then grouped the resulting characters in groups of four, juggling their order at random. On the third try, the blank screen suddenly dissolved into a blue background, displaying the name "*ROWALTER*" in a unique red logo. He was in. The next screen depicted four quadrants, neatly laid out with pictorial backgrounds. They were titled "FINANCIAL", "RESEARCH AND DEVELOPMENT", "THE FUTURE", AND "PHARMACEUTICAL". Each required a security code. Alton went straight to the pharmaceuticals quadrant and began wracking his brain for information. Another thirty minutes went by. With his photographic memory, Alton could call quickly to mind all of the background information he had culled about Rowalter. One tidbit he knew was that Rowalter had its agricultural operations in Bolivia, but major headquarters in Peru. When the word "Lima," Peru's capital, produced no results, he began working his way outward to smaller, more obscure towns. He then scrambled the letters of each one. After the fourth town he tried, he hit "Enter" and was immediately looking at list after list of drugs, described in pharmaceutical language. By clicking on each one, he pulled up the chemical formula, a diagram, and chart describing the drug's properties, and its uses. Alton went to "PHENYLZANADIOXIDETETRACHLORAMINE, otherwise known as 'PZT'," and began paging through furiously, memorizing. He had just arrived at a section labeled "Hazardous Properties" when he heard what sounded like footsteps outside the door. Nervously, he exited the program, and scurried back to the bed, positioning himself facing the wall with his back to the door. He heard the door knob turn, and measured footsteps that stopped at his bedside. Alton could feel someone hovering over him, and no longer able to suppress his curiosity, turned to look. Next to him stood a neatly groomed, well-dressed man who looked to be in his mid-thirties. He studied Alton for a moment with piercing blue eyes, then glanced at the breakfast tray, now devoid of food.

"Good morning, Mr. Dean. I trust you had a restful night's sleep and a good breakfast."

Besides a white shirt, tie, and a light blue laboratory jacket he wore a nauseatingly patronizing smile.

"It's pretty damned hard to get a 'restful' anything when your treated like a caged rabbit," Alton spat back. "When do I get out of here?" Alton knew the answer in advance, but figured he had to at least go through the motions to maintain his self-respect.

"Well, it's good to see you have some spunk. We were worried that you might be a little depleted after yesterday's activities. You know, jet lag and all. After all, we have a big day planned for you. Time to rise and shine!" Alton wanted to slap him right across that smirking face of his when he said that. "I have brought a change of clothes for you," the man continued, gesturing toward the shelf table. We'll be letting you tour the facilities here shortly, and you will have about thirty minutes to get ready. There is a lavatory directly across the hall, and your entry code is '306'." Alton sat up at this, suddenly realizing he needed to use those facilities very badly. The man cast a sidelong glance at the computer in the corner. "Ah, I see you have discovered our computer." Alton cursed himself for failing to black out the screen, which now displayed the "Password" box. "You'll have a chance to use our computer soon enough, and a much better model, I might add. But you won't get very far with this one without security codes, and those change every week. No need for concern, however. You'll have an opportunity soon enough to show us what you can do."

"Would you mind *terribly much* giving me some idea of the time of day?" Alton said, infusing each word with as much sarcasm as he could muster.

"Not at all. It is 8:30 a.m. You have till 9:30 to get cleaned up and ready for the tour. You'll want your mind as sharp as possible for all the day's activities." The man made it sound like summer camp, as if the volley ball courts were the next stop. He began fishing through a pocket in his lab jacket, like he had just remembered something. "Here's something you can use to let us know if you need us. In any event, I'll be back at 9:30 a.m. sharp." The man handed Alton a grey and white plastic device containing a button that must have been a simple transmitter. It reminded Alton of the vibrating gizmos they give you in some restaurants to call you to your table.

As the man turned and made his way out, Alton yelled suddenly, "How am I supposed to get out of this stupid room? The door's locked."

"Simply hit the little button on the back of the device, Mr. Dean. See you at 9:30." After the door closed behind him, Alton turned over the transmitter to examine the button. Resignedly, he pressed the little red button on the reverse side. The latch on the door responded with a loud click. Filled with disgust, Alton picked the clothes up off of the table and walked through the doorway. The hallway outside was uncarpeted, and fairly narrow with few doors. The one directly across from his room was nondescript except for the fact that it was made of heavy gauge metal, like his. There was a numerical keypad installed directly beneath the doorknob. Alton entered the numbers 3-0-6, heard another click, and the door yielded to his push.

* * * *

Except for the drive to the hospital on Natalie's delivery date, Dane had never driven so fast in his life. As he pulled up onto his street, he could see Susan's car parked in its usual spot. Dane's heart, already off the chart, skipped a beat as he burst through the front door and into the living room. He parked the car around the block toward the alley, all the while surveying the area carefully in the same manner as some of the investigators he had worked with.

Dane knew he had to do this quietly, with no slip-ups. He approached the house from down the alley, cutting through a neighbor's yard, and jumping a fence to avoid being seen. He entered his house through the garage, using the coded keypad. Susan was in the kitchen, humming a tune and cleaning the floor. Dane surprised her from behind, grabbing her and kissing her passionately. As he held her close, he placed his lips next to her ear and whispered, as softly as he could manage, "Something's wrong. Come with me and don't say anything out loud. The house may be wired." Susan's eyes were as big as dinner plates as she listened, nodding nervously. Dane quietly stole over to the front door, locked it, checked the french door, then deftly motioned Susan toward the garage. A moment later, they were in the alley, then back in the car. Dane rolled up the windows, checked the door, and made sure the telephone was off, while holding his index finger to his lips to keep Susan quiet. He pulled a piece of paper out of his pocket, and, checking his rear-view mirror, scrawled a note to her which read, "Don't say anything. This car may be bugged. We need to talk about Natalie. In ten minutes or so." Susan's expression mirrored her feelings and told the story: she was ready to explode with anxiety.

Taking a back route, Dane wheeled the Beemer onto a heavily traveled state highway, then after he had barely joined the traffic, exited abruptly. He checked his rearview mirror again—no car had followed him. Once on the access road, he took a circuitous course down some residential streets that brought him out on Cedar Springs. Still satisfied no one was tailing him, he pulled into a smallish building bearing the name "Cedar Springs Branch - Dallas Public Library".

Motioning Susan out of the car, they entered. Now speaking openly, Dane asked the desk librarian if there were any conference rooms. She motioned him to the back of the room. Dane took Susan carefully by the hand, his palms already heavy with perspiration. A moment later they were in the room.

"Dane, will you tell me what's going on?" Susan's face was flush with emotion, as she yelled the words. He launched into a fifteen-minute condensed description of the day's events, starting with his meeting with James Patterson, and ending with the phone call from the unidentified man at Rowalter. Susan listened with great effort, and when he got to the part about Natalie, became hysterical. "Oh, my baby!" she yelled, over and over again, tears starting to stream down her cheeks. "Dane, we have to do something. We have to get her out of that hospital tonight!"

"I've already thought about that, and I'm not sure that's the answer. If Rowalter is brazen and insidious enough to have infiltrated the hospital with this drug and somehow gotten the medical staff—or one of its own people—to administer it, who's to say they wouldn't do the same thing at whatever hospital we move Natalie to? I'm also very worried what could happen if we tried to transport her in her condition."

"Well, we can't just *sit* here—they've got her on this hideous drug, and we have to do something!"

"We will. I wasn't sure this morning whether I was ready to trust Patterson, with what he was asking of me and all. But things have gotten personal real fast, and ... what other choice do we have? If a client of mine is willing to go to this extent, and is this crazy, I can't fight the battle with a water pistol. I'm ready to go back to the FBI and ask for protection. And, I'm not sure I want you around where they can get to you— they don't even want me having this conversation."

"I'm not going anywhere without Natalie," Susan shot back, her posture stiffening. "I've waited long enough for her to come home!"

"Susan, you may not have a choice," Dane said softly. "I want Natalie safe, but I want you and Jackie safe, too. Hopefully, there's a way we can do both at the same time. We'll see what Patterson has to say."

"Just make him get those bastards away from our daughter!" Susan was like a cornered mother bear, surprising even him.

"Don't worry—but right now, I want you to go to Houston and stay with your sister. I'll see if there's a way we can safely move Natalie to another hospital. I've heard Cedars-Sinai Medical Center in California has the best neo-natal unit."

"Dane—you don't get it, do you? I won't leave Natalie, not for a minute. Can't we get something closer, like maybe in Houston? I already feel like I've put her in the hands of these evil people." The tears were welling up again.

"Susan, you must leave." Dane said, undeterred. "Either you go to Houston now, or you move somewhere within Dallas, and then move again if we end up bringing Natalie back here."

"Fine," she said. "Then Jackie and I will stay with Aunt Jeanne in Fort Worth. But we're not going to

Houston or anywhere else more than an hour's drive away, until I know for sure where Natalie will be."

"All right. We can go back to the house and get you packed. You call your aunt from my office...better yet, from a pay phone, if we can find one. Just tell her you and Jackie need to come live with her for a while, and that you can explain why later. If you can't trust her with a secret, don't tell her anything. We can't afford any mistakes here, since I don't know what these people are capable of doing."

Dane and Susan seemed to be moving the same direction now, and Dane leaned forward with his elbows on the conference table to wipe her tears away. He gave her a tender, lingering kiss. She yielded to his embrace and began to cry softly. He cradled her head in his arms for a minute, telling her everything would be all right, and trying desperately to make himself believe the same thing. Then at about the same moment as if on cue, they pulled apart and with renewed resolve, returned to the car. Dane took Susan to an old working phone booth in the historic district of downtown, dropped her at the curb, and kept his eyes glued to her throughout the call to her aunt. A minute later she returned to the car and silently mouthed the words, "it's all set." Dane had scrawled another note on the back of one of his business cards that read, "DON'T USE A CELL PHONE TO DISCUSS ANY OF THESE MATTERS: TOO EASY TO INTERCEPT." He held it up to Susan, who quickly nodded her understanding. He floored the gas as he reentered the road exiting the Turtle Creek area of Dallas. Soon, he was back on the Stemmons Freeway, training his car on the shortest route back to the hospital. As he drove, his mind whirled crazily with what he would say to Patterson when he next saw him. But that, he told himself, would come later. First, he and his wife would face the doctors.

CHAPTER SIXTEEN

Alton quickly finished his shower. He hadn't realized amidst the furor of the last twenty-four hours just how much he had needed one. It also afforded him a closer look at just how bruised his body was. In fifteen minutes he had donned the ill-fitting clothes provided for him. Using the toiletries left for him on the bathroom vanity he hastily shaved, gargled and generally shook off the last vestiges of the drug-induced stupor from last night. By his watch, he was running forty minutes ahead of "schedule." Heaving his dirty clothes back onto the bed in his assigned quarters, he began trying doors up and down the stark hallway. He scanned the walls and ceiling, looking keenly for evidence of video surveillance. He saw none, but accepted the possibility that cameras could be deftly recessed in a pinhole sized opening in a corner, or in a light fixture. None of the doors responded, and all had a security keypad like the bathroom door. Next, he tried the air vents. There appeared to be two intakes, placed along the length of the floor at opposite ends of the hallway. He peered down into them, hoping with everything in him that he was not peering directly into a camera lens. Both were blowing cool air. One vent was bolted firmly down and immovable; the other, the one farthest from his room, had a couple of loose corners.

According to his watch, he had thirty minutes left. Alton proceeded to the end of the hallway, which intersected a larger corridor running opposite directions. There was no sign of any living person, and the only sound was the gentle hum of the air conditioning compressors. Since there were no windows, it was clear to him the only light was provided by fluorescent bulbs that really didn't do the job, throwing off a sort of violet-tinged glow. Alton took the right corridor, got halfway down it, and through the dim light could swear he saw an "EXIT" sign. As he approached, he was sure of it, although a man looking for it in a fire would surely have never made it out of the building in time. Arriving at the door, he tried the heavy knob. It was a large, heavy gauge metal door, securely locked and unyielding. The latch assembly looked like it could be electronically controlled, but he couldn't be sure. The most distressing thing is that he couldn't tell whether the door led directly outside the building he was in, or whether he was upstairs, downstairs or underground. The door fit flush against the door jambs and the floor. He doubted if he could fit anything bigger than a dime between them.

Alton started back down the direction from whence he came, noting several doors along the way, and trying each one. The third one he tried, surprisingly, opened. His spirits rose, then plummeted, as he realized it was a janitorial closet. The smell of old ammonia mixed with musty dirt filled his nostrils. As he turned angrily to leave, the corner of Alton's eye caught movement. He turned back just in time to see the flash of a brown mouse scurrying under a mop bucket back into a corner. As his eyes followed the mouse, he noticed the faint outline of...what was it? He approached slowly, throwing open the closet door farther to allow the diffuse light to penetrate the closet. He reached over the dirty mops and buckets, shoving them aside to grope the wall. His fingers felt, then traced the line of what could not be a random crack, but rather appeared to be a smallish door about three by five feet, running down to the floor. The door had no knob or latch, and would have been missed by anyone who did not already know it was there. Alton's eyes quickly surveyed the shelves of the closet, looking for—there it was! A battered old putty knife was wedged between bottles of cleaning supplies. He seized the knife and inserted it midway down the seam in the wall. Prying with all the force the flimsy instrument would allow, he managed to pull the door out from the flush wall's surface a bare fraction of an inch. He then dug his fingernails into the protruding edge, and with great effort forced the door open. Alton wished with all his might that he had a flashlight, for the area behind the door was pitch black. He grabbed one of the mops and, like a swordsman, thrust it into the opening as far as he could reach. The handle hit nothing. Alton backed out into the hallway and peered at his watch – 15 minutes left. He reentered the closet, impatiently pushing aside pails, cans and mops with a clatter. The size of the diminutive opening forced him to enter it while bent sharply at the waist. Once inside, he dropped to all fours. It was immediately apparent that this was not just another closet. Within a couple of minutes, Alton estimated by the number of "steps" with his hands and knees that he had gone ten feet or so. It was equally clear that this was no spacious corridor. There was barely enough room to move, and he could feel each side of the passageway rubbing against his shoulders. A much larger person could have scarcely inhaled without fear of becoming wedged in place like a rock badger. There was no sign of light ahead, and no noise other than occasional scratching inside the walls, which Alton reckoned to be more mice. The luminous dial on his watch glowed an eerie 9:22, and decided not to risk it. He reversed direction, panicking for a brief moment when he feared he was stuck, then continuing on. At 9:26, he had re-hidden the putty knife, shut the passageway door, and quietly closed the janitorial closet. He surveyed the hallway quickly: just as quiet and deserted as ever. He half walked, half sprinted back to his "room", which appeared to be in the same condition as when he left it. Out of breath, he flung himself on the bed, and wondered silently how much of his little expedition had been caught on video camera. He couldn't escape the unfamiliar sensation that his every move was being watched.

Moments later, there were three quick raps on the door, then, right on cue, the man with the piercing blue eyes reentered the room. He held a clipboard in his left hand and a pen protruded from behind his ear, in the same manner as a doctor making his hospital rounds. He still wore the lab coat.

"Well, Mr. Dean, all scrubbed and freshened up, are we?" Alton wanted with all his nerdish being to smack the silly grin and knock the guy to the floor. *"Just drop the charade and get down to business, will you?"*

"Follow me, and get set for a most enlightening tour."

The man turned on his heel in mock military style and led Alton down the same hallway he had traversed moments ago. This time, however, the man took the left branch when they reached the T intersection at the end. They had nearly reached the end of that hallway, when the man extracted from his coat pocket a rectangular shaped electronic device that somewhat resembled a garage door opener. He pointed the device at a door that had an access keypad mounted adjacent to it, just like the bathroom. A tiny red light began flashing and the keypad beeped at them. Alton heard the door latch abruptly and noisily give way. The man opened the door and they entered a much more brightly lit area containing two large elevators, but which had no apparent buttons to operate them. Using the same device he had used for the door, the man aimed it in the direction of one elevator, which promptly and noiselessly opened, Star Trek style. Inside the elevator car, a rather spacious one that could have accommodated ten people or so, there were buttons for floors that the man used manually. He did not do so, though, until he had nimbly entered a lengthy security code by pressing the floor buttons. He did it so quickly that Alton, concentrating with all his might, was only able to memorize about eight of the ten numbers in sequence.

They ascended ten floors in only a few seconds. Alton still believed that they were underground; how, he didn't know. When the elevator doors parted, they were in a different world. They entered a spacious room that, to all appearances, could have been the data processing center for IBM or a Microsoft. Computer stations, separated by partitions, stretched in all directions, each manned by smartly dressed employees busily at work. People carrying stacks of paper and obviously on a mission were bustling between work stations with the seemingly undirected efficiency of a beehive. A ring of glassed offices encircled this area, with names written in Spanish, and men in business suits visible at desks or conference tables in several of them.

"Wait here," his host ordered. The man traversed the large room, wending his way between desks with the skill of one familiar with the terrain. He entered one of the larger glass-fronted offices, and from a distance Alton could see him conversing with a man in a dark business suit, seated behind a massive, burnished desk. Then, smiling, the blue-eyed man opened the office door, stepped half-way out and beckoned Alton to come with a gesture of his hand. Resentfully, Alton followed. When he arrived, the man ushered him inside, where the man seated behind the desk brusquely motioned him to a seat in front of the desk. His chair was positioned so that he was forced to look upward at the face of the man opposite him. "Señor Betaña, this is Alton Dean, the one I've been telling you about. Mr. Dean, Señor Betaña. Alton nodded curtly. "Mr. Dean" he continued, looking at Alton, is the one who will be assisting us in finalizing our research on the new product."

"Superb," answered Señor Betaña, with only a trace of an accent, "You have done your work well, Ramos." Thus, Alton's first indication his "host" had a name. Ramos took a seat by the expansive window on the wall opposite the door.

Betaña leveled his gaze at Alton and spoke carefully and matter-of-factly. "Mr. Dean, Ramos has spoken correctly. We have a need for your services".

"How utterly absurd; it's as if I've answered an employment ad in the Sunday Times. I wonder what the starting salary is?" thought Alton, mockingly. "Go ahead, I'm listening," he said circumspectly, trying his best to sound nonchalant.

"We don't have anyone like you in our operation here at Rowalter. Oh, we have plenty of staff, as you can see," he said, grandly gesturing toward the office outside the glass. "But what we lack is someone who knows the way to—how do you Americans say—'put your best foot forward?'" Quite frankly, we don't believe we have any 'foot' other than our best one," he paused to chuckle at his choice of words, "but we are greatly solicitous of your ability to marshal the data we need to get our products into your country. You see, we have been following your research closely. We have also studied your background in depth. Your achievements at Harvard Law were remarkable, and your subsequent clerkship with the District of Columbia U.S. Court of Appeals, and later the Supreme Court, were quite an honor. You have continued to distinguish yourself while at Salacuse & Lockridge." Alton couldn't help noticing the open folder in front of Señor Betaña which contained several sheets of paper. We would like to offer you substantial compensation, and very tangible benefits, to come to work for us."

"I have just a bit of a problem with your methods, Mr. Betaña. What makes you think I, or anyone for that matter, am going to respond to your overtures after your thugs take me by brute force from my home?"

"I am sure, Mr. Dean, that you can appreciate our position. While we are now a client of Salacuse & Lockridge, your first loyalty is to them. After all, they write your paycheck. If you are rigorously honest, I think you will admit that your research findings go both ways—some, in favor of the positive benefits of our new product, and others against. And, despite your duty as an advocate for our position, you also consider yourself an officer of the court. To you, this means you need to reveal certain negative findings about the drug to Mr. Ingersoll, who in turn discloses them to the court. Am I correct?"

"You could say that."

"All we are asking, Mr. Dean, is that you allow us to pay you, say, $500,000 per year to supervise our product research and advocate our legal position to your Food and Drug Administration. We could also throw in a very nice home and car, and some other, shall we say, intangible benefits." He grinned when he said this. "Simply ask, and it's yours—within reason, of course."

Alton suddenly noticed his breathing accelerate. *"Five Hundred Thousand Dollars? A Car? A Home?"* As only a first-year associate, he earned about a quarter of that now, *sans* car and home.

"As for your research findings, we are confident that, on balance, they will be extremely favorable to our product. We have had the best chemists in the world working on this for years, and they long ago worked the kinks out. It remains for you to simply assist us in getting the word out, effectively, so that we can move this product to market expeditiously." The man's English was flawless, and Alton guessed that he had attended a very good college somewhere in the northern hemisphere.

Alton had to admit he was tempted. All he had to do was accept Betaña's offer, work here for a year or so, get the drug approved, then quit and go back to the states. Yet, in that moment, for some inexplicable reason, Alton made a strategic decision, one that would have many implications. He decided to play along. There were two paths he could go down on this thing, he reasoned. One was to buck and fight and refuse to cooperate in any way, shape or form. He figured that, at best, that path would keep him here just as long as otherwise, gain him nothing but frustration, and spawn ill treatment from his captors. At worst, it could get him killed. On the other hand, if he played along, he just might be given, after a time, enough slack on the tether to find out everything he wanted to know about this place, catalogue it in his virtually boundless memory, and eventually funnel it to the outside world. He only hoped that this second path would not turn out to be the length of a marathon. And, he didn't want to be so cooperative that at some point he became indistinguishable from the slime bags.

"May I consider your offer for a couple of days?" he heard himself say.

"Why certainly, Mr. Dean! Take the time you need. We have prepared accommodations and a working environment for you that, I dare say, you will find quite suitable," continued Betaña. "Ramos here has been placed in charge of you and will be, in effect, your attaché during your stay. He will acquaint you with our operations, your role within them, and the physical layout. Please, if you have any questions which he cannot answer, I am here to help."

"I do have a couple of questions."

"Yes?"

"What day is it?"

"Monday, January 16th."

"Has the hearing begun before the FDA?"

"I'm afraid that is not my department, Señor Dean. However, I will see if I can get you an answer."

"Is Dane Ingersoll still on the case?"

"I believe so; at least, I have no reason to believe to the contrary."

"May I communicate with Mr. Ingersoll?"

"Unfortunately, that cannot be allowed. Although what we will be doing runs on a parallel path to Mr. Ingersoll's efforts, there can be no communication between or amongst you. That is also true of all of your former colleagues at the Salacuse firm. I trust you understand."

"No surprises there," thought Alton. But he had to ask.

"Allow us to show you to your office, Mr. Dean."

Señor Betaña and Ramos rose in unison and escorted Alton across the hectic work area to the bank of elevators. They ascended two floors, then lurched to a halt as the doors parted and Alton entered a spacious floor that contrasted sharply with the bustle and seeming chaos they had left behind. Rich oak paneling covered all of the walls, accented by plush two-tone carpeting, charcoal grey with a green border around the perimeter. "ROWALTER INDUSTRIES" appeared prominently displayed in gold lettering over the door through which they entered the spacious reception area. Betaña gestured with his hand to a pleasant young lady seated behind a large, matching wooden reception station. She smiled as if expecting them, then nodded to the left in the direction of a short corridor. Alton followed Betaña and Ramos down the corridor a short distance and abruptly found himself entering a spacious, beautifully furnished and appointed office. The desk was of heavy burl wood with leather inlaid across the top, with gold leaf carving around the edges. A matching hutch and credenza were behind the desk, and a separate computer station was to the side of the desk so that the user could swivel seamlessly into position. The computer adorning the computer station was, there was no mistaking, state of the art, boasting two large flat screen monitors with video, three hard drives including one solid state drive, two DVD drives and numerous USB and HDMI ports. He thought he spotted voice activation, as a small microphone was attached. He surmised the computer was part of a network with optical cable using HDMI connectors running to an onsite server. Peering more closely, he could see it was hooked up for Wi-Fi, though he wondered how well that could work if the facility were deep underground as he suspected. Shelves lined the walls, and they were filled with several legal sources, among them the CCH Federal Agency Reporter, which carried the latest FDA rulings. A small round conference table with four chairs sat at the opposite end of the office. It was at least three times as large as Alton's old junior associate's office at Salacuse & Lockridge. Noticeably absent from the office was a real window, though someone had made the attempt to ameliorate that effect by placing several pastoral paintings of beautiful woodland scenes on the walls. There did not appear to be any windows elsewhere on the floor from which they had entered, either.

"I am sure you will have everything that you need to accomplish your task here, Mr. Dean. And the best part is that your living quarters are nearby, just a few floors down. All very self-contained and efficient."

"How incredibly thoughtful of you," thought Alton.

"We have taken the liberty of procuring for you much of the research you completed at your firm prior to your stay here. You will find it in the lateral file cabinet, indexed just the way you left it. Now, we know you have much work to do, and we have some rather urgent deadlines for you to meet. And we will leave you to yourself. This floor is completely open to you, and you may feel free to roam around and familiarize yourself with it. That is not true, however, of the other floors in the building, which are off limits to you. You have security clearance for only this floor, and your residence floor. Remember, we know your whereabouts at all times, and I am quite sure you will observe the rules." Alton thought about asking for a hall pass, or maybe asking permission to speak with the RA, but suppressed the urge. "Oh and, before I forget, here are the passwords you will need to access the pertinent portions of our computer network." Ramos handed him a card with some numbers printed on it. "They are changed every two days, so don't forget to get them from Ramos as needed. You will have access to the company intranet for purposes of your research; you will, however, have no access to company files and computers for which you are not cleared. The file server can see all of your computer's files and activity; you can see only limited portions of it and the remainder of our network. Do you understand?" Alton simply looked at him and nodded noncommittally. "Why don't you try the office on for size, while I step across the hallway?" Alton obliged, and ambled toward the plush looking high-backed chair situated behind the desk. As he slid into the chair, his eyes fell on a wood and metal carved name plate on the front of the desk, with his name inscribed in capital letters. He wondered silently how far in advance they had prepared this little item in anticipation of his arrival.

Betaña vanished with his shadow, Ramos, and reappeared a few moments later in the doorway. Beside him stood an attractive looking young woman, light brown hair to the shoulders, about 5' 3", maybe 5' 4". "This is Celicia, your secretary," he announced with a noticeable hint of pride in his voice. While I am familiar with your capabilities on the computer, you will find her helpful for the more routine tasks, and her organizational skills are impeccable. Her work station is just across the hallway. And now," continued Betaña, studying his watch, "I have some pressing appointments. I will leave Ramos with you to get you settled in and answer any questions. Please explore your surroundings. I will have lunch sent in for you later. Work should begin in half an hour or so." Just what this "work" was Alton could only guess at, but figured he would learn soon enough.

CHAPTER SEVENTEEN

The meeting with the doctors and the hospital administrator at the East Dallas Medical Center offices was a stormy one. Dane would not be placated with patronizing answers or promises of an "investigation." Susan was so upset that at one point Dane excused himself, took her outside the building, and let her walk around the perimeter to blow off steam. In the final analysis, the hospital spokesman had said, it was too soon to conclude anything. They would need to run tests on Natalie to see if she exhibited any "uncharacteristic behaviors," and just what *was* in her system. All that they had to go on at this time was that Dane and Susan said there was someone in their facility who was surreptitiously adulterating the drugs they were using to treat little Natalie. "We will first have to either confirm or disprove this," stated the chief doctor, in just a bit too business-like a manner for Dane to stomach. "Then," he continued, "we will decide on a change in the treatment plan, if one can be supported."

"You have 24 hours to do that," Dane snapped, "and not a second longer. If I don't have firm answers by then, we're moving Natalie. And...." he added, almost as an afterthought, "there is no guarantee that will be the end of my dealings with your fine establishment."

With that over, Dane and Susan took the elevator to the parking garage, where Susan reluctantly got into her own car, still jammed with luggage from the night before. He bid her goodbye, kissed her through the window, and told her that everything would be fine. He would keep her updated on Natalie and, of course, she had the doctor's number also. Watching Susan wheel out of the parking gate, Dane prayed that she and

Natalie would be all right, and wondered what the day would bring.

Back at the office, with Dane and Alton both gone, Jenny had been at the helm. The Rowalter matter had been Dane's baby from the very beginning, and no other attorney in the office felt familiar enough with the facts to commandeer it in his absence. Jenny was up on the details, and in fairly regular touch with FDA support staff which monitored the hearing docket. Now that they had an additional two weeks to ready themselves, she was starting to believe they could pull it off. But her heart wasn't in it for obvious reasons, and God-only-knows what Dane was planning to do with the case when he returned. She wouldn't blame him for a second if he abandoned the case entirely, but she knew that would never happen now that a threat had been leveled against Natalie. What she really thought would happen now was that Dane would employ a philosophy that she had seen criminal defense attorneys use on several occasions when defending an accused that they knew to be guilty. You do the best you can for the sake of the legal system and the constitution and then, "let the chips fall where they may." The difference in this case, she reasoned, was that there *were* no constitutional rights, and Dane was not representing a criminal defendant. Though well-financed, what Rowalter was doing as a corporate client was every bit as sinister—perhaps more so—than any burglar or murderer or rapist acting on his own. She knew instinctively that, in order for Dane's daughter to have any chance of survival, they had to at least make a convincing pretense of putting on their best case for approval of PZT. Therefore, while awaiting Dane's arrival, she had busied herself preparing outlines of testimony and exhibits that reflected only the best evidence for the drug. She filed away the hideous pictures of victims writhing under the influence of the mutated permutations of PZT, steeling her will in order not to look at them.

Amidst the pressure-filled chaos, Jenny found herself wistfully thinking of a more innocent time, back at high school with Dane. How much had happened since those days when they would lie under a canopy of stars out in the meadow just behind the football field at Madison High! She had thought it would never end, and wished it never had. To find herself back here, now, with the very same Dane Ingersoll, but in these surreal circumstances. She just had to believe it was more than coincidence.

Jenny's day dreams were interrupted when Dane burst back into the office, sputtering out of breath. "Jenny, get us on the speaker phone with...do you have Patterson's phone?" Dane was frantically feeling through his shirt pocket, presumably fishing for a business card, and coming up empty.

"Yeah, I've got it right here, Dane." Jenny felt a flush in her cheeks. She wanted to tell him what she had been thinking moments ago, but suppressed the impulse. She lined up the four-way telephone speaker/mike in the middle of the conference table.

"What's the urgency?" she queried, then quickly realized how ridiculous the question must have sounded.

"You'll see. But don't dial just yet."

Dane abruptly held up a hand and beckoned through the doorway to a man Jenny had not seen standing in the hallway. The man entered compliantly, and began scanning the room with piercing eyes, intent on finding something. He pulled a device from his hip pocket that bore some resemblance to stuff she had seen airport security guards use when checking subjects for firearms, yet somehow different. He began sweeping the walls with it in wide arcs. This he followed by checking the light fixtures, smallish knickknack items on the conference table, and the telephone itself. Jenny had never before seen a room swept for bugs, and found it at once interesting and amusing, like she was in a James Bond movie.

The man looked at Dane and, almost imperceptibly, shook his head. Satisfied, Dane turned to Jenny.

"Okay, get him on the line."

Jenny complied as the man swiftly exited and closed the door. The phone rang twice, then answered.

"Patterson here."

"Mr. Patterson, Dane Ingersoll."

"Yes, Mr. Ingersoll. What can I do for you?"

"I don't know how much of this you already know from surveillance or whatever, but these thugs from Rowalter have now gotten to my family. I tried to fire them not long after speaking with you, and then they threatened my family, my little girl. Did you know that?"

"No, I didn't. I'm very sorry to hear that."

"I want FBI protection. I'll cooperate with you if you can show me how to do it without jeopardizing my family's life."

"Keep talking. What do you have in mind?"

"I've already got my wife staying with her aunt in Fort Worth. There have been no threats against her as of now, and she's okay. But these people seem to have eyes and ears everywhere. I would like at least a couple of agents watching her."

"I'm listening."

"My daughter Natalie is a premature baby, born only three weeks ago. She's had this...well, rare condition—from day one. The hospital and specialists working on her had told me they were using something experimental on her and that her condition had improved. And it seemed to have, at least to us."

"That's good news."

"True enough, except for one problem," Dane fought for control of his voice. "They've turned Natalie into an...an *addict*."

There was momentary silence, then: "Do you mean what I think you mean?"

"I've got the hospital doing testing. I should know more specifics later today, but Rowalter says they've been giving her PZT through an IV."

There was an even longer pause at the other end. "Mr. Ingersoll, that's hard to believe, even for them."

"Well, believe it, at least for now. And the worst part is they say they've introduced a stabilizer into it to keep it from mutating. If I don't cooperate in representing them before the FDA, they'll withhold the stabilizer from her. If that happens, they're saying it can mutate out of control."

"They're correct about its ability to mutate. As for the stabilizer, I've never heard of one, and our research chemists are pretty up to speed on such things. It could be a bluff, you know, to gain your cooperation. I'm sure you've considered that."

"I seriously doubt it. They'd have to have considered that I would follow up with exhaustive tests to get at the truth."

"I agree. But if they had a stabilizer that no one else had, the tests might not be able to detect it for what it was. I'll get with our people in Washington and see what they know anything about the subject. As for the PZT itself, the hospital would be able to identify a foreign substance, but might not know what it is without certain protocols being followed. I can put them in touch with our chemists."

"How fast can this all be done?"

"Maybe, 24-48 hours."

"Well, you'd better speed it up if you want my compliance. There's no way in hell I'm going to be able to take the position you guys want me to take if Rowalter's doing what it says it's doing to my daughter. And I need your people stationed at the hospital, whether we keep her at that wretched place or move her somewhere else."

"I think all your security concerns can be accommodated speedily. But please, for her sake, don't make any decisions to move her without our knowledge and input. It would not be difficult to infiltrate other hospitals in the area, and you don't want to jump out of the frying pan and into the fire."

Dane swallowed hard as he again considered this possibility. "Okay, I'll be back in touch as soon as I have the test results."

Dane gave Patterson the address and phone of Susan's aunt as well as his private number, then ended the call. He slipped his phone into his pocket and collapsed with a thud into a chair by the conference table next to Jenny. He planted his elbows on the table and buried his face in his large hands, his thoughts racing uncontrollably on just what to do with his daughter, and with this case run amok. Jenny gave Dane a minute to recover, then touched him gently on the shoulder.

"I know this has got to be tough, Dane, and I can't imagine what you are going through with the baby. But we've got a lot to do, and not much time to do it. Are you up to going through the hearing outline now?"

"Damn the hearing. I have some calls to make. You take care of it."

"OK, but I think I've gone about as far as I can go on my own; I need your help.

"And you'll get it. But not now. Find something else to do. Prep Zimmerman some more. Review the pictorial evidence. I'll be in my office."

* * * *

Dr. Norman Holloway was bone tired. He had just put in another long day's work at the little laboratory tucked away in the Rocky Mountains, the one that nobody knew about. As he entered the two-bedroom bungalow he called home in the outskirts of Colorado Springs, he thought of his classes, his students, and his research that he felt he was neglecting. The post-Christmas break was coming to a close, and he would soon be returning to his academic pursuits. It had been many years now since he opened the odd-looking letter one day after concluding teaching a graduate seminar class. He still recalled how, with hands trembling, the engraving on the envelope looked and felt to his fingers as he read the words, "Stockholm, Sweden" on the return address. The Nobel Prize in chemistry had been long in coming, but not totally unexpected, given the sweeping impact of his ground-breaking findings in organic chemistry. No one else had ever drilled down so deep as he in demonstrating the effects of mutating cells on organic compounds occurring in nature. He had led a team of chemists in doing so, brought untold prestige to the university, and gained wide acclaim. But that was ten years ago. His wife of twenty-five years had died last April after an extended struggle with cervical cancer. His money from the Nobel prize had long since run out, and, while he was a tenured professor, the monetary rewards of his position at the university were not particularly noteworthy. Missy's suffering had endured so long that insurance caps had been reached and surpassed, and their savings drained. Professor Holloway had been forced to start looking outside academia for paying work. He'd taken a year sabbatical, with the Chemistry Department agreeing that a period in private industry would enhance both -

his and the department's credentials. After working for a couple of main line American chemical companies on highly remunerative projects, he had returned to full time academic research and teaching, in that order. However, despite an increased salary from the university, he was still heavily in debt. So, during the summers and on extended breaks in his research and teaching schedule, he would supplement his income by consulting with companies who paid well. One such company was a South American firm that had run a blind ad in an insert to the *Journal of Advanced Organic Chemistry*. He had responded, and been retained instantly when Rowalter Industries, S.A. had recognized who they were dealing with. They agreed to pay him three times as much as any project he had done for a North American firm.

Dr. Holloway entered the little den where he had spent so many wonderful evenings with the love of his life. After making himself a modest meal of leftover roast and a Caesar salad, he sat down in his office to do some writing. His laptop computer was where it always was, on the secretary next to his favorite books. Missy's picture looked lovingly at him from one of the many nooks and crannies in the secretary. He laid his hands on the keyboard and began typing an encrypted email message. The message contained a string of characters and symbols that had meaning only to an accomplished chemist. He typed several uninterrupted lines of chemical formulae. Then, he entered the following message:

"Today, at your laboratory, for the very first time, I became aware that my energies were not been expended on the humanitarian objectives which I have heretofore thought."

He hesitated, hands on the keyboard, then took another bite of the roast.

"In all good conscience, I must halt this work. I will not be able to continue. I have worked all my life to do good for scientific endeavors and for mankind, and cannot change course now. I have been greatly blessed to have served in some capacity to ease mankind's pain—until now."

He concluded the email with his initials, then attached a couple of image files, and hit "Send," transmitting both email and images to their destination.

* * * *

The *Denver Post* got the story first, through a reporter on its city beat who had a friend that worked for the *Colorado Springs Gazette Telegraph.* The *Telegraph's* reporter had it to his news editor almost immediately, but the *Post* still scooped the *Gazette Telegraph*, rushing to press with its early morning edition. Dr. Norman Holloway, celebrated chemist/lecturer/scientist and local boy-made-good had, it appeared, taken his own life. He was found with a semi-automatic pistol still clutched loosely in his hand, slumped forward at his computer. Police declined to speculate on the reasons for the tragic incident, stating that no note had been left. The computer, whose hard drive would be confiscated and analyzed only if foul play became suspect, did not reveal any immediate clues. The screen saver had been running and password-protected. Naturally, said police, they didn't know the password. However, it did not appear the good professor had been in communication with anyone at the time. More facts, said the front-page article, would be reported as they became available. The name Rowalter Industries appeared nowhere in the article.

By 9:00 a.m. MST anyone in the world that mattered in the field of chemistry knew of the gifted Dr. Holloway's untimely passing by suicide. The university hastily put together a press release that honored him, lauding his scientific achievements. Though it alluded to his wife's tragic passing a few years before, the release deliberately excluded any mention of the manner of his death.

CHAPTER EIGHTEEN

Dane's bedside telephone jolted him awake. He sat bolt-upright in bed, disoriented, and realized he had been dreaming. He grabbed the phone, fumbled it, then grabbed it once again.

"Dane, were you asleep? What are you doing still in bed at 8:00?" It was Susan.

"I-I don't know." He squinted through bleary eyes at the alarm clock on the night stand, and confirmed that she was right. He threw back the covers and leaped out of bed, hitting the speaker phone button as he did so. It had been strange sleeping in the king-sized bed alone last night.

"Well, I'm calling to find out what hospital we're going to be moving Natalie to." She was anxious.

"Sweetheart, you know better than to call me here," Dane croaked, only somewhat awake. Although Dane had had the house swept for bugs by Patterson's people, he was still uneasy. There was no way he was going to disclose over their home phone information of that sort. "I'll call you back in thirty minutes from another phone." Dane raced through a five-minute shower, shaved, then quickly donned the suit he had hung on the closet door the day before. Grabbing his briefcase off the kitchen table on the way out the door, Dane was soon racing down the road in the Beemer. He pulled into the Stop and Go convenience store a half mile away, picked up a cappuccino and, clutching it for warmth, located an ancient car-high pay phone on the corner of the lot. Surprisingly, it worked. He called the number of Aunt Jeanne. Susan answered on one ring.

"I thought you'd never call!"

"Sorry. I spoke to the head honcho at East Dallas Medical yesterday. He was about as helpful as a stump. 'Told me PZT was a form of experimental drug that the hospital had used in 'only a very few cases' under close supervision and with several qualified physicians approving it. Said it was 'introduced' to the hospital as a non-formulary drug by an unnamed sales representative of a large foreign pharmaceuticals company late last year. In the few cases where they used it, they've had 'remarkable results'."

"Doesn't that miss the point? I mean, I don't care if it's the Salk-Sabin vaccine if it makes my little girl into a drug addict!"

"My thoughts exactly." Dane deliberately withheld from her, as he always had, the full, ugly story of what the drug was capable of doing. "I told him he'd better start looking for top legal counsel for the hospital, and that I'd be in touch with him later. Oh, and Patterson says he has an FBI chemist visiting the hospital today to help them test the PZT to see if there are any irregularities with it."

"But what about the transf—"

"I know; I know. I've got someone working on it at Jones-Petersmythe Hospital in Houston. All three hospitals I've contacted are very leery of taking a patient with Natalie's rare condition, and under these circumstances. They all want to know why she's being transferred from the hospital with one of the best neonatal units in the country. I'm keeping back from them the fact that I'm a trial attorney, and that we're upset. We obviously don't want them running scared."

"But Dane, when will we know if they can accept her?"

"By tomorrow afternoon, after certain doctors meet in committee."

After a long pause, "What will we do if *no one* accepts her?"

"I...I don't know. I prefer not to think about that. I'm not sure what would be worse: leaving her in the hands of East Dallas Medical and the three stooges, or starting from scratch with a facility whose doctors are unfamiliar with her case and just as unfamiliar with PZT.

"I know." Susan being crying softly. "And I don't want her several hours away, but we've got to do *something*."

"Don't worry," Dane assured her. "We will...we will," he said, as he fervently wished for something more hopeful to tell her.

Dane and Susan exchanged other minor bits of news, both trying in vain to act like it was business-as-usual, but always returning to Natalie. He hung up the phone and stepped on the accelerator. Remarkably, he was parked and at his office by 9.

* * * *

Jenny surveyed the three newspapers appearing in three different windows on her computer screen, *The Dallas Morning News, The Denver Post,* and *The New York Times.* Though she had missed the 10:00 news herself last night, one of the many law clerks working on the Rowalter case had told her about a story on the death-by-suicide of a Nobel prize winning chemist named Holloway. Apparently, the clerk had said, Holloway had been moonlighting from his position at the university, working for a private chemical concern based in South America. He thought there might be something here worth looking into, and Jenny agreed.

She scanned the articles, beginning with the front page Associated Press report in the *Post*. Her eyes instantly froze, riveted on the words "Rowalter Industries". Apparently, the distinguished chemist had been supervising lab testing work for Rowalter during the Christmas recess. Because the university had not known about the job, said the report, it was deemed suspicious enough to obtain a search warrant. Police investigators were now trying to decode the hard drive on his computer to rule out homicide. They might take the hard drive to the FBI crime lab. Just routine, of course—they didn't really expect to find anything significant. There was something awfully odd about all this: too odd for words. Dane's FDA hearing, the "expert witness" who did an inexplicable about-face, Alton's disappearance, Natalie's force feeding of the world's most potentially lethal drug, and now a suicide by a top chemist who—just by coincidence of course—had been working for Rowalter. If she didn't know any better, she would expect Goldfinger and Agent 007 to appear before her, then hopefully awaken from a bad dream. But, no such luck. This was stark, cold reality, not a spy flick.

She began doing research on Holloway. She got his full legal name, address, phone number and date of birth from the internet. His social security number was a little more tricky, but with the help of a few on line services the firm subscribed to, she soon had that also. Next she went for his academic background, and learned, among other things, that he had minored in experimental pharmacology. As a young man, he had pursued a pre-med curriculum and had been enrolled in Stanford University Medical School, but had left it after two semesters and channeled himself into a graduate chemistry program at Caltech. Hitting his stride there, he had obtained his master's degree in organic chemistry, *summa cum laude*. He earned his doctorate in Molecular Neuropharmacology at the Institute of Pharmacology and Toxicology, University of Zurich, Switzerland. Again, he graduated with highest honors. He had collected the Nobel Prize in organic chemistry five years later. Holloway had even crossed professional paths with Zimmerman the real Zimmerman, at one point. So much for the easy stuff. What about Holloway's connection with Rowalter? Tapping into a website for issuance of passports Jenny was able, for a small fee, to learn that Holloway had traveled to both Bolivia and Peru nearly two years ago, and returned barely a week later. He did not appear to have ever been to either country before, and a genealogical search verified Dr. Holloway had no family living in South America. It was shortly after that trip that he took a research/teaching position at the University of Colorado in Boulder. Suddenly Jenny heard the door open noisily and nearly jumped out of her chair. It was Dane, returning from a meeting. Her eyes met and searched his for an inkling of how things stood. They were calmer yesterday, but still could not be completely read.

"How 'bout some lunch, Jenny?"

"I'm game, I need a break. And I can tell you about some research I've been doing."

"Good. Lord knows, I need some fresh ideas right about now. I know a good deli down Lamar, in the West End that serves great Texas chili."

"I'm with you." Jenny's spirits perked up. It was the first decent mood she'd seen her boss in a week. Her research could wait.

<u>Somewhere underground in South America</u>

Alton eyed the plush surroundings in his new office. He got up and wandered out into the hallway, awkwardly gesturing a greeting to his new "secretary". A heavy uneasiness had settled over him. He knew what he had to do, but hadn't a clue how long he had to do it. He was unsure what day it was anymore. He didn't even know where he was. For all he knew, the FDA approval hearing was history, and he was being kept here for some pure profit motive or, worse, just to titillate someone's perverted sense of humor. Except for some occasional clerical personnel traveling up and down the elevators, it seemed like this area was cordoned off, separate from the rest of the company, and that he was the "bubble boy"—sterile, protected and isolated.

But he couldn't afford to let himself feel that way, couldn't allow himself to sink into despair. After all, no one was going to bail him out of this situation, so he had to depend on his own wits. He could either make a run for it or work from the inside. If he escaped, though, what route would he take out of this subterranean prison? And what would his chances be, with video surveillance in every corridor, security people blanketing the building, and him without any weapon? Clearly, he thought to himself, the decision he had silently reached in Señor Betaña's office was the right one.

He shuffled back to the tufted leather chair behind the imposing desk. It was time to get down to business. Working intently, he called up from his memory the series of security codes and passwords that he had used to get into Rowalter's system that morning. Within five minutes, he was browsing around in the "Research and Development" section of the company's intranet. A list of pharmaceutical compounds, denoted by their proper chemical names, appeared before him. He couldn't even pronounce most of them, much less get a grip on the chemical formulas which described them. In a separate directory where one would least expect to find it, he unearthed a group of drugs which seemed related to opiates like heroine and the like. The difference was that, by the descriptions appearing next to each, certain ones possessed unique healing qualities that were not dissimilar to the near-miraculous effects of steroids. Still, there was no sign of PZT. Acting on a hunch it was in a hidden file, Alton shifted into DOS and entered a few commands to pull up file attributes. A couple of commands later his screen was filled with a smorgasbord of now unhidden files. One by one he opened them, staying within the Research and Development/new drugs subfolder. Within fifteen minutes he had it: a file named "Phenyl.txt". There was only one problem. As the same moment that he tried to open it, another message popped up, "PASSWORD REQUIRED". Alton brought his fist down on the desk hard, and felt the smarting of the pain in the heal of his hand. All he needed right now was another damned password. He pondered it a minute, and then got up and walked across the hallway to Celecia, the secretary he had been "introduced" to a short time ago. His gait was a studied saunter, affecting a business-as-usual manner. He cleared his throat.

"Um, Celecia," he began, *very casually*.

"Yes, Mr. Dean, can I help you?"

"Yes, if you don't mind. Could I have the extension of the administrative staff for the computer network? I seem to be having a bit of, er, trouble getting used to your system."

"Certainly, sir." "It's extension 967. Would you like me to dial it for you?"

"Oh, no, no, that..uh..won't be necessary. But thank you for offering."

Moments later in his office, Alton took a deep breath, and quietly rehearsed a low-toned South American Spanish accent. He pressed the intercom button and keyed in 9-6-7. When a male voice answered, he said in the most routine tone he could muster, "This is Ramon in data processing. We seem to have lost our password for a certain file in the Research and Development drugs directory. One of the guys in research needs it. Can you help us?" Alton held his breath, praying that his accent had been convincing.

"What file is it for?" the man replied, sounding very Bolivian.

"Phenyl-dot-t-x-t," said Alton.

"I'll buzz you back in a minute, Ramon," said the voice. "I'll have to locate it. What's your extension number?"

Alton panicked, nearly falling off his chair. He recovered quickly, forcing his voice back into as even of a cadence as he could manage. "Oh, that's all right, I'll hang on for you."

"Suit yourself, Señor."

Alton heard keys being pressed on a keyboard, then the sound of some papers shuffling. After what seemed an eternity, the voice came back on.

"What's your classification level?"

Alton gulped and broke into a sweat. "Top clearance", he shot back, remembering the phrase from some CIA movie he'd seen.

"Very funny," came the reply, "but I got you covered. The password is '7llama24.'"

Alton repeated it back to make sure he had it right, then thanked the man and hung up the phone. He quickly panned the doorway to the hall to see if anyone was watching, and in so doing realized with a start that he had left the office door open. Once again, with forced nonchalance, he strode across his office, pretended to check his thermostat setting, then quietly closed the door. Back at his desk, he carefully entered the password. Before his eyes series of files expanded, all of them named for various chemical compounds. Every single one was in Spanish, but it didn't take a linguist to discern that the files were named after various stages of mutation of a compound: "Mutatión numero uno...Mutatión numero dos...Mutatión numero tres..." and so on. He opened and decompressed the files one by one, straining his photographic memory to its very threshold, but wishing all the while for a flash drive to supplement it.

Alton bravely ventured forth into the files. Each additional click of the mouse ushered him into pages of data describing the clinical effects on human subjects of a different mutation stage of PZT. These too were all in Spanish. Fortunately for Alton, he had taken four years of it in college—bucking the trend for students to take French while at Harvard. The files unmistakably and graphically chronicled the drug's degeneration into a lethal compound, beginning at about one month after it was first administered to a subject. What began as a morbid curiosity in Alton became horror as he read and mentally translated the descriptions in the files:

"Mutation numero uno—

...Thirty-one days and two hours after the first administration. Subjects begin to evidence excessive saliva production, mild skin rashes, some sporadic lack of concentration. Not all symptoms are noted in all subjects, but at least one symptom noted in every subject. (Sample size: 100)..."

"Mutation numero dos—

...Thirty-five days and ten hours after the first administration. Saliva production continues to be excessive, causing foam to appear around mouths of most subjects. Epidermal itching, accompanied by inflammatory rash, markedly increased in nearly all subjects. Lapses of concentration more frequent. Not known whether lapses are due to other symptoms or an independent phenomenon..."

"Mutation numero tres—

...Forty-two days and five hours after the first administration. New symptoms noted. Eyes of subjects becoming bloodshot, difficulty in sleeping. Shortness of temper in most subjects. Some subjects bleeding at situs of rashes, regardless of treatment through skin lotion...Tightness of throat accompanied by soreness and hoarseness...."

"Mutation numero quatro—

...Forty-seven days and zero hours after the first administration. Swollen eyes, loss of vision in 20% of subjects. Oozing wounds with deep infections. Many subjects unable to drink, eat or swallow. Convulsions occurring in 75% of subjects on average of every hour. Some beginning to have difficulty standing and walking..."

"Mutation numero cinco—

"...Five subjects deceased..."

Alton stopped. He had read enough. He had ventured up one directory level to browse around some more when, without warning, the office door swung open and some authoritative footsteps brought him nearly out of his chair, heart thumping furiously. He quickly, almost without thinking, exited all open directories, hit the monitor switch so that the screen went black, and pretended to fiddle with some connections running to the computer under the desk.

"Is there some problem with the computer, Mr. Dean?" It was the ubiquitous Ramos, cheerful and smiling. If they were onto him, they were decidedly not tipping their hand.

Alton thought quickly. "Y-yes, as a matter of fact. This damned keyboard has been skipping keystrokes and costing me lots of time."

"That is most unusual. We had everything thoroughly tested before we furnished your office."

"Well, it may have been a software problem. I've just begun rebooting the system, and we'll see if that fixes things."

"Be sure to let me know immediately if it does not. A new keyboard is, of course, no problem. We don't want any time wasted on equipment failure." Ramos was carrying something in his hand which looked like a portfolio of sorts. This he handed to Alton as if it contained government classified documents. "Here are some materials we believe will be helpful in getting you started in your work. Research protocols, time saving methods, and basic sources. I am sure that with your background, you are way ahead of us in many respects. But there may have been some methods in here you have not utilized in your prior research at the Salacuse law firm. We want to equip you with every tool to help us show your government that we have not only the safest product, but the best—indeed, the *only*—one out there. I'm sure I don't need to remind you that time is of the absolute essence, with several major competitors poised to enter the market."

Alton stifled a sigh. "Thank you. I will do my best to make use of them."

"Wonderful. If you need anything, here is my extension." Ramos handed him a business card with Rowalter's logo on one side and the numbers "98" scrawled on the other. The card smelled heavily of whatever brand of after shave Ramos' used. "Lunch will be brought up at 12:30. You'll find the menu in your upper left-hand desk drawer. You'll also want to mark your calendar for a meeting with Señor Betaña tomorrow at 10:00 a.m. You're expected to be prepared to discuss your findings at that time."

One could dress it up any way one wanted, but it was crystal clear that Alton had no real "choices" here. He simply nodded his acknowledgment to Ramos, who turned and glided through the door, nodding at Celecia on the way.

As he entered the hallway, Alton impulsively blurted out, "Say, Ramos, you wouldn't happen to have any USB flash drives lying around here, would you?"

Ramos looked over his shoulder patronizingly. "No, Señor Dean, I'm afraid we don't. Rowalter has the greatest of confidence in your retentive powers." He smiled a wolf-like grin and glided down the hall, taking his trilled "R's" along with him.

"So, they want some research, huh? Well, I'll give them some they won't forget any time soon." It was now noon, and he had twenty-two hours to whip up something. Alton unzipped the portfolio. It contained

some two sided, laminated sheets with references to numerous dot com and dot org web sites. Additionally, a whole section was devoted to a "Logic Tree", which depicted strata of colored blocks trailing down the page. Levels of blocks were separated by "If/then" statements which directed the user to different topics based on what, if anything, he found on the previous level. It was all hogwash, both condescending and insulting at the same time. Any eighth grader could follow a decision chart. He threw the book aside disgustedly. He would do this on his own, and in his own way, thank you very much. He already had virtually committed to memory all he needed to defeat Rowalter's application. Now, if he could just get it to someone on the outside. He could crank out what Rowalter wanted to hear all day long if that's what was necessary to buy him the time he needed. He phoned in his lunch order, then settled back in his chair to begin formulating propaganda. The funny thing was, just days before, in a different time and place, he would not have thought of this as propaganda at all. But in only a couple of days, all that had changed.

* * * *

Jack Heinz sipped his cup of cappuccino while Scruff readjusted himself in his seat and scanned his copy of *USA Today.* Mere slits behind Ray Ban look-alikes, his trained eyes did a wide-angle scan of the area surrounding the unmarked sedan where he sat. Reflexively, Jack felt under his left armpit for the holstered Sig 228 - 9 millimeter pistol he wore as if it were a bodily appendage. He had meticulously checked its operation this morning on the firing range, just as he did yesterday morning and would do tomorrow, and the next day. Jack Heinz had never particularly relished these civilian surveillance assignments. They were neither challenging nor career-builders, but they came with the territory when you were an agent on surveillance assignment. So far, there was nothing to report, but then again, they had only been here a couple of hours. Sometimes he wished again for his days back in the L.A.P.D. narcotics squad chasing drugs up the ladder from user to pusher to dealer to kingpins. Jack had methodically worked his way up the chain, to the point where he eventually was tracking down sources south of the Baja California—dealing with quantities of cocaine and heroin that could only be measured in plane loads. Then it had been off to the DEA, where he had gone undercover and quickly earned a reputation for one of the savviest agents to ever come down the pike. The only problem is he had, like so many others who did what he did, relegated his family life to last place, until it was too late to salvage it. One year and a divorce later, he had completely burned out, taken a leave of absence, and eventually transferred to the Bureau to seek whatever "low pressure" job would have him. After working awhile at a desk job, he had nearly called it quits, going completely stir crazy with the sheer boredom of it all. Earlier this year, a position in the FBI witness protection program had come open, and he had hungrily snagged it. A little surveillance was thrown in for good measure, and these days he spent his time about evenly divided between the two job assignments.

Jack studied "Scruff", whose proper name was Bernard Footman, the junior agent who'd partnered up with him on several surveillance gigs. He was an expert marksman, but could also take a man twice his size down and place him in a life-threatening hold in about 7 seconds...on one of his slow days. He was normally of a fairly placid disposition, but you didn't want to make Scruff lose his temper. One man had done that very thing about five years ago, and pushed him too far. At the time, Scruff had been on a one week leave of absence from his assignment as a Navy Seal working deep within Iraq. Outside of a bar in Tel Aviv, he'd been jumped by four thugs, two with Uzis and one with a Karambit knife. In the space of ten seconds, he disarmed two of the assailants, and round-house kicked a third, bringing him to his knees, writhing with pain. The man with the knife wasn't so fortunate. Before he had time to even pull back the blade and think about thrusting it forward, Scruff snapped the man's arm below the wrist, causing him to release the knife, then put his knuckles through his throat, severing his windpipe and killing him instantly. Precisely because he was such a lethal killing machine, the FBI was somewhat nervous about using him in deadly situations which required a steady hand and patient temperament. *Perhaps,"* thought Jack with a grin, *"if he proves himself here they'll turn him loose on some top international kingpins."* Scruff, clearly reduced to boredom for the moment, pulled a deck of cards from his shirt pocket and begin dealing himself a hand of solitaire.

Something caught Jack's eye in the rear-view mirror. A glint of sunlight...a change of color? He raised his sunglasses and peered over his right shoulder. *Nothing.* Just to be sure, he got out of the car and took a casual stroll around the circumference of a five-hundred-yard circle with the car at its center.

His jaunt took in a large enough area to be able to see the back yard of the smallish, unpretentious house. Nothing particularly unusual: just silvery leaves blowing gently on maple tree and five or six birds squabbling over a bird bath. Just as Jack rounded the far corner of the house, he heard it. Or did he see it first? In barely a millisecond of time, Jack saw a bright flash fill the sky, felt the heat of multiple blast furnaces, and heard the deafening roar of an explosion. The incredible force knocked him off his feet, face first and spread eagle on the ground. He raised his head just in time to see what was left of the car suddenly become engulfed in black smoke and flames. The steering wheel was off to his left about fifty yards. Ahead and to his right was a mangled suit jacket ablaze in flames tinged with orange and blue. Twisted and sheared pieces of charred metal were everywhere, and the mingled stench of burning chemicals and sickeningly burning flesh filled his nostrils. Jack forced himself to his feet, which were still numb and surging with adrenalin, and lunged with all his strength toward the burning wreckage. But the wall of heat and flames held him back, would not let him enter. It didn't matter, anyway. Scruff had been gone, he knew, since the moment of the explosion. Jack, now feeling his first knife-like stabs of pain, noticed his right thigh bleeding where a piece of door handle had dug into it. He limped to the hedges near the house, and collapsed in the landscape. With the blast still ringing in his ears, he fished his cell phone out of his coat pocket, and dialed 911. Then, he hit the preprogrammed key to call his office. The last thing he remembered before blacking out was a white-haired woman standing over him asking if he was hurt. He did not respond.

* * * * *

FBI Agent James Patterson sat at his computer in the upstairs office of the part-hotel-room-part-townhouse structure he'd called home for the last several weeks. Whenever he could, he exercised his preference for doing office work from this suburban location, insulated from the hectic comings and goings of downtown Dallas. Running in the background on a monitor was a chess game James had been playing for a week or so with some former chief of police in Pittsburgh. But that was idle for now, stuck in mid-gambit while Patterson stared at the other screen before him. Even as he watched, the words flashed across the monitor screen:

"Mutation numero uno—

...Thirty-one days, two hours after first administration. Subjects begin to evidence excessive saliva production, mild skin rashes, some sporadic lack of concentration. Not all symptoms are noted in all subjects, but at least one symptom noted in every subject. (Sample size: 100)..."

Patterson's eyes bored into the monitor screen.

"Mutation numero quatro—

...Forty-seven days, zero hours post administration. Swollen eyes, loss of vision in 20% of subjects. Oozing wounds with deep infections. Many subjects unable to drink, eat or swallow. Convulsions occurring in 75% of subjects on average of every hour. Some beginning to have difficulty standing and walking..."

"Mutation numero cinco—

"...Five subjects deceased..."

A look of shock, then disbelief crept across the face looking at the screen. He jerked his mouse onto a box called "User Code Verifier" and checked its contents— yes, there it was: the computer operator was located on the twelfth floor of the Rowalter underground complex. And the user code was a match with the office to which Dean had been assigned. *"But, how could he have broken into a protected area?"* He pulled up his list of contacts on another screen, hit "RO" for Rowalter, and selected a number next to "Betaña". He dialed the number nervously from his keyboard, heard two crisp rings, then the Bolivian accent directing him to leave a message. Patterson cursed the voice mail—then cursed all voice mail in general. His terse message underscored his worry: *"Betaña?...Patterson. There is trouble in Paradise. Call A-S-A-P."* As he completed the message, it suddenly occurred to him that the old idiom wouldn't make sense to the stupid Bolivian. No matter, though: his tone of voice would convey the urgency. Patterson idled his computer and got up, heart thumping, and grabbed the coat off of his chair. In his haste, he left spread across the top of the desk a copy of the *Wall Street Journal* dated January 17, 2002. It was opened to page 29. There, circled in red on the page of stock market quotes for the day was the ticker symbol "RowInd".

* * * *

Dane was wheeling his Beemer out of the Wong Sun's Chinese take-out when his cell phone went off. It was one of Patterson's underlings, named Agent Zachary. Dane, conscious his conversations might be bugged, parked and stepped outside his car to take the call.

"Mr. Ingersoll, the FBI Crime Lab instructed me to contact you as soon as we had word back on the test results from your little girl. They found PZT all right, and some other inert substance in about the same dosages. Although the PZT is not mutating at this time, she is..." he paused, uncertain how Dane would react... "addicted, and until we know more, she will need close observation. It's your call, of course, but we are suggesting you not move her."

It was nothing Dane hadn't expected to hear, but the news of Natalie's addiction hit him hard, nevertheless. "But what about this 'stabilizer' they were talking about? How are we supposed to keep the PZT from mutating if we don't even know what the stabilizer is?"

"I understand your dilemma. Our chemists are still working on Natalie's blood samples to try to isolate whatever substance it is that keeps the PZT from mutating. So far, they have had no success. In the meantime, though, if you leave her at East Dallas Medical, you're at least dealing with a known quantity. Natalie is surrounded by good security day and night, and no unauthorized personnel have access to her medications. The hospital has never encountered this before, but the doctors are now gaining at least *some* experience in the administration of PZT. Can you say that about the other hospitals you've been checking into, sir?" the agent asked rhetorically. "Also, you should probably consider the medical risk in moving her at all right now."

Inwardly, Dane grudgingly had to concede the logic in what the agent was saying. He never got to finish the conversation, however. To his immediate right and left two Dallas Police units suddenly appeared, pulling even with his car, lights flashing. He mumbled something nonsensical to the agent and hung up the phone. Dane's mind began racing, for he knew this was no routine traffic stop. He had already been outside the car talking on the phone for several minutes now.

"I-is everything all right, officers?" Dane asked, fully aware of the ridiculousness of the question.

"Mr. Ingersoll, there has been an accident..."

"Oh God, let Susan and Jackie be okay..." prayed Dane.

"There has been an explosion at your wife's aunt's house in Fort Worth. Your wife and son are all right, but your wife is being kept under observation at Saint Luke Medical Center in Fort Worth."

"What does 'all right' mean?" Dane asked, his voice shaking.

"So far, it appears she was not hurt by the blast at all. Here is her room number and telephone at the hospital. She's expected to be released later today." The officer handed Dane a business card with the numbers scrawled on the back. "We'll be happy to escort you to the hospital, if you'd like." The other officer stood by mutely, concern in his eyes.

"Um, er, that won't be necessary, officers. Thank you."

The officers smiled politely, then shuffled awkwardly back to their patrol units. Dane hurriedly did a 180 in the parking lot, and sped down Main Street toward the viaduct, past which he picked up Interstate 35. At the same time, his non-driving hand punched in the number at the hospital.

"Saint Luke Hospital."

"Yes, this is Dane Ingersoll. My w..."

"Oh yes, we know, Mr. Ingersoll, we were alerted you'd be calling. Your wife is being seen by the doctor right now. I'll put you through." Ten eternal seconds ticked by, then—

"Mr. Ingersoll! Hello, sir. Your wife is fine. Hang on..." He heard the phone receiver being passed, and a moment later he was speaking with Susan.

"Dane," said Susan's quavering voice, "What's going on?"

"I - I don't know Darlin,'" was all he could manage between waves of guilt which washed over him. "How *are* you?" He caught his breath.

"The doctor says I'm fine, though there's still some Godawful ringing in my ears from the sound of the explosion. Thank God, Aunt Jeanne and I were working on the garden in the back yard when it hit. Jackie was playing at a neighbor boy's house down the street. He's fine, and Aunt Jeanne's been checked out and is OK. But this horrible ringing in my ears..." Dane resumed breathing.

"But the two FBI agents were killed, and there is nothing left of their car." Susan's voice suddenly dropped to nearly a whisper. "Dane, they're calling this a 'gas pipeline' explosion, but I don't know if I believe them. I mean, why would just two agents be hurt and their car destroyed? And why didn't we smell any natural gas?"

"It sounds funny to me, too, but I'm just glad you're OK. I'm about five minutes away from you, and I can't wait to hold you."

"Me, too, sweetheart....How's Natalie?"

"They've confirmed she's a-d-d-ic-ted to the stuff." He tried to sound brave for Susan. Remembering that his car might be bugged, he added, "Susan, we'll talk about this later. I'm almost there. Lie down or something and conserve your strength."

"Okay. I'll see you in a moment." Dane heard the sound of Jackie's and Aunt Jeanne's voice in the background as Susan hung up the phone.

In minutes, Dane swung the car up to the Emergency Room entrance, found the space nearest the door, scanned the parking lot right to left, and ran inside. Susan and Jackie met him at the elevator door. Susan was in her clothes, not a smock, but was covered with filth and the smell of smoke. His eyes drank in their presence as he pulled first Susan, then Jackie close to him. Tears streaked Susan's cheeks and tremors visibly racked her body. "Dane," Susan managed, her head buried in his shoulder, "what is happening to us?" He wanted desperately to be able to give her an answer, but just wrapped her in his arms, then sighed resignedly, "I wish I knew, Susan." He guided her and Jackie to a nearby waiting area and made them sit while Aunt Jeanne went looking for some water. "One thing is for sure. The FBI had better start providing some answers. Now." A minute later, he looked up and saw Aunt Jeanne awkwardly holding several bottles of water not wanting to intrude on the family reunion.

"I am so sorry about all this, Jeanne. How are you—are you hurt?"

"No, Dane. I just thank God we weren't in the house when it happened. The entire front half of the house— the living room and two bedrooms—is gone. All of the windows are blown out. The police are claiming it was a natural gas explosion, and that they had had reports of a leak in the area. If that's true, why was mine the only house affected, and why didn't someone report it to us? Something is funny here."

You bet it is," shot back Dane, grimly. "Incidentally, have the Feds got a man here now?"

There was a man here for only a minute or so who identified himself as FBI," said Susan, "but then he disappeared. Supposedly, someone is on the way to talk about some accommodations for me tonight. But I was told that 45 minutes ago."

"Damn those worthless jerks! Their own agents are dead, my wife is nearly killed, and they don't even have a man here? To hell with 'em!" Dane forced himself to take a deep breath, and looked up at Aunt Jeanne, who was still standing.

"We'll find a safe place for all of you to stay tonight, until Jeanne's house is rebuilt."

"But where?" yelped Jackie.

Dane lowered his voice to a whisper, motioning Susan and Jeanne in close. "Don't worry. I know a place that is secluded, that no one else knows about. And the feds can't botch this one, because not even they know about it."

A look of consternation crossed Susan's face. "Dane, are you sure this is the best..."

"Yes, I'm sure. I'll hire body guards of my own."

"What about Natalie?"

Dane gave a look to Susan which clearly requested privacy.

"Aunt Jeanne, would you excuse us for a moment?" asked Susan. Jeanne, holding Jackie's hand in hers, politely stepped down the hall, leaving Dane and Susan together. Dane motioned her around the corner into a starkly furnished consultation room and shut the door. He surveyed the room for video cameras, and saw none.

"Susan, Natalie is addicted to an unstable, mutatable form of PZT. So far, whoever administered it to her has stabilized it with some other substance, to prevent mutation. The FBI, though I can't say I fully trust them at the moment, is saying to leave Natalie where she is. They're continuing to try to isolate the stabilizer that keeps the drug from mutating. For now, she's stable, and the drug is behaving itself, as long as they administer it to her. And they will keep on giving it to her because, besides her being addicted...er, dependent on it, it is helping treat her disease. Let's just hope it stays that way."

Susan's eyes were still teary as she nodded resignedly. "I guess you're right. I don't know what else to do. But I want to see my baby."

"I know, sweetie, but it's too risky. If they are willing to do that to our daughter, what might they be willing to do to you as my wife? I feel horrible that I've dragged us all into this, but we mustn't make things worse by playing right into their hands."

"Maybe I could figure out a way to visit her in a disguise."

"Don't be ridiculous. All this will come to an end soon, she'll come home, and you'll be able to see her as much as you want."

"I so hope you are right. Please be right."

That afternoon, while Jenny and other attorneys on his team labored to get ready for the FDA hearing, Dane contacted the owner of a security firm named, appropriately, "Body Guards". A former college classmate of his who was a green beret knew the owner personally. According to him, the owner hand-picked his body guards, each of whom were ex-special forces, highly trained in weaponry, hand to hand combat, and disarming of explosives. Using some of the money he had stashed away in the glove compartment, he hired two giants, and dispatched them to a place he called simply, the "Lake House." The Lake House was a fully furnished, three-bedroom cabin in east Texas, situated on a little known private lake. It was not in a high-priced resort area, as many such houses were. A few years ago, a well-to-do client had expressed his appreciation for Dane's services by giving Dane a long-term lease of the property—at

$1.00 per year. Dane did not own it, and therefore had no cost of upkeep. An added bonus was that the property could not be traced to him by anyone. He need only make it available to the owner for one month each year; the rest of the year he could use it as he pleased. Dane had never told Susan about the cabin—figured he'd surprise her one anniversary. He never dreamed he'd be using it for such an occasion as this.

By night fall, Susan and Aunt Jeanne retrieved all of the things they and Jackie needed, for the time being, from the Fort Worth home. The house was "locked" as best it could be, using a temporary construction door. Aunt Jeanne hired a company to clean up the mess, and told the Fort Worth Police to keep a close watch on the old homestead. By 7:00 p.m., Susan, Jackie and Aunt Jeanne had bumped their way through the thick pine forest of east Texas, and taken up residence at the Lake House. Two hulking giants who resembled Dallas Cowboys offensive linemen carefully escorted them, and watched their every move the rest of the evening. The body guards were in constant communication with each other by digital two-way radio and with their command station in Dallas on a secure channel. They brought with them a Doberman guard dog who looked like he needed no excuse whatsoever to attack. Susan felt secure, but—even with her aunt and her little boy there—indescribably, unspeakably, alone.

CHAPTER NINETEEN

It was Tuesday, and the day had begun like any other day at the influential Dallas law firm of Salacuse & Lockridge. The mood was somehow different on the 40th floor, though. There was less movement and less of the frantic air of impending deadlines, even though it was already 9:15 a.m. The firm would be having its monthly meeting, and there was certainly nothing unusual about that. But everyone knew, and Jerek Barbour as much as anyone, that this was no ordinary meeting of the partners. Jerek sat at his desk, spread with innumerable stacks of files and papers, and attempted to gather his thoughts for the stormy session he was sure was about to begin. He had seen, perhaps more than anyone, the change in that bright rising star known as Dane Ingersoll in the last couple of months. Dane's case load had suffered noticeably, and it had fallen to the more junior—and correspondingly less experienced—associates to pick up the slack. His work output, at least on cases which produced income for the firm, had fallen to near zero since taking on this Rowalter matter. But the biggest problem, the one which, Jerek mused, was bound to become the lynchpin of the meeting, was the waves Dane was threatening to stir up with other clients of the firm. Clients like the United States Department of Agriculture, Amalgamated Pharmaceuticals USA, Inc. and Chem Futures Bionics, EU. Substantial clients, to whom could be attributed hundreds of thousands of billable hours of work each year, meaning millions of dollars in billed and collected fees. Such clients would not be pleased, albeit for differing reasons, should it become generally known that their law firm was trying to get a volatile drug approved for legal use. Plus, it made for bad press. Those partners Jerek had spoken with believed that, while the cat was not yet out of the bag on the qualities of PZT, the lid couldn't be kept on it much longer. Among those partners was Rob Jenkins, Dane's mentor in the firm. "Once the general press gets ahold of the story, what effect will it have on our revenue stream?" Jenkins had asked. "After all," he'd pointed out, "this is no drug that has been in widely accepted or general use, like alcohol or even nicotine."

As for Jerek, he was reserving judgment. His relationship with Dane Ingersoll went beyond merely professional. They had been in each other's homes, gone out as couples, vacationed together. Derek could not predict what would happen in the partner's meeting. But his stomach told him that whatever it was, it would not be good for Dane. He collected his thoughts, then with a grim look of mixed concentration and foreboding, he crossed the hallway and stuck his head in Rob Jenkins' office. Rob was practicing his golf swing with a putter and ball in the middle of his floor. Jerek intercepted the putt by sticking his foot in front of the hole, drawing a surprised "Hey wh—!" from Rob.

"Coming to the meeting?" Jerek queried. I hear they're giving out some pretty nice profits to split this year." Jerek had heard no such thing, but it made for good conversation.

"Yeah...sure, I'm coming."

"Good. See you there." Jerek tossed the ball back to Rob, who looked at him quizzically. Jerek disappeared into the imposing firm conference room with the twenty-foot table and oak paneled walls at the end of the corridor.

The meeting was called to order by Preston Bernard, the ranking senior partner on the firm's Management Committee. Bernard's ponderous grey-black eyebrows gathered together in the middle of his forehead to form one uninterrupted line, while he peered around the room at the assemblage of some of the most moneyed professionals in the State of Texas. Word had been spreading for days as the agenda for the meeting began to congeal. There wasn't a partner in the room who couldn't read what was on Preston's mind and the air was silent, and heavy with anticipation.

"Men," began Preston (which was not at all politically incorrect, there being no female partners at the firm), "we have called this meeting because of a brewing storm at Salacuse & Lockridge. If the storm breaks, it threatens to cause us to lose our envied position as the leading Dallas law firm, and as one of the leading firms in the South. One of our aspiring young rising stars, Dane Ingersoll—who is on track to make partner within the year, mind you—has, like a moth venturing too close to a flame, gotten burned. In so doing, he has indirectly, and I'm certain without meaning to, invoked the scrutiny of the Federal Bureau of Investigation. In the process, one of our other associates with a gifted mind named Alton Dean, has mysteriously vanished without a trace while working almost exclusively on an FDA drug approval case." He paused for emphasis and his eyes swept the room, his weighty eyebrows rising perhaps half an inch. The other partners, save one who was reading an article in the *Wall Street Journal*, returned his gaze. "On the economic side of things, Mr. Ingersoll, while a very able trial and appellate attorney, has been out much more than he has been in, with the consequence that his billable hours have fallen off dramatically. And," he only partially suppressed a wince, "some of our other clients are beginning to make noise about his representation of this South American firm, Rowalter Industries, S.A. One of the largest and oldest pharmaceutical companies, represented by our partner John Lyons, told him last week they had heard something from a high-level bureaucrat in the FDA. Let's just say it was not a positive comment. Not-so-subtle hints were dropped that business would be pulled and sent to Harwood, Jenkins & Underwood across town. While we might prefer to do otherwise, if Dane can't divest himself of this client, we must divest ourselves of him.

Jerek had listened raptly. Nothing that Bernard said surprised him, but now he leapt in with all fours like an angry panther. "That is the biggest *crock* I have ever heard. Dane has done plenty for this firm for many years. He is tremendous partnership material. Now, he encounters some stormy weather, first from a very sick child and then from a very sick client, and you want to show him the door. Is that the way this firm rewards loyalty, just because someone hits a few bumps in the road? He paused for effect. Dane didn't ask for the circumstances that he's in, he fell into them. Besides, if you take this precipitous action, and some other firm down the road will be getting one of the finest litigators in the country." He noted with some satisfaction that several of the partners were staring uncomfortably at the table in front of them. "I've said my piece—for now."

Next Rob Weimer spoke up. "I think Jerek is right. We can't, and shouldn't do this to Dane. If he can extricate himself from his relationship with this unsavory client of his...er, ours—make a clean break— then things can return to normal. I have no criticism to offer of his earning power." He glanced at a spread sheet in front of him. "He has consistently brought in more than his share of fees. The way I see it, he's just spending way too much time away from the office, and way too much time on a case that could ultimately hurt us. He just needs to start billing again."

"I might be able to agree with you if it weren't for the fact that we've lost two valuable associates to this pharmaceutical client of his," John Lockridge, the oldest partner in the firm had spoken up, his throaty, authoritative voice commanding everyone's immediate attention. But that's 20,000 billable hours this year on Alton Dean alone. He was the most talented appellate staff associate we had. And we're paying an even heftier sum to Ingersoll, while he's out gallivanting around the city. Even worse, I think the damage to our reputation may soon be irreparable. I say we offer him a reasonable severance package and cut him loose now." Lockridge's tone was stern and cold. Soon, another partner threw in his two cents worth, then another, and another, until it was apparent that two contingents had formed: the old guard and the "under 45" set. Although the latter group was more articulate and unquestionably more empathetic with Dane's plight, the old guard, anchored by Preston, Michelson, and name partner Lockridge, had two distinct advantages. They were greater in number, and though they were equal partners with the younger set, to a man they tended to have the larger, wealthier clients.

The two contingents fought and argued back and forth for over an hour, ignoring all the other firm business on the agenda. The younger partners' contingent made a valiant last stand, but when it was time for a vote, Derek could see in advance what the result would be. A second, and then a third vote was called for, but it was clear that the few votes that switched sides were not enough to affect the outcome. In the end, it was clearly all about money, and money now rather than later.

* * * *

In the several days that had gone by since his arrival in this hell hole, Alton had managed to compile a formidable amount of research. Dutifully and obediently, he had handed over a couple of hundred pages of propaganda on PZT that would have made Joseph Goebbels himself blush. Some of it was factually based and well footnoted, but much of it was junk science, filled with hyperbole and conjecture, and phrased in such a way as to make it seem plausible to the undiscriminating eye. Most important from his forced-client's point of view, it all supported the legitimate medicinal value of their patented drug.

Alton had also been very busy in between "research" sessions. After making his computer blind to the remainder of the Rowalter network, he copied millions of bytes of sensitive company data from the Rowalter research and development library. This he stored on several USB flash drives he managed to smuggle from a nearby office without being detected. The four flash drives had found their way to an obscure spot under Alton's mattress in the depressing room where he slept at night. Each night, as he warily retired behind the closed door, he moved them to a different spot under the mattress. Sometimes he would put them inside his pillow; sometimes in his pajamas clutched between his thighs while he slept. The uneasy slumber to which he had become accustomed was punctuated by fitful starts during which he groped frantically for the drives, making sure they were still there, right where he had placed them that night. Once, he was sure he heard footsteps in the hallway...virtually certain they had found him out and were coming for him. He'd frozen with terror, like a wild hare caught in the headlights of an approaching automobile, wordlessly staring at the ceiling, sweating, trembling, not breathing. Then the steps had receded, and he had drifted uneasily back into a restless sleep.

But the day had arrived, nevertheless, as he had always known it would. It was now or never, and Alton was ready: ready to break free, or to die in the trying. If his counting was correct, it was January 26th, the tenth day since his abduction. He didn't trust Rowalter's computer operating system clock, so he had, Robinson Crusoe style, marked each days' passage on the wall of his bedroom near the computer.

This morning, he swung his feet over the edge of the narrow bed at 3:30 a.m. Alton knew his best odds would be under cover of the chilly winter night. He dressed hurriedly in the simple blue jumper of Rowalter employees—the same kind that he had worn every day since his arrival. He wanted nothing in his appearance to draw attention. He was just another Rowalter deep night shift employee, like the many faceless ones he had seen moving around the hallways at all hours. He carefully clipped to his lab coat pocket the magnetic striped security badge he had swiped from a coat hung on the back of a thirteenth-floor office door by an unsuspecting employee. Now, for the computer. He entered the passwords he had committed to memory on the first day, moving through one, then two and finally three levels of security. Deliberately avoiding the use of Rowalter's own email system, he pulled up his own web mail account and went directly to the "new message" screen. Next, he composed a fully encrypted email message to Dane. Each of the four gigantic files containing information he had gathered since his arrival, he now uploaded to the Salacuse & Lockridge secure cloud drive. Everything he placed on that drive would be encrypted automatically. Alton then placed a link to the files he'd just copied to the cloud drive in the email to Dane. He sent a copy of the email to his own computer at the firm. Last, he carefully took the four flash drives one at a time and, using packing tape he had smuggled from an office, attached them securely to his inner thighs. When he was done, the drives were in four different locations on his body. He refastened his pants, exited the program, and still operating in the darkness, felt his way to the door.

Alton had rehearsed and re-rehearsed his next steps probably fifty times, so that when the time arrived he would be able to do it without the benefit of any lights. His efforts had not been wasted. His mind and memory took over, and with the same sureness as if he had night vision, he followed the line of the hallway to its "T" intersection with the other hallway. The shroud of darkness kept the TV cameras from spotting him and alerting the security guards, but just in case, he kept his back flat against the wall of the corridor down which he now moved, silently. With the tips of his fingers acting like an insect's antennae, he discerned each door, then the break in the wall...turn right and follow the baseboard about twenty paces to—there, he felt it: the rough surface of the janitor closet door. His eyes had adapted to the darkness, so that he used what little light there was to pan the entire hallway for any shadow, however slight. He saw none, and so turned his full attention on the janitor closet door. He turned the door knob, swung the door open, and stepped warily inside. He had created a smallish pathway to the hidden doorway in the back corner, so he could maneuver between the mop buckets and other equipment noiselessly. He shimmied in sideways, nearly falling over when he stepped on a wet spot. He felt above him for the putty knife perched in its familiar place on an overhead shelf. With his left hand, he felt for the crack in the wall marking the 3 X 5 door. With the right, he jammed the putty knife hastily into the crack and pried the door open. This was the one time that Alton wished ever-so-fervently that he had a light—any light at all. He did not like being in tight, dark spaces, even when he knew where he was going and for how long. Before he entered the tunnel, he reached back to close the janitor closet door and nearly jumped out of his skin when a mouse—or was it a rat? —scampered over some refuse. Alton dropped to all fours and resignedly entered the passageway. From here on in it was just a matter of mind over matter, he thought to himself. The cold, dank smell of the passageway enveloped him and clung to his body. He could hear the blood coursing through his veins at his temples and feel each beat of his heart as it all but reverberated off of the walls. He crawled on his elbows and knees, praying that the passageway would be unobstructed, just as it had been the last time he rehearsed his escape. For what felt like about fifty yards, Alton breathed sparingly, since it hurt to do so. Then, not a moment too soon, a faint rectangle of light appeared ahead. He patiently crawled toward it until he was positioned underneath, so that the light shone on his head. He reached up, placing his hand in the middle of the grill cover that led into the heating duct. The duct was about 15" long by 12" high. This was the part Alton had never attempted before, but he had reasoned—no, hoped—that his bean pole build would manage to get him through it. Even considering his lanky frame, he still had to contort himself like a pretzel, placing first one arm, then his head, then another arm... and, finally, trunk and legs through the opening. Fortunately, the heating duct was large, as heating ducts go. Once he was fully into the duct, he still had to crawl, but could at least raise his head a few more inches. Ahead of him now he could see a very dim light permeating the darkness, probably from a service door, he speculated hopefully. Alton tried to block out the musty smell which hung heavily in the duct, breathing shallow breaths to limit the amount of foul air he inhaled into his constricted lungs. By now, his cramped limbs had begun to ache, and the stretch ahead of him could just as easily have been a mile as the hundred or so yards it appeared to be. He alternately moved knees and elbows, pausing to rest about every ten feet. He caught his breath when he felt a sudden surge of cold air, as the air conditioning kicked on. The strength of the air current made his journey even more strenuous, and Alton redoubled the strength with which he willed his hips and arms to move. He began to play mind games in order to motivate himself, pretending that he was in an old *Mission Impossible* episode, with several disguises in his pocket and electronic gadgetry waiting at the other end of the tunnel. *"It's a 'mission impossible', all right,"* he thought aloud, startling himself with his own speech. Once, when he had drawn within about twenty feet of his destination, he got stuck, and nearly panicked. Alton had never thought of himself as claustrophobic, but *everyone has their limits, and I've reached mine*, he thought. After more whispered prayers, slow breathing, and about three minutes which seemed like as many hours, Alton managed to slowly extricate himself from his position. In about another fifteen minutes his heart stopped, as he found himself at a dead end. Just to his right however, near enough for his hand to reach out and touch, was the service door he had so fervently prayed for. It was too dim to make out anything but the crack outlining the rectangular shape of the door, though there was a smallish window perhaps five inches square in the middle of the door. It didn't do much good, since there wasn't enough light from whatever lay on the other side to provide Alton any assistance. No matter— Alton was out of patience and out of time. With all the strength he had left in him, he drew back his doubled up right arm and rammed his elbow against the glass square in the middle of the door. It gave way grudgingly. Alton's rangy frame again came to his aid, as he was able to, like a moth shedding a cocoon, squeeze through the opening and into a room that appeared to be the repository of HVAC equipment. Other than that, Alton had not the slightest idea where he was, but was thankful just to be able to rise to his full six-foot four-inch height and wring the cramps out of his legs and arms. Glancing quickly around the room, he found a flashlight, which he put to instant use. The room was only about fifteen by twenty, and chock full of heating and air conditioning parts, tools, and a smattering of other nondescript items. Hanging on the wall by the entrance door were two uniforms, both grayish blue, with the word "*Mantenimiento,* which was Spanish for "Maintenance". He grabbed one of the uniforms and quickly changed into it, ignoring the fact that the sleeves were about an inch too long. He crammed the flash light into the uniform pocket, then cracked the door an inch to get his bearings. The hallway adjoining the HVAC room was deserted, lit only by flickering fluorescent lights. He noted no obvious television cameras, "*probably because it's a maintenance area,*" he thought. Nevertheless, Alton was alert to the distinct possibility that there were hidden cameras, and turned and grabbed a large crescent wrench from a shelf in the room. This he held in one hand, half to complete his disguise, and half for use as a weapon should worse come to worse.

Alton entered the hallway, keeping his head down but rapidly surveying both sides as he proceeded down its length. The walls were uninterrupted, with no sign of stairwells or elevators. The corridor came to a "T", and he hung a left, where he almost immediately stumbled onto a large elevator. Still no other persons in sight. He mashed the button for "Up" and the button light came on. He wished he could melt into the floor while he waited, listening to the deep, throaty sound of the elevator motor bringing the car down the shaft. Suddenly, Alton started as he heard the metallic echo of a door closing from somewhere off to his left. Trying not to appear too obvious, he stared straight ahead, but with his peripheral vision could pick out another maintenance worker, similarly dressed but wearing a cap. The man had on a tool belt and, Alton concluded with terror, had what seemed to be a walkie talkie strapped to one side. He held his breath, wishing with all his might that he wouldn't have to speak Spanish and thereby reveal his *gringo* accent.   Then it happened: the man said "Hóla."   Alton turned and nodded back to him with the best friendly grunt he could muster, but avoided like the plague speaking any words. He heaved a sigh of relief when the man shuffled on by him, and at about the same time the elevator doors lurched open with a squeak. The inside of the elevator car was lined with a heavy quilted material like the pads that movers use to separate furniture, and Alton realized approvingly that it was a maintenance or freight elevator.   As the man disappeared from sight, Alton glided into the elevator and waited an eternity for the doors to close. *"Now for some real fun,"* winced Alton nervously, as he scrutinized the panel containing the floor numbers. For the first time since his arrival in this God-forsaken place, Alton realized he had been a full ten stories underground. But where to go from here? He didn't want to come out on some main floor in full view of whoever might happen to be there.   Carefully, he pressed the elevator button marked "2". The massive elevator car came to life with a groan and he felt his feet press against its floor. He watched the numbers over the door flicker in succession, unsure whether the slow progress upward was real, or a dream brought on by his anxiety. The elevator lurched to a halt, and another set of doors behind him opened. In the palpable darkness Alton could make out only very little, but he surmised he was not in a publicly visited area since, usually, freight elevators don't service such areas. Moving carefully and deliberately, Alton reached into his pocket and turned on the flashlight without even pulling it out. The muted light created an eerie glow on the floor outside the elevator, like the lighted steps in movie theaters but not as bright. From the silhouettes created by the light he discerned he was in a vestibule, which connected to a short hallway. From the opposite end of the hallway came the reddish glow of an exit sign, which he figured marked a stairwell. Alton drew a bead on the sign and was almost there when he froze in mid-step. The hairs on the nape of his neck stood up as a figure emerged from the intersecting hallway and a male voice inquired in Spanish, "Señor, may I see some identificación?" The man carried a flashlight of his own. Instinctively, Alton knew that he couldn't fake this one. In an instant, before he could marshal the conscious thought, the bulky wrench was in Alton's hand. In the next instant, the *hombre* lay on the floor unconscious with a severe blow to his left temple. Surprising himself with the rush of adrenalin, Alton grabbed the larger man at his armpits and dragged him back to the freight elevator. It took several minutes to move him back to the elevator vestibule, since he outweighed Alton by over fifty pounds. Minutes later, the guard was headed toward the tenth subterranean floor, but not before Alton confiscated the walkie talkie clipped to his belt and traded his maintenance uniform for the man's security garb and badge. He made sure the walkie talkie was on, and turned up the volume, but it emitted no sound for the time being. Alton strapped on the guard's belt, which had a holstered semi-automatic pistol attached. He thought hard about, then rejected the idea of taking the small pistol strapped to the guard's belt. It was too heavy, and Alton didn't know how to use it anyway.

Immediately, Alton turned and headed for the stairwell. There was no one in sight, and he was grateful for the rubber soled shoes of the guard which, though a bit large on him, noiselessly met the cement steps of the echo-filled stairwell. Taking the stairs two at a time, Alton achieved the first-floor landing quickly. He figured it was now no later than 4:45, maybe 5:00 a.m., and no more than 90 minutes till sunlight. His heart pounded and his hands grew sweaty as he contemplated his next move. Flattening his back against the wall, he extended his hand just enough to pull the door open a half inch or so. His heart sank as he noted the first floor was lighted. Worse than that, he could see two guards from where he was standing, both armed. Alton felt for the spot on his hip where the pistol had been and cursed himself for leaving it behind. At least he would have looked like all the other guards. As he brought his hand back, he felt a lump and looked down to see a small can of mace in a sleeve attached to his belt. *"Now this, I know how to use,"* he thought to himself soberly. He made sure the cover on the sleeve was unsnapped for quick access.

Both guards were stationed near the entry doors to the building and were obviously focused on preventing entry by intruders from that direction. *"My only advantage,"* he thought, *"is that they don't expect anyone to come from the other direction."* As the guards continued talking, Alton waited until the one nearest him had turned his back and meandered over to say something to the other guard. The first guard, the one with his back to Alton, now completely blocked the line of sight of the second guard to where Alton stood in the stairwell. To his left, at the back of the building, Alton saw a door with one of those red emergency exit type handles on it. *"It's now or never..."* he thought. Alton side-stepped through the door opening, keeping his head down and carefully closing the door behind him. Not daring to look back, he hurriedly stepped down the hallway to the exit door. His walk became a run, as he traversed the hundred or so yards to the back of the building, gritting his teeth to prepare himself for what he knew was about to happen. His hands hit the bar without breaking stride like a running back stiff arming an approaching tackler. Instantly an alarm sounded, but the former low hurdles runner had already put a quarter mile between him and the building before the guards knew what was happening. The hydraulic hinge on the emergency door had pulled it closed again and the guards spent the first five minutes confusedly looking for a fire that didn't exist.

The warm, sultry air of the January summer night in Bolivia streamed against Alton's face as he settled into a steady run. As he approached the perimeter of the compound, he saw barbed wire, and a lighted tower with an armed guard stationed near a gate. Thinking at the speed of light, he unholstered his walkie talkie, pressed the button and summoned his best Spanish. *"Un detainee se ha escapado! Abra la puerta!"* Obeying the uniformed guard below him, the tower guard pressed a button which released the electrically controlled gate latch. Alton pushed on the gate, which swung open obediently. Minutes later, he was alone, an American running blindly through the mountains of Bolivia at 11,000 feet above sea level.

CHAPTER TWENTY

To say that James Patterson was worried would be putting it mildly. He booked a red eye flight out of DFW International to La Paz over his secure cell phone channel, all the while racing down LBJ Freeway at about 80 miles per hour. He redialed Betaña's number at least a hundred times. He fumed and fretted, yelling as if the man could somehow hear him from another hemisphere. "Damn fool—turn on your cell phone!!" But it was early, Betaña was still sleeping peacefully in his luxurious mountaintop home. The phone in his office rang unnoticed by the maintenance crew cleaning it, and the cell phone in his bedroom was set on silent mode.

In between such vain attempts, Patterson called Adam Zachary, his Assistant Special Agent-In-Charge. He knew Adam was still in bed, but, unlike some stupid Bolivians, would be sleeping with his phone on as always. It answered on the second ring.

"Zachary here." The voice was tired, but instantly alert.

"Adam, its Jim..."

"Jim...er...I mean Mr. Patterson, sir—where are you? I've been trying to reach you since yesterday. There was a terrible explosion!"

"Oh...I've been attending to a death in the family and I'm out of the loop. Tell me about it."

"Well Sir, as you know we had placed the house of Susan Ingersoll's aunt under surveillance in Fort Worth. Someone planted a timed car bomb which detonated and killed our two agents in place and destroyed half the house! I've been trying to reach you, but you weren't answering your phone!"

"As I said, I've had a death in the family, and I've been...out of sorts. As we speak I'm headed to the airport to get to Philadelphia for the funeral." Patterson's voice seemed remarkably calm, considering the circumstances. "Have you moved Mrs. Ingersoll and her aunt to a more secure location?"

"I'm afraid not, Sir. Mr. Ingersoll says he's lost confidence in our ability to protect them. He's taken matters into his own hands, and refused to reveal their new location to us—just says they are well protected. And, as you would expect, he wants to speak to you as soon as possible."

"Naturally. Yes, I can understand that." Patterson sounded distracted. "Adam, you are in charge while I'm gone. Continue trying to learn where Ingersoll has his wife. Security may have been breached once, but it won't happen again, and they're taking a huge chance that Rowalter will find them. Keep the surveillance tight at the hospital. Let me know any new developments. Finish up the status report I've begun to the deputy director. I'll be out of town for at least one, maybe two days. You know how to reach me. Out."

Patterson peered at his watch. It was later in Dallas than in La Paz, and the eastern sky was just beginning to show the first blush of pastel pink that foretold the sunrise. Though he continued to hit redial, Patterson knew his attempts were futile. "*If the subject were only in the States, I could have five men assigned to him right away. But I had to give in to the moronic Bolivians, with their vaunted security!*" Patterson chided himself. "*And now they've gone and messed things up big time,*" moaned Patterson inwardly. He had known that they might try to make a statement following Dane Ingersoll's attempt to withdraw from the FDA case. But taking out two of Patterson's own agents and nearly killing Mrs. Ingersoll in the process was overkill—no pun intended. "This is my job we are talking about now!" screamed Patterson at the inside of his automobile. Despite the lucrative nature of the insider information he had illegally been given by Rowalter, he still had not sold the securities he had received from them, or the thousands more he had purchased on his own government salary. He was highly leveraged into the stock, and he was not a wealthy man, at least not yet. He still needed his job and, he reckoned, his reputation. Patterson only hoped he had not miscalculated with Betaña and crew. Rushing into the airport terminal, he made one final unsuccessful attempt to roust Betaña before boarding the airplane, to no avail. The next flight out, said the ticket agent, left in twenty minutes. He would fly to Lima, with a brief stopover in Caracas, Venezuela. Patterson purchased a ticket under the name Jonas Worthington, one of several alias identities he'd used in undercover work, but one known to few within the Bureau. The ID presented by Jonas Worthington to the lady at the counter was authentic beyond question. He paid cash for the ticket, and checked no bags, carrying on his attaché. Within minutes, Jonas Worthington was airborne for South America.

Jerek Barbour tipped Dane off with the news of the partnership vote before it had a chance to be formalized in writing. "I tried, Dane, I really did, and so did several of the others. But the old bastards—you know who I mean—outnumbered us at the end of the day. We're losing a good man, one of the best. If there's anything else I can do...."

Dane knew Jerek had done all he could in his behalf, but that didn't make the news much easier to take. By Wednesday at 10:00, he had already arranged to sign a lease for 1750 square feet of office space almost directly across the street from his former employer. "I might as well do it in their faces," he told Jenny. It would be a huge leap for him into a solo practice, and something he had certainly never contemplated at this stage in his career. But what else could he do? He had about ten clients he thought would make the move with him, not counting the case from hell. He didn't expect the firm to fight him for those clients, but one could never be sure.

Jenny, who by now knew his case load inside and out, would be making the move with him, as would his secretary Linda. The severance pay and bonus he had coming from the firm would carry him through two, maybe three payrolls, and cover a couple of paychecks big enough to live on—if he was careful. But he still had to pay the monumental costs of the hospital, which the insurance company was fighting him on. Then there were body guards, which didn't come cheap either.

Jenny was his cheerleader. "We'll do it, Dane," she would say. "You'll see; we'll finish the Rowalter deal, tell them to take a hike, and start hauling in big fees from your other cases."

Dane wished he shared her optimism. Fighting utter, mind-numbing depression had now become a daily fact of life for Dane. He was truly torn in two, and felt like his gut was caught in a vice most of the time. It was as though he was wrestling with a sea monster with fifteen tentacles: when he cut one off, another grew to replace it and wrapped itself more tightly around his body. He couldn't dump Rowalter, for fear of his daughter's—and now his wife's—safety. He *had* to finish the matter, and he *had* to win the drug case. And this very fact threatened to suffocate his ability to grow his fledgling little practice at a time when he must either grow, or perish.

Dane had scrupulously avoided telling Craig Johnson about his dilemma. He knew Craig would feel badly about having sent him the case, and there was really nothing he would be able to do now, anyway. Craig had connected the dots, though. He'd heard about Alton Dean's disappearance, and it wasn't every day a promising young law-partner-in-waiting struck out on his own in solo practice. As if to assuage his conscience, Craig sent over three of his staff to help Dane get settled in, and Dane placed Jenny in charge of logistics. Dane called Jenny from the management office of the new building, where he had just signed all the paperwork.

"How's everything going, Jen?"

"Pretty good," she panted, still winded from unpacking boxes. "The phone people are here and hooking you up, and I and one of Craig's men have finished bringing over the second truckload of boxes. The other two are over there getting the computers and server ready to move. The furniture movers should arrive about 2:00."

"Roger. How many more boxes do you think we have?"

"Fifty-four, if I numbered them correctly."

"You're unbelievable, Jenny," he said, thankful for someone who was good with details. Don't forget to check Alton's office. There's still a bunch of stuff in there he was working on for us."

"Gotcha. We'll scour everything. I assume you want your computer data backed up one last time before the move?"

"Yeah. It's set to automatically back up at night, but let's do it one more time to be safe. And get Alton's computer files on Rowalter."

"Check."

"I should be down there in about an hour. I just want to check on Natalie, then I'll be joining you guys."

"'See you then."

Jenny had just hung up with Dane when Richard, one of Craig's law clerks, called her from Salacuse. "Jenny, do you want me to back up Dane's hard drives?"

"Yeah, I was just talking to Dane and he says it's a good idea. He wants you to copy Alton's Rowalter files, too."

"Well, I'd love to do both for you, but we have a problem."

"Oh, and what's that?"

"Well, I can't get into Dane's computer and Jack can't get into Mr. Dean's."

"But I gave you both passwords."

"That's not what I mean. When I hit the keyboard, there's a flashing message that appears on both of their monitors that says: 'Secure email, Open Immediately.' It won't let us go further, and I didn't want to violate confidentiality. But I wouldn't try moving the computers until we address the issue. I'd be worried about a virus or something."

"H-m-m, that's odd." said Jenny. I don't recall either of them using an email program that operated that way. I'll be right over." Jenny put the other clerk in charge of watching the new office, and hurried across the street and up to the 16th floor. She arrived breathlessly in Dane's office to find Richard and Jack peering wide-eyed at Dane's monitor screen, which flashed in bright red every second the words, "Secure email; Open Immediately." She dashed down the hallway, to find a similar message emanating from Alton's now-abandoned office. Jenny returned to Dane's office and politely asked the two clerks to wait out in the receptionist area. She opened Dane's email program, but had never looked at his email before and lacked the password to retrieve anything from the server. She decided to call him.

"Dane, have you finished checking on Natalie?"

"Yes, as a matter of fact, just now."

"Well, can you accelerate your schedule a bit? The guys can't do anything with your or Alton's computer until you open a confidential email that's flashing on your screen."

Dane's heart froze. His first thought? Rowalter. "I'll be right there."

Moments later, Dane was in his office, staring at the same phenomenon that Jenny, Rick and Jack had been mesmerized by moments before. With Jenny staring intently over Dane's shoulder, he ran an internet-updated virus scan on the hard drive. This took three or four minutes, but produced nothing of any consequence. Dane then opened his email program and entered his signature key for retrieval of encrypted messages—something he rarely ever used. The encrypted message converted instantaneously and a letter unfolded across his screen, from no less than...Alton! A yelp of surprise mingled with joy erupted from both simultaneously, as they hungrily read the message together:

"Wed.. 26 Jan 2011 03:35:00————————————

By the time you receive this, if I'm not dead, I will be on the run and out of the Rowalter complex somewhere in Bolivia (I think). Dane, they are in possession of the most powerful and addictive death drug in history. If there was any doubt about it before, there is no longer. Linked to this email are the test results and the data that you will need to incriminate them. I'm also including chemical formulae for the buffer drug that keeps the mutation from metabolizing. Get the buffer formula to the proper people, to at least counter the effects until distribution can be halted and people prosecuted. I presume crime lab chemists could duplicate the buffer. Please immediately put all this on secure media and get it to the authorities. I don't yet know exactly where I am, because they sedated me while I was transported here, but I suspect I'm in the Bolivian Andes. I know I will be hunted. I will try to go under an assumed name, find the

fastest way out of the country and let you know where I am as soon as possible. Not sure how long that will be, as I have no funds. You MUST keep this communication and the attachments secure and confidential until they are in the right hands. These people know what they are doing and mean business.

Your Friend,

Alton"

Dane and Jenny exchanged incredulous glances. Dane clicked on the link, which took him to the cloud drive, where he entered his credentials. He was no chemist, but after scanning several pages, it was clear to him that what they were viewing was clinical trial results of the drug PZT. Page after page of detailed formulas and notations followed. Of the portion of it that he could read and interpret, none of it positive for the drug, and some was downright frightening. This was followed by an equally lengthy section of mathematical formulas which appeared to show the degeneration—or mutation—of the drug over time. Clearly, this was what Rowalter had not wanted known. It would not have been discernible from even the most thorough-going research Alton could have performed from the law firm, the university, or anywhere else. Jenny ran over to one of the boxes strewn about the floor and extricated a new flash drive which she handed to Dane. His hands trembling with excitement, he slid it into the port and began copying the material. While this progressed, Jenny articulated what they were both thinking.

"Dane, you know this could be your ticket out of this whole fiasco."

"Exactly what I was thinking."

"But what about Alton? He's lost miles up in the Bolivian Andes and will either die from exposure or be shot on sight by Rowalter operatives...or someone else. We need to tell Patterson."

"That bungling idiot? Are you kidding? He nearly got my wife killed; there's no telling what he would mess up where Alton's concerned."

"Well, we've got to get this to *someone*."

"You don't know how much I'd love to make this Exhibit "A" in the hearing next week, and watch Gary Thompson's face when it comes in."

"But your hands are tied because of—"

"—Natalie," he said, completing her sentence for her.

"So where does that leave us, Dane?"

"Where it leaves us is having to find someone in the government, or somewhere, that we can trust without making matters worse than they already are."

"But who?"

"I don't have a clue right now."

"Well, we'd better start thinking fast. Time is running out."

* * * *

Professor Rupert Jenkins had been traveling abroad, taking his first real vacation in five years. The flight back from Moscow had been anything but restful, and he and his wife had arrived home in the wee hours, hungrily anticipating an uninterrupted slumber on a real bed. Dr. Jenkins slipped on a pair of moccasin bedroom slippers and padded sleepily to the front door. It was good to be back home again, good to be in America, and better still to be in California. The crisp January air bit his face as he reached down to pick up the Saturday edition of the Pasadena *Herald Tribune.* It was warm compared to Moscow. Anything was, but it was a cool 45 degrees for Pasadena.

After a brief detour to the kitchen for tea, Dr. Jenkins made his way back to the bedroom where Jana still slumbered peacefully. He sipped his tea slowly, casually scanning the headlines and front page. When his eyes landed at page 3, they ground to a halt, riveted to a particular article titled **"PROFESSOR TAKES OWN LIFE"**. He read on, first with interest, then captivation and finally horror as his mind awoke to the stark facts: Nobel prize winner Dr. Norman Holloway was dead. Stunned over the news concerning his former student, Dr. Jenkins took the newspaper with him to his office across the hallway. The computer perched on his desk had sat idle for an unusually long period. Jenkins began to go on line and check the *Herald Tribune* website for more details, but never got that far. His automatic email program came onscreen, alerting him of a full mailbox and at least one message flagged "Urgent." He opened the email message and his eyes were instantly transfixed. It read:

"Today, at the lab, for the very first time, I became aware that my energies had not been expended on the humanitarian objectives which I had heretofore thought." In all good

conscience, I must halt this work. I will not be able to continue. I have worked all my life to do good for scientific endeavors and for mankind, and cannot change course now. I have been greatly blessed to have served in some capacity to ease mankind's pain, until now."

Jenkins paused thoughtfully, his heart racing inside his chest. He had known through a mutual acquaintance at the University of Colorado that Holloway was pursuing some summer research outside his normal field, but not much else. There was an attachment, which was not in a typical format. Jenkins clicked on it, and tried to open it with four or five programs in succession. He finally tried a scientific notation program he sometimes used for lab work, and it did the trick. Unfolded before him were two pages of chemical reactions appearing as equations. He did not recognize most of the polymers, though it was clear that they were organic, and exceedingly complex. The hairs on the back of Jenkins' neck stood on end, like he was strolling through a cemetery talking to someone he had known from beyond the grave. "Because", he mumbled to no one in particular, "that's exactly what Norman is doing here." Jenkins knew and respected Norman as a peerless man of science, a brilliant and consummate researcher, and a decent human being. He had been honored to be his professor, even for the short duration of his class in Polymeric and Supramolecular Liquids. It sickened him to realize that Dr. Holloway's last moments had been spent in suicidal depression. Nevertheless, he had somehow maintained the presence of mind to attach what seemed to be the fruits of his latest research. Clearly, there was a message—or a directive—here, but what? Dr. Jenkins checked again, and confirmed that nothing accompanied the attachment. He printed out the attachment and placed it in the zipper pocket of the briefcase on the desk. Then he went to wake his wife and tell her the news.

* * * *

Jack Heinz winced in pain as he shifted in the bed which had been his "home" for the last week. His leg alternately ached dully or itched enough to drive him to tears, but he grudgingly supposed it was better than the numbness that he had felt at first. As for the remainder of his body, he had second or third degree burns over twenty per cent of it, most of it below his waist. It had taken three days for the awful ringing in his ears to subside, and he was only just now reaching the point where he didn't have to ask the nurse to repeat every other sentence. The worst part was the horribly painful "scrubbing down" of the burns that they had to do every single day to keep infection from setting into his wounds. He'd cried like a baby the first few times they did it. Now, he just gritted his teeth and prayed for death. He'd fallen so far from the proverbial stereotype of the tough, immovable FBI G-man that it was pathetic.

Through the blinding pain and numbness, Jack Heinz had managed to direct his mind onto a single, pervasive thought. In point of fact, his ability to keep this thought at the center of his being had been somehow therapeutic, and had helped him get through the hellish treatment, when he might otherwise have succumbed. That one thought: to seek, find and exact vengeance on the person or thing that had killed his partner and caused his own slow death. To the extent that he was capable of logical thought at all, Jack had, beneath all the bandages and in the stillness of the night at the hospital, arrived at the notion that the explosion was not the gas leak explosion he had at first supposed. It had been too neat, and far too "coincidental". His car had been gone through with a fine-toothed comb by agents before being deployed, as are all surveillance cars in a high-risk operation. It had been in the Bureau's custody at all times pre-deployment, and in his and his partners' custody every moment since then. Something smelled about this assignment, and it smelled a lot worse than the chemical explosive residue that still clung to his clothing.

The bottom line was that Agent Jack Heinz had become convinced that this little mishap which was the cause of his suffering emanated, not from some sinister outside force as he had been led to believe, but rather from within. This belief had started as an ill-defined feeling, nagging at his consciousness between the waves of pain and nausea that had first assaulted him hour after hour, and then day after day. At first his mind, writhing in agony, had not allowed him to dwell upon it or even consider it, for it carried with it a different kind of pain which was even worse to contemplate than the charred flesh which now covered his body.

Only yesterday had he been wheeled by hospital orderlies from the burn unit into a private hospital room with a telephone. The agency had sent only one person—that's right, one—who came on the second day. Or so he had been told. Burning with a fever of 106 degrees and body-wracking pain, it was as though a man had come to him in a dream and mumbled at him mindlessly through a "white noise" milieu. As he later reflected upon it, the man had mouthed business-like platitudes about how "unfortunate" it was that security had been "compromised", and how the explosion had "clearly been the result of infiltration by the opposition." Naturally, he had never been let in on just who the "opposition" was. So far as he knew from James Patterson, Special Agent-In-Charge by special assignment to the Dallas Field Office, he was just protecting someone in the witness protection program. The young lady and her aunt had just been relocated, he'd been told, and this accommodation was merely provided for a few days until they could get settled in. What assignment could be more routine? This was not underworld stuff, with John Gotti's henchmen lurking somewhere around the corner. That was why, as he lay numbly in the front yard of what had been a house moments earlier, the seasoned FBI veteran's mind was racing, probing, searching for logical answers which eluded him. That ceaseless search for answers had propelled him inexorably to one question: Where is James Patterson? When he had finally managed to prop a telephone on his hospital pillow and make a call, he had gotten the runaround. Where was the man who had placed him in this position? Why hadn't he, of all people, visited him in the hospital, instead of some briefcase-carrying flunky? These were questions that simply would not go away, and they had hammered at his thoughts every waking moment that he was capable of thought.

These questions, Jack knew, would not remain unanswered much longer. The agency knew, and in fact had told him courtesy of his hospital visitor, that they were no longer protecting Mrs. Ingersoll. Jack was aware that Dane Ingersoll, a successful and respected young attorney, had taken matters into his own hands and hired body guards, and that he had moved his family to an undisclosed location in east Texas. He even had a pretty good idea where it might be. But that was not really the issue, was it? If Ingersoll, a man who had resources and a measure of intelligence and discernment, had made up his mind he couldn't trust the FBI to protect his family, then why should he? Perhaps Ingersoll knew something that he didn't, maybe even where Patterson could be found.

Underneath the scarred flesh now covering his body, Jack experienced a brief quiver of excitement, though he wasn't quite sure why, as he reached for the bedside telephone. His own cell phone was only a memory, charred to oblivion. He buzzed the nurse's station using the hand-held gizmo they'd given him, and requested a business telephone directory. In a few moments, he was dialing the number of Dane Ingersoll, Salacuse & Lockridge.

* * * *

Jenny had barely had time to complete the backup of Dane's computer and rush the portable drives back to the new office, before the clerk appeared in her doorway, flagging her down. Dane was in the back of the office, he said, talking to a man from the telephone company. She beckoned the clerk over, laying the portable drives on one of several stacks of boxes near the window.

"Someone just called for Mr. Ingersoll, Miss Pemberton. Something from a hospital." The clerk said, trying to sound helpful.

"Oh, no! I hope Natalie's okay!" yelled Jenny, grabbing the note. All it said was: "Jack Heinz, Doctor's Hospital. Please have Mr. Ingersoll call 428-5319." Jenny heaved a sigh of relief. "Probably a med mal or MVA case," she said, dismissing the clerk. Dane was going to need all the new cases he could get, now that he was on his own. She bustled back to the phone room and stood by, waiting for a break in the conversation and holding the message conspicuously. In a moment she got it, and Dane took the message. Even though he was up to his rear in alligators, curiosity got the better of him, and he pulled out his cell phone and began dialing the number. The other phone emitted one ring, then answered at the beginning of the second. Sounds of clattering and shuffling followed, as if the party had been awakened unexpectedly.

"H-Hello." The voice sounded groggy.

"Yes, this is Dane Ingersoll, returning the call of a 'Jack Heinz'."

"This is Jack Heinz," the voice said more clearly now. Hello, Mr. Ingersoll, I'm glad you called."

"What can I do for you?"

"Mr. Ingersoll, I...I am one of the agents who was guarding your wife last week." The words came deliberately and with obvious difficulty. "The other agent died. And I almost did."

"Well, Hallelujah," thought Dane. *"A call from none other than the FBI."* Straining to maintain control, he said, "Thank you for your nobility, agent, but my wife very nearly died too, no thanks to you folks."

"I realize that, sir, and I am truly sorry. You don't know *how* sorry. But you must understand that I didn't know, which should be obvious from the fact that I myself was caught in the blast." The voice had a hoarse edge to it. "Are you on a wireless phone, sir?" Heinz asked, abruptly.

"I'm on my cell phone. We are relocating our offices today."

"Then I'm lucky to have caught you. Listen: I'd rather not talk with you on a cell phone, if you know what I mean. And I know you must be incredibly busy, what with moving your office." The man wheezed a little, and Dane heard him take a deep, labored breath. "But, could you possibly meet with me here, at the hospital. I have a matter of some urgency to discuss."

"Concerning what? My wife?"

"I have a matter of some urgency to discuss," the voice repeated, much more slowly this time.

"Um...I see. Yes, I can be there in—where did you say you are?"

"Doctor's Hospital, Room 4-2B."

"I'll be there in one hour."

"All right, I'll see you then." Dane pocketed his phone.

"What was that all about?" Jenny queried.

"I'm not exactly sure," mused Dane. It's one of the FBI agents that was watching Susan's aunt's home. He wants to meet with me."

"This is getting too weird."

"Tell me about it. I've got to be at Doctor's Hospital in an hour. Do you want to come?"

"Not unless you feel you need me. There's plenty to do around here right now. I'll continue unpacking, and we can talk more about the Alton situation when you get back."

"'Sounds like a plan." Dane felt a sense of appreciation sweep over him at having someone he could count on. Jenny also looked especially attractive today, as she bent over the boxes in her blue jeans, shuffling through files. For a fleeting moment, he wondered what it would have been like...then reality jerked him back as he headed out of the building. As he got in his car and sped to his destination, his mind began whirling in a thousand directions: Natalie, Alton, Susan, new office, and now FBI agent Heinz. How could he have known a scant few weeks ago that he would be in this position today? Who would have dreamed?

* * * *

The NICU at East Dallas Medical was deafeningly quiet. Three staff nurses glided noiselessly about, checking incubators called "isolettes" as well as monitors and other assorted gadgetry. When one of the nurses arrived at the one marked "Natalie Ingersoll", chart in hand, she was especially careful. Another nurse watchfully shadowed the first, looking over her shoulder as she wrote. For Natalie's protection, but at least as much to protect itself, the hospital no longer allowed merely one nurse at a time to monitor this particular baby. Everyone in contact with Natalie was checked and double checked. An FBI agent, dressed in a business suit, looking and feeling strangely out of his element, stood outside the NICU entry door around the clock. At least once an hour, but never at regular intervals, he would enter the NICU, being careful to stay out of the hospital staff's way. Lingering near Natalie's isolette, he would check the label on the intravenous bag suspended above her tiny body. Sometimes, he would wander over to the supply cabinet where the medicines were kept and ask a nurse to show him Natalie's medicines. When the bottle was shown him, he would peer at it closely, scribble a few notes in a spiral pad, then return to the incubator. If any of the bottles was unmarked or contained ambiguous information, the agent promptly confiscated them. No boxes, nor the bottles they contained, were allowed to be discarded. Instead, they were routinely and fastidiously collected by the agent and deposited at some undisclosed location.

Natalie's color was good. Her cheeks were pink, and her skin tone better than it had been in weeks. Her pulse was strong and her breathing regular. But for her incessant dependence on the mysterious "experimental" medication, the doctors who had charge of her might have let her go home by now. There was only one problem, however, best illustrated by what had occurred ever-so-briefly only two nights previously. The digitally calibrated machine which monitored the flow of drugs into little Natalie's arteries had, at precisely 2:17 a.m., ceased to function. No one knew exactly why. There were no power outages, and, like all such hospitals, there was a fully capable auxiliary power generator in the unlikely event of such a failure. None of the other meters had stopped working, either. But, for thirty-nine minutes, the slow, steady drip of liquid medication entering Natalie's system had trickled to a halt. The second nurse who worked the deep night shift that night had been out ill. The head NICU charge nurse had been busy with paperwork at the nurse's station. With remarkable speed Natalie had first drifted, then plummeted downward into a semi-conscious state, reaching a near-comatose condition in less than fifteen minutes. Her heart rate had dropped to a staggering fifty b.p.m., her respiration to "shallow and sporadic," and her pallor to a morbid gray blue. When the shrill alarm of the heart monitor pierced the darkness that evening, the charge nurse was instantly at the bedside, issued a code blue, and the neonatal specialist was called. Within two minutes of the IV drip being restored, the baby looked brand new again, as if nothing had happened. The phenomenon was at one and the same moment amazing and deeply frightening. The charge asked to be relieved from her shift that evening. Of course, there was no need to tell the parents of the incident, after all, everything had been properly restored to normal, hadn't it? The FBI agent had been excluded from the room in the bustle of the emergency, and the doctors, who greatly resented the agent's presence anyway, simply remarked that it was a false alarm on one of the other infants. No harm, no foul.

So, in retrospect, one could easily discern why Natalie Ingersoll could not go home. In fact, to even consider her going home under the circumstances was unthinkable. Explaining the reason for her having to stay to Mrs. Ingersoll, who called two and three times each day, was a different matter, entirely. When she showed up at the hospital the next day and Natalie was looking almost as healthy as a normal baby, it was difficult indeed for the doctors to convince her that Natalie was anything but healthy. But she was totally, utterly dependent on the bottle which dangled perpetually above her delicate little body.

* * * *

Dane arrived at the hospital room of Jack Heinz with not a little trepidation. He knew that the man he was about to talk to had been in a terrible explosion. Dane had never seen anyone who had come through such an experience, and had certainly never been in the armed services, let alone a war, where he would have been most likely to encounter it. He tried to prepare himself for what he might see as he walked down the stark, echoing hallway, studying the room numbers on each door. He came to a halt at Room 4-2B, the door to which was ajar. He checked the name on the door. It said "Jack Heinz," and Dane appreciatively noted that this was a private room. Gingerly, he swung open the door and entered.

"Come on in, Dane Ingersoll. Pull up a hospital chair. That's about all the furniture there is in here." There was a labored chuckle from the direction of the voice.

"Thank you, I will." The smell of hospitals and medicine permeated the room. The light was much dimmer than in the hallway, Dane noticed. Even in the subdued light, the man in the bed appeared grotesquely scarred. "I believe you wanted to talk to me."

"Talk? Oh, yes, I very much want to talk with you. You know, I never met your wife. Is she all right? How did she take the explosion?" Dane could hear clearly in Heinz' voice that these were no casual conversational questions. The man really was interested to know.

"Oh, she was shaken up a bit," Dane downplayed things for the sake of Heinz—no use making a very ill man feel worse—"but she's doing much better right now. Of course, your employer is no longer involved in her safekeeping."

"I'd heard that very fact, and I can't say that I blame you one bit. Nossiree, I would have done the same thing if it were my wife." Heinz paused awkwardly, for what seemed like an extraordinarily long interval. When he spoke again, his words were poignant. "I'm sorry that we blew it. Please believe me when I say we never saw it coming."

"Of course I believe you. If you knew about it in advance you wouldn't be talking to me from a hospital bed. But that doesn't change the fact that someone in the Bureau didn't do their job. And now you are paying for that fact—just like Susan nearly did with her life."

"True enough." Any disorientation Heinz had shown initially was now gone. He raised his head slightly from the pillow, with obvious effort. "And it sickens me. It sickens me because it shouldn't have happened—I'll go farther than that—it *couldn't* have happened without ...close the door, will you?"

Dane was poised on the end of the chair, bolt upright. He closed the door with his foot.

"Without what, Mr. Heinz?"

"Without some complicity," Heinz spoke in a much lower tone.

"What are you driving at?"

"Very simply this. There is no way in God's green earth than an FBI vehicle, under its constant supervision and custody, could ever have a bomb planted without some cooperation from the inside."

Dane scowled, as the implications of this statement catapulted through his mind. "And you have proof of this?"

"I don't need proof. I've been with the Bureau too long, and seen too much. Believe me, there is no way this can have happened without someone being bought off, or ordering it done. I can't put a good face on it, because it's pretty ugly."

"Even if what you say is correct, why would someone in the bureau want my wife dead?"

"There are many possibilities. Whoever it is may have wanted her dead, or only to scare her—or more likely, you—into doing something they wanted very badly."

"Do you have any clue what you are suggesting, Mr. Heinz?"

"I'm not suggesting anything. Why don't you tell me what you are thinking?"

"What did your superiors tell you about why you were watching Susan in the first place?"

"That she was in the witness protection program."

"Nothing more?"

"Nothing, except I remember hearing somewhere that some nondescript group from South America might be a threat."

"Can you keep a secret?"

"Is it legal?"

"Yes. But the information I am about to reveal to you is known to only two other individuals, and my and my family's ability to go on living depends on absolute confidence." Dane wouldn't have gone this far already if he didn't trust Heinz.

"Fire away. My lips are sealed."

"All right then. My wife was no witness waiting to testify in a federal trial. She—along with our newborn baby girl—have become unwilling targets of Rowalter Pharmaceuticals. In actuality, they are hostages to my willingness and ability to get a highly unstable and virulent drug approved by the FDA in a matter of a few days." Jack Heinz listened with rapt attention as, after this intriguing introduction, Dane launched into a half hour story of the amazing events of the last several weeks. He left nothing out, right down to Alton's email and apparent escape that very afternoon. When he was finished, Heinz face held the look of a trance, as though he'd been watching a fascinating movie for several hours. Then, slowly, his dry chapped lips puckered and he let out a whistle.

"That is some incredible story. He paused. "How'd you stand the pressure?"

"I don't know. It isn't over yet by a long shot, and the pressure is just beginning. Wait until that hearing."

"I'd like to help."

"How could you possibly help? Besides your obvious condition, and with all due respect, your employer has already botched things up pretty good."

"Well, the way I see it, we both have a whale of a beef with my employ—with my *ex*-employer." He paused, displaying a knowing half-smile. "I don't think for a minute that Patterson didn't know about that bomb. Oh, I'm not sure he actually *planted* it—he's certainly too smart for that. But I have a hunch he knew all about it. I'm just not exactly sure yet why he would allow it. But, no matter. I would be willing to run interference for you, get to the bottom of who is pulling strings at Rowalter, and most importantly, who is protecting them within the Bureau."

"And what, pray tell, would all this cost me?"

"Just my out-of-pocket expenses. I would be doing it for the sheer satisfaction of evening the score. Besides, I don't need the money. I have a pension from the LAPD and an uncle that died and left me a ton of money a couple of years ago."

"How do I know I can trust you any more than Patterson?"

"You don't. Feel free to thoroughly check out my background, though. You can have my social security number, driver's license, date of birth and the like.

You're an attorney. You know how to get the lowdown on me. Bear in mind, though, that the only other option you've got is to keep on running. Granted, you may have damning evidence on Rowalter from their computers, but they've still got Natalie—or at least, we have to assume they still have access to her. You could turn in the evidence and she could die or disappear in a heartbeat, especially if you're turning it in to an enemy rather than a friend. If my theory about Patterson is correct, he may have some help within the Bureau. Even if he doesn't have knowing assistance from on high, he has access to the Bureau's resources, and he knows how to use them without tipping his hand to anyone. You should regard him as a formidable adversary."

"Even if I were to accept your offer, how would you be up to doing anything in your condition?"

"You'd be surprised. The worst is behind me. They tell me I'll be out of here in two days. All I have to do is come back for some occasional skin grafts—you know, cutting skin from my ass to paste it on my face or my arm—that sort of thing." Heinz smiled wryly. "Actually, I believe my perceived physical condition to be an advantage. Who would expect a 47-year-old ex-cop burn victim to still be in the game? They will never suspect. They don't realize this old body made it through Desert Storm in '90."

Dane thought a moment. "I don't need to check you out. You've already heard my whole story. If you were working for Rowalter, you'd have only to pick up the phone when I left and tell them everything, and there's nothing I can do about it now. I would want to see a copy of your letter resigning from the Bureau, though."

"Consider it done. Give me your card and I'll have it faxed to you as soon as I'm out, along with proof of mailing."

"All right then. We've got a deal." Dane stood. "I've got a hearing in five days, and a new office I'm opening in the meantime. I'll be in constant preparation. Here's my card if you need to reach me," he said, reaching out to place it on the table beside the hospital bed. "Tell me what you need and I'll get it to you. And thanks." Dane was hoping Heinz wouldn't ask for the USB flash drives he'd received from Alton, and he didn't. They shook hands, and as they did Dane noticed that Heinz' grip was strong and his hand appeared to be unscathed by the fire.

As Dane exited the room and returned by elevator to the main floor, he reached into his coat pocket and turned off his cell phone voice recorder that had been running for the last thirty minutes. It never hurt, he told himself, to have a little extra insurance, just in case.

* * * *

Alton's breath came in shallow gulps, and he was soaked with sweat. His heart thumped against his chest like a jackhammer, until he thought for sure it would come right out of his body. He had been running for what had to have been at least five miles without pausing. The mountain air at this altitude was so thin that it left him lightheaded and unsatisfied, like a thirst that is never quenched. But Alton couldn't stop. He pushed himself ever onward, with the baying of hounds piercing the summer night and coming ever louder until it seemed that they were climbing up his back. It was a terrifying sound, made more so by the knowledge that, no matter what the strength of his will, his body could not keep this up much longer. Tripping over a fallen log, Alton felt his foot sink into water, and realized he was on the bank of a stream or lake—which, he wasn't sure because of the darkness. Exhausted, he ripped the all-important flash drives from the inside of his thighs, and held them in his teeth. He then waded out into the water, forcing himself ever farther until he could no longer feel the bottom. In the stillness of the moonless Bolivian night, he slowly treaded water, waiting for what seemed an eternity for the barking to recede. Eventually it did, and he cautiously side-stroked his way to shore, keeping his head, and the precious flash drives, above water. He made it back to the shoreline, surveyed the area as best he could in the starlight, and decided to try to find a place to sleep until daybreak. This wouldn't be easy, and Alton was frightened to death of sleeping out in the open when he was completely unfamiliar with his surroundings. Worse, Alton hadn't a clue as to what body of water he was on—though by now he surmised it was a lake—or where he was along the shoreline relative to anywhere else. All he knew was that he was more tired than he could ever remember, law school finals included. His legs and arms ached, and his lungs screamed for relief. He stumbled around the shoreline, lost and disoriented, until a large tree branch slapped him in the face. Through the starlight he could make out the shape of a large looming cocillana tree. He fell to his knees underneath the tree and, with what little energy he had left, scraped together a small pile of what felt like leaves. He curled up in a fetal position, resting his head on his hands, which in turn rested on the leaves, and was instantly asleep.

Hours later, Alton awoke with a start. Sunlight illuminated his little resting place, but he was too tired to move or to care. As his eyes fluttered open and his vision cleared, he became strangely aware of the presence of another, and scrambled to a sitting position, his heart beating furiously. Three people, two children and a man of smallish stature stared curiously, silently at Alton from a few feet away. They were dark skinned but not black, and dressed in colorful clothing. The man wore a hat, and held something Alton would guess to be a fishing net. A boat made not of wood but of a reed like material, almost like wicker, bobbed against the shoreline a short distance away. Struggling to gain composure, Alton forced a smile and tried out some Spanish on the Aymara Indian.

"*Hola. Como esta usted?*"   No reply. The man looked around shyly.

"*Cuál es el nombre de este lago, por favor?*" queried Alton, looking over his shoulder and gesturing at what he had by now discerned was a lake rather than a river. At this, the man's eyes showed a glint of recognition. "*Titicaca,*" the man replied, simply.

"*Ah, now we're getting somewhere,*" thought Alton. "*I'm on Lake Titicaca, which means I'm near the Peruvian-Bolivian border!*" Alton was equally uplifted by the fact that this Indian at least seemed to understand some Spanish. Still unsure whether he had responded more to his body language than his words, Alton tried out some more simple Spanish phrases on him.   The man did not respond to any of them. Suddenly, he motioned to the two children, a boy and a girl, to follow him. They proceeded to the boat, obviously having more productive things to do than stand here staring at an outlander all day. They rummaged through the vessel, which smelled of fish even from this distance. Alton got up from his sitting position, amazed as he did so at the fact that he had slept undisturbed in such an uncomfortable spot for so many hours. He felt for the four flash drives and found them inside his waistband where he had placed it last night before dropping off to sleep. As he stood to his full height and began to stretch, Alton felt pain in muscles he hadn't even known he possessed. Today, he reminded himself, was Wednesday, January 26th. It was important to him to keep track of the passage of time, since he had so precious little of it and he knew the crucial FDA hearing was not far away, if it wasn't already too late. If the decision didn't come out the way Rowalter wanted, it could appeal to the courts, but Alton couldn't count on a court holding the line against Rowalter. Besides, who knew how many more could die from the drug in the interim? Nope. He knew he had to get out of this country quickly, and to a decent sized city, to find his way home. He wasn't too up on this part of the world, but he figured if he was on the border it couldn't be too awfully far to Lima. On the other hand, he seemed to remember La Paz was nearer to the border, and it was an awfully long trek to anywhere through the high Andes. He decided the Aymara might be his only chance of getting where he needed to go anytime soon, whether they understood only a few words of Spanish or not. Perhaps, if nothing else, he could hitch a boat ride to the side of the lake nearest the border, then hope to hit a highway or small airport that flew into Lima. The only problem was: with what? Alton was penniless, and painfully aware of it. Stripped of everything when he'd been apprehended by Rowalter, he didn't even carry any identification. If he told anyone he was an American lawyer, he was certain they would break out laughing. He almost laughed himself at the very thought.

Humbly, he approached the Aymara man once again, and using the best combination of Spanish, English and sign language he could muster, he said he was lost, was an American trying to get to Lima, and needed a ride. The man's eyes grew large, and to Alton anyway, he gave the appearance of someone who at least seemed to comprehend some of what he was saying. At least, that was what Alton hoped it meant. The man let out with some unrecognizable gibberish and pointed with his right hand to the far end of the lake. The last word in his utterance, though, was clearly spoken: *"Perú"*. Alton repeated back *"Peru?"* and pointed to the far end of the lake, away from the sun. The Indian repeated the word, and nodded his head. Alton reached down to the boat, uncertainly put one foot in it, and made a frantic motion like rowing while asking in Spanish if the man would kindly take him to Peru. The children laughed at Alton's motions, while playing with the fish in the boat. The man appeared to think reflectively for a moment, then motioned broadly the children to be quiet. He spoke again, more slowly this time, and Alton caught a few Spanish words amongst the mass of native language. One was *"casa"* and the other *"allí"*. Alton took that to mean that the Indian's house was "over there". To make sure where "there" was, Alton pointed in the same direction as the man had pointed before and asked, *"Su casa está allí?"* The man nodded and said *"Sí,"* then followed it with some other words that were clearly not Spanish. Alton breathed a sigh of relief, and then bravely settled into the back of the smelly boat, repeating *"gracias, gracias"*. He knew he was being presumptuous, but given the language barrier and his current circumstances, this was no time for manners or deferential behavior. He would take his chances with being blunt.

The trip across Lake Titicaca was, in a strange way, exhilarating after a night on the hard ground. The spray laden breeze felt refreshing on his face, and the sky was blue, the day pleasant. Alton sat between the man and the two children, afraid to shift his weight even slightly to the right or the left in what seemed to him like a flimsy vessel. He tried to ignore the powerful fishy smell wafting upward from the boat bottom, where the morning's catch lay plainly in view. It appeared to be catfish—very large catfish not unlike what Alton had seen many times in Louisiana, where he grew up. The Indian man applied the oars smoothly, rhythmically, like the expert that he obviously was. In no time at all, it seemed they had covered a thousand yards, and in another few minutes, the shoreline from whence they'd departed had disappeared from view. White native birds hovered and swooped over the boat, as if to escort them to their destination. Within what could not have been more than forty-five minutes, they were pulling into the far shore of the lake, in an inlet where several other reed boats were moored. The Indian grunted and motioned his children out of the boat, and Alton followed suit, as he pulled the boat ashore and tied it up to a large rock. The children gathered up the fish in some kind of cloth sack, as if they knew it was expected of them. The Indian spoke a few words hurriedly to Alton, and motioned him to follow, then started up the inclining shore toward some unknown destination. The kids scampered excitedly ahead of him, with Alton bringing up the rear.

Within moments, Alton saw the object of the Indian's striving. Dead ahead, just over a short rise, was a series of ramshackle "houses" some with metal roofs and some with straw. The Indian vanished into one of them, while Alton waited impatiently about twenty yards away. His eyes scanned the horizon for any sign of aircraft, on the outside chance that he could figure out where an airfield might be. Seeing none, he returned his attention to the group of huts before him. It seemed like another ten minutes before the Indian emerged with another man, slightly taller, and clearly older. The younger Indian grabbed the elder's arm and guided him over to where Alton stood, chattering something utterly foreign. The elder man stopped dead in front of Alton, and gave him a good looking over, top to bottom. With a partly suspicious, partly critical look in his eye, the Aymaran asked in a funny sort of Peruvian Spanish dialect where Alton was from. Except for the accent and a couple of words Alton had to guess at, the Spanish dialect was really quite understandable. Pleasantly surprised, Alton replied. The man seemed puzzled until he heard the word, "Texas," which he then repeated back to Alton with the American pronunciation rather than *"Tejas"*, the Spanish equivalent. Alton gathered his courage, and, looking directly into the brown eyes of the old Indian, asked in Spanish how he could get to Lima, Peru. He pointed in the direction he surmised it could be found. The man seemed surprised at the question, and turning his back abruptly to Alton, began furiously jabbering away at the younger Indian, who responded in kind. Alton stood waiting awkwardly, wondering how far it was to the nearest telephone or other form of electronic communication. After a few minutes, the elder Indian whirled back to Alton, stretched out his arm and pointed his finger on a southwesterly heading and began making strange noises. He stretched out his arms to full length and made banking movements with them. He mentioned what Alton knew was an attempt at the Spanish word for "airplane," but it came out differently. Growing excited now, Alton asked a series of intense questions. The elder Indian seemed to comprehend the majority of them, but could only respond in Pigeon-Spanish, leaving Alton to piece together information with much effort. In several more minutes, Alton had established to his own satisfaction that there was a man with a small plane who visited the Indian village from a small town in Peru. Apparently, the purpose was to trade with the Aymara. He came, as best Alton could discern, about once each "moon", and there was a small landing strip several miles away. While the younger Indian set down on a stump nearby and appeared to work on his fishing nets, Alton cajoled the elder to stoop down on the ground and draw him a map of where the airstrip was. He then asked him how many "suns" since the man's last visit. The wizened face of the old Indian lapsed into concentration, then came the reply, "Don't count suns. Count moons." Ready to blow a gasket with excitement and frustration, Alton asked whether the man had come on a "full moon" or a "new moon?" His companion grew perplexed, and Alton could see the English terms were not getting across. Hurriedly, he cleared a spot on the ground and drew pictures in the earth with a finger. He scratched out a full moon, a crescent moon, and a completely shaded or "new" moon. The Indian immediately thrust his finger into the middle of the "full moon." Some more chattering later, and Alton confirmed that the man with the airplane had last arrived during the full moon.

With nothing in his possession but what he was wearing, Alton hadn't a clue what the status of the lunar calendar was at this moment along the Peru/Bolivian border, and he really hadn't thought to bring an almanac. He did, however, recall it being a moonless night when he had swum ashore hours earlier—that very fact had probably saved his life. But was it a new moon, or just clouds obscuring the moon? Alton culled through his memory, and seemed to recall there being no stars in the sky last night. That meant heavy cloud cover, which in turn meant he had no way of knowing the whether it was the beginning or the end of the lunar month. He pressed the old Indian again, but all he could get out of him was that the man with the plane was due back "soon." And, thought Alton, there is no way I can be sure I'll get a ride with him this mysterious pilot without a dime to my name. And with that realization, Alton suddenly became intensely aware that he was ravenously hungry, even starving. Out of the corner of one eye he noticed an Aymara woman—or should he say squaw?—huddled over a fire a couple of hundred yards back to his left. He hoped she was cooking, not performing some time-honored artistic or religious ritual. He was not disappointed when, a fraction of a second later the breeze touched his nostrils with the tantalizing aroma of frying fish. Alton had never been a big fish-eater, but he was hungry enough to eat a proverbial bear, and fish would do quite nicely under the circumstances. The younger Indian, children tagging alongside, beckoned him over to join his family in a meal. Alton was grateful for the hospitality, and hungrily headed up the hill, leaving the boat bobbing in the lake.

CHAPTER TWENTY- ONE

The meeting with Betaña was not a pretty sight. Patterson arrived at 6:00 a.m. in La Paz, hailed a lonely looking cab curbed outside the airport, and made it to the compound about thirty minutes later. Patterson placed his hand on the digital scanner at the door to the compound. The security guards monitoring the videocams around the perimeter of the Rowalter compound saw him, and did not recognize him. This man was not an expected visitor according to their logs. They immediately placed a call to Betaña's quarters on the first underground floor of the compound, asking who the visitor was. Meanwhile, Patterson strode boldly to the main security entrance of the building, placed his hand on the digital scanner panel at the door to the compound. The computerized entry system immediately "recognized" his hand print, and requested his alphanumeric security code, which he promptly keyed in. The door disengaged, allowing his entry. By then, Betaña was fully awake and was in the process of checking his messages. He was part way through the one from Patterson, when the guards stationed outside his room rushed in and in unison announced the presence of an unknown and unexpected visitor—one Señor James Patterson. The only I.D. he had presented, they reported excitedly, was an official badge of the Federal Bureau of Investigation of the United States of America. And, to their surprise, he had entered the compound with ease. Betaña ordered them to stand down and finished flinging on his bathrobe, as he went to the front door. The guards disbursed back to their stations, except for a small contingent of house guards and personal body guards, who always shadowed their employer.

One of the guards had ushered Patterson into Betaña's first floor office, an imposing room where Patterson now stood, red-faced. Betaña approached him with studied caution, yet affected the ingratiating manner which was his trade mark.

"James! 'So good to see you!" Betaña effused, smiling. "Come, come, have a seat. Ricardo, get Mr. Patterson some café. Pray tell, good friend, what brings you here at such an unusual hour?"

"Cut the crap, José. You know exactly what I'm here about. There was unauthorized computer activity from the 12th floor of your compound last night. I called last night forty or fifty times and got no answer. What the hell has been going on here?"

"Why, nothing but the normal business activity. Oh, we had a minor breach in security last night, but nothing we can't handle, and it won't be repeated."

"Does this 'minor' security breach involve a certain Mr. Alton Dean, per chance?"

Betaña's face became pensive as he cocked his head, lips pursed. "The name sounds familiar, though I can't verify it at this time. I can contact the head of security if you like," he said, reaching for his intercom. It was a good act, but Patterson wasn't buying.

"That won't be necessary, Señor Betaña. I know precisely what was going on. I know, and you *know* that I know, Dean's exact location and his capabilities. Because of your stupidity and incompetence, he has now compromised Rowalter's computer files and read—perhaps recorded—its most sensitive and potentially damaging research." Patterson paused, as if to punctuate his next remark. "Where is Dean now?"

Betaña almost faltered, then without missing a beat, recovered. "We have him under surveillance."

Patterson wasn't fooled. "Surveillance implies absence. I *said,* 'Where *is* he'?!"

Betaña caved. "H-he escaped last night, and we lost track of him in the mountains near the border." The man's face was red, his eyes sheepish. "But we have an all-out search in progress."

"You cursed fool. You've jeopardized a lot more than my investment, though that's bad enough. You've put my career on the line, together with all we've worked so hard for. Need I remind you that it was I who recommended against apprehending him in the first place?" Patterson was nearly yelling now. The servant arrived with the coffee, but Betaña waved him off.

"I remember. But nothing is to be done now but to gain your FDA's approval. It is nearly in hand, true?"

"The odds are in our favor, yes. But just imagine what will happen if Alton Dean surfaces at just the right moment with whatever he has pilfered from your computer. Has that thought even so much as occurred to you?"

Betaña had tried to put the thought completely out of mind. His only answer to Patterson's question was frustrated silence.

"Think about it, Señor Betaña. Think about how you are going to explain this to your board of directors and your precious investors in São Paulo and Río. Then think about how prison is going to look when you are extradited for a long and painful trial. Remember Manuel Noriega?" Patterson paused, and his eyes drilled directly through those of Betaña and into his soul. "What, I wonder, is to be done?"

Both men knew precisely what was to be done. What FBI blood remained flowing through Patterson's veins wouldn't let him utter the words, but there were some words that simply didn't need to be said. Patterson excused himself, and was soon back on a plane to the states. Betaña picked up his phone, and placed a call to somewhere in Bogotá, Colombia. After reminding the person at the other end of the line of some transportation favors Rowalter Industries had provided for his bustling cocaine trade, Betaña called in a long-standing IOU. The transaction completed, he hung up the phone, and returned to bed, leaving the untouched coffee sitting in the corner.

* * * *

It was a cold, bright Saturday morning when Jack Heinz was wheeled down to the elevator at the end of the fourth floor of Doctor's Hospital. A few moments later, the wheels bumped over the threshold of the south entrance as the broad electric doors lurched back to welcome him into a world he had nearly forgotten existed. The morning sun made Jack squint, and the cold made him wince with pain, as the skin recently grafted onto his face and arms rebelled. Jack had no relatives in the area, and his ex-wife resided in Pennsylvania with her second husband and children, so he was attended completely by nurses. Courtesy of the insurance afforded him by the U.S. government,

Jack would have as much home convalescent and rehab care as he needed. He was to have round-the-clock help for the next several weeks. Doctors' orders. Only, Jack didn't plan on following doctor's orders. He had a much more demanding timetable—and strong motivation with which to accomplish it, no matter the pain.

Safely at home in an easy chair with legs propped up on the footrest, Jack allowed his male nurse attendant to give him his meds, then asked for some coffee. The attendant made him decaf, which he hated, but didn't squawk about since he didn't feel like arguing about "doctor's orders." He then summarily dismissed nurses to the next room. For the moment, Jack Heinz remained an agent with the Federal Bureau of Investigation. That would change very soon, but in the meantime, Jack fully intended to exercise all the benefits of membership in that elite fraternity. He grabbed his laptop computer which was within arm's reach, just where he had left it the day of the fateful explosion. Jack up-linked to the security check site used by all agents, and entered his pass word. Within ten minutes, he had performed complete background checks on each home nurse that had been assigned to him. Just to be sure, he cross-checked the information through several other website links he and his investigator friends utilized. Soon, he had everything he could ever want to know about them, verifying to his satisfaction that they were clean. Then, ignoring the unfamiliarity of the first chair he had sat in for weeks, agent Heinz typed out a tersely worded resignation letter. It was easy to justify, and no elaborate explanation was necessary. Lots of years of service followed by a catastrophic accident, couldn't faithfully discharge his duties after such a traumatic experience: that sort of thing. This he emailed, and saved to his disk in letter form for printing and mailing to James Patterson later today, certified mail, with a blind copy to Dane Ingersoll by fax. He would qualify for disability, a pension, and a host of other benefits.

"Now, down to business," thought Jack. The FDA approval hearing, he remembered, was to take place this coming week. Today was Saturday. The luxury of time was something Jack did not have. He placed a call to the number on Dane's business card, which he extracted from his shirt pocket. Ingersoll was, as be expected, not there at the moment, but a girl named "Jenny" took the call.

"This is Jenny; may I help you?"

"Yes, this is Jack Heinz, and I believe..."

"Oh, Mr. Heinz, he's been awaiting your call! Are you home?"

"Yes, I am, and 'resting comfortably,' as they say. Ready to get to work."

"Great." Jenny lowered her voice a notch. "Have you submitted your resignation yet? Dane wanted me to ask."

"It's done. Do you want a copy?"

"Please, if you could maybe fax it along with a copy of the certified mailing."

"Boy, they are none too careful, are they?" thought Heinz.

"Yeah, I'll have that done in the next several minutes."

Though he could tell she wanted to, Jenny would not continue the conversation until she received the fax—she had her instructions. Jack forced himself out of his seat and across the house to his office, where he ran out the letter, readied the mailing and faxed the copy. He re-called her from his office.

"Did you get it all right?" asked Heinz.

"I sure did, and everything looks fine." Jenny left unspoken the fact that she had already checked everything that Heinz had ever done that was publicly available, and some that wasn't, back to the LAPD and beyond. "Everything seems to be in order. What's our first move?"

"Well, obviously that's Mr. Ingersoll's call, but I was thinking it might be wise to check into Natalie's care, then do some surveillance on your friend and mine, James Patterson. I'd be very interested to see how he explains the explosion at the in-laws."

"Sounds like a plan."

"Do I need Mr. Ingersoll's authorization to proceed?"

"Nope. He said if your paperwork checked out, to give you a free hand. He's buried in preparation for the FDA hearing, and can't spare a moment."

"Fair enough. I'll begin immediately."

"Let me know if you need anything, Mr. Heinz."

"Oh, you'll know right away. And, it's Jack. Call me Jack."

"As you wish, Jack."

* * * *

Alton peered impatiently at his watch for the third time in as many minutes. The automatic calendar had stopped working after his swim in Lake Titicaca that first night, but the watch itself was one of his few remaining links with civilization and the fading memory of his former life. It was 10:00 a.m. He squinted at the horizon and made a conscious effort to shut out the sounds of the gulls swooping down on the lake in the distance. Was it the outline of a plane that he saw breaking over the edge of the mountains—or merely a cloud formation? He had sighted such a "plane" before and been wrong at least three times in the last couple of days. He was beginning to doubt his own sanity. Was he losing it—or hallucinating perhaps? Then...he heard it. The steady droning, the one that sounds like lawns being mowed on a Sunday afternoon in the suburbs...or like the sleepy sound the electric clippers make just behind your ears in the barber shop. His heart leapt, and he unconsciously let out a whoop. He wished vainly for a pair of binoculars. In the distance, several children in the Aymara village heard his jubilation and curiously ventured up toward the outcropping where Alton was perched. A group of Aymara children, seasoned veterans at such sightings, ran out to where Alton stood and followed the line of his gaze. The old man, too, materialized under a scraggly tree near the village. The bare hint of a smile showed at the edges of his mouth. "*No,*" Alton concluded, "*I'm not imagining it this time.*"

He continued to track the plane with his eyes as it grew to a clearly discernible image, banked to its left and broke through a low ceiling of clouds. It then leveled off at a thousand feet or so, and for the first time he could make out a cockpit and then the landing gear. Alton recognized the Cessna 172 Skyhawk at this distance, principally because his dad used to train other Civil Air Patrol pilots in them. Within a few more minutes Alton could read the alphanumeric on the visage of the small fuselage. An excited yell went up from the children, many of whom now had the approving smiles of parents who had drawn alongside. The plane came in low and flat, just over the knob of the outcropping which separated Alton and the crowd of Aymara from the crude, hand-cleared "runway". The outcropping seemed to be generally regarded by the tribe as a sort of safety barrier, but once the plane touched down, restraint gave way to pandemonium. Alton was little different. He broke into a half jog, half sprint, carried along by the wave of fleet footed children surrounding him. They mounted the cliff to which the outcropping attached and dashed down the other side, ignoring the slope.

The Cessna had rolled to a stop and its pilot was already out of the plane, blocking the wheels with some nearby rocks. He was a young man—perhaps thirty—Alton thought, tall, tan and blonde haired, and dressed in a loose-fitting khaki outfit. He finished blocking the second wheel, then stood and waved, smiling at the welcoming party. Within minutes, the poor fellow was surrounded by a sea of little urchins. Alton stood a short distance away with what had now become twenty or so Aymara adults. The man spoke a few words in the Indians' language, then put up a finger as if to say "wait a minute." He reached back into the plane, whose door was still open, and extracted two large drawstring bags. A collective scream of excitement went up from the children as the man thrust his hand into the one of the bags, pulled out a wad of candy, and broadcast it to the crowd. Hands, arms and legs were everywhere as the children dove for the treasure. Amidst the dust and excitement, the eye of the visitor immediately met Alton's. *"I must be an incredible sight, a white man out here in the middle of nowhere,"* mused Alton. If the pilot was surprised to find a *Gringo* among the Aymara Indians, he kept it well hidden. The pilot shouldered the military-style duffle bag he had brought, closed the plane door without locking it, and began walking in the direction of the tribal camp. En route, he abruptly turned to Alton and greeted him, not in Aymaran, but in Spanish. Alton responded in kind, but asked if the man knew English, as he was an American. To his surprise, the man, calling himself Roger, shifted seamlessly into American English.

"What brings you all the way out here—are you a trader, or an anthropologist?" Roger queried, a good-humored twinkle in his eye.

"Neither," Alton replied cautiously, not yet sure if this man could be trusted. "This is my temporary stopping place on a trip gone bad back to the states. I'm hoping to persuade somebody to get me to Lima, or at least to some place with a commercial airport."

Roger's eyes were at once friendly and penetrating. Alton could tell he was being studied. "How long have you been here?"

"About a week." Alton thought it best to keep things vague till he knew more about this fellow.

"'Sounds like you have an interesting story to tell."

"Oh, not really," Alton lied, "Just your typical mechanical breakdown on a hike through the Andes. I had some companions who went for help, but I haven't heard from them since they left. How about you? Is this a regular stop for you?"

"I'm a former missionary to these parts. Church of Christ. 'Did it for several years during grad school while I was working on my Master of Divinity degree—I like to tell people I'm an M.D." Roger flashed a toothy grin. "At some point, it got pretty risky flying into the Peruvian rain forest. One of the American missionary planes was even shot down by the Peruvian air force, apparently in the mistaken belief it was carrying drugs. So, I became a trader with some of the indigenous Indian tribes. It's been fun, and I still get to share my faith. Oh, but I didn't exactly answer your question, did I?"

Alton had become interested enough in Roger's story, especially the "drugs" part, that he had momentarily forgotten what he had asked. He flushed with embarrassment.

"The answer is 'yes'," Roger continued obligingly. I usually make it out about once a month. If I can't for some reason, I have a friend who can sub in for me."

"Are you based in Lima?" Alton wasted no time.

"As a matter of fact, I am. I live there at the moment."

"How far is it by air?" Alton persisted, as they reached the camp.

"Oh, about three hours or so. You have to fly at a pretty high altitude to be safe in these mountains," Roger made a panoramic sweep of his hand, "so it takes a bit longer than in the rain forest."

"I can imagine," said Alton, attempting to be conversational. Alton struggled with how to phrase his next request, so much so that he didn't realize it registered plainly on his face.

"Do you need a ride somewhere?" Roger queried helpfully.

"Do I ever!" Alton replied, relieved.

Roger flung his duffle bags onto the ground near the Aymaran hut at which they now stood. He unsnapped a canteen of water from around his belt, and thrust it out toward Alton. "It's the only pure water you're going to get around here, which I'm sure you've already discovered."

Alton couldn't agree more, and thanked Roger as he drank directly from the canteen. He had forgotten what potable water tasted like. Roger than took a long draught. He didn't want to sound too pushy with this new-found savior, but he had gone through too much to be concerned with niceties. "Roger, how long do you plan on staying to trade with the Aymara?"

"Well, I could stay and drag it out until tomorrow, though the actual trading itself only takes a few hours—you know, fish for trinkets and clothing, that sort of thing. But lots of times I like to stay the night.

That way, I get to know the tribal people better and build some relationships."

"Please understand—that is, I don't mean to rush you or anything, but I have a bit of an emergency back home, and I have been stuck here in the mountains ever since—", he hesitated, continuing "since my car broke down. I'll make it worth your while, if you could just trust me on it till I get back home. You see, I lost my wallet and everything on the hike up here."

Roger, nice as he was, was not stupid. He could tell as well as the next guy when there were gaps in a story, and it was clear that there were many in Alton's. But he didn't particularly want to step into the role of grand inquisitioner. Besides, there was something in Alton's manner that, while obviously desperate, was worthy of trust.

"I don't have any pressing agenda or anything," Roger chuckled light-heartedly, "and it's still early in the day. We should be able to get our trading done by this evening, sack in tonight and be back in Lima in time for lunch tomorrow. 'Sound like a plan?"

"You have no idea how appreciative I am."

"Don't mention it. As for 'making it worth my while,' I have to go back to Lima anyway. One more passenger will make for some pleasant conversation, which is more than I usually have. But, if you don't mind my asking, how do you plan on getting a flight from Lima back to—where did you say you were from in the U.S.?"

"I didn't. It's Texas, and I haven't a clue what I'll do to get back. But I've got to, and quickly. If I can just get to Lima, somehow I'll figure out something." Alton was the picture of resolute determination.

"I admire your grit. Well, I'll do *my* part, at least. Something tells me you'll make it back." Roger was smiling again. "Do me a favor, will you, and help me unload these bags over there." He pointed to a level spot on the ground about fifty yards distant. Alton promptly obliged. A few moments later, the two men were stooped under a shady tree, emptying the contents of the two large bags, one at a time, onto the ground. There were bolts of colorful fabric, pocket knives, fishing gear, firewood, rope, some boys and girls clothing, candy, and the kind of trinkets and simple toys that Alton supposed had interested the Indians who traded away Manhattan island. As he helped Roger set up, Alton had an indefinable, yet very tangible feeling that this was a man who he could trust. Logical thinker that he was, Alton reasoned that a man who would do this for an isolated group like the Aymara, with very little pecuniary gain, had to be a rather decent fellow. But it wasn't entirely logic that made Alton want to trust Roger. It was his openness, his unabashed transparency, and apparent lack of any agenda that pulled Alton to him. Since he was the only other *gringo* within a thousand miles, Alton mused, the feeling was a comforting one.

Within moments, the children who had scouted out the plane's arrival had drawn the entire tribe, which now engulfed Alton and Roger like a sea surrounding an island. They were literally awash in people, and in noisy, happy shouts as adults and children alike maneuvered their way up to the two men. Alton, just for a moment, forgot the urgency of his mission, as fish and trinkets began changing hands with furious rapidity. He could afford to relax a little now. After all, Roger had said they would leave in the morning. There was nothing more he could do until then.

CHAPTER TWENTY-TWO

Dane was all in a fever. He had worked throughout the weekend without let-up. Jenny and a junior associate named Nick, on loan from the old firm, ran out every few hours for pizza, subs or what-have-you. They kept Dane's thermos filled with hot coffee as he pored over every case file memorizing essential facts. Dane worked furiously, scrawling out on yellow pad after yellow pad the outline of his examination of each witness. Jenny, for whom Dane was especially grateful, had seized the task of indexing, cross-indexing and triple cross-indexing the trial notebooks and supporting exhibit books. They now numbered about ten and weighed at least five pounds apiece. At the same time, she was in regular contact with the witnesses, all five or so of them, who could substantiate with their live testimony the experience with the drug PZT. Some of the witnesses appeared to Dane, at least outwardly, to be perfectly normal. For example, there was Julia Chatsworth, a middle-aged woman from Cincinnati, whom you had to engage in conversation for a couple of hours to discover what was wrong with her. Julia had been head of systems management over the entire electronic data processing department of a sprawling national bank. She had contracted, at 40 years of age, a form of lymphoma for which there was no known treatment. So, Julia had flown to Mexico to try some experimental treatments, among them a course of intravenous PZT. Not only had the treatment had no noticeable impact on her lymphoma, but it had caused massive cerebral hemorrhaging. This, in turn, produced short term memory loss so severe that she had to surrender her promising and lucrative career. In her interview with Julia, Jenny found her interesting, apparently quick-witted, and friendly. But as soon as she ventured into what she did yesterday, or last week, or a few hours ago, it quickly became apparent that Julia's was a serious case. Jenny had seen early Alzheimer's patients that had better recall than this woman. Ironically, a trait that would normally make a terrible witness capable of being decimated on cross-examination, became instead an asset.

Next there was Lenny. Dane and Jenny had both interviewed him on several occasions. Lenny was a New York City taxi cab driver, about twenty-seven, with a live-in girlfriend. He had two kids, one by the girl friend, and another from his ex-marriage to a high school sweetheart. Lenny was, simply put, a mess. He drooled when he spoke—that is, when he attempted to speak. His speech had become so slurred that it was hard for an observer to determine whether he had cerebral palsy or was inebriated. He was neither. About two years ago, Lenny had responded to a mail order solicitation promising a more potent, steamy sex life. Like other naturopathic remedies, this one was not regulated by the FDA. Lenny had not noticed or cared when he received a brown bottle listing ingredients like ginseng, yohimbine, and at the bottom, a non-descript drug called PZT. And, of course, he wouldn't have blinked an eye had someone told him that the small, South American manufacturer/reseller had bought a huge lot of the substance from Rowalter Industries, S.A. Within six months after first use, Lenny had experienced heart palpitations and seen his doctor. The doctor ran a few tests, pronounced him healthy, and told him to lighten up his work schedule. Lenny complied, but then began awakening in the middle of the night with his chest pounding and severe headaches. Thirty days later, he could no longer concentrate well enough to drive his taxi, and he filed for social security disability. That case was still pending.

The other case histories were similar, yet different. All involved episodes of rapid, uncontrolled bleeding, manifested in different parts of the body depending on the victim. Yes, that was the word which was to be used by Dane and all the witnesses: "victim." For there had been no doctor and no patient, since PZT was a hard to obtain, non-approved drug. No Physician's Desk Reference contained it, and 99.9 per cent of licensed physicians had never even heard of it. Jenny's job, with the help of a technical assistant, involved placing carefully edited video interviews of each witness on a DVD ROM disc, indexed by digital codes. The technical assistant could then, on the appropriate cue from Dane at the hearing, immediately access an interview by punching into a key board the appropriate alphanumeric code. A second later, the interview would be projected onto a screen at the front of the court room.

Dane, Jenny, Nick and three of the witnesses retired across the street to a mock court room which Jerek Barbour had finagled for them at Salacuse. It was fully equipped with screen, computer console, counsel table, lectern and, should it have been required, a jury box. Dane had never used this particular facility in his years at the firm. In another epoch, before his life had been turned upside down, he would have been impressed, if not awed, by the facility. But he was too far beyond that. He had a job to do, and that was all that mattered now. Get the damned drug approved, reclaim his wife and daughter, and move on with his life. Yeah, that's what he craved: normalcy, predictability. These were now terms that seemed as foreign and unfamiliar to him as the smells and sounds of the intensive care unit where little Natalie lay.

Jenny commenced running the witnesses through their paces. Out of the corner of his eye, Dane could see her prepping the witnesses, seated in the sound-proof witness room in the back.

He began assembling his opening statement notes, which he never really used anyway, except as a prop. He then dress-rehearsed his opening statement, launching into it awkwardly at first, since there was no judge and no jury. Dane picked up steam as he went, though, willing himself to believe the unbelievable: that PZT really did deserve to be approved and be sold in every American pharmacy. He *must* be persuasive, he kept telling himself as he pictured Natalie wrapped up in IV tubes. What choice did he have? He concluded the opening statement in just under twenty minutes. It was a little long, but it would improve with practice.

Next, Dane began calling his witnesses. Jenny trotted out each witness in succession, placed them on the stand, and sat in the back to critique. Dane fired salvos of questions, beginning with simple ones which allowed each witness to tell his story. Sometimes their mere appearance spoke volumes more than words could. He had to lead Lenny like a child, and keep a handkerchief handy to wipe his mouth when he drooled. To adjust for his child-like comprehension level and slurred speech, Dane caught himself having to retrench and slow down several times. He knew, both from the erratic pauses and the quizzical looks that swept over each witness' face without warning, that Jenny was making odd facial gestures and visual cues in response to each twist or turn of their testimony. It would have been most amusing to watch her histrionics, had he not been so immersed in the process himself.

Somehow, in spite of all the fits and starts, they made it through two hours of drill. When the last witness began to stumble over her words to the point that he couldn't make them out, Dane raised his hands in a "T", like a football referee's "time out" gesture. Jenny acknowledged with a relieved smile from the back of the room, and everyone headed to the back of the "courtroom" for a coke break.

"Hey, stud, I heard your opening statement out of one ear. Pretty darn good, I'd say, for a first try." Jenny smiled encouragingly.

"Thanks, Jen." Dane didn't tell her that his stomach had been in knots the entire time.

"What I really need now is something that will convince the Administrative Law Judge to disapprove the damn thing, while making it appear to Rowalter that I pulled out all the stops—gave it everything I had."

"Of course, I'm just brain-storming here, but...what about the stabilizer?"

"Uh huh, what about it?"

"Didn't you say they have Natalie on it?"

"Yes. And–?" His voice trailed off in an exaggerated tone.

"Well, doesn't the existence of a stabilizer presuppose that there is something that needs to be stabilized...that is, that it is currently *un*stable?"

"Obviously."

"Couldn't you show them what a great drug PZT has, all its medicinal uses and such, but then spend the bulk of your time on the stabilizer?"

"Jenny, I know I'm not the brightest lawyer around, but I don't follow. Where are you going with this?"

"Dane, if I were administrative law judge, I think it wouldn't take a whole lot of discernment to figure out that if a drug needed a stabilizer to be safe, I wouldn't want to approve it. It would be something that, in my mind at least, was basically unstable, like uranium or plutonium or something."

Jenny saw a flash of comprehension appear in Dane's tired eyes. But right alongside of it was worry.

"There's only one problem with your idea, Jenny. Right now, I'm the only one who knows about any stabilizer. If I reveal that knowledge to the court, they'll realize what I'm up to in a heartbeat."

"Then put it in your brief."

"What?"

"You heard me. Put it—no—*highlight* it in your brief. The ALJ will have to ask you some questions about it. You'll simply be responding to his questions, and Rowalter need never know."

"And what about the email from Alton?" Dane voiced what they were both thinking.

"What about it? You yourself said we can't use it in the hearing. At least not without jeopardizing Natalie."

"True enough. But now that I know about it, I'll be concealing critical evidence from the government if I sit on it." A look suddenly spread across the lawyer's face, not unlike what must have been on Edison's face when he conceived of the light bulb. "But," Dane continued, "Who says I have to sit on it?" "*So simple, yet so profound. Why didn't I think of it sooner?*" he wondered.

"That's *right*, Dane! The Solicitor General has included a request for emailed data in his discovery requests anyway, and you'd simply be complying with them, just like the rules require. You can fight brilliantly in favor of approval, and still be guaranteed to lose as long as the S.G. has that evidence!"

"Get me a clean disc," Dane ordered, his mouth half-smiling in relief.

"Roger that."

CHAPTER TWENTY-THREE

Jack Heinz heard the phone ring in three crisp bursts. "FBI, Dallas Field Division, James Patterson's office. May I help you?"

"Yes ma'am. May I speak to Agent James Patterson?" Jack was just a bit nervous.

"I'm sorry, sir, but Mr. Patterson is out of town. Can someone else help you?" Heinz had expected this response, of course.

"No ma'am. This is his travel agent. Somehow, there was a mix-up in his flight plans, and we may have given another client his plane reservation and him theirs. We are trying to correct the error before someone is greatly inconvenienced." Jack knew he was making a calculated gamble that Patterson had flown a private airline, not government. "Perhaps you can help us. I show Mr. Patterson on Pan Am flight 793 to Paris outbound yesterday and flight 890 returning on an open-jaw from Rome to Dallas today at 9:05 p.m. Is that correct?"

"Oh, no, sir. Mr. Patterson flew American flight 267 through Philadelphia early this morning. He had a death in his family. Your records are incorrect—he never went to Paris."

"I can't tell you what a relief that is. We handle all his personal flight arrangements, and we just got a call from another client that had James' name on it. Whew! Just to be sure his return arrangements are in order, could you verify those for us?"

"Sure. He's returning on flight 461 from Philadelphia tomorrow—wait a minute. Who did you say this was?" *Bingo.* The girl suddenly woke up to the fact that she had already said way too much. *"Thank you very much, ma'am,"* Jack smiled to himself as he hung up on the non-traceable phone line.

His next call to an American ticket agent confirmed exactly what Jack had theorized. Patterson had boarded neither of the Philadelphia flights, though someone named "James Patterson" had originally held reservations on them. Acting on a hunch, Heinz checked American flights routed to Bolivia and Peru departing early this morning. Fortunately for him, there weren't very many. Jack knew from years of being in the Bureau, and his knowledge of Patterson, that he most definitely wouldn't travel under his own name. He also had a hunch about the name he would use.

"Hello, flight reservations? This is Hockaday Travel, and we're trying to verify that our client, Jonas Worthington, made his flight this morning to La Paz, Bolivia?"

"Let's see...*computer keys clicking*...we show a Mr. Worthington flying out on flight 297 through Caracas, then on to La Paz, arriving around 7:30 a.m. But", the agent sounded suddenly perplexed, "we don't show you as the booking agent."

"Oh," offered Heinz deftly, "that must be because he made a last-minute change in his flight plans. He was originally going to fly through Bogota. He sent us an email to notify us. He is coming back on flight 790, isn't he?"

"No, sir. We don't have a flight 790. He's already airborne on flight 341 arriving at DFW this evening at 8:30 p.m."

Bingo again. His luck was holding...so far.   Heinz glance hurriedly at his watch, which read 11:03 a.m. *"Not much time, and lots to accomplish in the next couple of days,"* Heinz thought urgently. His next stop would be the public library. He arrived thirty minutes later, and managed to hole up in an obscure corner of the second floor. He found a carrel. To his right he placed his laptop and, without bothering to plug it in, logged onto the Wi-Fi network which he'd obtained from the desk clerk. Inside of a minute, he had tapped into several sources cataloguing the world's foremost public and private pharmaceutical firms. A minute later, his monitor displayed complete financial and corporate data on Rowalter Enterprises, in living color. He traced Rowalter's ownership to a certain "HSL Industries Group", a parent corporation with principal offices in Los Angeles. A couple of more clicks revealed a footnote indicating that Rowalter was now wholly controlled by the American company, which had acquired 55% of corporate shares in 2007. In another five minutes, Heinz had located the list of major shareholders, officers and directors of Rowalter Enterprises and saved it to a file. *"So much for basics. Now, for the good stuff,"* thought Heinz. He pulled up the web pages of the New York Times, Chicago Tribune, LA Times, and Dallas Morning News, minimizing each window as he acquired it. Then, he entered each website in succession, pulling up the "Archives" file for each newspaper. Beginning with the New York Times, he performed word searches on all articles three years back using simply the term "Rowalter". Heinz excluded the financial pages from his search—he wasn't interested in stock performance at this point. What he found surprised him. He hadn't expected it to be quite this easy, but there it was, plain as day. A squib from an AP press release appearing in page 51 in the *Times* just last week. The headline read: "Nobel Prize Winning Researcher Takes Own Life". Heinz scanned the brief article, which reported the suicide of distinguished chemist Dr. Norman Holloway. It seems Dr. Holloway had put a gun to his head one evening while seated at his computer. But the significant thing was that, at the time, Holloway had been finishing out a year-long stint working for Rowalter Industries at some remote location in the Rocky Mountains. This fact took Heinz' breath away for an instant, as he downloaded and saved the article. It wasn't every day that your average Nobel Prize winner offed himself. The article didn't say whether Holloway left a note, but Heinz' instincts told him he must have. His search of the *Chicago Tribune* archives gave him no new information, and it was the same for the *Los Angeles Times*. When he got to the *Dallas Morning News*, however, his luck changed. The article appearing a week ago Monday on the second page of the News stated, not surprisingly, that the *Denver Post* had broken the story. "*Simple enough,*" Heinz mumbled to himself as he entered the *Post*'s website. In a few more key strokes he had the article, complete with news file photos of Dr. Holloway. These he printed out, while saving the article to his thumb drive. While there was nothing especially remarkable about Holloway, Heinz considered it an extraordinarily provocative fact that, during the relatively brief period of his life that he'd been a consultant with Rowalter Industries, the good professor had ended his own life. Hungrily, he devoured the *Post* article for every factual tidbit to fill in the gaps in his knowledge. When he'd wrung as much stuff as he could from the article, he jumped onto their website to comb for any back story that hadn't made it into the published article. Sure enough, there was, complete with some helpful biography on the scientist. It seemed Holloway's wife had died a couple of years earlier of cancer. He had no children, was 58 years old, and apparently completed his undergraduate work at USC and at least one post graduate degree at California Polytechnic. Heinz' brow momentarily furrowed. Could Holloway have taken his own life while in a depressed state over his wife's death? The bio indicated that they had been married twenty-five years. *Unlikely*, Heinz almost said it aloud. She had been dead two years at the time of his suicide. He grunted. If he was despondent over her death, he would have done the deed much sooner. No, it had to be something else. Heinz went back to the bio, and thought hard about what might be his highest percentage shot, as the minutes which were flying by.

"Who might he have contacted before his death?" Heinz strove mightily to get inside the dead man's head, and to think like he imagined a scientist would think. Then, seemingly out of nowhere, the answer popped into his thoughts like a light slicing through darkness. *"Of course! I would share it with a colleague. Perhaps another professor or scientist."* But finding the deceased scientist's colleagues would be no easy task, Heinz surmised. With the ticking of the library wall clock sounding like thunder, he reckoned it was time for a personal appearance. He'd reached the limits of what he could accomplish by a computer and public access, at least for the time being. Time now for a little Sherlock Holmes strategy. There was really no substitute for that kind of gum-shoeing when you really need to dig out the hidden kernel of a case. Heinz packed up his laptop and thumb drive and stuffed

them, together with the print-outs, into his briefcase. He willed himself to his feet, and as he did so, felt the dull pain ripple like shock waves down his legs and into his feet. It was a sobering reminder of the reason for his mission, and of the seething fury which drove him resolutely toward his objective. Ignoring the pain, he pushed through the haze of the medications the doctors had him on. Heinz struggled his way to the desk downstairs, and requested the local phone directory from the elderly woman behind the desk. He had his cell phone out and ready as he located the phone number for the airline he normally used, and placed the call. Moments later, he had booked a flight to Los Angeles. In another 2-1/2 hours, he was on the aisle seat of a 767 preparing to take off for LAX. As the flight attendants closed the hatch and ran through their last pre-flight checks, he called the number on Dane Ingersoll's card which he'd pulled from his wallet. He got voice mail. *Probably in trial preparation,"* he reasoned.

"Mr. Ingersoll, this is Jack Heinz. I'm headed out of town to a place I can't discuss at the moment. I will be in touch with you once I get there. I feel like I'm on the scent of a trail." Jack ended the call and returned the phone to his pocket, unwilling to run any further risk of informing others about what he was doing. Who knew how many eyes and ears his former employer had, and where they were?

CHAPTER TWENTY-FOUR

The pale grey of predawn yielded to the first warmth of the sun's rays as grey horizon turned to pink, then orange. A rock had lodged itself uncomfortably under the rolled blanket that Alton used for a pillow, making him wince at the twinge of pain in his neck. He squinted at the rising sun, fervently wishing—like so many other mornings in the Andes—to pretend away his circumstances. He rolled back over, closed his eyes, and told himself it was a dream from which he would soon awaken. But a moment later he felt a hand on his shoulder, shaking him gently. He shivered violently in response, and burrowed more deeply into the sleeping bag for warmth.

"Mr. Dean, we'll ready to leave in about an hour. I'll have breakfast ready in just a few minutes." Alton could not express the feeling that swept over him from hearing the American English, and in Roger's cheerful voice, at that. He rousted himself out of his sleeping bag, which, during the cool Andes night, had developed a fine layer of dew covering its entire top. He felt his thigh again, to make sure the flash drives were still in place. Relieved that they were, he began rolling up the sleeping bag that Roger had kindly lent him for the night. It beat the hell out of sleeping in one of the Aymara huts again. Alton's nose twitched as he smelled...what was it?...A smell that he had almost forgotten could be so wonderful: bacon. He looked up to see Roger with a Coleman camp stove set up on a collapsible table, gas burners glowing. There were two pans—one for eggs, one for bacon. A separate burner held a pot of coffee. The sizzling and popping of the bacon, and the aroma of the coffee mingled with the eggs extinguished the last vestiges of sleepiness and awakened in Alton a voracious hunger.

"Say there, Mr. Dean."

"Call me Alton."

"All right, Alton. You slept pretty soundly, but you are quite a conversationalist in your sleep."

"Oh," Alton froze, yet tried to appear nonchalant. "What did I talk about?" His face felt suddenly warm and flushed.

"It was pretty hard to understand you, and I was trying to catch some winks myself. But I thought I made out something about a 'Dane' and some sort of drug."

"Oh, really? Just the insane ramblings of an overtired American tourist. My dreams, when I have them, never seem to make any sense. Especially to me."

"Yeah, I know what you mean." If Roger suspected anything, he was keeping it well under wraps. "Well, grab a plate and let's get started. There's some bad weather coming in later today, and I want to beat it back to Lima."

Alton tied up the bed roll and, at his host's instruction, stowed it in the open compartment under the wing of the waiting Cessna. Roger had paper plates, napkins, and plastic forks set out by the fragrant food, and he eagerly partook of the first American food he had seen in over a month. They ate in silence, savoring the *huevos rancheros* that Roger had expertly prepared, and watching the sun steadily climb in the Andes sky. From their vantage point in the camping chairs that Roger furnished, they looked down on the valley below and watched the last shadows of night recede into the warm yellow of the morning sun. Despite the striking beauty of the panoramic view, Alton's mind began whirring through the next moves he had to make when he got to Lima. Somehow, he had to accelerate the pace, or else he would never make it in time. There would be, he reminded himself emphatically, no margin for error.

After breakfast, Alton helped Roger break camp, and pack everything securely in the stowage compartment. By now, they could hear the first sounds of activity in the Aymara camp which was just across the ridge from them. Some of the children began to romp and crow with delight as they popped their heads up over the ridge to have another look at the *gringos*. Clearly, everyone knew about Roger's departure, and had been through this event before. Soon, a little crowd began to form within fifty feet of the plane, including the Aymara men and women he had seem yesterday. Roger spotted the wizened old Indian who had been so helpful at the outer fringe, and went out to meet him. He thanked him for his help, and shook his hand—a gesture which seemed foreign to the old man, who stared as he did so. Roger hailed Alton back to the plane, where he'd become nearly invisible beneath a squirming mound of excited Aymara children. In spite of this, Roger managed to say proper goodbyes to several of the Aymara tribesmen and women. About the time Alton navigated back to the plane, Roger had begun entering the cockpit, and gestured to Alton to get up on the wing and enter from the other side. Inside the plane, Alton looked around uncomfortably, nervous at the prospect of flying in something not much bigger inside than a Volkswagen beetle. He fastened the shoulder harness and belt. Roger showed him how to adjust the head phones, and Alton slipped them into place while Roger ran through his pre-flight check list. This done, he cranked on the engine, which sputtered to life with a kick, and Alton felt the vibration run through his body. The earphones crackled to life as Roger announced, "Taxiing down north runway," and then called off some bearing number to no one in particular. Roger executed what Alton thought was a smooth take-off, at least for a single prop plane. About five minutes later, they leveled off at an altitude of 3,000 feet. As they flew beneath the cloud cover which blanketed the sky 500 feet above them, Roger gave Alton a travelogue tour of the surrounding countryside.

"To be safe in the Andes range, you have to fly quite a bit higher than, say, your State of Texas." No further explanation was needed, as Alton peered intently just below the right plane wing to the mountains which, even from this height, appeared steep and treacherous. He mouthed a silent prayer that nothing would disturb the fragile balance between gravity and lift that held their craft suspended between heaven and earth.

"How much longer to La Paz?" Alton yelled over the engine, which seemed necessary even with the earphones on.

"Couple of hours," crackled back Roger, checking the global positioning system instrument attached to the cockpit windshield. "I love this thing," he smiled, as he glanced over at Alton. "Nothin' like the old days. All I do is punch into the GPS the number assigned to the Lima airport on my flight map, and it gives me the bearing to fly. Piece of cake."

With nothing to do for a while but watch the scenery, Alton was alone with his thoughts. He wondered what his next step was when he made it to Lima. He had to bum some money somewhere, somehow, and get on a plane to the states. Alton cursed himself for not memorizing at least one of his credit card numbers. Maybe he could hitch a ride on a military aircraft. *"Right. Sure. In Lima, Peru!"* He nervously fingered the floppy disk which he now carried inside of his belt, beneath his shirt. He would come up with something. *"After all, I've come this far, and I must have been put in this position for a reason."*

An hour and a half later, Roger banked the Cessna left and began a wide circle to bring it around for the descent to Lima. In a valley ahead of him, Alton could see a moderately sized city, with not a few skyscrapers jutting from its nucleus. The cockpit radio crackled to life again. "This is Cessna C-F-4-5-3-L, approximately nine kilometers out, approaching Northwest to Southeast. Calling for landing clearance."

"Roger, Cessna C-F-4-5-3-L," The voice was English tinged with a Peruvian accent. "I'll bring you in before the Piper. Stay at 2200 feet. You should have runway 9, but check with me again as you get closer."

A couple of more exchanges between Roger and the control tower, and they leveled off for final approach. Roger brought the plane down at what seemed to Alton like a pretty steep angle, but he reminded himself this was no Boeing wide body. The airport surface raced up toward them as the landing gear came down. Alton gripped his seat hard, and felt the jolt as the landing gear hit the ground. At least they were on concrete this time rather than a mountain pasture, thank God. After a long run down the half mile runway, the plane's brakes brought them to manageable speed. Roger taxied east to a large lot near a hangar area where a myriad of small planes was congregated. He brought the plane to a halt between a twin-engine Piper and an older model pontoon plane.

"Well, Alton my friend, we made it in one piece. How do you plan on getting to Texas from here?"

"You don't know how much I wish I knew the answer to that question."

"Well, you're in God's hands, because I'm praying for your safe return. Somehow, I know you'll be fine."

Not used to being prayed for, Alton, blushed, but felt good inside that someone cared enough to do something like that for him. "Thanks a lot. I can use all the help I can get."

The men got out of the plane, and started toward the small airport terminal. As they got inside the double glass doors, Roger turned to Alton. "I'm parked in the south lot on the other side of the terminal." He broke into his easy smile. "I wish you weren't in such a hurry. We could have coffee together." He nodded toward the coffee shop, waiting for Alton's response.

"I'd love to. But you're absolutely right. I have...a...er family waiting on me I have to get back to." He had almost let it slip, which was easy to do with Roger. The man had a face that anyone would trust.

Roger reached out to shake his hand, and as he as their firm grips met, Alton felt something in the palm of his hand. He drew it back to see a $50.00 bill, and a small slip of paper.

"What is this for?", Alton said, incredulous.

"Just consider it an investment. It's not much, but I've found that if I sow seed where it's needed, I reap it back tenfold. Not from you, but from elsewhere. You know what I mean?"

Alton could only nod, dumbstruck. Somehow, he not only believed Roger, but felt it was the right thing to do to keep the money. Roger's words made him feel as if he would be violating some cosmic purpose to give it back. He glanced at the folded slip of paper.

"Just my phone number and an email address. Once you get back where you belong and things settle down, I'd like to hear how things came out. I sense that there's a lot more to your situation than meets the eye." He flashed that disarming smile again.

"S-sure. I'll be in touch. A-a-and thanks for the...investment."

With that, Alton turned and headed toward the main ticketing area while Roger meandered through, then disappeared into the crowd. As quickly as he could, Alton found his way to an airport shop where he purchased some packing tape. He then slipped into the men's restroom where he gingerly removed what was left of the tape holding the four flash drives in place—a process not entirely devoid of pain—then reattached them securely in place. He then returned to the ticketing area, with absolutely no clue as to how he was going to get back home.

* * * *

Dane and Jenny bent furtively over the computer screen in the make-shift office on Cadiz Street. Boxes and stacks of paper surrounded them. The computer desk and station were the only semblance of order in the place. The computer beeped to let Dane know it had successfully transferred the first data file linked to Alton's prolific email.

June, the legal temp he had hired for the transition, appeared, seemingly from nowhere, and thrust something in front of him. "Mr. Ingersoll, sir, here is the certified letter you requested me to prepare. You said it was important."

"Thanks, and you're right," Dane said tersely, extracting a flash drive ever-so-carefully from his computer with one hand, while he handed over the certified letter to Jenny with the other.

Jenny scanned the letter hurriedly. "Yep, I'd say that should do it. Do we give this to the government prosecutors?"

"Absolutely not. We're under no obligation to do so, and I'm at least going to make *some* pretense at appearing to represent my client's interests." Dane noticed the temp still standing awkwardly in the same position, holding something in her hand. "Is there anything else, June?" he said, anxious to get on with his preparation.

"Y-yes, Mr. Ingersoll. Your mail has arrived. I put the certified letter from the government on top, along with the fax that came in from them." She thrust the stack of papers and envelopes toward him. Dane took them with trepidation, silently praying for no curve balls this late in the game. His hopes were dashed when he read the letter, which bore the return address of the U.S. Attorney's office in Dallas. It read:

Dear Mr. Ingersoll:

An injunction proceeding has been initiated in Federal Court seeking the immediate cessation of all manufacture and distribution of the drug PZT. Service of a temporary restraining order has already been obtained on your client, Rowalter Industries. An emergency hearing is set for February 3, 2011 at 10:00 a.m.

The fax which the temp had placed directly underneath the U.S. Attorney's letter was from Gary Thompson of Rowalter. It read:

"I just received a set of papers from some damned U.S. attorney telling me the government has obtained a restraining order halting all shipments of our product. I'm also holding another letter from our director of U.S. imports informing me that three shipments of PZT have been seized in El Paso and impounded. What the hell is going on up there??? I'm sure you don't need a reminder of how much is riding on this."

Dane could feel his heart stutter step, but only for a moment. Then his instincts took over. "Jenny," he barked. I want all my evidence up here immediately. Put our witnesses on immediate standby for the trial." *There, he had said it. The word he had longed for; the thing he was good at. No more of this "administrative hearing" crap.* "Call the U.S. Attorney and the ALJ in the approval case and tell them we will need to reschedule the approval hearing—another matter has come up."

"Sure Dane. You realize, of course, that under the ALJ's pretrial order they may dismiss the approval case, rather than grant another continuance of the hearing."

"Absolutely. But that simply cannot be helped. We—that is—Rowalter, is now on the defensive. And we have a federal judge to get ready for."

"What are our chances, Dane?" Jenny asked, wide-eyed.

"At beating the injunction? Three to one against us, at best. At getting Natalie home healthy? Don't ask. Pray."

"I will, Dane. I will."

CHAPTER TWENTY- FIVE

The man in the chair shifted his large frame and let his head flop backward. His eyes rolled back in his head, the hand that had held the two-way radio resting by his side. He began to snore. "*Some bodyguard!*" Susan sneered to herself. She clicked off the TV, stood up and, hands trembling with anger, strode to the kitchen to use the "secure" telephone.

"Hello, Dane? Where did you get this security outfit? And *why*? Can you hear the snoring in the background? Well, get a good earful, because that's the guy that's supposed to be protecting me!" Even as she spoke, the giant hulk of a man awoke with a start, and looked sheepishly in the direction of the kitchen, where Susan stood, just out of sight. She peeked around the doorway corner and, noticing him awake, lowered her voice to a whisper. "This is ridiculous and absurd, Dane! What would happen if someone tried something up here and this defensive lineman was in dreamland? Not that I'm worried, you understand. I think I should be with Natalie, anyway. But how comfortable would *you* feel if the guys who were supposed to be protecting you were sleeping on the job? And when am I going to get to see my baby, anyway?" All of a sudden, Susan felt like crying, something she hadn't planned to do at all.

"Let me talk to him," said the voice on the phone.

Susan, still tearful, got up and walked over to the chair where the big galoot sat watching, nervously. "It's for you," she said, thrusting the receiver in the man's face. Susan returned to her vantage point in the kitchen, where she nursed a half-consumed Pepsi and observed the big galoot.

"...uh, no sir...um-m-m absolutely...Oh, yes Mr. Ingersoll." Susan could hear Dane's voice rising and falling even from ten feet away. The security guard's face reflected embarrassment, and more than a little concern. After a couple of minutes, he handed the telephone back to Susan, accompanied by a penitent "I'm sorry, Mrs. Ingersoll." He checked the clip in his side arm, holstered it, then began speaking into his walkie talkie to check the property perimeter.

Susan took the phone and spoke into it with emotion. "Dane, when are we going to get Natalie home? I can't take another day of this!"

"As soon as I can, Sweetie. I miss her as much as you do, but there's been some recent developments in the case that prevent me checking on her personally. I've got a man on it. And you've been staying in touch with the hospital, haven't you?"

"Every day. But the nurses never tell me anything. All I ever get is 'She's holding even,' or 'There's no change, Mrs. Ingersoll. Dane, I want to *see* Natalie, to *hold* her! I'm cooped up out here until God-knows-when, with no end in sight. Something has got to give before I go crazy."

"I know, Susan. You have every right to be wound up about this. But the people I've had checking Natalie say she's stable, and that's my big concern until we make it through trial. Then we'll find a way out of this mess. We'll take Natalie out of that hospital, and bring her home, and you can start being a Mom to her." Susan heard computer and offices noises in behind Dane's voice.

"But Dane, how long—"

"Not much longer, Babe. Go with me on this one, Okay. Just give me another week, all right?"

No reply.

"All right?" Dane was louder this time.

"Well...I suppose," Susan whispered hoarsely from way back in her throat somewhere. They said their goodbyes and she hung up the phone. The body guards had begun making their evening rounds before retiring for the evening. She heard the crackle of the walkie talkies and the low mutter of men's voices as they exchanged their signals. Weary with emotion, she turned in for the night.

Heinz arrived at the Delta terminal at about 12 midnight on Monday, 10:00 p.m. Sunday, Dallas time. He found a motel next to the airport and checked in for the night. Then he swept the room thoroughly for bugs and, finding none, turned in and drifted quickly into a much-needed deep slumber. The last thing he remembered was dictating a closing day's entry into his cell phone log.

In the morning Heinz rose at five sharp. He felt clumsily around the night stand for his phone. Strange, he thought he'd left it by the lamp, but it was pushed up against the clock. He dismissed it from his mind, and dictated the opening entry for the day. Six o'clock found him sipping coffee at the Waffle House next door, poring over a map of greater Los Angeles, red pen in hand. Despising public transit systems for their utter lack of privacy, Heinz rented a car—a burgundy colored Buick—paying for it in cash. He tucked the map inside his newsstand copy of the *Los Angeles Times,* left a five on the table, and followed the map route he had traced to Pasadena. Heinz had alternate routes planned in case he was tailed, but his repeated checks of the rear-view mirror showed that to be unnecessary. On the front seat, next to his laptop, lay a biographical sketch of Dr. Norman Holloway. Circled in red was his last postgraduate degree, from a school known as University of California Polytechnic at Pasadena, or, more commonly, "UCPC". Cross town traffic was heavy, but he made it to the university by eight without incident. With persistent effort, he found a vacant graduate student slot to park in, laying claim to it with a doctored graduate sticker he placed on the dashboard of the rental.

Heinz locked the Buick, leaving his usual marker in the door hinge: a blade of grass snatched from the nearby lawn. He carried only his attaché, containing the Holloway bio, his laptop, a yellow pad and his cell phone. Next stop was the library, where he figured he could find an internet hook up. After a couple of false starts, Heinz found a smallish library annexed to the graduate college which, he was surprised to note, contained a bank of T-3 internet portals. Furtively, he surveyed the area and, seeing no one, logged onto the internet connection. Fortunately, the person he was looking for was not hard to find. He had pulled up the faculty web page and was delighted to find that each professor had a photo, bio, classes taught, and even a home address. Heinz knew what he was looking for. It had been a scant six years since Dr. Holloway had done advanced post-doctoral work at UCPC, according to his bio. The additional research Heinz had done on the internet revealed work in a curious field that meant utterly nothing to him: polymeric and supramolecular liquids. So, reasoned Heinz, he need only find who taught that course, and hope that it was the same guy who had taught Holloway. *"I mean, how many guys can there be who teach polymeric and supramolecular liquids?"* he mused.

Then, suddenly, he had it. There it was, under "Department Heads": "Dr. Rupert Jenkins, Department of Supramolecular Studies." He saved the page to a file, then went via the site map to the office of the Registrar, where he pulled up class schedules. From there it was a short hop to the courses taught by Jenkins. Sure enough, four days a week, Jenkins taught Polymeric and Supramolecular Liquids. As it happened, today was a Monday, and the class finished at 9:10 in the Owens building. That was a half hour and about five hundred yards away, if he was reading the university map correctly. Heinz wondered whether he should try to buttonhole Jenkins before the class started, or instead sit through the two hour, seminar level class and then approach him. After a moment's thought, he dismissed the idea of approaching him now. There would be too little time to talk, even if he was fortunate enough to catch Jenkins before class. Better to busy himself now, getting his interview organized. Since he really had nothing to go on except Jenkins's former student-teacher relationship with Dr. Holloway, and what with Dane Ingersoll's FDA hearing imminent, there could be no time for beating around the bush. On his yellow pad, Heinz busied himself lining out ten questions he felt were "must asks." If these produced fruit, he'd follow the trail wherever it led; if not, he'd be on his way.

* * * *

"So, Mr. Simpson, where was it you said you were going?"

"Dallas," Alton replied tersely. He fought off the insane urge to smile as he thought of the inspiration for his fictitious name: Homer Simpson.

"Nice town, Dallas." The bewhiskered charter pilot shifted the chaw of tobacco tucked in his cheek. Alton had never thought of Dallas as a "town", but he decided to oblige small talk with his new host.

"Yup. I've always liked it."

"You married?"

"Yeah. Two kids." *"Might as well play it to the hilt,"* thought Alton. "What about you?"

"Married twice. Two kids by the first wife, one by the second. Child support's killing me. That's why I'm working two jobs, including this charter flight service. I could fly for the airlines, but the charter service lets me both run freight for them *and* work my other job. Bottom line is I make more money net to me than I could flying full time as an airline pilot. Not as many benefits, mind you, but great pay. Now, you computer sorts, I guess you pull in a pretty penny, don't you?"

"When business is strong, there's plenty of consulting work. As long as my clients are paying their bills, I do pretty well. It's a living." The deception was starting to get easier now.

"'You fly to South America much?"

"No, this was my first job south of Mexico. With the breakdown of my car and my wallet being stolen, I think I'll make it my last." Alton had grown quite comfortable with the fictitious story, and the words flowed out of him effortlessly.

"Oh, I wouldn't be too quick to judge. We could work something out with your firm and make your next trip a better experience. I fly out of DFW and Love Field all the time."

"Is that so?" Alton still couldn't get over his good fortune at finding a pilot going to DFW that he could, in effect, hitch a ride with.

"Yep. Well, we'll be putting down within the next ten minutes. Make sure you're buckled in." The pilot checked his GPS coordinates, then spoke into the mike. "Dallas control, this is BD 1-5-7 Niner, charter, approaching from south-southeast, requesting landing clearance."

The mike was silent, then crackled to life into Alton's head phones. "Roger, BD 1-5-7, we have you. Hold your altitude and we'll come back to you in five." Even with the headphones, it was difficult to hear over the roar of the two turboprop engines. Alton's stomach began to churn, but not because of the impending landing. Nope, he felt like a seasoned veteran at flying now. He was far more worried, though, about what he was going to do once he got on the ground. They maintained altitude, then trimmed off a couple of thousand feet as they broke through a blanket of clouds spread out beneath them. Abruptly, the sprawling airport known to the world as simply "DFW" came clearly into in view.

"BD 1-5-7 to tower, holding altitude at 2,000 and awaiting your further instructions." The as-yet-anonymous pilot seemed perfectly at ease. Alton fingered the flash drives which, amazingly, remained taped to his legs. They chaffed uncomfortably at the points of contact.

"BD 1-5-7, you are cleared to land on runway 7W. Watch the jumbo jet coming in over your head 1000 feet headed on a bearing 044."

"Roger, tower. Beginning approach."

The pilot lowered the flaps and gradually took the charter plane into a bank left. Next the landing gear came down and Alton both felt and heard it lock into position. The altimeter registered the plane's descent, and Alton watched it spiral downward to an altitude1500, then 1000, then 750 feet. The engines seemed to go into a lower RPM, and the vibration they generated invoked a sympathetic vibration in Alton's face that made his teeth buzz. The plane's rate of descent was not particularly fast, but seemed so because of the sheer size of the airport that seemed to rise up to envelope them. Alton said a silent prayer as he always did on landings, then felt the jolt of the wheels meeting concrete. The turboprop engines reversed speed, and the pilot began applying the brakes. After what felt like about fifteen hundred feet of runway, the plane taxied right to a group of hangars clustered in an area bearing a sign which announced "CHARTER PLANES." The plane slowly rotated to a stop outside of a hangar marked "Viol Charters". The pilot cut the engines, but motioned to Alton to stay seated while he ran through his post flight check. A few minutes later, Alton climbed out of the plane to the tarmac, and nearly let out a whoop of rejoicing like the one he had given after graduation at Harvard. The feeling quickly faded when he realized what still lay ahead of him. Alton was tired down deep in the marrow of his bones. He would like nothing better than to step into a long, hot shower, have a decent meal and sleep for twenty-four hours straight. But he dared not think about such things. Dane Ingersoll's hearing must by now be...he paused and looked skyward, ticking off the days in his mind...oh God...tomorrow! His exhaustion was instantly squelched into some distant recess of his mind as he considered his next move.

"Listen uh...what did you say your name was?"

"I didn't. Samuel Coggins. Call me Sam."

"Er, Sam, I want you to know I am very grateful for the ride, but I have a bit of an emergency and have to be going now. I'd offer you more, but I have to pay cab fare back to Dallas." Alton held out a twenty and a five, keeping his remaining twenty tucked away. His hands broke into a sweat.

Sam waved his hand dismissively. "I enjoyed the conversation—you broke up the boredom. Besides, I had to refuel here anyway on my way to Corpus Christi Put your money away."

"You don't know how appreciative I..."

"Don't mention it. Well, I guess you have to be going, and I have a plane to unload, so 'Hasta la vista.'"

The two men parted without further ado, Sam striding to his hangar, and Alton making a beeline for the terminal with the urgency of a man on a mission. Alton fought hard against the urge to sleep as he entered the huge and bustling terminal. He hesitated momentarily as, incredibly, he passed a bank of old payphones. Four took credit cards but two—which looked in a state of disrepair—took coins, with one occupied. Should he call Dane now? He willed himself to walk to a magazine stand about twenty yards away to get some change. Returning to the pay phone, Alton nearly panicked when he couldn't remember the firm's phone number. Somehow, he pieced it together and fed the coins into the dilapidated phone.

"Salacuse and Lockridge. May I help you?"

"Yes. Dane Ingersoll please...and, hurry, it's important."

A moment's hesitation ensued, and then...

"I'm sorry, but Mr. Ingersoll is no longer with this law firm."

Alton gasped audibly. *"Had they gotten to Dane? Could something have happened to him in so short a time?"*

"Er, um, do you have a new phone number for him?"

"Just a moment please." Another pause. "Yes, sir. It's 2-1-4-5-5-5-4-9-3-8."

Alton thanked her and hung up, squirreling the remaining two quarters from his pocket, and almost dropping them. He threw first one, then the other into the phone and dialed the number hurriedly. It rang four times and—*curse the day*—the *damned voice mail came on.* Alton let the generic factory-recorded message play through and virtually yelled into the phone.

"Dane, it's Alton! I'm back in the States." His voice was breathless. "Call me at my apartment in an hour. If I'm not there yet, just hang up—don't leave a message. I don't know what I'll find when I get there. We need to talk right away!"

Somehow, Alton managed to stumble his way through the north terminal exit. Along the way, he noticed the long lines of passengers being searched by federal baggage inspectors and was grateful he wasn't one of them. *"I probably fit the profile of a terrorist myself,"* he mused grimly. Alton wasn't sure whether his filthy, stinky clothes and disheveled hair and beard provided him the perfect disguise—something he fervently hoped—or whether it was like having a target painted on his back. Once he reached the sidewalk on the terminal's north side, he hailed a cab that was just dropping off a couple of businessman types. Alton collapsed gratefully into the empty back seat and began gulping out staccato directions to the driver.

"Greenville & Lovers Lane, Dallas. And I only have twenty-four dollars," Alton fibbed. Can we make it for that?"

"Yeah, sure," the driver replied in the clipped accent of someone from India or perhaps Pakistan. As they pulled away from the curb, Alton did a 360-degree visual scan of the area to see if he was being followed. No one seemed to be looking his direction, but he kept a wary eye on the rearview mirror just the same. As soon as they hit Interstate 635 off the north airport exit, the monotonous hum of the taxi set in and, in spite of himself, he began to doze off.

Heinz glanced at his watch. It read 8:45. Less than half an hour to go until Jenkins' class ended. Time was precious, and he felt like a caged cat with nothing to do. He closed his laptop and placed it in his attaché, then slid the little reporter-sized spiral notebook into his coat pocket. He was ready. *"Might as well see what good ol' Jim Patterson is up to,"* he thought, wryly. He exited the library to find less conspicuous surroundings from which to make a phone call. The walk to the Owens building was short, wending through a heavily treed park-like area en route. He arrived at the two-story brick building at 8:50, and satisfied himself that he could easily find Dr. Jenkins' classroom. Then he backtracked to the park-like area and found an empty bench. He surveyed the area and saw no one but a group of students at least a thousand yards off. Perfect. He pulled his secure cell phone out of his pocket and began dialing a number from memory. It answered on the second ring.

"Hello."

"Reggie?"

"Who's this? Jack—is that you?"

"Who do you think it is, you ol' grizzly?"

"I thought that was your voice! How're you doin'?"

"'Depends on your point of view. Pretty good, I guess. I've retired from the Bureau."

"You what?"

"You heard me."

"How come? You were always a Lifer."

"I don't have time to explain now, Reg, but let's just say an occupational injury sidelined me."

"I'm dying of curiosity. We've got to get together."

"Oh, we will, sometime soon. But, listen—I need a favor."

"Name it."

"You mean it?"

"Of course I mean it. You and I go way back, and God knows you've gotten my ass out of a crack more than once. What's up? D'ya want me to bug the Pentagon or something?" Reggie chuckled.

"Actually, you're not too far off." Heinz paused to gather himself. "Reggie, do you remember Jim Patterson?" There was silence for a few seconds.

"Was that the guy who was at Quantico with us in ITU, and then went to DC for a while?"

"That's the one. Organized crime training. He got a cushy assignment to the Washington bureau as an intelligence analyst right out of the Academy."

"He was a bright one, if I recall. A real driven fellow. What's he doin' these days?"

"That's what I aim to find out."

"What're you drivin' at, Jack? He's still a Fed, isn't he?"

"Oh yeah. He's running a special investigation out of the Dallas field office. From what I've heard, it's a pet project of Director Stockman, who's pulling the strings. But I think Patterson has taken a turn."

"You mean...(*long pause*)...on the take?" The voice became a loud whisper.

"That's my hunch."

"That's mighty serious stuff, Jack. 'You got any proof?"

Jack scanned the area where he sat once more, and satisfied that no one was near, launched into the entire story. He told of the car explosion in Fort Worth, Rowalter's drug peddling, Natalie Ingersoll's addiction, and Professor Holloway's suicide. Within twenty minutes he had brought Reggie fully up to speed. When he was finished, Jack heard a long, low whistle.

"I've heard some crazy stories since I left the Bureau, but that...*that* tops them all. So, you suspect Patterson, huh?"

"Yeah, and I can't put my finger on exactly why. But ever since the car bomb...You know, Reggie, when the Bureau puts a car out there, it's clean. And no one had access to that car but Patterson's people."

"I agree. It would seem no one else could have done it. But why Patterson? What would he have to gain by taking a car out and a couple of agents with it?"

"I'll tell you what. If he's in thick with the very folks he's supposed to be protecting Ingersoll from, he has to make it look like there's one or two things out of his control. You know, if only to throw people off his trail. If everything goes a little too perfect, it's going to seem way too convenient whenever folks come around asking questions about him and Rowalter. This way he can act like he was doing his best job, but that, in spite of his efforts, the bad guys hit back."

"All right, Jack. It's a bit of a reach, but I'll go with you that far. But tell me this: Why would Rowalter ever want to pull something like that in the first place? I mean, trying to kill or maim the wife of the *very lawyer* they've hired to get the drug FDA approved doesn't sound like the brightest strategy in the world. Nor does administering an addictive drug to the newborn child of that same lawyer."

"Conceded. But, you must remember a couple of things. First, it probably wasn't Rowalter, as I said. They may not even have instructed Patterson to do it as a ruse. I'll put my money on a bet that he did it totally on his own, in the misguided belief that it would make it look like Rowalter were the bad guys. Second, Rowalter does have a twisted reason to be angry at Dane Ingersoll. He dug up some nasty stuff on them and then tried to withdraw from the case, like I told you. They have a reason to remind him of both their power, and of their resolve to see this thing through. And Patterson would be well aware of that if he were in cahoots. So, he'd simply set things up to make it look as though Rowalter were sending off a warning volley."

Reggie snorted. "Some 'warning'! To hear you tell it, it was a damned close call."

"Tell me about it," Heinz said, wincing with pain as he shifted his weight on the park bench.

"So, Jack. This is all very interesting, but why the call? Why me?"

"I think you know why, my man. I now have a deep, personal interest in this case, and I need your help."

"I know I owe you, Buddy. But I'm just a private investigator. No federal badge anymore, remember?"

"That's true enough. But both you and I know you're still the best in the business. What I need is a guy to search Patterson's place while I'm out here in California."

"Are you out of your mind? I can't search the home of an FBI bigwig. I may be good, but I'm not stupid. Besides, I'd kind of like to live into my old age, if that's not asking too much."

Heinz decided to alter his approach. "Gosh, Reggie, I never knew you to be afraid of anyone, least of all an FBI Washington jock. I suppose I'll just have to get someone else."

"Hold on, Jack. That mind game thing won't work with me. Anybody in the Bureau, let alone someone at Patterson's level, is going to have his house locked down tighter than Fort Knox, with surveillance that is world class."

"Maybe; maybe not. Either way, I'm going to have to get it done, and I figure it might as well be you. After all, you are the best there is."

The line fell quiet. "All right Jack, you know I'm not one who forgets a favor. If it weren't for you stepping between me and a bullet a few years back, I wouldn't be here. But Geez.... "

Heinz still recalled vividly the drug raid on the Venezuelan cartel in New Orleans back in 1986. He was gratified to know that his old friend's memory of the life-altering event hadn't diminished. Still, he admitted to himself it was indeed a tall order he was asking.

"I haven't checked with Ingersoll, but I'll see if I can scare up some expense money to help out."

"Gee, thanks."

"Don't mention it," Heinz side stepped the sarcasm. "Oh, I almost forgot. I need you to check on this little girl at a certain hospital. Natalie Ingersoll."

"The daughter of Dane Ingersoll, the Dallas attorney you mentioned."

"It's good to know you're listening. You always were a good one with detail.

"Flattery will get you nowhere, Jack. Just give me my assignment."

Heinz proceeded to give Reggie all the information he had on Natalie, which was quite a bit, followed by a condensed dossier on Patterson which was somewhat trivial in comparison. He then left him his own secure cell phone number. They chatted about old times for another ten minutes, swapping war stories and discussing family. It turned out that Reggie now had a rather large private investigation firm, with several ex-FBI working on staff and a rather select clientele. Heinz liked the sound of that; he could use the contacts. He ended the call, then glanced at his watch, which now read 9:08. Pocketing his phone, he retraced the steps he made before the phone call, back to the Owens building, and took the stairs two at time until he reached the second floor, panting heavily. He located the seminar class room, just in time to be jostled about by throngs of graduate students that came gushing through the door and into the hallway. When the doorway finally cleared, he stuck his head in tentatively, and noticed a balding man packing up his briefcase. The man must have felt Jack's gaze, because he turned and looked up, peering over the rims of his glasses.   *"Probably thinks I'm a student."*

"May I help you?

"Yes...or, at least I hope so. My name is Jack Heinz." Heinz, to be safe, punctuated the announcement by flashing his FBI badge. "You are Dr. Rupert Jenkins, I trust?"

"Is there..." the Professor blinked nervously at the badge, "some kind of problem?"

"You might say that. I am investigating the death of one certain Dr. Norman Holloway. You knew him?"

The professor's eyes grew profoundly sad. "Yes, I knew him. We all knew him. Such a brilliant man, and such a tragic loss. Do you know anything about why he took his own life?"

"Actually, I was sort of hoping you could tell me that."

"I haven't seen Dr. Holloway since he was a student in my doctoral level class five or six years ago. The only contact I've had with him is..." Dr. Jenkins paused, struggling hard to keep his composure.

"I'm sorry, Doctor Jenkins. Take your time."

"Yes, of course. I meant to say, the only *personal* contact I've had with him. I received a very strange email message from him on my home computer last Sunday—the very same day I read in the paper about his suicide. I had just returned from my vacation, so it appeared his message had been on my computer for several days and I simply hadn't had time to check it." He paused and looked at Heinz quizzically, as if to inquire whether he thought this fact was significant.

"Go on."

"Well, naturally I opened the email. The text was very odd, indeed. It read like some sort of confession, only—he sounded like he was halting his work because...because he'd learned that it was being used for the wrong purposes."

"That is very interesting. May I— "

"—And there was an attachment to the email containing organically based chemical equations."

The man had his attention now. "Doctor Jenkins, this is more important than you can possibly know. Do you still have the email?" He held his breath, praying for the right answer.

"Why, yes. Yes, I do. I backed it and the equations up to my hard drive. I suppose I did this because it seemed so eerie. Here was a distinguished former student who I hadn't seen in years, sending me a seemingly posthumous email. I had just read of his horrible death when I opened it." He hesitated, then asked the obvious: "Do you think it was some sort of...suicide note?"

"That's a distinct possibility, professor."

"The equations are quite different than anything I've seen before. Unfortunately, Dr. Holloway isn't here to shed light on them."

"That's certainly regrettable. I wonder if we might have a look at the email." It was a more a statement than a question.

"Of course. Anything that will help in your investigation."

"Are you available now?"

"I don't teach another class till this evening, and I live just a few blocks away. I'd be more than pleased to have you look at it. Anything at all that I can do to help..."

"Consider your offer accepted."

CHAPTER TWENTY-SIX

The Neonatal Unit of East Dallas Medical Hospital was dark and still, but for the eerily rhythmic sounds of the respirator units and the hum of the fluorescent lights. It was early morning: 7:00 a.m. to be exact. The change of the nurse shift had yet to occur, and the one nurse who had held down the fort since 11:00 the night before looked, to the FBI agent at least, bone tired. He studied the nurse's bleary eyes as they strained to focus on the screen where she entered progress notes on the twenty-two frail infants under her care. The only reason he was able to notice such detail without nodding off himself was the remnant of thick, strong coffee in the mug which sat on the floor below his chair. It was the agent's fourth since midnight. He had asked that his chair be placed in a corner of the room somewhat removed from the incubators but with a good view of them. The staff had obliged him. He had opened the top button of his obligatory starched white shirt, loosened his neck tie, and hung his suit jacket over an unused IV unit. He forced his eyes to scan the room in a conscious effort to stay awake for the last thirty minutes of his shift.

Unnoticed by the agent, a man dressed in light blue scrubs shuffled up the corridor toward the double doors of the Unit, pushing before him a shiny stainless-steel cart carrying various and sundry hospital supplies. As he pressed the button and the doors parted, the agent looked sharply in his direction, riveting his gaze on the man's face, or at least what could be seen of it. He glanced at the nurse for any look of recognition, but she barely looked up from her charts, then sullenly returned to her work. To be safe the orderly nodded briefly in her direction anyway, and then continued along a deliberate path toward two supply cabinets in the corner. He arrived at the cabinets, opened them, and slowly and methodically unloaded the supplies, carefully placing them in organized rows on the cabinet shelf. Satisfied that the orderly was no different that the many he had seen doing the same thing during his stint in Neonatal, the agent went back to scanning the room. This fact did not escape the notice of the orderly, nor did the fact that to the orderly's right only a few feet lay Natalie Ingersoll, resting peacefully in her incubator. Her eyes were closed, her breathing frequent yet calm, and tubes and wires seemed to protrude from virtually every part of her frail little body. With the bottom shelf of the cart still full of supplies to be unloaded, the orderly turned his back to the agent, reached in his scrub pocket and extracted an object about the size and shape of a safety pin. He spotted a stuffed panda bear which was smiling down at Natalie from the adjacent window sill. In a matter of five seconds, he grabbed the panda, shoved the tiny object into its nose, and returned it to its resting place. He then resumed unloading the cart, stealing a sidelong glance at the agent. The man's head had nodded downward, his chin resting on his chest. Only when the orderly closed the supply cabinet doors did the noise rouse the agent, who looked around the room as if embarrassed. His work finished, the orderly nodded at the preoccupied nurse and shuffled out of the room the way he had come. Once in the hallway, he pushed the cart into another room an*d stepped into the nearest restroom. There, he hastily shed his scrubs, revealing street clothes underneath. He pulled a digital video receiver out of his pocket, looked at it, smugly satisfied at the clear, wide-angle image of Natalie's incubator and the surrounding area. *"This should do very nicely,"* he mused, a smile crossing his lips. He then returned the receiver to his pocket, and vanished from the hospital as quickly as he had appeared.

* * * *

The office which Dane Ingersoll now called home was quiet. Gone was the hum of daytime activity, with secretaries and paralegal temps bumping and jostling each other in a futile attempt to avoid the stacks of evidence, briefs and motions. What remained was the lone figure of the wiry attorney, his sleeves rolled up, hunched over a laboriously penned response to the temporary injunction that had been sought by the United States, and ordered by a federal judge against Rowalter Industries. Jenny glanced up from the make-shift desk where she was completing the cataloguing of exhibits, just in time to witness Dane's head nodding forward, then collapsing onto his folded arms. The man was clearly exhausted, and she hadn't the heart to wake him. The thermostat from the furnace in the run-down building was again stuck in the "on" position, to which Dane's sweat-soaked shirt and absent necktie bore testimony. Jenny rose, and walked quietly over to Dane's desk, where he had begun to snore. Impulsively, before she had time to develop conscious thought about what she was doing, she bent over and pressed her lips gently against his. Her shoulder-length hair fell loose upon his chest. Dane stirred and, she thought for a moment, his lips responded to her kiss. Was he dreaming, or awake? Long forgotten feelings rushed through her body in a torrent—prom night, Dane's twenty-two-point all-time high scoring basketball game, the unforgettable rendezvous behind the stadium on the practice field. But the feelings she had now were different, deeper, less girlish. She fought with herself inwardly. With a lingering glance at the closed eyes and the face resting peacefully in the crook of his arm, Jenny stood and walked slowly back to her desk.

"Wake up, sleepy head," she said. "I think it's time to head home." Dane barely stirred. Walking back to his desk, she gave his arm a tug.

"C'mon, Dane. We can't stay here all night. You'd best get home and get a good night's sleep. We've got that injunction hearing day after tomorrow, and you can't afford to be without your rest."

Dane stirred, then groggily raised his head. His hair looked just exactly like he'd just gotten out of bed, and Jenny laughed at the sight. Dane squinted through bleary eyes at his watch, but before he could focus them, Jenny announced, "It's 1:00 a.m. for Pete's sake. Enough is enough. Let's get out of here." Dane didn't attempt to argue, so she knew he was tired. She helped him assemble his briefcase, outline and exhibits, then stuff them into two giant catalogue cases. They got them on a hand truck, turned out the lights, and beat a hasty retreat.

* * * *

Alton had the cab driver drop him a block away from his apartment. He slipped out of the cab furtively, stuffing a twenty into the driver's hand before he could change his mind and grab it back again. That left him twenty-four bucks to his name. He decided to walk to his place by a circuitous route, and hung a left at Waltham instead of going straight down Wisteria as usual. He took a couple of more turns, and approached his apartment building from the rear. So far, so good. Nothing appeared unusual, just some street workers jack hammering near a sewer line. He hid out near the shrubbery which wrapped around the back of his building, and peered around the corner to make sure no traffic was coming. At precisely the right moment, Alton dashed like an Olympian sprinter to the front door. In another moment, he was pulling open the massive glass doors trimmed with ornate brass, then inside the foyer looking squarely at the attendant. The attendant's face evinced, first shock and surprise, then a sneer.

"What are you doing on this property, may I ask, sir?"

Without a shred of patience left in his being, Alton shot back," It's Alton to you, Jerry. And if it isn't too terribly much to ask, I'd like to get into my apartment."

A look came over the black attendant's face that could only be described as other-worldly, his eyes as big as saucers. "Alton D-Dean?" he asked, slowly and deliberately.

"None other than. Now, I need a shower, a change of clothes and a myriad of other rather basic things, so would you mind letting me into my apartment? I seem to have lost my keys."

"S-sure, Mr. Dean." Jerry placed his face within an inch of Alton's, the more closely to inspect it beneath the layer of caked-on dirt. He appeared to stop breathing for a moment. Then, reluctantly satisfied Alton's claim was truthful, backed away to a more appropriate distance. "But, Mr. Dean, your apartment...that is, well—"

"Well, *what*? I don't have all kinds of time!"

"Your apartment is...well, not available anymore."

"What d'ya mean? *You rented it out*?"

"N-not exactly. There was a fire."

"A *what*?"

"A fire, a very bad fire, Mr. Dean. It destroyed your apartment, and smoke damaged the ones on either side of yours too, before they got it under control. The police was out too, 'cause they knew you were missing. Everyone thought that with you missing and the fire and all, that you were dead for sure. The police had crime scene tape up and everything. I think they've still got that whole section of the floor sealed off. They've moved some of the other residents to other apartments while they check things out." Jerry's eyes had melted into a mixture of disbelief and compassion.

An uncontrollable shiver started at the nape of Alton's neck and ran down his spine. He tried to utter words, but they got stuck down deep somewhere in his chest. Something akin to grief engulfed him. For a couple of interminable moments, he thought he would sink to his knees and break into unashamed, body-racking sobs. *"No,"* he thought. *"They must not have their way!"* Summoning all his strength, Alton's despair was transformed in an instant into uncontrollable rage.

"Jerry, I need change for a dollar." The words came through clenched teeth with a subhuman growl.

Jerry, his face still marveling at the filthy figure standing before him, dug in his pocket and produced four quarters. He refused Alton's proffer of sweaty, wadded up dollar bill with a wave of his hand, and handed him the quarters.

"Mr. Dean, I'm sure we could come up with a place for you to stay temporarily. Why, I could even put you up in my apartment—"

"Thanks, Jerry, but that won't be necessary." Alton had already turned and headed toward the lobby pay phone—one of the few still functional in the city. He pulled from his pocket the piece of paper that bore Dane's new office phone number. Seconds later, Dane's voice penetrated the haze that now enveloped Alton. The voice sounded surreal, even other-worldly, but Alton had grown to accept such momentary departures from the normative and predictable. He wasn't even sure what words the voice spoke. Like Alice in Wonderland, anymore, nothing was quite what it seemed.

"Dane, is that you?" *One can't be too careful*, thought Alton. *After all, it could be an impostor.*

"That's what I asked you! You answer first. Is this really Alton?"

"You bet your bippy it's Alton! Um, listen Dane— there isn't much time. I've got to see you right away."

"Sure, Alton. A-a-re you all right? Did they hurt you? Where are you?"

"Whoa, slow down there, Counselor. There will be plenty of time to answer the first two questions later on. But the answer to the last one is: at my apartment. Can you pick me up?"

"Sure. I'll be there in 15 minutes."

"Dane—don't hang up!" Alton's voice dropped abruptly to a course whisper. Listen: I'm a wanted man. Certain people want me dead. Don't pick me up on the street. In the alley, out back down toward the corner, at Vinyard Street."

"Roger that. I'll be right there."

Alton cradled the phone and, with a new surge of energy coursing through his frazzled body, cut catty corner across the marbled floor of the apartment building to the door which exited onto the alley. He cracked the door a bare half inch, just enough to peer through. There were hedges out there but, he firmly told himself, he would not set a foot outside until he knew Dane should be at the corner. That, he calculated, wouldn't be for at least ten minutes. While the time ticked ponderously away, he occupied his mind dreaming up creative ways to torture Señor Betaña and Ramos. When it seemed as though enough time had expired, he flattened his body and slid through the door. He kept his back, arms and legs up against the high stucco facade of the apartment building, staying in the shadows afforded by its towering height. He cloaked himself wherever possible with the trees and shrubs which bordered both sides of the alley. In a few minutes, he reached the corner. He leaned against the leeward side of an oak tree, taking care not to venture into the open intersection ahead. He couldn't have timed it any better, for in an instant the familiar black Beemer pulled up to the light at Vineyard Street. Before the car could slow to a complete stop, Alton dashed from his protective cover, flung the door back, and dove in next to Dane.

Dane accelerated quickly, and checking his rear view, snaked through a series of lane changes and turns that would test the stomach of an astronaut. It wasn't until he pulled out on a straightaway and was convinced that they weren't being followed, that he finally turned to look at Alton. His jaw dropped and his eyes seemed to Alton to grow visibly bigger.

"I must be quite a sight, huh, Dane?"

"You could say that...yeah. I'm sorry to react that way, Alton. Hey, buddy, it's just great to have you back. Until we got your little mystery email package, we all thought you were a goner."

"You don't know how close I came to being one. There will be time to fill you in on the details later. Say," Alton glanced nervously around the car, "Have you had this swept for bugs?"

"As a matter of fact, I have. Several times."

"Good. Did you look at the flash drives?"

"Yes, many, many times. How in the world did you get—?"

Alton didn't allow him to finish. "Never mind how I got it, just be thankful that I did. What are you going to do with the information? Am I too late?"

"Well, in the order you asked: we're sitting on it; we'll probably use it in the hearing, but I'm not sure how; and no, you're not too late, but you managed to cut things awfully close." Dane's clumsy attempt at humor fell flat. "A lot has happened since you were here. We have postponed the hearing for FDA approval twice. But now the Feds are on the offensive.

They've brought a full-scale injunction proceeding, and the hearing is on the 3rd at 10:00 a.m. It's big—real big. This thing should tell us if PZT can be distributed for sale, or shut down at least until the approval hearing can go forward. We should be able to fry them pretty good with the stuff you got us. You don't know how much we appreciate it." Dane deliberately omitted anything concerning Natalie—Alton had enough to contend with as it was.

"Don't mention it; you could say that I had nothing better to do. Listen, Dane, on another subject. I need a place to stay. After I escaped, the Rowalter boys thought it would be fun to torch my apartment."

"Do what?" Dane nearly ran off the road, then steadied himself.

"You heard me. They torched my apartment, and I can't even go up on that floor. I'm told that an arson investigation is in progress."

Dane struggled for words. "A-are you sure it was them?"

"Well now, let me think. Only my apartment was destroyed, the rest of the building is untouched, and it just happens to coincide with my kidnapping and later escape. What do *you* think?"

"You're right, of course. 'Just making sure. Listen Alton, you can stay at my place, such as it is. I'm keeping Susan elsewhere, for obvious reasons, so don't mind the mess. I'll get you home so you can clean up, get something to eat, and get a change of clothes. You're about my size, so feel free to grab anything you need out of my closet. For now, though, just get some rest. I'm going to need everything you can give me for the hearing."

"You can count on it. And thanks for the help." He had barely finished the words when Alton leaned his head back, and was snoring away by the time Dane hit the next traffic light. Dane suspected that Alton was going to remain that way for a good little while.

CHAPTER TWENTY- SEVEN

"Over there, on the cul-de-sac," Dr. Jenkins gestured to the two-story house with the nearly all glass front. Heinz wheeled the Buick around to the left, tracing the curb of the sidewalk and coming to rest in front of the residence. The neighborhood was quiet as Jenkins swung open the front door and bid Heinz to enter. Inside, the house design was contemporary, with crisp, modern lines leading from the terrazzo tiled foyer into a hallway on the right. Heinz followed his host around the first corner in the corridor, and narrowly missed stepping on the tail of a charcoal colored cat who scampered out of the way as he did so.

"Don't mind Midnight," muttered Jenkins," the computer is in here. And so it was—an impressive late model Apple, Heinz noted, the choice of scientists. The desk was neatly arranged, and Dr. Jenkins reached gingerly to open a drawer to the right of the keyboard. "I thought this might end up being valuable, so I backed it up onto a thumb drive. But the original email is also on the hard drive. Here, I'll show you." He clicked the email icon on his desktop, and two clicks later, he had the email open for Heinz to read. Heinz quickly absorbed the email portion, which began:

"Today, at the lab, for the very first time, I became aware that my energies had not been expended on the humanitarian objectives which I had heretofore assumed."

The email continued in the vein of what was obviously the confession of a man who felt the need to purge his soul. "What about the attachment?" queried Heinz.

"That is the most remarkable part of all." The professor moved his cordless mouse over the

attachment noted at the top of the email and clicked on it. A huge spread sheet unfolded across the screen which contained what, to Heinz at least, appeared to be page upon page of undecipherable gibberish. As a "C" student in high school chemistry, Heinz had barely gotten by with the help of his lab partner. The equations might as well have been hieroglyphics lifted from King Tut's tomb.

"Uh, pardon me, Prof," Heinz began, embarrassed, but could you give me a hand with what all this means?"

"Why, certainly, at least in broad terms." Dr. Jenkins handed Heinz a print out of the attachment he extracted from his briefcase. "This is the cataloguing of an organic molecular 'meltdown.' In layman's terms, it shows what appears to be a healthy organic compound, probably from a living organism, that has begun to mutate into many variant forms. While there is no time line attached to this chemical progression, I would make an educated guess that the mutation seems to be quite rapid." He paused, peering more closely at the bottom lines of the second page of formulae. "And...I just now caught this...by about the fiftieth mutation, some rather toxic, non-organic compounds have begun to appear. This is most interesting, most interesting indeed." the Professor mused aloud, rubbing his chin as if he was viewing some major new discovery.

"What did you know about the dearly departed? Was he eccentric, or given to—"

"If what you're driving at is whether Dr. Holloway had all his marbles, to use the vernacular, he was well grounded in reality. He was probably saner than you or me."

"I was hoping you would say that. Do you mind if I take these materials with me?" The question was merely a formality.

"Oh, please do. That's why I saved them."

"I have one other great big favor to ask."

* * * *

Reggie Andrews had placed several exploratory phone calls to Patterson's house from random telephones over the last twelve hours. Based on the information provided by Jack Heinz, he was pretty certain the agent was still out of the country, but *"One can't be too careful about these things,"* he thought, as he cased out a three-block radius surrounding Patterson's house. Reggie was neither foolish nor reckless enough to try the most reliable method of all— a hard wiretap on the phone line. Not only was it likely to be detected by an agent as good as Patterson, but there was "just a slight problem with a wiretap with no court order, and some major pen time," as he had told his wife when he left the house. It was now 3:00 a.m., and Patterson was due to arrive late this morning, according to Heinz. "Well, it's now or never," muttered Andrews, wincing painfully at the thought of casing out, let alone searching, a veteran Bureau agent's castle. At the steering wheel mutely sat Rick Hennings, junior partner in Andrews & Hennings Investigators, LLC. On this job, Rick was to speak only when spoken to. The panel van had front and rear windows only, and bore the sign "Henderson Plumbing Supply", with a large pipe wrench logo painted in red on both sides. As they drove without headlights or running lights, Reggie nervously watched Rick park the van about five hundred yards down the alley running behind Patterson's house, facing in its direction. This was the plan they had rehearsed, but actually executing it placed all Reggie's senses on edge, like a stag in the forest on opening day of hunting season. Reaching into the equipment bag beside him, he withdrew a long-range thermal infrared camera—the same type used against Al Queda in Pakistan. He positioned the camera, powered it on and set the rangefinder. The view which materialized on his flip-out screen glowed reds, oranges and yellows from various household appliances and heat-producing objects. To his great satisfaction, however, Reggie noted no moving, breathing beings, whether human or animal. He flipped the screen back flush and returned the camera to his bag. Restarting his car but running with headlights off, Rick did a U-turn and exited the block, turned left, then drove down the adjacent street. He brought the van to a halt, roughly parallel to the spot where Patterson's house was located. To any casual observer, his was simply a plumbing supply company van parked in front of an employee's house for the night. There were no street lights to illuminate the area, and the moon, as forecasted, was almost completely obscured by clouds. Exiting the van, Reggie glided silently on foot down to the end of the block, circling back up the alley which ran directly behind Patterson's house. He was dressed entirely in black, from the running shoes on his feet to the baseball cap on his head. Though he wore a walkie talkie on his belt which matched the one

Rick had in the van, he maintained absolute radio silence for the time being.

Dressed in complete black and moving with the panther-like stealth of the ex-Navy SEAL he was, Reggie approached the subject's back yard deliberately. Peering through small gaps in the privacy fence, he did a visual check for animals. Finding none, he trained a telescopic surveillance microphone on the home to detect any unusual activity. The hypersensitive mike transmitted back only low-level noise probably associated with wall clocks and the refrigerator compressor. Andrews pocketed the device, took a deep breath, set his jaw, and whispered to himself, *"Well, here goes nothing. Patterson, this had better be worth it!"* He flattened his body and silently rolled over the top of the fence. His profile he kept sleek and low as he dropped noiselessly to the pool deck, landing in a crouched position. Immediately, he dropped to his belly and shimmied military style across the deck to the back landscape. His eyes scanned the back yard rapidly. He knew very well it would be impossible to see any active infrared security system, but there was no sense in taking any chances. When he reached the patio door, Reggie knew he had to make a choice. Clearly, he couldn't cut any wires leading into the home. That would-be suicide, since in even the most basic home security system would then trip an audible or silent alarm and electronically notify the police. No, he would have to go through a door or through glass. Glass entry was usually less risky, because no circuits had to be broken. But Reggie knew it wouldn't insulate him from an active infrared alarm once he made it inside. He trained his night vision binoculars on the patio door. The door had a large deadbolt on it. *"That makes the decision easy,"* he thought, as he crept behind the bushes to the nearest large window to the right. He extracted from his pocket a small glass cutter and a heavy magnet. Before he began, however, he checked for concealed circuitry in the glass itself. There was none. Moving swiftly and precisely, he etched around the perimeter of a small framed section of the window. Using a rubber suction cup in his other hand, he applied gentle pressure to the glass until it stuck firmly, then pulled, while re-tracing the outline of the etching. The glass came loose with a pop, and Reggie scooted the rectangle out of sight underneath the shrubs. Slipping a tiny penlight from his shirt pocket, he illuminated the inside sill area near the window latch, and located the magnetic contact for the security system. He then placed his stronger magnet carefully next to the weaker one in the security contact, and attached it to the sill with pliable adhesive. With the contact safely neutralized, he reached his other hand through the window, disengaged the window latch and slid the entire window fully upward. Reggie paused, listening carefully for any sign that the alarm had been tripped. He heard nothing, and his equipment showed no evidence of a silent alarm being transmitted. He slithered through the window. The room was completely dark, but silhouetted shapes of gray in the blackness and the hum of a compressor told him he was in the kitchen. Flattening himself against the wall, he peered through the night vision glasses again, and surveyed the upper corners of the room. In one corner, directly above what he surmised was the refrigerator, was a mounted device no more than four inches long. It emitted a dim, LED glow. He cursed when he saw it, because it made his job only that much harder. The field of view of the infrared device seemed to cut a swath along the middle of the kitchen floor, but also came perilously near to the window through which he'd just entered. There was only one way to deal with such a sensor, and that was to, in effect, defeat its ability to "see" infrared movement. This Reggie accomplished by utilizing another handy military device. He trained it on the infrared sensor, neutralizing its detection capability. Next, he used a pinpoint laser to burn its circuitry, putting it completely out of commission.

Andrews keyed the walkie talkie, and whispered hoarsely into it. "Rick–I'm in and moving through the kitchen. I've neutralized the perimeter alarm and am taking out the motion detectors as I find them. Check back with me in 15 minutes if you haven't heard."

"Roger that. I've got you covered."

As Reggie moved to the kitchen doorway, he could see into the next room, which appeared to be a living room. Through the night vision glasses, he could see a hallway beyond. He would love to just flip on some lights—it would save so much time—but nothing would be more foolish. There must be absolutely no evidence of an intrusion for the neighbors to talk about—or for some hidden camera to capture. With the skills he had learned first in combat and then honed in the Bureau, Reggie glided seamlessly from room to room, neutralizing the motion detectors as he went.

He saw nothing particularly suspect. But then, he found himself in a room that had the smell and feel of a study. There was a good-sized desk and chair, shelves stocked with books, and stacks of papers.

"Rick," Reggie spoke staccato into the two way. "Ready for search. Activate the video gear, and we'll go live."

The room contained no exterior windows, and the door was visible only from the hallway. He shut it, and in one smooth motion turned on the lights and stowed the night vision, laser and other gear back into his belt pack. He extracted a tiny head-mounted videocam which would allow his hands to operate unhindered. This he slid into place around his scalp, then flipped the tiny switch to "transmit." The invisible data stream emitted by the camera burst to life, and Reggie knew that Rick was now seeing full color images on the van monitor. Back in the van, Rick pressed the button that began recording the images.

Andrews scanned the room looking for any evidence of a connection with Rowalter. Seeing nothing obvious, he extracted some latex gloves from his jacket pocket and quickly put them on. He looked through the papers on the desk, halting over a folded copy of the *Wall Street Journal* flipped open to the NYSE quotes table. The symbol "Rowlnd," circled in red ink, jumped out at him. Next, he slipped open the desk drawer. A semi-automatic 9mm pistol lay there, with clip inserted. Nothing unusual there. In a lower drawer, he found a spiral notebook. Flipping through it, he found pages of scrawled notes, with the letters "PZT" appearing in several places. Dane Ingersoll's name occurred again and again, but most prominently in a section labeled "Surveillance". About ten pages in were written the words, "Natalie - East Dallas Medical Center, Neo-Natal unit." Andrews produced a tiny camera no bigger than two inches square and digitally photographed every page of the notes. The rest of the drawers yielded a variety of fairly nondescript material, except for two items. One was a product label of some kind with the words *Rowalter Pharmaceuticals, S.A.* emblazoned across the bottom and the letters "PZT" in bold print above. The other was some odd sort of device that piqued his curiosity.

"Hey, Rick. What do you make of this?" Reggie looked directly down at the item lying in the lowest right-hand drawer.

"'Looks like some sort of timed exploding advice to me, boss," came the reply. "Can you zoom in closer?"

Reggie dropped to all fours and brought his face to within inches. "I think you're right, Rick. But you're the demolitions guy. Not my cup of tea."

"Yeah, I've got it now," came the voice over the walkie talkie. "I thought so. That's a pretty sophisticated control for a remote demolition bomb. We saw something like it in Baghdad. It can be set to a particular GMRS frequency, then coded and used to detonate from distances of up to 100 miles."

Reggie let out an unbelieving whistle, then chuckled. "Heinz ought to be very interested in this."

After taking more digital photos from several angles, Andrews stowed the camera and decided to explore elsewhere. He knocked out the motion detectors in the remaining rooms and, finding nothing of interest, made his way to what he believed would be the garage. It was. The room was a large rectangle of the three-car variety, and contained an SUV, a sedan, a workbench, and stacks of boxes. Most of the boxes were empty—probably, he figured, the residue from the agent's recent move down from Washington. Then Reggie noticed a couple of smaller ones stacked in the corner adjacent to the overhead door. They were unsealed but closed, unlike the others. Opening them revealed stacks of perhaps tens of thousands of product labels bearing the ponderous but unmistakable name "PHENYLZANADIOXIDETETRACHLORAMINE". At the bottom left corner of the labels, in small print, appeared "ROWALTER PHARMACEUTICALS, S.A." In the opposite lower corner was stamped a number in the form of a fraction, which, Reggie guessed, must be a product lot number. He fanned the labels to set up for the photo shoot and to depict as many of the lot numbers as possible, though he wasn't quite sure why.

"Why would a man assigned to halt importation of this stuff have unused product labels in his garage?" he mused. *And where there are labels, there should be product."* Reggie smirked to himself wryly for his investigative brilliance as he shoved the boxes aside, looking for clues. One of the boxes had—*what was it—some handwriting?* Scrawled in felt pen on the underside of one of the top flaps where it would be easily missed was the word, "truck", and another word he couldn't decipher. *"What truck?"* he wondered.

Suddenly, an image of car keys flashed into Andrew's memory—something he had seen in the office but dismissed as unimportant. He pivoted on one foot and backtracked to the garage door.

"Rick, 'you still have that video running?"

"In living color, sir."

"I'm headed back to the office for a minute."

"All right sir, but it's approaching 15 minutes, and you said—"

"I know what I said, Rick. But we're almost done here. While I'm wrapping up, will you do a complete scan of the area and make sure we're all right?"

"I'm on it." Rick checked the police frequency scanner and simultaneously deployed his night vision glasses to sweep the block on which they were parked. Nothing.

Within less than a minute, Reggie was back in the office again, where he pulled out the top center desk drawer. There, in plain view, was the set of two shiny keys on a nondescript key ring attached to a plastic tag. The tag read simply, "Truck." The writing, though small, looked remarkably similar to the script he had seen on the box flap. Hurriedly, he snapped four or five close-ups which highlighted both the writing and the index numbers appearing on the keys. This done, Reggie returned to the garage and scanned it once more for anything remotely interesting. He checked to make sure all his equipment was in place, and all the boxes were returned to their original position. Then, realizing Rick would soon be in a panic, he returned quickly to the dining room where he swiped several items of sterling silverware and generally made a mess of the contents of the hutch. The mahogany box which held the silverware Reggie left open in plain sight on the dining room table. He took the silverware down the hallway to the master bedroom, and thrust the pieces deep in between the mattress and box spring. Next, he backtracked to the family room and, using a tiny flashlight, disconnected the Blu-ray disc player. Then he tucked the player under one arm and made a last trip to the garage, where he stashed it in one of the boxes in the stack of empties. Nervously, he keyed the walkie talkie.

"Rick, I'm exiting now. What's status?" Andrews could hear the static and chatter of the police band scanner in the background.

Reggie's walkie talkie crackled to life. "Reggie, you need to boogie, fast." The police have a burglary call within—" he listened to the chatter for a moment "— within about five miles of here. They'll probably wrap that up in ten minutes or less. I'll cruise up the alley to pick you up."

"No! Andrews barked back. Stay put. I don't want to draw any attention. I'll let you know when I need you." Several minutes passed as Andrews checked the perimeter. He glided swiftly back the way he came, exiting the window. *"No one should expect— "*

"Reggie!"

"Damn that radio!" "You'll wake up the neighbors! What is it?" Andrews said in his loudest whisper.

"I show two squad cars headed this direction on Southland Street, about three blocks away. They've cleared the burglary."

"Sit tight. I'll be there soon." Reggie was on a dead run, stooped low, then shimmied and rolled over the back fence, snagging his shoulder on a nail as he did so. Another minute ticked by while he began racing down the alley. The radio at his belt crackled again, startling him.

"What *now*?" he whispered.

Rick's voice had taken on a panicked tone. "Reggie, they've turned east from Southland. Someone has called in with a suspected burglary on Landsford!"

"That's this street—

"Tell me about it, man." Rick had already cranked up the engine as he spoke the words, and the radio emitted the rumble of the engine followed by the squeal of tires against road.

"Meet me at the end of the alley, Landsford and Colfax." Reggie only hoped they weren't picking up this frequency, a unique one he used for such special occasions.

"You read my mind." With no time for finesse, Reggie sprinted the rest of the way to the corner, and now flattened his body like a gecko against the alley fence, waiting. The sound of the van approaching from a block away pierced the heavy silence enveloping the neighborhood. No sirens, though. *"'Probably hoping to catch me in the act,"* thought Reggie.

An eternity passed before the van rounded the corner, nearly flipping over in the process. It slowed to perhaps fifteen miles per hour, as the sliding back door flew open. Reggie ran low and hard to meet it, then planted his left foot and long jumped for the back with his right, catching the door handle just as Rick floored the accelerator. The force of the van pulling away swung the door open just enough for Reggie to grab the headrest on Rick's seat and pull himself in. He yelled over the roar of the engine when his foot, balanced precariously on the edge of the step, slipped, turning his ankle. A big hand appeared over the front seat, grabbed his right forearm, and pulled him back up. Wincing in pain, Reggie reached out and pulled the sliding door shut, while Rick continued to drive like a demon. He took a winding route out of the neighborhood, and back onto the freeway, taking care not to use headlights, but testing the limits of the lumbering van.

"I figure we had a minute and a half, maybe two, head start," Rick yelled. "They should be getting to Patterson's house about now."

"Way too close for comfort," Andrews shot back. "I haven't pulled off a garden variety break-in for a while. Why'd you have to pick a neighborhood that's already being burgled?"

"'Guess you've got me there. But we did get some goodies, didn't we?" Rick chuckled.

"We did, at that." Reggie didn't exactly share his partner's exhilaration yet. Although the adrenalin was somewhat muting the pain for now, he knew in a few hours it would be killing him. He couldn't wait to get back to the office of Andrews & Hennings, debrief and unwind. Then he would permit himself the luxury of assessing their find. At the moment, he was just grateful to have satisfied his IOU to Heinz, albeit at great peril to himself and his reputation. 'What kind of crazy fool would break in and pilfer a senior FBI agent's house?" he muttered to himself, disbelievingly.

"What was that?" asked Rick.

"Oh, nothing," muttered Reggie through the pain. Nothing at all."

CHAPTER TWENTY- EIGHT

Jim Patterson squinted at his watch in the pre-dawn darkness. It was the third time in twenty minutes he'd checked the luminescent dial. The cabin of the 767 Jumbo was quiet. Most passengers were dozing, lulled into a stupor by the vibration of the massive jet engines. A few were reading magazines under reading lights. They had just passed over El Paso, and Patterson calculated that landing would occur about 5:35 a.m. at DFW. He turned his attention back to the lap top computer on the tray table in front of him. The screen emitted a low but distinct glow, contrasting markedly with the surrounding darkness. He clicked on the envelope icon next to the email which read "Injunction Hearing". It was a day old, from Newcombe in the Dallas office:

> *"I just received word from Washington that an injunction hearing is scheduled for February 3rd at ten. The purpose is to shut down all sales of product. Ingersoll will be there with staff. Government counsel is Rick Saunders, a ten-year vet. 'Thought you'd like to know. Please confirm your arrival time."*

Patterson cursed himself for not checking his email sooner. He clicked the "Create Mail" button and began typing in encryption:

> *"Dean is working for Rowalter. Repeat: working for Rowalter. He has been to their HQ in S.A. and I believe he is now back in Dallas. Track and apprehend for questioning immediately. He must not appear for the hearing. I will arrive at DFW at 7:10, and should be at the office by 8:00 a.m.*

Patterson clicked "SEND", then watched the pop up box tell him the message was encrypted and transmitted. He then opened his web browser, opened his "Favorites" menu and brought up Blumberg's real-time stock quotes site. He typed in the symbol "Rowlnd". Instantly, several sets of numbers and a moving, colored graph flashed before him. Yesterday's closing was, he noted, down $1.30 over Monday's. He'd have to check back about an hour after the market opened, and made a mental note to do so. The price should continue its slide downward due to the uncertainty of the court case. He figured he needed about five thousand more shares—yes, that ought to do it. Then, he'd sit back and watch while the price went through the roof. He smiled. After all, who would ever suspect that a veteran FBI agent in Dallas would have access to this kind of information?

* * * *

It was gloomy and dark in the smallish apartment. A man with reddish-blonde hair stretched his neck back over the top of the chair where he had positioned himself for the last half hour. He rubbed his eyes tiredly through closed lids, then squinted them open just enough to get another look at the monitor before him. He hit the pause button on the remote; then rewind, stop. Play, rewind, stop...freeze frame. With the deft flip of a switch and a couple of key strokes on the computer, he digitally enhanced the image, blowing it up to twice the normal size on the high definition monitor.

"Hon, come over here for a minute. I want you to see something," he muttered. A woman left some work she was doing in the kitchen and appeared at his side.

"What do you make of this?"

The man left the image on the laptop computer screen, but gestured toward the monitor. He hit "Play", and the two found their eyes riveted on Natalie Ingersoll's incubator. The time displayed in the upper right-hand corner of the screen was "0220". A hand appeared at the left the side of the screen, clearly that of a man, and unhooked the IV bag. Another hand appeared and unscrewed the cap on the bag, placing the cap to side, out of the camera's view. The second hand returned, and while the first held the bag steady, poured liquid from a brown colored bottle through the opening and into the bag. It set the bottle aside, replacing the cap. The right hand then squeezed the bag several times, and replaced it, inverted in its holder. At that point, the man stopped the tape.

"Now watch," said the red-haired man to the woman. He rewound the tape to frame 36, and froze the frame, then turned to the laptop. "Look at the digital enhancement." Before them, in the amorphous darkness of the hospital room, was depicted the brown bottle. The enhancement software, they noticed, played up markedly the contrast between light and dark. The man pointed with his pencil to the lower half of the bottle, being careful not to give away too much to the woman. "What do you see?"

"A number. It looks like...4...8...no, make that 3...5...7...9...Z."

"You're quicker than I thought," said the man to the woman.

"Gee, thanks."

* * * *

"Rick, I have an assignment for you."

"C'mon, Reggie, it's 4:30 a.m. and we've been up all night. Don't you ever take a break?"

"Not when I think I'm onto something. You know me better than to ask. Go get those labels we pulled in from our little burglary tonight. I want you to check each and every number against this one. Get me anything even close." Rick nodded reluctantly, and went for the labels.

"Say, Rick, when does that warehouse home improvement place down on the corner open?"

"I think at 7:00, but the contractor entrance may open at 6."

"Well, this morning, I'm a contractor. I'm going to take these truck keys down, and try to narrow the field on what we're looking for."

"What do I do with the rest of the stuff we pulled in last night?"

"Keep it under lock and key. That detonator especially. Oh, and when the receptionist comes in, tell her to interrupt whatever I'm doing if Heinz calls. I can't imagine why I haven't heard from him yet. Have her contact me on my cell phone."

* * * *

Wednesday morning dawned as any other. The sun's rays made it somewhat warmer than it had been, but the air was still crisp and cold against Jenny's face. Jenny watched the movers she had hired for the occasion finish packing the last two file boxes into the rental truck. That done, she made them load the computer, projection screen, and document presenter into the trunk and back seat of her car to prevent damage from shifting. Photographic exhibits she would trust to no one but herself, she laboriously and painstakingly wrapped, packed and arranged so that they were impervious to any conceivable mishap. She dispatched the movers, then glanced at her watch, which read 6:55 a.m. Jenny suppressed a gasp, and motioned hurriedly to John, the remaining aide, to get into the car. The plan was to arrive at the federal courthouse at 8:00 sharp to survey the courtroom, then coordinate the unpacking and setup with the aide immediately upon his arrival. Dane would arrive about forty-five minutes thereafter, allowing them just over an hour before the hearing. There was no time for dilly dallying, since it would probably take most of an hour to get through traffic, and an additional ten minutes after parking to get all this stuff through security at the north entrance. Then, too, they had to have everything set up before the court started its docket at 9:00 sharp.

Dane was downing his second mug of strong coffee by 7, having been awakened by a call from Susan three hours earlier. She couldn't sleep, thinking about Natalie and about the hearing. Dane slept fitfully himself, but not to worry, he'd assured her with a manufactured confidence he did not feel. He had left Alton alone, slumbering like a rock in his guest room. The loyal associate, he knew, could serve no useful purpose in his physically and emotionally exhausted condition. He also had not heard from Heinz despite having left several cell phone voice mails, and became aware of a gnawing worry at what might be going on there. And then there was his little girl. How he missed her! Yesterday, the doctor told him the same thing he'd been saying every day for weeks: "She's stable, vital signs normal—but not viable." Translated from doctor-speak, that meant they dare not disconnect her from the IV for fear of the near fatal episode she had experienced before. *"What do we pay these guys for? They're so godawful ignorant!"* Dane fumed, while he dressed nervously. Dane mused on the reasons for his jumpiness. For sheer size and difficulty, he'd tried many cases more challenging than this one. But just what, in God's name, was he supposed to do? He detested his client—"detest" was too mild a word, in fact. Yet, he had to find a way and a will to win this thing, anyway. But how did he know that Natalie would ever be normal, even if he did? If the drug-from-hell was approved because of his efforts and millions of Americans suffered the consequences, Rowalter would have no further use for him, anyway. Why should its operatives keep their word, for what little that might be worth? What incentive would they then have to administer the "buffer" drug that alone kept his daughter from dying a horrible death? And what guarantee was there that her frail little body wouldn't have some permanent residual effects when all the smoke cleared?

"But," his mind screamed at him, *"you can't afford to take that chance! What other choice is there?"*

It was dead-on true, he knew. He had no other choice. The sobering realization, which he faced squarely for the first time, weighed down on him like an iron anvil. Dane tightened his neck tie and pulled on his jacket, downing the last gulp of coffee. He looked at himself in the mirror. It was time. He grabbed two briefcases—one, his usual attaché and the second, a monster containing the binder which was the nerve center of his trial presentation—and threw them into the trunk of the waiting Beemer. Soon, the sleek automobile was streaking through the rush hour traffic of Turtle Creek, en route to the Cabell Federal Building downtown. The hands-free phone rang and Dane took it on the speaker.

"We're here, and we're ready," came Jenny's matter-of-fact voice.

"Good. I'm en route now, and my ETA is ten to fifteen minutes."

* * * *

Time was running out; a fact of which Heinz was excruciatingly aware. It was 5:00 a.m. California time, and they hadn't even crossed into Arizona yet. Dr. Jenkins was resting with his head back and eyes closed. Thankfully, thought Heinz, he'd agreed to testify without a subpoena, provided an assistant professor could stand in for him for no more than a week. Twice Heinz had tried to use his cell phone to call Dane. The first time, he earned a stern look and a comment from the flight attendant. The next time, the bitch threatened to confiscate the cell phone. He now regretted not taking the time to call from the college campus or from Dr. Jenkins' house; but things had been so rushed, he told himself. He nervously fingered his pen, wondering how to do something constructive while the trial was beginning. Suddenly, it occurred to him that he had his digital pager with him. He rummaged through the attaché he'd tucked under the seat in front of him, retrieving the pager from a zipper pocket. With a furtive glance around for the crabby flight attendant, he flipped the switch to "vibrate". "*I may not be able to send, but maybe someone has tried...*" He checked the little screen, which lit up, then began scrolling. It read:

"Have completed ops at Patterson's house. Couldn't reach you by cell. Found very helpful information. Call soon. Reggie."

Heinz' heart skipped a beat. "*What information?*" His mind postulated a thousand questions. Had Reggie unearthed evidence of Patterson's participation in the car explosion? Did the conspiracy go higher than just Patterson? But there was no way for him to contact Reggie without his secure cell phone—the useless phone attached to the seat ahead of him was, well, useless. Besides, there were too many ears at too close a range to have that kind of a conversation anyway. He grabbed a magazine and resolved himself to fitfully sweating out the rest of the flight.

The landing gear bumped hard as the Boeing 767 hit the runway and the retro thrusters kicked in. Patterson glanced at his watch, and noted with satisfaction that they were five minutes ahead of schedule. The plane taxied without stopping to the gate at terminal C. Patterson fought back the wave of tiredness that swept over him as he bent over to retrieve his briefcase, then stood to exit the plane. As he walked out of the jet way into the terminal, he immediately felt a hand on his shoulder and glanced over to see Jon Newcombe.

"Hello, Mr. Patterson. Follow me, I have a car curbside." They whisked past the businessmen waiting for their flights, through the revolving door to baggage claim, out the automatic doors to a grey sedan with emergency lights flashing.

"I just got here. You were early."

"Thank God. The approval hearing is at 10:00 a.m., and I need a shower and shave. Why don't you run me by the house before you go to the office?"

"Sounds like a plan."

Patterson's tone changed from ragged to serious. "Did you find Alton Dean?"

"I'm afraid not, sir. Did you know the apartment building he was living in had a major fire? His apartment and two or three others were gutted."

"Is that so?"

"You got it. I visited the site, and questioned the onsite security. The man said Mr. Dean came by yesterday for the first time in a couple of weeks, talked with him, made a phone call, then disappeared. He hasn't seen or heard from him since."

"Well, he certainly can't be far away if he has no place to stay. My people south of the border tell me he went to work for Rowalter on the PZT project. Obviously, he's a man with very valuable information, and needs to be apprehended."

"No question there. About all we could do right now is question him. Do you have anything on him to support a warrant?"

Patterson hesitated. "Not exactly. But that's why we need to locate and question him. I'm confident he'll lead us to something. Have you tried Dane Ingersoll's place?"

"Not yet. I figured it wouldn't look too great to be prowling around his house the day of the injunction trial, especially after his wife was nearly blown up."

"Figure out a way to do it and not get caught. I'm going to clean up and head down to the courthouse." Just as he said this, they pulled up in front of his Patterson's home.

"I'll get right on it." Newcombe laid a little rubber pulling away as Patterson hurried up the front walk to the sedate looking home. The sun was now all the way up over the horizon, and its rays streamed onto his back, providing noticeable warmth amid the chill of the frigid winter morning. He fumbled for his house key, found it, then with the aid of the sunlight mated the key to the deadbolt. He swung open the heavy wooden door, turned to his left and disarmed the security system. He headed straight for the master bathroom and turned on the shower as hot as he would be able to stand. While the water was coming to temperature, Patterson's stomach noisily reminded him he hadn't eaten since early last evening. He made a bee line to the kitchen to grab something from the fridge. Mid-way there, as he entered the dining room, something tugged at the corner of his eye. Then he spotted it...the silverware! *"What is it doing...I didn't...A burglary?* Patterson wondered if he was tired enough to be experiencing hallucinations. But he felt and saw the missing silver, and noticed the contents of the hutch, won from his ex-wife in a divorce, thrown about.

He glanced around, pacing from one room to another, wondering what they had seen, and what they had taken. From what he could discern, little had been taken. And yet, an uneasy feeling had settled over Patterson that couldn't be fully explained by the petty theft. They had been smart: the security system had been left armed, and that meant that no wires were cut. He took a quick inventory, and found nothing else disturbed. It was almost *too* good a job, almost as though it had been purposely made to look amateurish. It was precisely this fact that unnerved him. He reached for the phone and started to dial 9-1-1, then caught himself. *No,"* he thought. *"Not worth the risk."* He put the phone down and returned to the master bedroom. Once there, he went to the night stand by his bed. Reaching under some papers inside, he pulled out a Beretta 9mm semiautomatic. He opened the magazine and checked the clip, leaving the safety off. Satisfied, he went into the bathroom and placed the gun on the back of the commode, within easy reach of the shower. He left both the bathroom and bedroom doors ajar, so that from the shower, and with the use of the dresser mirror, he could view the doorway to the bedroom and the hallway beyond it.

Patterson soaked himself for several minutes, letting the hot, steamy water pound the tension out of his body. He dried quickly, then shaved and dressed in ten minutes. Taking the Beretta from the bathroom, he holstered the weapon, then slipped an extra clip into his coat pocket. He was ready. On his way out to the car, he made a mental note to get the biggest, most ferocious junkyard watchdog he could find.

* * * *

While Dane parked the car in the ten-story parking garage across the street from the federal building, it occurred to him that he hadn't heard from Heinz yet. He had just been too damned busy to think about it. He still was, but curiosity nagged at him.

Dane arrived at the courtroom as scheduled, at precisely 8:45 a.m. Judge Fitzhugh would be presiding. Dane glanced at an imposing portrait of him which graced the courtroom wall, obviously taken in his younger years. The huge, wood paneled courtroom accomplished what its designers obviously intended: to create a sense of awe and respect, and yes, just a touch of healthy fear for the United States judiciary. At the moment, the place was teeming with support staff, for both sides of the impending case. He spotted Jenny instantly, running checks on the exhibit projection system. They exchanged quick half-smiles as Dane gratefully relinquished his brief cases, parking them under the defense counsel table. It was too soon to begin unloading them; he would only be kicked off the table by defense attorneys on the case which preceded his. Jenny turned over the running of the computer system to an aide, and appeared at Dane's side.

"How are things going?" queried Jenny.

"About as well as can be expected, given the circumstances," Dane replied dryly. "Alton is sleeping it off at my place, and I haven't heard a word from Heinz."

"Do I detect a note of worry?" she said, obviously trying to lighten the mood.

"Gee-whiz, whatever must you be thinking?"

"Listen, Dane. All you can do at this point is put on the evidence and let the chips fall where they may. The judge will make up his own mind."

"I wish it were that simple, Jenny. The government gets to go first, since they carry the burden of proof. This is an injunction hearing, so they have a heavy burden to prove probable injury. That means, of course, that they will go for broke. Which, in turn, means that we have to put our best cards on the table."

"Meaning?" she asked, although she knew.

"Meaning, that there is no middle ground. Either we show the drug is the greatest thing for health care since penicillin, or we fall on our sword. And I can't take the second option, for reasons with which you are very familiar."

At that point the bailiff, who had momentarily left the courtroom, boomed out, "All rise! The United States Federal District Court for the Northern District of Texas is now in session, the Honorable Charles Fitzhugh presiding." A rather imposing figure robed in black entered immediately behind him, turned and motioned the spectators to be seated. Jenny and Dane took seats in about the third row back on the left, the better to see how his honor handled himself. Dane recalled sitting second chair in a trial in this court years before, but to a different judge. He seemed to remember Fitzhugh being appointed to the bench shortly thereafter. The man stood about six foot two, perhaps six three. Judging by his neck, the only part of his frame not obscured by the robe, he was rather lanky. He was very young for a federal judge, perhaps no more than thirty-three or thirty-four, Dane estimated. They had only met once, briefly at a Salacuse & Lockridge reception thrown for the newly appointed Judge by some well-connected senior partners. Dane wondered if he remembered. He was politically well connected. You didn't get appointed to the federal bench unless you were. But he had a reputation for being a quick study and no schlock, very knowledgeable in the law. He would be prepared. Dane adjusted his yellow pad as Fitzhugh settled deliberately into his chair behind the bench, smiled in the general direction of the gallery, then nodded curtly towards the clerk, a young man who had dutifully seated himself below but directly in front of the judge. The clerk then began reading the court's docket. For the moment, that consisted of only two cases: *McKinley vs. United States*, and *Food and Drug Administration vs. Rowalter Industries, S.A.* The clerk announced that the afternoon docket would be read at 1:30 p.m., but Dane knew those cases would probably never be reached. There were just too many witnesses and too much evidence. In fact, it was entirely possible the trial would continue into a second or even a third day.

"Dane," Jenny's whisper shook him out of his doldrums.

"Huh?" he whispered back.

"How're you going to get the contents of Alton's flash drives into evidence…w-without Alton?"

"Jen, you just don't get it, do you?"

"Well, I suppose not."

"The flash drives expose Rowalter for the greedy SOB's they are, true?"

"Sure."

"Rowalter wouldn't like that evidence, now would they?"

"No, clearly not. And they'd hold you accountable and do who-knows-what to Natalie. But supposing the evidence came, not from you, but from the prosecution."

"And, how, pray tell, would the Government happen to come by such information?"

Jenny smiled slyly.

"Jenny, you can't do that. First, it's unethical. Second, I've never helped the government win in any case, and I'm not about to start now. And third, if you planted the flash drives, who is to say they'd know what they had, or be able to figure it out fast enough to do anything with it?"

While the question still hanging on his lips, a hand tapped Dane on the shoulder, and he glanced up to see John, one of the litigation aides. Looking apologetic, he leaned close to Dane's ear and whispered, "There are members of the media here. I just thought you'd want to know." Dane winced, and nodded his thanks.

The absolute last thing he needed on his mind at a time like this was the media. "*How in hell did they get wind of this low-profile case, anyway?*" he wondered.

* * * *

Heinz glanced urgently at his watch for about the fifth time in the last several minutes. It read 8:55 a.m. as the 737's landing gear met the runway. Jenkins looked wide awake now as he had for the last half hour, and was fidgeting with his glasses. Heinz didn't wait for the seat belt sign to go off when they arrived at the terminal. Holding his bag out front and with Dr. Jenkins in tow, he fought his way down the aisle behind a string of loud *"Excuse me"* s and *"I have a medical emergency"* s. It worked like a charm, and within five minutes they had made it through the jet way, the north terminal, and to a taxi stop out in front. The first chance Heinz had to use the phone was when, frazzled and gulping air, he and Jenkins landed in the back of a yellow taxicab. Between gasps, Heinz told the driver the best directions to his house. On his secure cell phone, he quickly dialed Reggie at the office, whispering *"thank you"* to no one in particular as the phone answered on the second ring.

"Andrews & Associates Investigations," said a female voice.

"Get me Reggie," he barked." Tell him it's Heinz, and its urgent."

"Yes sir; right away sir." Barely a moment passed before Reggie's voice clicked in.

"Hey, bro, where you been?"

"Stuck on a plane for several hours. I got your page, but couldn't respond till now. The curiosity is killing me. What'd you get?"

"Well, would it mean something to you if I told you we found empty PZT shipping boxes and serial numbers which match the stuff that was used on Natalie at the hospital?"

"You're kidding, of course?"

"It's a tad bit late in the game to be playing jokes like that isn't it?"

"That's better than I ever hoped for," Heinz said, as he felt an indescribable rush through his body.

"Me too. But there's more, at least we think. Found some truck keys, and we're still trying to track down the matching vehicle. Could be there might be some other incriminating information there, too."

"How quick can you get something on the truck?"

"'Dunno. But we're working hard on getting it done today.

"Well, work harder. The injunction trial should be beginning as we speak."

"I know it. Oh, there's another thing."

"There's *more*?"

"Well, if my gut is right—and it usually is—this guy has some sort of financial interest in the company you're interested in. 'Found a copy of the Wall Street Journal, opened to the stock index page. Yesterday's stock quote for Rowalter Industries was highlighted. This guy, I figure, has more than a passing interest in the company."

"Reg, you're incredible."

"I also found a spiral notebook containing his surveillance notes. He mentions Natalie Ingersoll in it, along with her exact location in the hospital."

"That could be explained by his assignment to protect her."

"Sort of like he protected you in that car in front of Mrs. Ingersoll's house?"

Heinz flushed at the remark, and felt a twinge of pain in his leg to remind him of that horrible experience. "Yeah, sort of like that."

"So, do you want a written report, or shall I just box up the evidence and turn it over?"

"No time for a report, I'm afraid. Pack it up and have it ready for me to pick up within an hour. And step it up on the truck. Oh....and be ready to testify."

The phone grew silent. "Be *what*?"

"You heard me. Be ready to testify. You were there, I wasn't. If Patterson's up to what I think he's up to, I want his ass hanging on my trophy wall. You're going to help me nail it there."

"If you say so, *Capitan*. But I've never testified in a federal case. What's it like?"

"Never mind that. You'll do just fine. Clean yourself up, and I'll see you in about an hour."

* * * *

Dane Ingersoll stepped out into the hallway and flipped open his cell phone. He dialed the cell number that Heinz had given him, and got rings, then voice mail.

Moments later, the phone rang in "vibrate" mode, and Dane answered.

"Dane, was that you trying to call me?" It was Heinz.

"Bingo. Where have you been? Trial is about ready to begin!"

"I know, I know. They don't let you use cell phones on air planes, and that's where I've been for several hours. But the time hasn't been wasted. I've got a witness you may want to at least interview. Name is Dr. Rupert Jenkins, and he's a professor who used to have Norman Holloway as a student. It seems he received a rather odd email from Holloway on the day of his death."

"Yeah? What's the upshot of his testimony?"

"From what I gather, he's got a handle on how PZT mutates. And he's the only one who could testify from personal knowledge about the email Holloway sent him, which ties his work on PZT to his suicide."

"That's just terrific," Dane moaned. Another person to nail shut Rowalter's coffin. And Nat—" his voice trailed off.

"And what?" Heinz said, confusedly.

"Oh, nothing. Yes, you're right. I'll have to interview him. When can you have him here?"

"Just say the word."

"Get him here in fifteen minutes, but keep him away from the Government, whatever you do."

"You got it. Oh, and Mr. Ingersoll?"

"Yes."

"We may have something real strong developing on James Patterson. If I were you, I'd be careful around him. I'll bring you up to speed on it later."

"Don't worry. I stopped trusting the FBI when I had to hire body guards to protect my own wife."

Dane killed the phone call and returned to the court room, just in time to hear Judge Fitzhugh finish the morning docket and declare a fifteen-minute recess. It was 9:45. Scanning the court room, Dane saw chief federal prosecutor Nathan Smith, together with a couple of his underlings, in a standing huddle at the counsel table. A man that he guessed to be an FDA technocrat or perhaps a chemist, was seated beside them, leafing through documents. Dane caught Jenny's eye and motioned her over. She appeared instantly at his side.

"Anything new? Did you hear from Heinz yet?" Jenny whispered, her anxiousness showing.

"You could say that. He's managed to corral a surprise witness." Dane kept his hand cupped around Jenny's ear, eyes fixed on Nathan Smith. "Remember that professor who you said offed himself last fall? It seems he had a friend, another professor, to whom he emailed a suicide note as his final act. Heinz is bringing that friend over right away. 'Says he knows something about how PZT mutates. I'm not sure what he has to tell us, but I'm betting it's not good for my client." The prosecution team was looking in their direction, so Dane huddled closer to Jenny.

"Then why do you want to talk to him?" Jenny whispered.

"I learned a long time ago not to judge a witness' testimony until you've talked with them. Some who I thought were my best have turned out to be the worst. And some I would have sworn would make the other side's case have hit a home run for me. At worst, I can find out what he knows and be better prepared for the government's case."

As the courtroom cleared, Dane spread out on the counsel table, and got everything primed to start. He dispatched Jenny upstairs to an undisclosed location where she had the witnesses stashed, away from the prying eyes and ears of their opponents. Then, he looked around, took a deep breath, and waited. It was time. He knew what he had to do; now, the only thing was to do it. He thanked God that the Government went first. *"Perhaps they will let the cat out of the bag,"* he wondered.

John Newcombe had not the slightest idea of where to begin looking for Alton Dean. *Check the hospitals? Stake out the airports? Check the homeless shelter?* After some thought, he settled on getting a bunch of agents to watch strategic locations. From what he'd heard about Dean, asking folks a bunch of questions would probably drive him away from, rather than toward them. He picked out a surveillance team of five agents—all but one with under five years of Bureau service, but all good men. One he assigned to watch Dean's old apartment building. A second was stationed inside the Salacuse & Lockridge office building, just down the hallway in a temporarily vacated office. Two more agents were to watch the entrance and exits to the gigantic skyscraper, one on the south side of the block and one on the north. The fifth was to watch Dane Ingersoll's house 24/7. That one was strictly on a hunch of Newcombe's that Alton Dean would had to have looked up Ingersoll once he got back to the States. *"After all,"* Newcombe imagined his boss saying, *"Dean worked for Ingersoll, and had no wife, no kids."* Finally, he assigned a desk agent the job of checking out all of Alton's friends and associates, and getting good addresses. All of the agents were given secure, scrambled radio channels on which to communicate with each other instantaneously. By 9:45 a.m., each agent had already been dispatched, some of them pulled off of existing assignments. Newcombe told each one that Patterson meant business, and that this was priority. By 10:00 a.m., every assigned post was manned.

Agent Moore shouldered the assignment of watching Dane Ingersoll's house. He had not the slightest inkling who Dane Ingersoll was, or why this case might be deemed so important as to pull him off of the wiretap counterfeiting job he'd been working. Moore parked his car down the street about two hundred feet, settled himself in to read the Dallas Morning News, and waited.

Inside, Alton was dead to the world. Gathered in a heap on Dane's guest room bed, he slept the sleep of one who had been deprived of rest for days on end. His slumber was interrupted only when the telephone rang, and then only because it was inches from his ear. His head jolted upward an inch off his pillow and, managing to force one eye open a slit, he located the phone and grabbed it. "Wh-h-ho... is it?" The phone clicked in his ear. Only vaguely aware of his surroundings and utterly disoriented, Alton returned the receiver to its cradle. Outside the home, Agent Moore smiled ever so slightly. Much better than he had hoped for. He jumped onto the two-way and told the other agents of his find, then relayed the word to Newcombe himself. Newcombe, who seemed to Agent Moore to be preoccupied, had a terse response:

"Secure a warrant and execute it."

"Who's our informant, Sir?"

"Agent-in-Charge James Patterson. But start the ball rolling and I'll have him contact you."

Moore called the legal boys at the office and began work on it. Inside Dane Ingersoll's house, unbeknownst to Agent Moore, Alton Dean was beginning to stir. He stretched, he yawned, and then suddenly, he remembered where he was.

* * * *

Dane stood uneasily in the hallway outside Judge Fitzhugh's courtroom. It was 10:05 by the courtroom clock, and the Judge was uncharacteristically tardy. He could see Jenny at the far end of the corridor, watching the elevator in case Heinz came in there. Dane riveted his eyes on the entrance to his left, the elevator vestibule nearer the judge's chambers. He tapped his foot nervously. Abruptly, a man who was obviously a reporter approached him from the courtroom door.

"Excuse me, are you Mr. Dane Ingersoll?" Dane almost denied it, but realized the guy would find out soon enough anyway.

"That's me."

"Justin Jackson with the *Morning News*, sir. May I have just a moment or two?"

"Not when I'm about to step into this injunction hearing and I'm waiting on a witness. No offense, but now's not the time. Maybe afterward."

The man nodded, handed Dane his card, and moved down the hallway searching for other potential interview victims. A bare moment later, the elevator doors parted and there stood Heinz, looking breathless and a bit haggard. At his side was a grey-haired man, tall and thin, looking about forty-five-ish. He approached Dane like a political advance man, smiling and pumping his hand vigorously.

"Mr. Ingersoll, I'm sorry it's last minute like this. Hopefully, it's been worth the wait." He lowered his voice and glanced about. "Dr. Jenkins here can tell us something about how PZT works, based on an email he received from Dr. Holloway, God rest his soul." The tall thin man extended his hand with a gracious smile and shook Dane's warmly.

"I'm not sure what you can tell me that I don't already know, but I'll at least listen." Just then Jenny, who had seen them from the other end of the corridor, appeared.

"Jen, station yourself in the court room, and snag me as soon as the judge enters. I'll be over here." Dane gestured with a nod toward a witness room a few doors down.

"Don't worry, boss. I just spoke with the bailiff and the Judge is delayed in a chamber conference with about five attorneys. Some kind of emergency matter. It'll take about twenty minutes at least, I figure."

"Good. We'll need every minute, no doubt."

With that, Dane, Heinz and Dr. Jenkins headed into the witness room. Dane closed the door, motioning both gentlemen to sit on one side of the plain wooden table. He took the chair on the other side. When everyone was in place, he extracted a plain yellow pad and pen from his portfolio, laying them on the table in front of him. Then, he cut to the chase.

"All right, Dr. Jenkins. How do you know, er...how did you know Dr. Norman Holloway?"

"He was a student in my advanced graduate class at the university where I teach. An exceptionally brilliant student."

Dane watched Jenkins closely as he spoke. So far, he appeared credible. "How well did you know him?"

"We became friendly. Not the best of friends, certainly, but more than just teacher student. Like peers. I believe it was based on mutual respect. Speaking for myself, I was awed by his abilities."

"All right. Now, I understand you received an email from him. Posthumously, correct?"

"Well, yes. I received the email, in retrospect, the night of his death if the newspaper accounts are correct. I didn't open it until after I had returned from a short vacation."

"And what, if you please, is significant about this email?"

"Well, first the fact that he chose to send it on the eve of his death. Second, that it contained somewhat of a confession, if you will, about his work. Third, it had an attachment to it that showed some complex molecular equations. The last is, in a way, the most puzzling."

"Okay, but tell me what the confession said."

"Certainly. I use that word advisedly, but it said— well, I have a copy with me. Would you like to read it?"

"Absolutely."

Dr. Jenkins reached into his sport jacket pocket and extracted a crumpled piece of computer paper. He unfolded it and handed it to Dane with trembling hands. Dane took the paper and read aloud:

"Dearest Dr. Jenkins:

Today, at the lab, for the very first time, I became aware that my latest energies had not been expended on the humanitarian objectives which I had heretofore thought. In all good conscience, I must halt this work. I will not be able to continue. I have worked all my life to do good for scientific endeavors and for mankind, and will not change course now. I have been greatly blessed to have served in some capacity to ease mankind's pain—until now.

NH."

Dane paused with the awkward silence of one who witnesses a dying man's last words, and eyed Rupert Jenkins thoughtfully across the table. "All right. So we have a suicide note. So what?"

Heinz jumped right in. "The doc says there's something pretty important attached to the email, Mr. Ingersoll."

"Oh? And what might that be?" Dane's eye brows rose just slightly.

Jenkins obligingly reached inside his coat pocket once again. This time the paper he handed Dane was unintelligible gibberish—signs, symbols and letter combinations he hadn't seen since his college chemistry class. He smiled apologetically. "These are a progression of chemical equations that explain the way in which the drug you call PZT mutates. I studied them on the plane trip over here. This drug has remarkable qualities," Dr. Jenkins paused, lowering his voice for emphasis, "extraordinary qualities."

"Could you elaborate, Doctor? We don't have much time, you know." Dane glance nervously toward the door. No Jenny.

"Certainly. It appears that PZT has near-miraculous healing properties. In fact, its molecular architecture is not that different from those of some powerful human hormones. And, it seems to remain stable for periods of up to one year with no ill effects. Then, it begins to throw off electrons and certain subatomic particles, causing the bond within the weakest part of the molecule to disappear. Once that portion separates, mutation accelerates rapidly: exponentially, in fact. The result is that the host—the organism which is using the drug, begins to dehydrate and have the very life sucked out of it. You see, the mutating molecules absorb all the hydrogen and oxygen they can to supplant the now-absent portions of the original molecule. The organism more or less implodes on itself, quite rapidly."

"Does this happen in every case?" Dane was raptly attentive.

"No. That is the part that is perhaps the most perplexing. There is a certain randomness to it. More study is needed to reveal the definitive criteria which trigger it."

"Well, we don't have a whole lot of time for more study at the moment. What about its addictive qualities?" Dane was driving hard for solid answers now.

"Of course, every individual is different. But if I had to make an educated guess, I'd say this compound would be extremely addictive. It bears certain chemical similarities to the opiate class of drugs. You see, the hydroxyl ending—"

"Look, Doctor, I appreciate the chemistry lesson, but what I want to know—what I *need* to know is: Can a person who is addicted to PZT ever expect to kick the habit?" Dane surprised even himself with the directness of his question. He glanced at Heinz, who did not seem fazed.

"As a matter of fact, yes, I think they can. He held out the piece of computer paper toward Dane. The email Dr. Holloway sent me before he died describes a process which I believe was the foundation for an antidote."

"An antidote? You mean, to stop the addiction."

"That, certainly, and hopefully to arrest the mutation process. While I can't be certain yet, it appears that Dr. Holloway's dying wish was for me to formulate an antidote. He was a brilliant man, and based on his last writing, I believe it would be quite possible to produce an antidote for the drug PZT."

The little room suddenly fell quiet. Dane lowered his eyes to his hands which rested on the table in front of him.

"Dane," Heinz offered in a hushed voice, "Dr. Jenkins knows about Natalie."

"Yes, I do, Mr. Ingersoll, and I can't imagine what you must be going through at the moment. Of course, it would be experimental, and a bit risky without the time for clinical trials, but—"

"I want that antidote for my daughter, and to hell with the risk! I've been living with risk for weeks now. When can you put it together?" Dane's voice broke.

"If you have a good laboratory nearby, I could try to get something together by tomorrow—"

"Tomorrow isn't good enough. She may be dead by then. How much money do you need?"

"Mr. Ingersoll, I'm not going to charge you for my services. I'm more than happy to do this for Natalie and for the legacy of my good friend, Dr. Holloway. As for materials and the laboratory usage fee on short notice, you might be looking at $10,000."

"Done. If you need more, I'll see that you have it." He wrote his cell phone number on the back of one of his cards, and slid it across the table to Jenkins, who picked it up. Heinz, I've got my hands full here," Dane motioned toward the door and the hallway beyond. "Can you find a lab to set Dr. Jenkins up in?"

"Well I, er, I-I'll see what I can do."

"Well, see to it immediately. I want him in a lab equipped with everything he needs, before noon." Dane handed Heinz a credit card. "Book him a hotel room near the courthouse and, if possible, near the lab. I don't care about cost, just get it done." In spite of all the pressure, Dane looked for a moment like a two-ton load had been lifted off of his shoulders.

"Sure, Mr. Ingersoll. Uh, I know it's a little off topic, but isn't Dr. Jenkins also going to be a witness in the trial?"

"Heinz, what you've just provided is better than any expert witness testimony. If this antidote works, then we may actually be able to have a trial that matters."

There was a knock at the door and Jenny's head protruded half way through. "Are y'all ready? The judge is taking the bench." With those words, the meeting broke up, Dane leaving first. As he did so, he shouted back over his shoulder to Heinz, "I'll have my cell phone set on vibrate. Text me as soon as you have Jenkins set up. I want results today."

"Dane, I have another wit—", Heinz began. But it was too late. Dane had disappeared, slipping between the massive courtroom doors.

* * * *

James Patterson pulled up to the government employee parking lot adjacent to the federal building that housed the FBI field office. The building was only two blocks away from the courthouse, and he could cover the distance in minutes. As always, his assigned courtroom seat as agent-in-charge on the case would be waiting for him. He did not want to miss one second of the injunction trial, and glanced at his watch nervously. As his feet hit the ground and he felt the cool January air against his face, his cell phone rang.

"Patterson."

"Boss, we have Dean." It was Newcombe.

"Is he in custody?"

"Might as well be. We've located him right inside Mr. Ingersoll's house, asleep. 'Woke him with a phone call. He's moving around now; we figure he'll exit the premises in fifteen or twenty minutes. That should give us time to get the warrant and take him without raising any eyebrows."

"That's perfect. Once you get him, hold him for questioning. Mine only. And I want that warrant to be air tight. No miscues." Patterson knew all warrants went through Justice before issuance anyway, but he decided to punctuate the point.

"Not a problem. I'll be back in touch with you when we've served him."

"Great." Patterson hung up the phone with a satisfied feeling, and launched out on a brisk walk to the courthouse down Griffin Street, his satchel tucked under one arm. *"It's going to be an interesting trial,"* he smiled to himself. *"A foregone conclusion on how it will turn out, but interesting."* He covered the distance to the Cabell building in a mere seven minutes.

CHAPTER TWENTY- NINE

"Your Honor, may it please the Court, we have a motion for a continuance of the injunction hearing. May I approach the bench?" Dane's polished demeanor betrayed nothing of the unsettled stomach churning underneath.

"Yes, you may. But I must say a continuance of an injunction proceeding is rare indeed." Dane handed the hastily typed motion to the Judge, who peered skeptically at it through his glasses. He then took several steps to the Government's counsel table and handed a copy to lead counsel. Dane waited patiently for his honor to digest the motion before speaking again.

"I realize, your Honor, that this request is unusual. However, we have a critical witness that we have just learned about in California, who is performing some highly relevant laboratory analysis of the drug which is the subject of the hearing. We expect to have his results some time tomorrow."

Judge Fitzhugh's eyes squinted as he scanned a document which Dane was certain was the morning's trial docket. "What says the Government?" he queried, glancing their direction.

"Your Honor, we have witnesses who are prepared to proceed today, and who are from outside the Dallas area. It would be inconvenient indeed to have to postpone. The government would have to put them up extra days in a hotel. Besides, we bear the burden of proof and will proceed with evidence first. Mr. Ingersoll will not have to put on evidence until we are through. Therefore, he will have all the time he requires."

Dane was ready with a response. "Judge, that might be true but for two things. First, the witness we have is an expert, who needs to be present to hear the testimony of the Government's experts. He cannot do so while he is conducting the laboratory tests of which we speak. Secondly, if the Government finishes its case today, we would be still required to proceed with his testimony before we are ready to do so."

"Don't you have any other witnesses you could put on? And why the last-minute lab testing when you've known about this hearing for several months?" inquired Fitzhugh.

"Judge, we absolutely have other witnesses, but their testimony may also be affected by the lab test results. The last-minute development occurred with some newly discovered evidence in the form of a suicide note left by Dr. Norman Holloway, famed chemist familiar with the drug in question. All we are asking for is a one-day continuance to develop this vital evidence, your Honor."

"Gentlemen, I see that I have a couple of matters on my docket that will take about an hour or two each. I can keep busy for today without reaching your case, and it is 11:00 a.m. already. But I will start at 9:00 a.m. sharp tomorrow morning. See to it that you are both here before then, and ready to proceed. Motion granted."

"Thank you, your Honor."

Moments later, Patterson arrived at the courthouse to see Dane Ingersoll, his staff, and a group of several federal prosecutors swarming into the corridor. He approached a U.S. Marshall he happened to know.

"What's going on, Mick? I thought the trial in Judge Fitzhugh's court was getting underway."

"So did everyone else. At the last minute, Mr. Ingersoll moved for a continuance, and Fitzhugh granted it."

Patterson cursed.

"That Ingersoll must lead a charmed life. I never seen his Honor grant a continuance on anything the day of trial, much less on an injunction."

"Did the Judge say why?"

"I couldn't hear it all. Something about a witness from California is all I could catch. I was way in the back of the court room, you know."

"Really? Well, much obliged, Mick."

"Don't mention it."

Patterson made it back to his office even more quickly than he'd come, and arrived to the news that Alton Dean had just been served with a warrant and was in custody. It helped dampen the disgust he felt at the postponement of the injunction trial. He called Jon Newcombe to his office, and Jon arrived a few moments later, warrant in hand.

"Let's see it," said Patterson.

"Why the concern over the warrant?" Newcombe wanted to know.

"In case you hadn't pondered the issue, Jon, Dean is one of the brightest young attorneys with one of the most powerful law firms in the country. They are going to make a huge issue out of this—and if they don't, mark it down that Dane Ingersoll will. This warrant must be completely bullet proof." Patterson studied the warrant, and the affidavit upon which it was founded, for several minutes. He noted that it relied on the sweeping power granted by Congress after September 11, 2001 to detain and question witnesses who were deemed a national security risk. Clearly, it seemed to the FBI veteran, a man who had recently cavorted with South American drug kingpins who had possible terrorist connections was precisely such a risk. Dismissing his doubts about the propriety of using the terrorist connections as a basis for the warrant, Patterson peered up at Newcombe and emitted a staccato grunt. "This will do for now. Where is Dean being held?"

"At the county facility, in a special area for 'white collar' detainees. I'm ready to dispatch our two best interrogators, at your word."

"Who did you have in mind?"

"Jack Feeney and Wayne Hollins. Jack has worked with the DEA for twenty years and been instrumental in prosecutions of the Medellin drug cartel. Wayne transferred here recently from Corpus Christi, but has similar experience with the Cali cartel. Both of them can get to the bottom of things pretty fast."

"Look, Jon. We are not dealing with your garden variety drug trafficker. Alton Dean is an attorney at the top of his game, with very good connections. And we're not talking about a drug cartel here, but about a large, reputable pharmaceutical company—probably right behind Eli Lilly, Pfizer and Glaxo-Wellcome in size and reputation. We need to tread lightly and carefully.

We are Alton Dean's friend, and he is not a suspect, at least not yet. All I want is information about Rowalter." He spoke the words emphatically, though he hoped not so much as to seem contrived.

"I understand perfectly, Sir. I will make sure the interrogators stay strictly within those parameters."

"See that you do."

* * * *

Heinz surveyed the modest hotel room with a mixture of satisfaction and concern. It had plenty of room to spread out, including a study in the corner that could be used for a table if that's what Professor Jenkins wanted. There was a double-sink vanity in the bathroom. But a laboratory it most certainly was not. There would be no stainless-steel sinks, Bunsen burners, beaker holders or agar plates here. If Jenkins pressed him he supposed he might find him some lab equipment, but he hoped fervently this wouldn't occur. Time mattered mightily now. This place was the third hotel they'd visited, and far and away the roomiest. Clearly of 1950's vintage, it sat off the beaten path with a large lot around it and nothing within at least a hundred feet in any direction. but Heinz liked this because he'd had crazy visions of some horrific explosion, a sort of mad scientist's experiment gone wrong.

The door behind him swung abruptly open, and Heinz leapt nearly a foot in the air.

"Doc! Say, do you mind giving a guy some warning? You scared me half outa' my mind!" His heart was a jackhammer, still unconvinced it wasn't FBI.

Jenkins grinned sheepishly. "I'm sorry about that, Mr. Heinz. I didn't realize you'd be jumpy. I got everything I need from University Lab Supply near SMU. I even managed to rent a microscope." Jenkins held out the large box he supported on his outstretched arms as if it were a trophy.

"That's super, Doc. Do you really think you'll have enough room to conduct your work? I mean, it's kinda' cramped and all—"

"Nonsense,"Jenkins replied dismissively, depositing the box on the bed. "We'll make do just fine. Believe me, I've seen much worse during my graduate school days." He jabbed a finger in the direction of the desk. "How about clearing off that desk for me, and I'll set things up."

"You got it." Heinz' heart had begun slowing to normal again. He ignored the pain still tearing at his muscles and cleared off the desk, placing lamp, pads, phone books and phone on the floor in the far corner of the room. Dr. Jenkins, exhibiting a sense of purpose that was new to Heinz, pulled out the microscope. This he placed adjacent to an odd-shaped, high intensity lamp with a flexible neck, and plugged it in. Next, he extracted from the bag an assortment of bottles of different sizes, microscope slides, and something that looked to Jack like culture plates. In ten minutes, he'd been transformed into Dr. Frankenstein himself.

"Have you got the material?" Jenkins queried, ready to begin.

"I'm glad you asked. I was able to procure some while you were out running your errands." Heinz left unsaid that he had gone half-crazy trying to run down

Reggie Andrews, who claimed to have a bottle of the stuff. He produced a brown bottle from a coat pocket and handed it to Jenkins. Jenkins was visibly excited, even invigorated, as he donned a lab coat and began extracting samples of PZT from the bottle.

"How long do you think you're gonna need to hit pay dirt on this thing, Doc?"

"I'm not sure, Mr. Heinz, but since I've got classes to get back to, so it'd better be soon. Why don't you run along and find something to do, so I can concentrate?"

"I can take a hint, Doc. Consider me outa here."

Heinz knew precisely where to go next, and was grateful for permission to do so. Though he had the secure cell phone with him, Heinz walked quickly down to a pay phone he'd spotted at an Exxon station on the street corner. There was no way he was going to risk this call being intercepted. A female voice answered on the third ring.

"Er, pardon me, but is Mr. Ingersoll there?"

"Heinz, it's Jenny. Dane handed me the phone cuz he's tied up right now." Heinz heard the sound of papers being shuffled in the background.

"Well, tell him I've got some important news he's gonna want to hear." *More shuffling, then static.*

"Dane here. What's up Heinz?"

"Are you on a secure cell?"

"Yes, of course. It's scrambled. Why?"

"Well, Dane, I'm pretty sure James Patterson has got his own private agenda going on PZT."

Silence. "What do you mean, 'private agenda'? Elaborate."

"Well, you see, I took the liberty of contacting a friend of mine in the investigation business. He's no small timer—high end stuff, you know. We cased Patterson's house, and, well, I think we obtained enough to show he's not just working for the FBI on this thing."

Longer silence.... "Just exactly what do you have, Heinz?"

"We've found bottles of...well, PZT... in his house."

"So? I'd expect that if he's investigating the stuff, he'd—

"No, I don't think you understand, Dane. There are boxes full of product labels and bottles in his garage. He has a notebook filled with notes, and it mentions Natalie and her location within the hospital. He's been following the movement of Rowalter stock on the stock market. And," Heinz paused for dramatic effect, "we found a truck."

"Yeah?" the voice on the line was breathy and uncertain. "What kind of truck?"

"A box truck—the delivery type—parked at a warehouse and loaded to the gills with the stuff. The key to the truck was found in Patterson's home. We have complete video and still shots. I think you'll wanna see these." Heinz both sounded and felt triumphant, like he'd snagged a trophy-winning bass.

"We need to meet. I'm at the office now, but I can be home in twenty minutes. I have to check on Alton anyway. Bring whatever you have to show me then." Dane proceeded to give directions.

Heinz arrived first, and sat in his car at curbside till Dane entered the house, as they had agreed. He let five more minutes pass, then slipped out of the seat, quietly closed the door, and carefully mounted the front steps. He had barely cleared the threshold when Dane grabbed his shoulder and said hoarsely, "Alton is gone."

"What do you mean 'Alton is gone'?" Heinz struggled to shift his mind from what he had to tell Dane to what Dane had just told him. he'd just been told.

"I mean he's not in the bed where I left him after I picked him up yesterday."

"There are no signs of forced entry," said Heinz, examining the front door, then heading for the back of the house. He heard Dane's steps moving hurriedly behind him. "Nothing from the patio door, either", he announced with an air of someone who should know. Dane returned to the bedroom with Heinz close behind. The sheets and covers on the bed were all askew, and the phone off the hook. Dane reached over and hung it up. "Sit down," Dane motioned to Heinz, who promptly complied by sitting on the bed. Dane took a seat next to him.

"Show me what you have."

A bit surprised at the shift of focus away from Mr. Dean, Heinz haltingly complied. He opened the legal-size envelope and emptied it on the bed. Out came several photographs, a video tape and product labels. Dane noticed some of the product labels were covered with dust obviously used to detect fingerprints. Hurriedly, Dane picked up the photographs, thumbing through them. His eyes grew narrow, then wide as he saw the huge stash of PZT in the truck. He craned his head back left over his shoulder to look another time at the empty bed where Alton had lain.

"Do you want to see the video?" Heinz offered cautiously. Dane shook his head and muttered simply, "Tell me what's on it."

"Well now, let's see...it shows copies of the *Wall Street Journal* in Patterson's study, highlighting stock quotes for Rowalter Industries. It shows hand-written notes in a diary of sorts and—" Heinz fixed his gaze on the floor and paused for what seemed like several minutes— "Here it, uhm...mentions....Well, it mentions Natalie and her location in the hospital."

"'Nothing out of the ordinary there. The FBI is supposed to be watching my daughter around the clock. More than they did for my wife. What else did the diary show?"

"Well, the investigator isn't sure about this but..."

"But *what?*"

"There are little numbers written in the diary margin where the entries about Natalie are. 'Looks like they could may be milligram or milliliter dosages." Heinz had rattled off this last part rapidly and with a 'business-as-usual' tone, hoping to somehow lessen its impact. It didn't work. Dane suddenly sat bolt upright, pupils dilated. His eyes drilled through Heinz'.

"Why in God's green earth would the FBI be in possession of dosages of Natalie's medicine?"

"*For a rising star attorney, this one ain't very quick,*" thought Heinz. "Dane, I'm not so sure it's **medicine** dosages—at least not as we understand the term."

"What are you saying?" Then, suddenly, it was as though a veil had parted. Dane's eyes widened with the realization as he began to connect the dots, and his mind ignited in hot fury. "That f— bastard." Heinz could only nod his agreement. Dane's brain was now working overtime. He glanced back at the pillow where Alton's head had rested a few hours ago. And that's not the only thing, Dane. I can't prove it at the moment, but my guess is that Patterson is doing some insider training. He has information that would obviously cause Rowalter's stock to plunge. That would explain why he gave all those photos and stuff to Jenny at Schneider's Deli. If we use that evidence and prove the drug is dangerous, the stock takes a dive and he can sell short, making millions after the stock bottoms."

"You said there was no sign of forced entry?"

"That's correct, sir. And no note either. Either someone very, very good extracted Alton from your house, or Alton left of his own accord."

"Alton wouldn't have left on his own. Not after what he'd just been through. The guy was paranoid of his own shadow. He was...taken by the Bureau." Dane mouthed the words slowly and deliberately, as if trying to convince himself. He stood from the bed. "Give me that videotape. We have work to do, and not a second to spare. What's going on with Dr. Jenkins?"

"He's hard at it in a make-shift laboratory. I'll check on him." Heinz began punching buttons on his secure phone, glad for the diversion. The phone gave two short rings.

"Dr. Jenkins." Heinz set the phone to "speaker" so they could both hear.

"Hello Doc. Heinz here. Mr. Ingersoll is with me. Could we get a status report?"

The sound of clattering glass and lab ware could be heard through the phone. "Gentlemen, I haven't tested it yet, but I do believe I may have an antidote."

With a hopeful glance at Dane, who reciprocated, Heinz replied, "Well...how sure are you?"

"About as sure as my knowledge of biochemistry can make me, which is pretty sure. But, of course, all such potions should be tested on a live host." More laboratory noise.

This time it was Dane who shot back, "Doctor Jenkins, if what you're saying is that you need a lab animal, or a human volunteer, we don't have any. All of the animals and humans we have evidence on are long dead. We only have one live person who is a—" Dane paused, then forced out the word: "host."

"Mr. Ingersoll, with all due respect, sir, I wouldn't advise trying an untested, first-formulation antidote on your daughter." Jenkins' tone sounded like a mixture of paternal and downright ominous.

"He's right, Mr. Ingersoll. What if something went wrong?"

Dane's big hands obscured his face, and his elbows rested on his knees as he hunched forward. A painful silence set in, only broken by Dane abruptly lifting his head and looking straight at Heinz. "There is no time for clinical trials." His words were crisp and decisive. "We have to make our move *now*. Natalie may not have till tomorrow, and doing nothing will only ensure her death." Dane turned to face the cell phone like it was human. "I want that antidote prepared to administer to Natalie as soon as possible. She needs to get it *today*." The other end of the phone was silent, with only Dr. Jenkins' breathing audible.

"Pardon me for asking, Mr. Ingersoll, but once we get an antidote, how should we get it to her? Through her doctor?"

"I'm afraid not, Heinz. The doctors at EDMC are useless, and they'd never subject themselves to liability by using an unproven, untested drug. We'll have to do this ourselves."

"But how? She's being guarded 24/7 by an FBI agent!"

"That's precisely where you come in, my friend. You wanted to help us. So, you think you got the goods on Patterson, do you? Well then, now's your time to shine. You're the man."

Dane's message could not have been any clearer. Heinz had received his orders, and he was a man with a singular mission. He would do anything humanly possible in order to square accounts with James Patterson. "*And If I can help a little girl in the process, then so much the better,*" he reasoned. "Don't worry, Mr. Ingersoll, I'll handle it. You concentrate on the trial tomorrow and on Mr. Dean. I'll check in with you as to how things are going." Heinz rose and began reassembling all of the investigator's evidence strewn about the bed. "I've got to get back over to the hotel-lab. Here, you'll need this," he said, handing Dane the envelope of material.

CHAPTER THIRTY

Heinz burst breathlessly through the hotel-lab door, causing Jenkins to spin around and nearly drop the beaker of liquid he was holding on the floor.

"Well, is it ready?" said Heinz, unapologetically.

"In truth, no. As I said on the phone, this is a first batch, untested and unproven. I would not want to—"

"Understood, Doc. But this is the Boss's orders, and I'm sure he'll take full responsibility if things don't turn out just so. Time is not on our side, if you follow me."

"Well...I...I suppose so."

"Now, we need to get this into some form to dispense into a little baby. What do you suggest, hypodermic, I.V., or what?"

"Well, I'm a chemist, not a physician. But I should think a premature baby would be very hard to inject with a needle. Also, a sudden high dosage of an untested antidote could be a terrible shock to an already very ill child. Perhaps you might substitute an IV bag containing the antidote for the one she's now using."

"Brilliant solution, Doc. I couldn't have said it better myself. Now, just how much of this potion should we need?"

"As I said, there is no way to know how anyone, much less an infant, would respond, or how soon. But I would imagine it will need to be diluted with saline solution, probably starting with at least a 1:10 ratio. I should think, oh, three IV bags of 1 liter each should be more than adequate."

"Where do I get this saline solution and IV bags?"

"Any medical supply establishment would carry them."

"Consider it done, Doc. I'll need the antidote ready to mix as soon as I return. We need to get this stuff up to the hospital tonight."

"I'll do the best I can."

"Just make sure the 'best you can' is having the entire batch ready to go. There's no room for error on this one. We're counting on you, Doc." Heinz ignored the pained look on Dr. Jenkins' face as he made a bee line for his car.

* * * *

Alton squirmed uncomfortably in the straight-backed wooden chair. His blue jeans-clad knees were just inches away from the knees of the man in the business suit seated directly across from him. Another man stood a few feet away. Both men had nearly identical haircuts, and both men were government agents cut from the same piece of cloth. The man named Feeney, who was standing, looked to Alton to be about 45, with touches of grey at his temples. Wayne Hollins, the one sitting uncomfortably close, appeared about a decade younger. Alton was the center of both men's attention, the object of their gaze. The atmosphere was cordial, but clearly no-nonsense. Hollins began the questioning.

"Mr. Dean, we apprehended you by federal arrest warrant because we are concerned about your recent trip to South America: what you saw, who you met and spoke with, that sort of thing."

Alton was now fully awake and at least somewhat refreshed, even sassy. "It would seem to me that if you were all that 'concerned' about my 'trip', gentlemen, you would have dispatched some agents to thwart my kidnapping."

"So, you were taken against your will?"

"No. Actually, I was on the midwinter vacation I'd been saving up for. Of course I was kidnapped, you morons! The real question of the hour is, where were you guys, and why aren't you sitting in this seat with me asking you the questions?" Alton looked directly at his interrogator and could see Hollins was caught completely off balance.

"Mr. Dean," interjected Feeney, the older agent. "I'm not sure you fully appreciate the seriousness of this matter." Feeney paused, his back side propped on the edge of a table. Do you have any witnesses of this alleged kidnapping?"

"Generally, Mr. Feeney, when someone is nabbed in a parking garage in the wee hours of the morning, people aren't standing around waiting to witness the event." Alton hoped he sounded condescending.

"Granted. Then you'll understand why we could not have known about this alleged kidnapping, either."

"Dammit, quit calling it "alleged."

Feeney ignored the comment. "We have records of your plane ticket purchase, your hotel stays, and your movements once in Peru and Bolivia. This evidence is completely inconsistent with your kidnapping story."

"What?!" Alton's reaction was both instantaneous and volcanic. He was standing now.

"You heard me correctly, Mr. Dean. We don't believe the kidnapping story. And, frankly, you're telling of it makes us quite concerned about your level of involvement in international drug dealing." He and Hollins traded knowing glances as he said this.

Alton's felt hot blood rush to his face, and he could hear his heartbeat pounding in his ears. Still weak from his ordeal, he steadied himself by gripping the back of the chair. Through clenched teeth he said, "I want a lawyer. Now."

"That can be arranged. 'Just a few more questions."

"Apparently you don't hear very well. I want a lawyer, NOW. And you are not getting another word from me."

* * * *

Heinz peered at his watch in the darkness. It read "3:55". Perfect. The nurses in the NICU would be changing shifts in five minutes. He would look like just one more male nurse or hospital orderly coming onto the floor to clock in. Following Heinz' instructions, Doctor Jenkins circled the hospital slowly without headlights, then quietly dropped him near the back of the employee parking lot. Jenkins exited the lot and made a wide arc, slowly circling the block on back streets while Heinz walked to the employee entrance. Heinz had purposely left his wallet and all forms of identification back in the hotel-lab. The sheer weight of the I.V. bags, filled to capacity, pulled downward the deep pockets of his hospital coat. He moved slowly to avoid them swinging conspicuously as he walked.

Silently, Heinz slipped through the sliding electric doors, and glided into the employee elevator. There was no information desk at this end of the hospital, no inquiring eyes to elude. The numbers above the elevator door blinked green at each successive floor until they stopped at "5". The doors parted, and Heinz found himself face to face with a nurse who was pushing a cart loaded down with bottles and instruments. Across the hallway to his right, he saw the supply room from whence she had come. He stepped quickly out of the elevator to allow the nurse to enter, taking care to keep his eyes angled toward the floor. In spite of his cool exterior, he felt drops of perspiration gathering in his arm pits and beginning to trickle down his side under the loose-fitting scrubs. Stifling his jitters, Heinz shuffled across the hallway to the supply room door and tried the knob. It opened, just as he'd expected. Inside, there were three carts. He grabbed the nearest one and backed out of the room into the hallway. Heinz let his eyes scan the corridors, surveying each room as he passed. There was bustling activity throughout the hospital wing as medical staff began gathering their things, chattering among themselves and trickling toward the elevators and stairwells. Heinz could not have timed it any better. He slid, unnoticed, past the Nuclear Medicine doors, through the pediatric wing, and finally arrived at the point where the corridor dead-ended. To his right was a door bearing a single name plate: "NEONATAL INTENSIVE CARE". He pushed the door open. The solitary nurse at the watch desk, a woman in her mid-forties, was noting her final entries in a chart. She looked up from the monitor, smiling at the "orderly" as he walked by. "'Starting your shift?" she asked.

"Yeah, just doing some restocking." *"Damn! Wanted to avoid talking to anyone!"*

"Well, I don't envy anyone who has to start working at this hour. At least *my* shift is over." The nurse packed up her things, and grabbed some kind of large hand bag. At that moment another, younger looking nurse entered the unit. Thankfully, Heinz noticed, the two began chatting by the doorway. Their backs were angled at about a two-thirds turn toward the entry door, which meant they faced away from the incubators on the opposite side of the long room. He glanced quickly at the FBI agent seated near Natalie's incubator. Incredibly, the agent was asleep. Seizing the moment, Heinz walked the fifteen or twenty feet, and quickly identified Natalie's incubator. A backward glance through the dimly lit room told him the nurses were still debriefing their cohorts from the last shift. The IV bag already in place above Natalie's head was nearly empty. He deftly exchanged it for another identically marked bag which he extracted from his pocket. The old bag he slipped into the same pocket. He then placed a spare bag, which he had marked "Ingersoll" in the supply cabinet beside Natalie's incubator. As he worked, he couldn't help noticing the shallow, quick breathing of the tiny girl, and the flushed cheeks. "*Not too long now, Natalie,*" he whispered, sub audibly. To complement his act, Heinz rummaged through the supply cabinet, feigning replacement of sundry supplies from his cart. Then he wheeled around, head down, and made a beeline for the entrance. A peripheral glance told him no one appeared any the wiser. Back in the car, Heinz used the secure phone to call Dane. "The deed is done," he spoke in monotone.

"Good. Thanks, Heinz." Dane hung up the phone and stared soberly at the wall of his office, where he would stay till the trial. Now it was a waiting game.

CHAPTER THIRTY-ONE

Judge Fitzhugh was running late this morning, according to his clerk. That was fine by Dane, Jenny, and the other members of the trial team bustling about the courtroom. An air of tense, breathless excitement filled the place...the kind a football player feels before the game opening whistle is blown. The adrenaline permeating the court room was palpable, and although Dane had been through many trials of greater complexity, he had never had so much riding on one. Dane unloaded his two large brief cases of material, while Jenny lined up the boxes of evidence in consecutive order along the railing which separated the public gallery from counsel table. They exchanged nervous glances, and Dane knew she had to be thinking what he was thinking: "What direction will this trial take?" It was one thing to try a case against the government for a big, well-financed client knowing what the risks were. It was entirely another to have no idea from the opening gavel whether one would be advocating his client's position or abandoning it.

Nathan Smith smiled smugly in Dane's direction as he took his chair at the government's table. There were four others with him, three male and one female. He guessed the two thirty-ish looking men were assistant prosecutors who would conduct questioning of some of the witnesses. The youngest man and the woman, both of whom appeared to be in their early twenties, were briefcase carriers: law clerks who were there to observe, shuffle exhibits and run errands.

There was a brief commotion at the front of the cavernous courtroom as the attractive young court reporter entered and set up the machine, cranked in her roll of paper and adjusted her chair. Her long, slender legs were nicely tanned and sported a short skirt that came to half thigh. She was closely followed by the docket clerk, a young, wiry, bespectacled man who sat to the right of the bench on a slightly raised table. That made him and the bailiff, who remained standing, all of the court staff on that side of the courtroom. The judge's law clerk, a young freckle-faced attorney who doubtless graduated in the top five of his class, entered from the far right and took a seat roughly parallel to the docket clerk. Everyone was present now but for Judge Fitzhugh.

Dane heard the creak of the gigantic doors to the court room open and, turning around, saw none other than Gary Thompson, the twit who first acquainted him with Rowalter. His eyes met Dane's ever so briefly, while his face wore a grin as silly looking as it was uncharacteristic of him. It turned Dane's stomach, and he quickly returned his gaze to the front of the court room, locked on the judge's bench. At that moment, the bailiff intoned the familiar, "All rise, the United States District Court of the Northern District of Texas, Chief Judge Charles Fitzhugh, presiding." Judge Fitzhugh entered deliberately, judicial robes flowing. At the same moment, Jenny glided noiselessly into the chair to Dane's right, smiling at him as she did so. "I apologize to the lawyers for my tardiness this morning," began the Judge, "but I had to conduct a brief telephonic hearing in chambers. Now for the matter at hand. We have the specially set case of *Food and Drug Administration vs. Rowalter Industries, S.A.* Are both sides ready to proceed?

"The government is ready, Your Honor," Nathan Smith said tersely, now standing, his demeanor cocky.

"Rowalter Industries is ready, Your Honor," Dane stated, rising. He mustered the most confident tone he was capable of.

"Good," continued the Judge. "The Court's file reflects no pre-trial matters currently pending which need my attention. Is that correct gentlemen?" Both counsel assured him that it was. "Fine, then let us begin. I will allow each side twenty minutes for opening statement, since this does not seem to be an especially complex matter and we have no jury. Mr. Smith, do you wish to make an opening statement?"

"We do, Your Honor."

"All right, then, you may proceed."

"May it please the Court, this is a drug approval case seeking approval by the FDA to market the new drug 'PZT', more properly and scientifically known as phenylkerozotetracarboxide. The application for its approval has been filed by the Defendant, Rowalter Industries, S. A. It is the government's position, supported by abundant and competent expert testimony, that this drug, though possessing some medicinal qualities, mutates randomly over time into a lethal substance, the dangers of which far outweigh any possible benefits." At this point, Smith paused for dramatic effect, glancing in Dane's direction. "The government," he continued, "will show that this mutative behavior is a predictable event, and that Rowalter Industries has marketed the drug knowing full well that it possesses these destructive characteristics. Moreover, Your Honor, Rowalter has withheld information from the Food and Drug Administration that tends to show such lethal propensities. It has attempted to deceive the FDA by reporting the medicinal qualities of the drug, but withholding vital information concerning its harmful qualities. Finally, it has illegally introduced PZT into the stream of United States commerce, selling it under various names, and marketing it after deceptively altering or manipulating the results of numerous clinical trials and required independent laboratory studies..."

Nathan Smith proceeded to outline his case in broad strokes. Judge Fitzhugh, though giving the appearance of listening, seemed to Dane to be preoccupied with something on the bench. Jenny, on the other hand, took copious notes just as he had instructed, while he made final adjustments to his own opening statement. That statement came down with both feet on the side of marketing the drug. Merely thinking about it made his hands break into a cold sweat. Just then, his right hand was seized by a tremor, perceived by no one but Dane. His mind raced, feeding back into his consciousness vivid, full-colored pictures of children dying, then of Natalie in her incubator. Before he'd had time to solidify his thoughts, he heard Smith say "We ask the Court for immediate injunctive relief." Then he sat down.

"Mister Ingersoll, do you wish to make an opening statement?" Fitzhugh looked casually attentive, peering over his glasses down from the bench.

"Yes...yes, Your Honor." Dane heard himself say.

"You may proceed."

Dane glanced at Jenny, who was smiling encouragingly. Since there was no jury, he stood at counsel table pressing his right hand flat against his legal pad, to quell the tremor. He could feel his sweat against the paper. An interminable moment passed, during which he was sure he heard the courtroom wall clock ticking away the seconds. Then, abruptly, Dane looked squarely at the judge.

"Er...Rather...Your Honor, Rowalter Industries at this time waives opening statement."

His Honor removed his reading glasses and peered curiously a long moment at Dane, but said nothing. Nathan Smith gave no outward hint of surprise, although his underlings could be seen staring, obviously puzzled. Dane only hoped they saw it as a strategy move: *"Let's dive right into the evidence. I'm so confident of my case, why waste time with opening?"* After all, there was no usual jury to impress—only Judge Fitzhugh, who knew the law and needed no outline to work from.

"Very well then, Mr. Ingersoll. Mr. Smith, call your first witness."

"Judge, the United States calls Walter Johnson."

Dane jotted the name at the top of his legal pad. This had been expected. Walter Johnson was the Chief of Compliance for the Food & Drug Administration. He would be a boring witness, but still necessary for the prosecution to set the context and to admit certain critical documents into evidence. As Dane began taking notes, Jenny handed to him his cross-examination folder on this witness. Smith took nearly half an hour just laying the groundwork— background, job description, credentials, everything but what Johnson had eaten for breakfast. He then spent the next two hours teaching His Honor the processes a new drug must go through before it can be test marketed, let alone distributed whole hog into pharmacies. Jenny stared at her laptop, dutifully keyboarding any significant statements. Although Judge Fitzhugh looked at the witness, his face depicted total unconcern. Dane, however, knew better. Fitzhugh, as was well known, would be on top of every detail; nothing got by him. By the time Smith passed the witness to Dane for cross-examination, it was noon. Judge Fitzhugh looked up, shifted his spectacles, and said, "Mr. Ingersoll, unless your cross examination is going to be extremely short, I intend to break at once for lunch." It was a question spoken as a pronouncement.

"Judge, I will definitely require full cross examination." *"Which sounds a whole lot better than, 'I need to buy my client some time at any cost',"* thought Dane.

"As I expected. All right. We are in recess until 1:30 p.m."

Dane and Jenny barely made it to the steps outside the courthouse before Heinz accosted them all in a dither. The Doc trailed behind.

"Dane, I switched the I.V. bags no problem." Heinz was gulping cold air from jogging up the many steps.

"Terrific—how's she doing?"

"No change as of a few minutes ago. In fact, when I called the NICU nurse, pretending to be you, she seemed to think Natalie looked worse." Heinz expression turned apologetic. "I informed Mrs. Ingersoll by phone of what we're doing, as you instructed. She's fit to be tied."

"Of course she is," Dane mumbled. His face was set in a grim look which didn't disguise his dejectedness.

"Should we get some lunch?" Jenny posed, hoping to brighten the mood.

"I'm not hungry," replied Dane.

"That's understandable, but we need time to regroup anyhow. Let's huddle up over at Sali's. Heinz and the Doc agreed, and they braved the freezing January Northern rattling down Commerce Street, crossed over Kennedy Plaza, and ducked in to the bustling Italian luncheonette. Jenny spied a large booth in the back and herded everybody into position. To make matters easier, she took everyone's orders and conveyed them to the waitress. She ordered Dane a personal pizza, but he didn't touch it.

"What do we know about Alton at this point, Heinz?"

"Only that he is still being questioned. My source on the inside doesn't know much about it, except that Patterson is personally supervising it, and has two of his top men on it. If I had to guess, I'd say they are trying to set him up. No one expected Alton to escape from Rowalter, least of all Patterson. Now that he's out, he's got to do some damage control. My thinking is, Patterson's worried about what Alton saw, and what he knows. He'll debrief him as much as possible. If he knows too much, they won't call him to testify. They won't risk it: just keep him out of sight. And of course, if we call him, Smith will do his level best to discredit him."

"Well, we can't very well call him if we don't know where he is, now can we?" Dane commiserated.

"Poor Alton," moaned Jenny. He's been through a lot.

"No kidding," Dane seemed to have temporarily suspended his depression over Natalie. "We've got to find a way to get him out of there. There's no telling what Patterson will do at this point. Alton could easily break right now. They may brainwash him, frame him, who knows what all. Heinz, see if you can come up with a plan to get him out of there."

Heinz' eyes grew as large as half dollars. "I'm good, but I'm not a miracle worker. This is the FBI you're dealing with, Dane."

"I'm aware of that. But somebody's got to rally for him. He's in this mess because of me and this crazy case. Can't you get some of your running buddies from your days with the Bureau to help you?"

"I dunno, Dane..." Heinz' voice trailed off.

"Well, what else have you got to do at the moment?" asked Dane, his irritation showing. The trial certainly won't be very entertaining. "And," he added, "Alton has information we could use. I'm not sure where it would lead us, but we could use it."

Heinz hesitated for a long moment, then blurted out, "I guess you're right. I can't promise anything, but I'll see what I can do."

Dane's cell phone rang. It was Susan.

"Hello, Susan? I'm in the middle of trial. What's going on?"

"Dane, the hospital just called, and they're saying Natalie's temperature is up, and she's acting strange. They're not sure what to make of it..." Susan broke into tears. Dane scooted out of the booth went to the open area outside the men's room for privacy. "Dane," Susan managed between sobs, "I have to go to her, and I can't stay in this God-forsaken place any more. I'm leaving now."

"Susan, listen to me. Your life is in danger, and you're lucky to be alive as it is. It won't help anyone to do something stupid and leave Natalie without a Mom."

"I'm not worried about *me*. There's nobody there except a bunch of strange doctors, and they don't know what they're doing anyway. Either you tell these security apes to let me go, or I'm leaving anyway and they'll have to chase me down with dogs and shoot me or put me in a strait jacket. I refuse to stay at a lake cabin with my daughter hundreds of miles away."

The phone grew quiet and Dane hung in indecision. Then, as much to break the tense silence as anything else, he said, "Put George on the phone." A moment later, a crisp, professional voice came through the receiver. "Yes, Mr. Ingersoll, this is George Fleming."

"George, our daughter is down at East Dallas Medical in the NICU. She's in a bad way right now, and I know you've seen how Susan is climbing the walls. I want you guys—all three of you—to personally escort her to the hospital. Keep her in your sight at all times, and be ready for anything. She can spend the rest of the day, but escort her back tonight. Be ready for anything. Station two guys outside the hospital, one on either side. You stay with her the whole time inside. At the first sign of trouble, contact me. 'Got it?"

"Got, it Sir. You can count on us." Dane heard rustling and muffled sniffling, then Susan's voice.

"Dane?"

"Now, Sweetie, you have till tonight, but you have to go back. No spending the night there; it's too dangerous. OK?"

"OK...OK...but I'm leaving *now*, before something bad happens."

"Good, then get going. And don't worry, nothing bad is going to happen." He made a superhuman effort to sound confident. "I love you."

"Me too," she responded tearfully.

Back at the booth, the food had come. But Dane wasn't hungry. He never was when he was in trial. The adrenaline suppressed his appetite, and that was even more true now. He was sure everyone had changed the subject when he reapproached the table. Natalie was on everyone's mind almost as much as on his. The difference is that they just didn't talk about it when he was around, because no one was sure what to say. Heinz was already on the secure cell phone, apparently talking to some friend from the Bureau. Everyone else was chattering, but the chatter died as Dane arrived.

"How's Natalie doing?" queried Jenny.

"Not good," Dane said flatly.

"You know," Dr. Jenkins broke the awkward silence," an antidote like the one I prepared would not necessarily show results immediately. Please don't conclude it is not working." Dane cracked a half smile and replied simply, "I know. Thanks." The group ate hurriedly, with the clerks trying to talk it up and Jenny joining in the banter. They spoke of the boring testimony of the FDA official, and how Dane would cross examine him. Dane was vaguely aware of this conversation whizzing around him, but felt strangely more like a spectator than a participant. He simply couldn't get his mind off Natalie and Susan. The group finished lunch with Dane having hardly touched his meal, and stood to leave. At that moment, Heinz' cell phone rang. The group crossed the street to the courthouse, with Heinz talking on the phone all the way, saying things like, "Yes," "Uh huh, and "I see." The group reached the courthouse steps at about the same time Heinz ended the call. Dane paused before they mounted the steps, the blustery wind contorting his hair in a comical fashion, and wheeled around to face Heinz.

"Well?"

"My source says there's no way they will release Alton at this point. They are still grilling er, 'debriefing' him, and will be for a while. It's all under Patterson's orders. He'd like to help me but doesn't have the authority."

Dane's mouth became a grim line of resolution, his jaw set in determination. "Alright then, we'll have to subpoena him. James," Dane beckoned the law clerk mounting the step next to him. "I want a subpoena ready to serve in thirty minutes on Alton Dean at the FBI field office. Make it returnable here at 3:30 p.m. Work with Heinz here on having him served personally. Use the United States Marshall's service. Now go!" Dane tossed the clerk a key. Before the group reached the top of the stairs, Heinz and James vanished to retreat to Mr. Dean's office. Back in the courtroom, Nathan Smith was again at counsel table, looking as though he'd never left. He seemed to Dane impatient to get on with things, and each of his minions were busy shuffling papers or scribbling something of momentous legal significance on a yellow pad. One had his notebook computer flipped open, typing away. Dane and Smith exchanged glances. With Jenny seated to his left, Dane pulled out his trial binder and got ready for cross of the first witness. He stared at the outline on his yellow pad—one of two he had prepared for the occasion. This one read simply "Natalie Sick" across the top. The rest of the page had only a few scribbles denoting topics he wanted to cover. He stared at the bold block print along the bottom margin which declared, "BUY TIME".

"As if I needed the reminder," thought Dane. Dane's musings were abruptly interrupted when his Honor entered from his chambers.

"On the record. Well, Gentlemen, I trust everyone had a fruitful lunch hour. I believe we left off with Mr. Ingersoll, counsel for Rowalter Industries. The witness has been passed. Mr. Ingersoll?"

Dane approached to stand at the podium. "Thank you, Your Honor. I just have a few questions for Mr. Johnson."

"Mr. Johnson, as Chief of Compliance for the FDA, you do not have involvement on a day-to-day basis with drug testing, correct?"

"That is correct."

"So you wouldn't know from your own personal knowledge whether phenylkerozotetracarboxide, also known as PZT, is harmful, beneficial, or some combination thereof. Isn't that accurate?"

"That's accurate. I wouldn't know that from my own personal knowledge, no."

"So, anything you know about the qualities of PZT you could know only from reports you had received from others acting under your authority, either directly or indirectly?"

"That is correct."

"And, in fact, you haven't reviewed any such reports, because that is not within your responsibilities as Chief of Compliance, true?"

"That's right."

"Your job, if I understand it correctly, is to monitor compliance with FDA procedures generally?"

"That's right."

"And you are here today principally to educate the Court on the requirements, that is, all of the 'hoops one has to jump through,' so to speak, to obtain FDA approval for a new medicinal drug. Am I right?"

"Yes."

CHAPTER THIRTY- TWO

The phone buzzed. Heinz, seated on the corner of the desk piled high with law books, answered it in mid-ring. The wall clock said 1:30.

"Law Office."

"Heinz? James here. They've served the subpoena."

"Great! Any trouble along the way?"

"A little. I had to go through the U.S. Marshall. They called up to somebody at the FBI office to verify Mr. Dean was there. He was, but I could tell someone at the other end of the phone was pretty surprised that anyone knew that Dean was with them. I was thinking they were going to try to pull some strings, but when the Deputy Marshall saw that the subpoena was for 3:30 p.m. they moved their rears pretty quick."

"Great." Heinz smiled at Dr. Jenkins, who sat in an overstuffed chair across Dane's office, using Heinz' secure cell phone. "Deliver the proof of service to Dane at the courthouse, pronto. This may change his witness line-up."

"Consider it done."

At almost the same moment, Dr. Jenkins ended his call, and locked glances with Heinz. From his eyes, Heinz could tell he had news which trumped serving subpoena on Alton.

"Natalie is exhibiting marked improvement. I just spoke with Mrs. Ingersoll, who is with Natalie's chief physician. Her respiration is evening out, her blood pressure is stabilized, and her color is coming back." Jenkins paused and let out a long sigh of relief. "The antidote appears to be working!"

Heinz leapt from his perch on the desk, grabbed a reluctant Dr. Jenkins from his chair and began doing a silly dance around the room, the pain from his injuries temporarily forgotten. After a minute, they plopped down on the sofa in the cramped office's waiting area, and caught their breaths.

"Mrs. Ingersoll was, of course, ecstatic," Jenkins continued. After talking to the doctor with her permission, I cautioned her not to get her hopes up yet, it was too soon. Naturally, the doctor knows nothing of the antidote and therefore has no explanation for the turnaround."

"But you—" said Heinz, still gulping air, "What do you think?"

"I think she'll continue to improve. Once the drug is completely counteracted, the doctors will have to assess whether any damage was done while she was under its effects."

"You can't imagine what this will mean to Dane, Doc. And now that Alton is subpoenaed to trial, it oughta' be a real dog and pony show."

"Yes, I can imagine that it might," mused Jenkins.

* * * *

Dane's cross-examination continued apace, unrelenting, parsing through a maze of seemingly endless and equally irrelevant details of Mr. Johnson's FDA Compliance duties. It occurred to Jenny that if his goal was to buy time, he was certainly succeeding. Under the circumstances, she couldn't blame him. And no judge would ever deny a lawyer the opportunity to do what lawyers do best: overkill on detail. Jenny took no notice of a courier who slid silently into the courtroom until, with Dane still questioning, the boy reached over the railing, tapped her on the shoulder and handed her a plain, unmarked envelope. Assuming it was for her, she opened the unsealed flap, and slid out a folded piece of paper. It read:

"*Dane,*

As of 1:30, Natalie is breathing normally, blood pressure normal, and color coming back. Doctors are cautious, but I am thrilled. It sounds like our little girl has turned the corner and is recovering!

Your Loving Wife,

Susan"

Embarrassed at the breach in privacy but elated at the news, Jenny couldn't suppress a broad smile. She quietly slid the note across counsel table to Dane, and waited for him to notice it on his own. It took a couple of minutes for this to happen, as Dane waited for the long-winded witness to finish an especially convoluted answer. Between questions, he glanced downward at the note. With nearly superhuman self-control and without breaking rhythm, he said simply, "I pass the witness." That done, he permitted himself a broad grin. This was closely followed by a sigh of relief. Then, as Smith began redirect, he leaned over and whispered into Jenny's ear, "We'll try for a break after they're done with Johnson. I want Natalie out of that hospital as soon as she can be moved. No FBI anywhere near her. Have Heinz take care of it. And find out if Alton's been served. Oh, and check my phone for messages," he said, handing her his cell. "Aye aye, Captain," whispered Jenny, stealthily sliding out of her chair behind counsel table, and exiting the court room.

From the end of the hallway, as far away from the court room as she could get, Jenny dialed Heinz on Dane's phone. She quickly confirmed service of the subpoena on Alton, then talked about Natalie's condition. This, she knew, changed everything. How did they find out? When? How much better was she, and was it permanent? Most important of all, could she be moved? With that, Heinz handed the phone to Doc, and Jenny began plying him for still more details.

"Well, what do you think, Dr. Jenkins?"

"Of course, Miss Pemberton, I can't comment on the security aspects, but medically, I think it prudent that she not be moved for 24 hours, minimum. She probably is not fully stable yet, and the antidote has only had an effect for a couple of hours."

"Gotcha. Give me Heinz again." Shuffling sounds.

"Heinz here."

"Heinz, we need a guard stationed at the hospital until Natalie can be moved. Doc thinks it will be a day or so. Can you handle it?"

"You mean, while the Bureau agent is still there?"

"Whatever it takes. I suppose we need to 'guard the guard,' and whoever else might try to undo what Doc has just accomplished."

"Alrighty, I'm on it. How's the trial going?"

"We're about ready to call—"

While she was in mid-sentence, there came the beep from another call.

"Hang on a moment, will you Doctor?"

"Sure. That's all I have for you, anyway. Do you want to just call me later?"

"Yeah, sure." Jenny pressed the flash button.

"Hello, Mr. Ingersoll." It was an unfamiliar voice.

"No, I'm sorry but this is his legal assistant, Jennifer Pemberton. May I help you?"

"Y-yes, perhaps. Is Mr. Ingersoll in trial?"

"As a matter of fact, he is. Who is this?"

"My name is Jon, and I work with James Patterson."

Instantly, Jenny's gut went tight. "Oh, yes. I've heard your name from Mr. Ingersoll. What can I—er—do for you?"

"Well, I'm not exactly sure. Could we meet somewhere, maybe?"

"Deja vous. Hadn't this happened to her before?" "Well—we're in the middle of a trial right now—" she spoke cautiously.

"Yes, you said that. This may have something to do with the trial..." He paused, and his voice grew suddenly quieter. "Something that you might be interested in."

That got Jenny's attention. "All right, Jon" she said, trying to sound non-committal. There was no way to check with Dane at the moment, so she said the only thing she really *could* say. "I'll see what I can do to arrange something. But whatever it is will have to involve Dane, and he's completely tied up right now. In fact, he'll be tied up for the rest of the day. I'll need to check with him first." Jenny took a deep breath as she waded in. "Where do you want to meet?

"How about the Elmo's at Field and Forest? Do you know the place?"

"Yeah, I think so."

"Good. I'll meet you there in an hour."

"Wait—! I don't think Dane—" But it was too late, as she heard the phone click in her ear. Jenny stared blankly at the LED on her phone as if it bore an alien message. Perplexed, she jolted herself back to reality and stuck her head inside the courtroom door. Smith seemed to be winding things up with his witness on redirect. She snuck back in and tiptoed to the counsel table. She ripped off the corner of a yellow pad, scribbled something on it, and thrust it into Dane's palm. Dane glanced at it and gave her a perplexed look which she returned with a shrug. He glanced behind him and did a quick scan of the courtroom. Gary Thompson, Rowalter's operative, was back in his familiar spot. There was no FBI evident. No reporters, either. He'd have to work a way for Jenny to meet with Jon, but not alone. That would be stupid; not only for the obvious reasons, but for evidentiary ones. There must be another witness along, a man. One kidnapping on his conscience was quite enough, thank you, and though Jon was FBI, Dane didn't trust anyone anymore. He took a large sticky note and wrote, "Get Heinz and take him with you. Record the meeting. Go. now." Just then, the Government passed the witness.

"No further questions of this witness, Your Honor," Dane announced. As he did so, he heard Jenny slip out of her chair. As the massive courtroom door closed slowly behind her, Dr. Graham Studdard, the government's chemist expert, mounted the witness stand. The time on the big courthouse clock above the jury box read 2:05 p.m.

"*This is going to be close*," he thought.

* * * *

Patterson turned the subpoena in his hand over, then over again, slowly, deliberately. This simply would not do, would not be tolerated. Dean was his, and if things had been handled properly by Betaña in the first place, he would not be confronted with this situation. He was furious at the incompetence of it all. It was totally unnecessary. But it was what it was, and the only thing to do now was to stop it dead in its tracks before things got out of hand. Suddenly, breaking out of his trance, Patterson picked up his intercom.

"Judy, get me Earl Johnson."

"Yes Sir." Patterson rapped his fingers impatiently on the holstered gun he'd been fingering just before the call.

"Johnson here."

"Earl, I have a subpoena I urgently need you to look at. We need to protect a witness of ours from it."

"No problem, Mr. Patterson. Can you fax it over?"

"You'll have it in a few minutes. Call me when you've looked it over. Oh, and I need you at the federal courthouse, Judge Fitzhugh's courtroom, at 3:30 sharp. I'll be there, too. Can you make it?"

"Yep, sure can. Fax away."

* * * *

"Jim Patterson's underling wants to *what*?" Heinz' face was contorted in amazement. He had just completed the phone calls to the body guards at the lake house, and was still trying to work things out with East Dallas Medical.

"That's just it: I have no idea. But I don't trust these Bureau people...sorry, Heinz, no offense. I trusted James Patterson once before. I took the bait hook, line and sinker. No more; you're coming along with me." Jenny's tone was resolute, immovable. It was clear there would be no arguing with the woman. "Aye, Aye, Madam. I don't know Jon Newcombe, anyhow. 'Never met him in my long and sagacious career working with his boss. Besides, what have I got to worry about anyway? I'm so deep into this deal now, I'm not even worried about what the Bureau thinks anymore."

"My thoughts exactly. Dane wants you wearing a wire for the occasion. Between you as a live witness, me, and the tape recording, we should have it fairly well covered. I'll drive, but let's get going. I don't want to miss any more of the trial than I have to."

Twenty-five minutes later, Jenny pulled into the Elmo's parking lot. It was only ten till three by her watch; they were fifteen minutes early. She hoped the agent was early too, so she could get whatever nonsense he wanted to discuss over with and hustle back to the court room. Heinz sat next to her in the front seat. Doc Jenkins had decided to come, for lack of anything better to do right now. There were only three other cars in the lot, testimony to the fact that it was between the lunch and dinner rushes. She was glad for that, but impatient to get started.

"Well, I sure don't wanna sit and watch my hair grow for fifteen minutes. Why don't I go inside and see if he's here? What's he look like, Jen?"

"Heck if I know. I've never seen him, and never talked to him till today. My impression from Dane is that he's a younger man than Patterson, say, 27 to 30, Caucasian. Other than that, your guess is as good as mine."

"Gotcha." Heinz fumbled in his inside coat pocket to make sure his cell phone recorder was in pause mode. He exited the car and as he did, cursed `both the pain that seized his leg and the man who caused it. Moments later inside the restaurant, Heinz had a clear view of the thirty or so tables and booths in the place. He noted one couple in a booth, and two grubby construction workers drinking coffee at a table across the room. No one in here fit the profile. He began turning to exit, then stopped when he detected movement at the rear of the restaurant, near the telephone. He turned and strode in that direction. A man with reddish-blonde hair wearing a blue sport coat and slacks walked out to the nearest booth. He fit the description.

"Are you Jon Newcombe, the one who called Jenny Pemberton?" queried Heinz.

"Yes I am. Who are you?"

"Jack Heinz." Heinz extended his hand and Newcombe shook it.

"You look familiar. Have we met before?"

"Probably. I was with the Bureau for a few years after leaving the DEA: in the witness protection program, and some surveillance. Miss Pemberton brought me along for the ride. She's outside." Heinz didn't feel much like chit chat, and got right down to business. "We're a little early, but ready to get started if you are. Shall we grab a booth?"

"Sure. I'll be back here in the corner. We need quiet." Newcombe spoke in guarded tones.

"I'll get Miss Pemberton."

Heinz returned to the main entrance, pushed open the door and beckoned to Jenny and Doc. Doc waived him off, content to stay in the car. That was okay with Heinz, since he had his cell phone recorder ready and two live witnesses. In moments, Jenny and Heinz were in the restaurant, seated on one side of the booth and Newcombe on the other. Newcombe ordered drinks for everyone while Heinz hurriedly introduced Jenny. Then Jenny propped her elbows on the freshly wiped table and leaned forward, cradling her chin lightly in her hands.

"All right, Mr. Newcombe, you have us as a captive audience in the middle of an important federal trial. Would you mind telling us what is so riveting as to warrant our coming out here?"

"I can't blame you for being upset, but I think you'll find it was well worth the interruption." Newcombe's eyes darted furtively around the room. The old couple in the nearby booth was busy eating. The grubby construction workers across the restaurant were talking loudly. He continued in a hushed voice, "I have evidence that my superior, officer-in-charge James Patterson, has been actively involved in the illegal use and sale of PZT."

"What do you mean?" Jenny opted to play dumb for the time being.

"Well, you know the 24-hour watch he placed on the little Ingersoll girl at East Dallas Medical? I thought something funny was going on almost immediately. I mean, Mr. Patterson seemed to take a very personal interest in the girl, always talking about her condition at inappropriate times, in the middle of meetings, and so forth. He seemed to start this right after the car exploded in Fort Worth. I don't know what gave me the hunch, but his behavior started changing. Not just a little, but radically. So, since I have the means and the ability, I planted a video camera in the NICU and placed it where no one would ever find it." Heinz quickly exchanged glances with Jenny. He hoped the tape was getting all this. Jenny leaned forward farther, her eyebrows raised.

"I've been recording now for several weeks on an infrared activated camera. It only runs when there is movement within two feet of it. I've been able to identify no less than nine times that the bag was changed."

"Nothing particularly remarkable there," commented Heinz.

"Not until you consider that practically all of those times they were unscheduled changes, and the person doing the changing was a male, not a nurse on staff."

"How do you know?" queried Jenny.

"Simple. In the NICU the charge nurse makes all the IV changes within a one-half hour period, so that none ever gets missed. It's always done at 7 a.m., 1 p.m., 7 p.m. and 1 a.m. Like clockwork. But the video shows the IV bags for Natalie were *again* swapped out within an hour of each scheduled change on a number of occasions. The tape also clearly shows it's a male nurse doing the changing in every case. Not a single nurse working in the NICU is male at this time. I've checked the employment records and weekly schedules as part of our due diligence on Natalie."

"Well, we already suspected someone was drugging her. But this: this is incontrovertible. Someone got past FBI security." Jenny said this with a note of disgust.

"The only problem with that theory is that no one outside gets by FBI security, at least not without cooperation. I'm certain this is an inside job by some renegades within the Bureau."

"I'd have to agree with him on that one, Jen," commented Heinz. "The agents assigned to the NICU were changed out regularly, and would have been strictly instructed as to which nurses were, and weren't, allowed to change the IV bags."

"I have some other evidence that is intriguing, as well. The camera picked up numerous serial numbers off of the bottles being emptied into the IV bag. Those numbers could prove useful in tracking down the source of the stuff." Heinz' eyes narrowed. Newcombe just kept talking.

"Look, I'm risking my career by telling you this, and all the more by what I've done. But I wouldn't be able to live with the thought that I was part of some crazy scheme to hurt a baby." He hesitated, then reached into his coat pocket for something. Placing a flash drive on the table, he slid it across to Jenny. "Here is the video. I suggest you view it as soon as possible. I have an extra in a secure location. Watch it completely through, then go to frame 36, then the rest. That's all I have. Good luck. And, y'all never met me here, all right?" The man's eyes locked onto Jenny's, waiting for an answer.

"Right," replied Jenny and Heinz, virtually in unison. Newcombe scanned the room once again, then displayed a satisfied look. He rose from the table, nodded in Heinz and Jenny's direction, and exited noiselessly through a side entrance to the restaurant. Jenny looked at Heinz, her face bewildered. Heinz was certain he looked the same, because he certainly felt it. He fingered the flash drive, slipping it inside his left pocket. Next, he checked his cell phone recorder, which showed just under five minutes expired. A fast meeting, indeed. As if awakening from a trance, Jenny looked at her watch and freaked. "Oh my gosh! It's three o'clock! Alton's due in court in half an hour." With that, she sprinted for the car, with Heinz struggling to keep up. They found Doc Jenkins, who was engaged in some call with the university on his cell phone. When he saw them, he abruptly hung up and queried how things had gone at the restaurant. Heinz began filling him in while Jenny laid rubber in the parking lot. By the time they arrived back at the courthouse, the Doc had been brought fully up to speed.

CHAPTER THIRTY-THREE

One thing was crystal clear to Dane. He had enough evidence to keep the dreaded drug off the market. But how to deal some measure of justice to the Rowalter kingpins, to see that they got their just deserts, that was now his challenge and his goal. The time was near at hand. It was almost 3:30. Just as he was musing over which of his former PZT victims to call to the stand, he heard the massive doors behind him open, and felt a rush of air from the hallway. In shuffled a government attorney: a new one that Dane had not seen before. He was a weaseled-looking man of short stature with mousey brown hair, wearing an ill-fitting gray suit. Nathan Smith was nowhere in sight. Mentally, Dane dubbed the new attorney "Weasel." Moments later, Dane noticed the leggy court reporter was back in place. Judge Fitzhugh soon followed, looking pleasant enough. He nodded greetings to both counsel, then gathered himself importantly at his seat. He peered over the ubiquitous spectacles. "Gentlemen, my clerk informs me that the government has something it wishes to take up with the court before we proceed further with its case. Is this true counsel?" The judge leaned inquiringly over the bench to look at the newcomer for the government. The attorney shuffled a few papers before him and stood to address the Court.

"If your Honor pleases, the United States, specifically the Federal Bureau of Investigation, is holding a witness for questioning and investigation in connection with other matters not necessarily related to this case. The defense has, only this afternoon, served subpoena seeking production of and testimony from this witness." He said this looking sidelong at Dane as if to imply he had committed some heinous crime. Weasel paused for dramatic effect and took a deep breath, glancing ever-so-briefly at the judge to gauge his reaction. None was forthcoming, and the attorney continued. "Your Honor, this witness, a Mr. Alton Dean, possesses highly sensitive government information subject to the Patriot Act. Until the government is through with its examination and detention of him, it is improper to subject him to subpoena. We have filed the appropriate motion seeking to quash the subpoena." At this point, the attorney strode over to Dane, and handed him a copy of a several page document entitled, "Motion to Quash." Dane scanned the motion hurriedly, hoping to dampen the effect of this all-too-common tactic. The attorney continued. "We ask that the Court quash the subpoena on the grounds stated in the motion."

Judge Fitzhugh turned to Dane. "What says the defense?" "Your Honor, I was just handed this motion moment ago, as you saw. From what I can tell from my brief review, it is grounded exclusively on concerns for national security. Stated simply, the government is trying to characterize Mr. Dean as some sort of international terrorist. This is nothing short of ludicrous, and a shameless attempt to obstruct the testimony of a critical witness with highly relevant testimony. Mr. Dean is an associate attorney employed by Salacuse & Lockridge, a firm I have been associated with for many years." Dane paused just long enough for this to sink in. It was a preeminent law firm with which Judge Fitzhugh was quite familiar. "Mr. Dean's testimony will show that he has intimate firsthand knowledge of the testing performed by Rowalter on its own drug and the scientific literature it has compiled on such tests. In fact, he will be the only sponsor for certain critical pieces of evidence which the government has produced to the defense." As he spoke these words, Dane held up for His Honor's viewing the first of several flash drives bearing an exhibit sticker.

Judge Fitzhugh stroked his chin and peered with somber deliberation down his ponderous nose at Dane. It occurred to Dane that, just now, His Honor's face resembled that of a large barn owl. Just as it appeared he was about to say "Who-o-o," he opened his lips and spoke, "Motion to Quash denied." I will allow questioning by the Defense of Mr. Dean on all matters pertaining to the drug PZT, as well as of the contents of the USB flash drive exhibit, provided a sufficient predicate is established." The owl face paused, and turned its head to face the government attorney. "I will entertain appropriate objections from the United States on the topic of national security," he paused dramatically, "but they'd better be good."

Dane opened his mouth to call Alton Dean to the stand, but only got out the utterance "Your H—" before the Weasel broke in. "Er–excuse me, your Honor, but the government has another problem." At the attorney's side could be seen an associate, barely more than a kid, whispering something in the Weasel's ear.

"And just what might that be, Counsel?"

"Well, it seems we are having...that is...difficulty locating the witness."

Judge Fitzhugh's eyes first widened, then narrowed, and he wore a pained expression. "If I'm not losing my hearing, you just told this court the FBI is detaining this witness for questioning. Did I hear that correctly, counsel? You said 'detaining'?"

"Y-yes, Your Honor."

"How is it, if you could please explain to me, Counsel, that the Government has suddenly lost track of a valuable witness that they have 'detained'?"

"Begging your Honor's pardon, Mr. James Patterson indicates the witness is, well...unavailable."

"And just who is this James Patterson?"

"Acting chief of the Dallas Field Office of the Bureau, Your Honor."

His Honor leaned forward over the bench and riveted his eyes on the Weasel. "Well, you tell Mr. Patterson, that he'd better damned well find a way to get Alton Dean here in the next few minutes, or *he'll* need to be 'available' for contempt of this court. The notion of the FBI not having a witness available who it is urging is a national security risk is not only highly suspicious, but absurd."

At this, there arose a commotion in the back of the court room, followed by two men in suits scrambling for the door like halfbacks on steroids. The next five minutes ticked slowly by as an awkward hush settled over the courtroom like a suffocating blanket. No one breathed or moved, though some distant, muffled voices could be discerned from the direction of the hallway. After what seemed like an eternity, the monolithic doors again opened. This time, Alton appeared, looking every bit as scruffy as he did when he'd hitched a ride with Dane yesterday. He half-ran, half-walked up to the front of the spectator section and seated himself directly in front of the witness stand. Only then did he permit himself the briefest of sidelong glances at Dane, who flashed a smile at him, which Alton quickly returned. *"Why that little squirrel! 'Gave them the slip, did he?"*

Alton twitched and squirmed and pulled at a collar which seemed rather too tight. He was in the same clothes in which Dane had left him that morning. He probably smelled. The Weasel suddenly entered the courtroom, accompanied by the now-not-so-smug chief prosecutor Nathan Smith, and flanked by two burly FBI agents. Judge Fitzhugh, who was clearly upset, said simply, "Gentlemen, I think we have found your detainee."

Suddenly, Alton's small frame erupted upward and he stood erect like a soldier. "Your Honor, may it please the court, I would like to testify."

"And so you shall, Mr. Dean, at the appropriate time. Since there has been some question raised about your availability under subpoena," his Honor said, casting a stern glance at the government's table, "I am going to remove all doubt and place you under oath. You will remain on call to the attorney who subpoenaed you, that is, Mr. Ingersoll. Alton dutifully raised his right hand and swore to tell the truth, the whole truth, and nothing but the truth, and to remain at the defense's disposal until released from the subpoena. At the conclusion of the oath, Alton seated himself in the back row of the court room while Judge Fitzhugh continued, "I hereby admonish the government that I had better not see any more shenanigans like I just saw regarding Mr. Dean, or I will not hesitate to issue an order holding its counsel in contempt for witness tampering. Mr. Dean, I see that you are in the back of the courtroom. You may remain seated there, or you may leave the courtroom if you wish. But stay close by for when you are needed by the defense.

Dane cast a backward glance at the ubiquitous Gary Thompson, who was shifting nervously in his seat, fidgeting with his collar that was an inch too small. Dane could also have sworn he saw a *Morning News* reporter, pen and pad in hand, in the back of the courtroom. "*Interesting. Is he merely on the courthouse beat, or has someone leaked something about the case?*" At that moment, as he turned around again, he felt Jenny slip back into the chair beside him. She leaned over and whispered into his ear.

"There's a videotape. We think it may implicate Patterson in Natalie's addiction."

"Have we seen it?"

"Not yet. I've got Heinz busy moving Natalie to another hospital."

"Then look at it, right now. Heinz has some investigation materials he seized—he'll need to compare them—"

"Call your next witness, Mr. Smith," boomed Judge Fitzhugh.

"Your Honor, the government calls George Barnhardt."

As the government's chief chemist rose and strode deliberately to the front of the court room, Dane sized him up. He looked to his right to make a comment to Jenny, but she'd already vanished.

* * **

James Patterson hung up the phone. The fellow agent at the courthouse had just told him the news— that they'd lost the skirmish over the Alton Dean subpoena, and Dean would probably take the witness stand sometime in the next hour. Patterson glanced wildly around the room. He nervously fingered the holstered Beretta under his left arm, then opened his desk drawer, exposing two loaded magazines. He grabbed both and dropped one into each coat pocket of the suit jacket draped over his chair, then stood and put it on. It wouldn't be long now, Patterson acknowledged to himself. There was little time to waste. He quickly moved across the hallway and down a couple of offices till he came to a door which bore the name, "Agent K. Dickerson". "*I can count on Kevin if I can count on anyone,*" he thought, pushing the door back several inches with his left hand as he rapped on it with his right. "Yes, who is it? Mr. Patterson, is that you?" The young man was looking up from a stack of nondescript documents. Protocol dictated that he address the higher-ranking agent by his last name.

"Kevin, I need you to round up five agents. Make them your best marksmen and snipers. Bring them to the federal courthouse with you. I need you all there in forty-five minutes. Meet me at the Kennedy Memorial across the street. Got it?"

"Sure, Sir, but all the agents except two are on assignment."

"Well, pull them off of their blasted assignments. There's already one up there, so you should only need four more. Tell them this is both urgent and immediate. No excuses. And no questions or briefing: I'll tell them everything they need to know when we meet down there."

"Roger that, Sir, 45 minutes." Dickerson had already picked up the phone and his keys were flying over the keypad. Patterson turned abruptly, checked his weapon yet again, and left the building. The wind that met him at the exit was half gale force. Its ominous howl brought a sudden sense of foreboding, which washed over him in waves.

* * * *

"Mr. Heinz! Over here!" Susan hailed him from the other side of the long hospital lobby. Heinz fit the description Dane had provided her. Heinz traversed the twenty feet between them in seconds and extended a hand to Susan Ingersoll, who grasped it exuberantly.

"Dane said you'd be here. I'm so glad to meet you. Isn't the news about Natalie wonderful?"

"No question about it, Mrs. Ingersoll. Why don't we go see her together?"

"Yes, yes, you must come. I've been up there the whole night, and her color has returned, her breathing is normal, and...well, it's just a miracle!"

"I can't wait to see her. Lead the way."

The newly acquainted pair hurriedly made their way up the elevator, then down the long hallway to the neonatal unit. Heinz caught the strong scent of alcohol as they approached the unit in fluorescent-bathed sterility. No words passed between them as they arrived in the unit. The 50-ish looking nurse behind the desk peered over the top of her spectacles at Mrs. Ingersoll and gave a fleeting look of recognition, followed by a quizzical glance at Heinz. "Oh, he's a family friend," offered Mrs. Ingersoll. Heinz stifled a smile as he recalled how, just days ago, he'd walked brazenly past the old bird without drawing so much as a sideward glance. Satisfied, the nurse motioned her head in the direction of the incubators against the opposite wall. Mrs. Ingersoll practically sprinted to the same incubator which Heinz had visited only two days earlier. As he caught up to her, Heinz did a double take. Even with the news he'd already received about Natalie, he was astounded at the little girl's appearance. The tiny cheeks were crimson. Her breathing, though no longer audible without the respirator, came in regular cadence, smooth and unlabored. Heinz' gaze fell on several plastic tubes hanging limply over the side of the incubator. A flurry of motion pulled his attention back to her face, where her now-raised arm brushed against her cheek. The skin on little Natalie's hand, though less flushed than her face, appeared a healthy pink, and Heinz noticed none of the beaded perspiration that he had seen before. It was, he thought, indeed a miracle of the highest order.

"Mrs. Ingersoll, now that she's better, we need to move her, don't you think?"

"You'll get no argument from me on that. If it weren't for those incompetent fools at the FBI, she'd have been out of here weeks ago." Susan virtually shouted the words, fixing a contemptuous look at the agent seated several feet away. He pretended not to notice, but squirmed uncomfortably in his seat.

"Do you have a place to put Natalie?"

"We have an old friend at Doctor's Hospital. He's the administrator there. I don't know why we didn't think of it in the first place."

Heinz hadn't wanted to intrude on Susan's moments with Natalie, so he was grateful when, after another moment, she suddenly looked up and declared, "Let's go see the doctor."

"Which one?"

"Dr. Weinberger. He's the one who admitted Natalie, before all the so-called 'specialists' got ahold of her. He's the one who can discharge her."

"How do you know if he's here today?"

"Because I called his office and I know when he makes his rounds. We can wait by the nurse's station and flag him down, or just wait here for him to show up."

They didn't even have time to decide on which, before Heinz was startled with a robust, "Good morning, Mrs. Ingersoll," coming from behind him. Both he and Susan whirled around as one, and stood face to face with a distinguished-looking man who reminded Heinz of an elderly uncle he'd once met. Weinberger was a head taller than Heinz, and did not fit his stereotype of the Jewish doctor—at least not that of his German relatives. He wore no hospital coat, but sported a tie.

"Dr. Weinberger, we need to move Natalie immediately to Doctor's Hospital."

"I had anticipated a similar request, Ms. Ingersoll. I heard that you were dissatisfied with our level of care of Natalie. Is this so?"

"That's putting it mildly. Natalie has been at death's door for weeks now with no improvement, until yesterday. Your hospital had not a clue of what to do to improve or even treat her condition. It was only because of Mr. Heinz here—"

"—What Ms. Ingersoll means, Doctor, is that you did a fine job as far as you were able, but that the hospital's lack of knowledge of this, uh, new malady greatly, er, impeded Natalie's recovery." Heinz felt the heat of Susan's glare, but ignored it. Susan was clueless of the big picture, and needed to be closely managed at this point.

"Well, we will miss Natalie and the opportunity to treat her, but I certainly understand your decision. In our defense, though, I would simply say that this is a rather novel case. I don't believe I've ever seen anything quite like it before."

"Neither have we, but we're not the ones with the medical degree," said Susan bluntly. "Now, where do I go to sign her out?"

"Second floor, behind the glass doors. Again, I'm sorry things didn't work out better, and I hope Natalie continues to improve."

"Oh, I'm sure she will. Come on, Heinz. Let's go."

CHAPTER THIRTY-FOUR

The Blu-ray player whirred as Jenny punched the rewind key again and again. There was no time to wait for Heinz, who was busy at the hospital. So, she had enlisted the help of Dr. Jenkins, and managed to jerry rig the TV hanging on the wall of the hotel room which had so recently served as Doc's laboratory. It wasn't the sharpest picture in the world, but would do just fine for viewing agent Jon Newcombe's investigative video. The video only lasted perhaps two minutes from beginning to end. Suspicious of that fact, Jenny had alternately cued forward, then rewound, to make certain she hadn't missed anything. Having assured herself she'd seen everything, and with Doc's concurrence, she now freeze-framed on the screen what obviously had been the focus of agent Newcombe's attention. Proceeding slowly, one frame at a time, she watched a gloved hand slowly disconnect the IV tube, invert the bag, and pour a bottle of some unknown substance into the bag. The hand replaced the cap, inverted the bottle, then reconnected the tube before squeezing the bag and placing it back on the IV holder. She was now at frame 43, so she carefully back-pedaled to frame 36, just as Newcombe had instructed.

"I'm not sure what I'm supposed to be seeing," mused Jennie.

"Look again, Miss Pemberton," Doc spoke thoughtfully, slowly.

"All I see is the brown bottle we saw in the rest of the footage. So, what else is new?"

"Look on the bottle. Of course, I could be wrong, but I make out the characters 3-5-7-9....Z. Was the agent trying to give you some information off the label of the bottle that could prove useful as evidence?"

Jenny's eyes narrowed to mere slits as she squinted hard and leaned toward the screen. "You're...you're right. But of what use are the num— wait a minute!" Jenny's face bore the expression of an inventor who has stumbled upon a new discovery.

"What is it, Miss Pemberton?"

"Didn't Dane say that Heinz had used an investigator that got into Patterson's house? I thought they found some information: took some still shots of bottles or something. Something about serial numbers, maybe."

"I don't believe I was present for such a conversation, Miss Pemberton. But it would certainly be worth checking with Heinz, since Mr. Ingersoll is in trial."

Before Doc had even finished speaking, Jenny had begun dialing her cell phone. "Hello, Heinz?" Heinz' voice was breaking up, no doubt because he was in the hospital. She was lucky, she knew, that he had it on, since cell phones were *ver botin* in such places.

"Do you remember the stuff you got out of James Patterson's house?"

"Yeah whe- *[inaudible]*..s..n..."

"You're breaking up."

"I said 'Yeah, what about it?'"

"I need the photos. Didn't your man get some still shots of bottles somewhere in that place?"

"Yep. In the garage. Lots of 'em"

"Lots of photos, or lots of bottles?"

"Bottles. Why do you ask?"

"Well, we've looked at the video Agent Jon Newcombe gave us, especially the particular frame he mentioned. It probably doesn't mean anything, but I think we should compare the bottles in the still shots of Patterson's garage with the one appearing on the tape. What about you?"

"I follow you...and yes, you absolutely should compare them. Say, I'm at the hospital right now moving Natalie. I can't get you my copy of the photos—they're at my place. But I can let you pick up copies from the investigator who did the job. His name is Reggie, Reggie Andrews. His phone number is 5-5-5-4-8-3-7. Tell him I sent you over and that you need it right away. Let me know how things went, once you get it, OK?"

"Sure thing."

Within twenty minutes, Jenny had not only made contact with Reggie, but was sitting in his office, Doc in tow. Reggie was out on a job, but his assistant, Rick, quickly got him on his cell phone. He authorized the assistant to produce the material, and moments later Doc, Jenny and the assistant were huddled in a small conference room, scanning the photographs. Halfway through the stack of monotonous close-ups of bottles, Jenny halted, then turned to Doc for confirmation of what she thought she had just seen. He nodded, his knowing eyes locking on hers. That was plenty for her. The photos were actually quite sharp, and she knew down in the depths of her soul exactly what she had just seen. Her heart beat quickened as she contemplated the significance of their find. Suddenly, it occurred to Jenny just exactly how much courage it had taken Newcombe to turn over this tape to them.

Maybe there *were* a few good people left on the planet.

It was 3:40 p.m. An uneasy hush settled over the courtroom. The reporters, whose ranks had now swelled to five or six, leaned forward as if O.J. Simpson himself was about to take the stand. The scratching sound of a courtroom artist's pen against sketch pad was all that broke the silence.

Nathan Smith stood slowly to his feet. "Your Honor, the United States rests." There followed a moment of uncertainty when everyone held their breath, expecting something to happen from Dane's side of the Courtroom. Dane felt the eyes of everyone on him. He turned to Brett, a young law Clerk seated behind him and, cupping his hand to his ear, whispered simply, "Is it safe?"

"Yes, Mr. Ingersoll. I just spoke with your wife, sir. Your daughter is now out of the hospital." Dane's relieved sigh was audible.

From the corner of his eye Dane could see Judge Fitzhugh's head was cocked in a quizzical expression that said, *"What are you waiting for, a written invitation?"* A smile flashed across Dane's face as he took a deep breath, stood erect and deliberately faced the bench. All at once, Dane suddenly felt as if a two-ton anvil had been hoisted off of his chest. "Rowalter Industries waives opening statement, Your Honor. "At this time, it calls its first witness, Alton Dean."

"Very well then. Mr. Dean, please come forward and be sworn." Alton had appeared in the back of the courtroom, flanked by a couple of expressionless government agents. As if on cue, they faded to the sides and took a seat, while a gaunt Alton walked somewhat tentatively to the front of the cavernous courtroom and raised his hand.

"Do you swear to tell the truth, the whole truth, and nothing but the truth, so help you, God?"

"I do."

"All right, then. Mr. Dean, please take the witness stand up here to my left."

Dane couldn't help but notice that Alton looked a good deal more rested than yesterday, when he'd picked him up off the street. At least his eyes weren't bloodshot, and he had shaven. Skinny as he was, the park bum look was gone.

"Please identify yourself, Sir," began Dane, obligingly.

"Alton Dean, 30 years old, attorney employed by Salacuse & Lockridge of Dallas, Texas."

"*Not bad. He still sounds sharp*," thought Dane.

"Where have you been the last couple of months?" Dane decided to waste no time with preliminaries.

"In nearly solitary confinement in Bolivia, South America, where I was taken by the Defendant against my will."

"How is it you came to be here today, Mr. Dean?"

"I was subpoenaed by you."

"I understand that, but how is it you came to be here in Dallas, Texas rather than in Bolivia?"

"I escaped from the Rowalter compound, and at great peril to life and limb, I might add. I almost didn't make it."

"You say you were kidnapped. By whom?"

"They were disguised, so I don't know, exactly. They blind-folded and drugged me. Later on, it was dark. I never did get a good look at their faces."

"Mr. Dean, did you ever learn why you were taken against your will?"

"Yes, higher-ups within Rowalter told me that they wanted my help to...well, essentially, to research favorable findings on the effects of their new pharmaceutical product, PZT. I was then to act as an 'advocate' on behalf of Rowalter in getting the drug approved by the FDA."

"Mr. Dean, how did Rowalter become aware of you and conclude that you might be useful to the company?"

"I haven't figured that one out yet. I was doing research for you on this very case at the Salacuse firm when I was kidnapped, and strange things had begun happening to my computer at the office. I had the sense that I was being followed; that my motions were somehow being watched."

Dane's eyes fell on a note hastily scrawled by Bret and shoved his way. It read: "Gary Thompson just left the court room." Without breaking stride, Dane jotted back, "Follow him/report."

"And, just how did Rowalter indicate it planned to secure your cooperation?" Dane knew he was way out on a limb now, but there'd been no time to prepare Alton.

"They offered me money, lots of money. But I got the distinct impression that if I'd refused the offer, it would've made no difference. They weren't taking no for an answer. I was kept under constant surveillance."

Dane paused for just a second, and then decided to get to the point. "Mr. Dean, did you ever have access to any Rowalter data or formulas in the course of your forced servitude?"

"Well, no, I wasn't voluntarily given access. But I managed to compromise Rowalter's security codes and break into their chemical formula files."

"What sort of information were you able to procure?"

"All of their formulas. Oh, there could be a few I missed, but I doubt it. I think I got a peek at everything, including the first prototypical molecular studies for PZT. And, of course, the final formula for PZT."

"What became of that information? Did you memorize it?"

"Memorize? Yes, some. But my memory isn't 100% photographic. So, I copied the files over to some flash drives."

"Meaning USB flash drives, also sometimes known as thumb or pin drives?"

"Exactly."

"Would you recognize the flash drives if you saw them?"

"I am sure that I would."

"Are these the ones?" Dane held four drives up high for the Court to see. One was red, two blue, and one green.

Alton peered closely. "May I see them?"

"Certainly." Dane approached the witness stand, handing four flash drives to Dean.

"There's no question that those are the flash drives I recorded. They're manufactured under a Brazilian label. I also sent an email back to your office as soon as I managed to get to a computer, which contained a brief summary form of the same data."

"What are on the flash drives, Mr. Dean?" continued Dane, methodically.

Nathan Smith sat with rapt attention at the government's table, chin resting on clenched fists, hanging on every word.

"To my knowledge, every formula and experiment Rowalter has run in its pharmaceuticals Research & Development Department for at least the last five years."

"Does that include all the work done on the drug known as P-Z-T?"

"It does."

Dane hesitated before asking the next question. "And what did you discern, Mr. Dean, from your perusal of Rowalter's research and development material?"

"Quite simply, that PZT is one of the most inherently lethal drugs ever created. It masks itself as a healing agent, causes its victim to become an addict, and then mutates itself quickly into a destructive, virus-like organism that never appears the same way for more than a few minutes." Out of the corner of one eye, Alton noticed a new figure glide into the back row of the court room. The man tried to evade Alton's gaze, but he was able to see just enough to recognize the man entering the huge court room. He had glimpsed this man just before being interrogated at the FBI office down the street. It was a man named James Patterson. He thought he saw several other men behind Patterson—no, probably not—and noted that no one else had entered the huge courtroom with Patterson. Alton adjusted himself in the witness chair, and swallowed the lump that had just appeared in his throat. He didn't like this one bit.

Sensing his witness' tangible level of discomfort, Dane stole a backward glance over his left shoulder. *Damn.* Patterson had seated himself in the very last row, near the center. His face bore a scowl. Undistracted, Dane resolutely resumed his questioning.

"Were you able to learn how this drug manifests itself? That is, what symptoms it can cause in humans?"

"To...to some extent I was, yes." Alton's eyes darted uneasily from Dane to Patterson, to the Judge, then back to Dane. The descriptions I read were most disturbing."

"Please elaborate, if you can."

"All right. I seem to recall that the patient often will do fine, and actually improve dramatically for weeks, sometimes months. This is sort of an incubation period, if you will. After that, and the timing varies greatly between patients, the drug begins to radically alter its molecular structure and becomes hostile to its host. At that point, symptoms range from severe stomach cramps to vomiting relentlessly, a sensation of burning in the eyes and throat...shall I go on?"

"Yes, please do."

"Progressing then to dehydration, sunken eyes, inability to eat, loss of bodily functions, writhing in pain, loss of cognitive ability and ultimately, an agonizing death."

"Mr. Dean, did your research yield any information regarding what subjects were used in the experiments that produced the symptoms you've just described?"

"Yes, as the flash drives reveal, human subjects were used. Though names were omitted from the records, it appeared as though the subjects were indigenous natives, probably poor." More men had appeared in the aisle seats. Alton looked up at his Honor, who seemed oblivious to the newcomers.

* * * *

Bret the law clerk trailed Gary Thompson by about one hundred yards, walking casually along so as not to be conspicuous. He figured he wasn't noticed anyhow, since Thompson had a cell phone plastered to his ear and was talking into it without even pausing to breathe. When Thompson stopped under an overhang in a building across the courtyard, Bret quickly slipped around the corner of the large brick edifice, and flattened himself up against it. There was no noise at this time of day, and they were far removed from the traffic on Commerce Street, so Bret could hear Thompson quite clearly.

"...I realize that, Sir, but things have bottomed out. Ingersoll has Dean on the stand, and he's telling all...Yes, Patterson's here, but he can't do anything thing about it...Uh-huh. All right, I'll see if I can speak with Patterson. Right. Okay then, Mr. Harte. I'll call you back at the next break." Bret saw Thompson pocket his phone, and then with narrowed, blood-shot eyes meticulously scan an arc around where he stood. Abruptly, with a double-time gait, he strutted back to the courthouse. Grateful that he had chosen a spot out of Thompson's line of sight, yet knowing he'd dodged a bullet, Bret followed at an even greater distance than before. As soon as Thompson slipped through the court room door, Bret moved down the hall way out of hearing range and extracted his phone from his coat. Jenny was on his speed dial, and he hit the number 3. The phone answered on the first ring.

"This is Jenny."

"Miss Pemberton, this is Bret at the courthouse. 'Sorry to bother you, but Mr. Gary Thompson just left the courtroom and Mr. Ingersoll had me follow him. I did, and he made a phone call to...well, I don't know who. Some guy named Harte. They mentioned something about Mr. Patterson, as though they knew him somehow."

"Is Patterson there now?"

"I'm not sure. I don't know what he looks like."

"He's about 6'1" with red hair, thin, no glasses. Pale blue eyes, I think. Go look for him now, Bret. I'll wait."

Racing to the court room, Bret cracked the heavy door open and peered carefully inside. Alton Dean was still on the stand, and Mr. Ingersoll was questioning him concerning some writing that was displayed on a wide screen LCD monitor in the front of counsel table. As his eyes swept over the pentagon-shaped chamber, they fell on the only red-headed male he could find, in the back and to the center. He returned to his station in the hallway, and placed his phone to his ear.

"He's in the court room near the back," Bret whispered with hand cupped over the bottom of his cell.

"I can't believe the balls of that guy. How far is Dane through Alton's examination?"

"I can't be sure, but I think he's nearing the end. He's had Mr. Dean on the stand for about forty minutes now."

"All right, we don't have long, then. We'll be right over. I'm very uneasy about Patterson being there, especially with Thompson's phone call and all. You sit tight, and let Dane know somehow that we're coming."

"Right, Miss Pemberton. Goodbye."

Bret swallowed hard. His stomach was all butterflies, and he felt the strong undertow of something very strange swelling, building pressure just beneath the surface of this trial. He stole into the courtroom as inconspicuously as he could manage, taking his position next to Dane's chair at counsel table once more. Dane was just finishing up the presentation of the technical looking material on the wide screen monitor, and stood in the circular area between defense counsel table and the bench, wielding a laser pointer. He was, it seemed to Bret, perfectly in his element. Bret did his best to sit patiently, becoming so absorbed in Dane's command of the courtroom that he nearly forgot his mission. It was only a couple of minutes before Dane leaned over the table for a last-minute check of his notes, then, with a studied nonchalance, uttered the words, "Pass this witness, your Honor." Without a moment's hesitation, Bret edged his chair close to Dane's and cupped his hand to his ear. "James Patterson is in the gallery," he whispered. Mr. Thompson, Rowalter's Mr. Thompson, just left to make a phone call to someone named 'Mr. Harte' from Rowalter. I followed him. During the call, he mentioned something about Mr. Patterson...I'm not sure what, but it seemed as though he knew Patterson." Dane listened raptly, his right ear all the while straining to concentrate on the cross-examination of Alton Dean, which Nathan Smith had just commenced. "I just talked about it to Miss Pemberton by phone. She says she is coming right over."

Bret had barely finished and was resuming his position when Dane heard the 'whoosh' sound of the big courtroom door closing and his eye caught sight of Jenny Pemberton slipping stealthily down the defense side aisle. She had a data disc in one hand and a stack of photos in the other. Dane's eyes briefly met hers, and in that fleeting second he knew that something big was in the air. Jenny took her seat beside him and, with Alton's cross-examination still in full swing, began scribbling something to him on his yellow pad. Dane read the words upside down. They said simply, "PATTERSON'S IN ON IT."

Dane thought Smith's cross of Alton was pretty basic, which stood to reason since, after all, Dane had made the feds' case for them. So, with only a slight break in concentration, he jotted back on the corner of his pad, "How so?" Jenny seemed poised and ready with a response. She wrote, more deliberately this time, "numbers on bottles in Reggie Andrews photos match those on secret hospital video."

The condensed phrasing left much out, but Dane filled in the gaps; or at least most of them. "*Secret video???*" he scrawled back.

"Jon Newcombe provided," came the answer. Dane hesitated another long moment, processing the information.

"Snitch?" he wrote?

"Yup." she responded.

Dane could barely contain his astonishment. Despite his disgust for Patterson since the house explosion, he'd had him pegged for the straight-as-an-arrow type. The fury that welled up within him now was a mixture of personal hatred of the vengeance variety, and the sort of contempt that one reserves exclusively for a traitor. He stuffed the feeling down deep inside his gut, but maintained a controlled exterior, impervious to Jenny's piercing stare. Nathan Smith's examination dragged on for another half hour, characterized by questions that had Dane yawning. Basically, he was just culling for even more detail the material that Dane had already elicited on direct. No bombshells remained to drop. Dane had, in one coup de gras, made his own client look like the murderous cesspool of corporate greed that it clearly was, and committed the unpardonable sin: gutting his case and his client in the process. And the heck of it was, it felt good...oh so incredibly good.

"Counsel, any redirect?" Judge Fitzhugh peered over his glasses.

"Just one question, Your Honor."

"Proceed."

"In light of all you've seen, both while captive at Rowalter and from your own independent inquiry, do you have an opinion as to what would happen if this drug were allowed to be sold for pharmaceutical use in the United States?"

Nathan Smith shot up. "Objection, Judge. This witness is not qualified as a scientific expert. Inadmissible opinion testimony."

"I'll allow it," growled His Honor. Judge Fitzhugh's face reflected impatience.

All eyes turned to Alton Dean, who paused to reflect, then carefully chose his words. "It would cause millions of people to become hopelessly addicted, and perhaps be hailed as a miracle drug by some. However, it would then ravage the population with a level of death and suffering not seen since the Black Death." Alton's words hung in the air. A look at the now-packed gallery told Dane that it'd had the desired effect.

"We pass the witness, Your Honor."

"Re-cross?"

"Nothing further from the government, Your Honor," answered Smith.

"In that case, Mr. Dean, you may step down, but you are not excused, since I understand you are still in government custody. The court will stand in recess for 10 minutes."

Counsel and the press and gallery stood in unison while Judge Fitzhugh and his entourage exited. Before the door to his chambers had shut, Dane and Jenny virtually ran down the aisle to the war room Doc had staked out for them previously. Someone had clearly tipped off the press, since several reporters nearly tackled Dane as he fought his way through the rear courtroom exit and down the hall.

"Mr. Ingersoll, can you comment on why you put on testimony adverse to your client, Rowalter Industries?"

"No comment."

"Mr. Ingersoll, did you sabotage your client's case deliberately?"

"Mr. Ingersoll, can't you get in trouble with the bar for taking a position adverse to your client's interests?"

"No comment. Let us through, please; we have work to do."

Their questions pierced him to the core, but Dane shut them out of his consciousness as he muscled his way through the crowd to the war room. Doc and Jenny were already there, with the DVD cued up and ready to play. Heinz, who had just arrived from checking Natalie into her new quarters, stood at the end of the table looking eager. A group of photos were spread out on the table, depicting stacks of boxes. Safely behind the door with everyone crowded around the small table, Jenny nodded to Doc, who hit the 'play' button. All eyes trained on the T.V. screen. First, they viewed the hand that reached up in darkness and emptied the bottle into Natalie's I.V. bag. Then, repeated rewinds of the numbers appearing on the brown bottle in the hospital. On frame 36, which correlated to 2:20:36 a.m., Dane could clearly make out the alphanumeric, Lot 45: 3-5-7-9-Z. Next, Jenny slid in the disc she'd gotten from the investigator. She quickly cued it up to the spot where Reggie had entered Patterson's garage. She let the disc play at normal speed to give Dane the sense of the place. Dane watched the camera pan the area, then pause on some open boxes filled with thousands upon thousands of product labels bearing the word

"PHENYLZANADIOXIDETETRACHLORAMINE". The camera then zoomed in to focus on tiny fractional numbers appearing on the corner of each label.

"Lot numbers," commented Jenny out loud. Dane grunted his tentative approval.

Jenny began narrating, and slowed the tape speed down to a crawl at the point where Lot 45 began appearing on a group of labels.

As the footage concluded, Dane said, "OK, it's good, I admit, but where's the smoking gun?"

"Hold on to your horses," said Jenny, with a knowing smile. She slid three photos across the table to Dane, who spread them out in front of him. "The first photo," narrated Jenny, "is of two keys found in the office desk drawer in the home of James Patterson. Notice the word appearing on the key chain." Dane had already picked up the faded word *"truck"* scrawled in black ink on the key chain tag. "The next two photos," Jenny continued, are of the inside flap of one of the boxes near the garage door in Patterson's garage." Dane studied the handwriting on the flap, which also bore the handwritten word, 'truck.'

"The handwriting appears to be the same," Dane observed.

"Exactly." smiled Jenny smugly. "Reggie Andrews took the serial numbers off the truck keys and made duplicates, then found the truck in an abandoned warehouse parking lot on the edge of South Dallas."

Jenny nodded at Doc, who slid a third and final disc into the video deck. "This is one we didn't even know existed until we visited Reggie's office this afternoon." Dane felt the intensity of multiple sets of eyes fixed on the flat screen TV, which now flickered momentarily before displaying a box truck parked in a remote lot, illuminated by a single flood light. A hand, presumably one of Reggie's helpers', appeared and inserted a key into a padlock on the rear door latch, then raised the sliding door. The hand trained a flashlight on the inside of the cargo area, revealing stacked rows of boxes of PZT. Scattered randomly on the floor were some empty bottles. The camera zoomed in on the bottles, displaying the numbers on each label, in succession. The fifth number clearly displayed "Lot 45:3579Z".

"Yes!" said Dane exuberantly, pumping one fist.

"I thought you'd like it," gloated Jenny.

"The dirty bastard," grumbled Heinz, disgustedly.

"Where do we go from here?" queried Jenny.

"Well, this is very juicy stuff, but obviously doesn't add anything to what's already in evidence about the characteristics of PZT. We need to get this into the hands of law enforcement." Dane's voice settled into a more serious tone.

"But who?" asked Heinz. "I can tell you that if you give it to the FBI, they'll back their man...cover it up. Patterson's been with the Bureau a long time, and I think he's squeaky clean, till now."

"I don't care if he's Mr. Clean himself, he's committed attempted homicide, illegal international drug dealing, and is an accessory to kidnapping, not to mention conspiracy and obstruction of justice. And don't forget the car bombing, Heinz."

"Believe me, I haven't!" Heinz winced in fresh pain at the memory.

"How is Reggie at testifying, Heinz?"

"Superb. I've seen him back up his work very well several times on the witness stand."

"Good. I think this trial is about over. The feds have what they need, and now we have what we need. All we need to do now is get it into the right hands. We go back in there, rest our case, and decide what we're going to do with Patterson." Doc, Heinz, Jenny and even Bret all nodded their approval. "Let's get back in the court room." Dane served as point man of a phalanx of legal eagles who struggled upstream against the tide of obnoxious reporters still flooding the corridor. He slipped through the doors a dozen "no-comments" later, red-faced and panting. As the Judge called the court to order, Dane stood even before his Honor had a chance to finish the words.

"Are you ready to proceed, Mr. Ingersoll?"

"Quite so, your Honor. However, it will not be necessary for Mr. Dean to testify further. The Defense rests." A look of surprise flashed momentarily in Judge Fitzhugh's eyes, but fled almost as quickly as it came. Dane knew that Judge Fitzhugh had already connected the dots. Why prolong the "agony of defeat?" Dane had been defeated before, but never had he fallen on his sword. Yet, somehow, he didn't feel at all badly that he'd done just that. Never had he hated a client quite so much as Rowalter.

"Very well, then. Does the United States close the evidence?" The Judge asked this with raised eyebrows and a tone of voice calculated to communicate that any other evidence would be an utter waste of his time.

"Rest and close, your Honor" said Nathan Smith, appearing rather disappointed at how easily his opponent had laid down his arms.

"Rest and close, your Honor," echoed Dane.

"In that case, there being no evidence before this court supporting the safety and reliability of the drug PZT, this court hereby grants the injunction requested by the Government. Rowalter Industries shall forthwith be enjoined from any import, distribution, or sale of any kind, directly or indirectly, of the drug commonly known as PZT within the United States of America. A written order will be forthcoming to the parties within 72 hours. Mr. Smith, if you wish to submit a proposed order before then, please have it to me by tomorrow morning. Court adjourned."

CHAPTER THIRTY- FIVE

Dane and crew exited the dank emptiness of the federal courthouse and walked slowly, directly into a crisp and cold winter's night. It was already almost dark, but the reporters were still swarming like bees, each hoping to put the story into the late evening newscast as 'breaking news.' Dane didn't exactly feel much like heralding his defeat, so he sent them all away with a brusque "no comment." When the last of them had resigned the effort, Dane's group made its way to a distant lot where he had parked his car. Each member of the trial team slowly trailed off to his car, one after another, exchanging thank-yous. Doc bade his farewell, indicating he had a plane to catch back to the coast. Jenny gave Dane a big hug and a smile, lingering just a moment too long to be appropriate before walking to her car a block away. In a moment, all that remained of the trial team were Dane and Heinz. Dane was exhausted. The thought suddenly occurred to him that he'd been unable during the trial to ask Heinz any details concerning where Natalie was, how Susan was and so forth. So he asked. Heinz had just begun to answer when the crunchy sound of shoes on gravel made them both glance up, startled. It was none other than James Patterson, flanked by two agents on either side.

"Mr. Ingersoll. How are you this fine evening?" Patterson's half smirk was worse than nauseating.

"Couldn't be better, now that your partner Rowalter Industries has crashed and burned. What's your business here, Patterson? Shouldn't you be out chasing some good guys?" Dane couldn't—no, wouldn't—disguise his contempt. "Doing a little insider trading, or poisoning children, perhaps?"

"I think you know why I'm here," Patterson said without breaking stride.

"No, he doesn't, Patterson," said Heinz. Exactly why *are* you here?" Heinz fingered something inside his jacket pocket as he spoke. Patterson's men saw it and tensed up, looking ready to pounce until Heinz returned his hand to his side, empty.

"Let's just say you have something I want." Patterson's gaze never wavered from Dane's.

"Oh? And what might that be?" Dane sneered, playing along for the moment.

With a sweeping motion of his arm, Patterson dismissed the agents flanking him on either side. Obediently, they fanned out to positions about a hundred yards distant. Patterson lowered his voice perceptibly, but spoke in a calm, measured tone.

"I've been watching you, Mr. Ingersoll. And so has the Bureau. We know, for example, that you've been trafficking in illegal pharmaceuticals yourself. Sort of a 'payment in kind' from your client. A little extra 'bonus' paid for your work, before you deliberately tanked Rowalter's case."

"That's a lie from the pit of hell, and you know it!" Dane's face contorted in rage.

"Is it? We have a reel of video and a whole gallery of photos to prove it." 'Want to see some?'" Patterson provocatively, mockingly extended a hand which held a group of photos fanned like playing cards.

Dane swallowed hard and his heart stopped. "You *planted* it, you stinking bastard, and you know it. When did you break into my house?"

"Oh, about the time your people broke into mine. Don't you think I've been in this business long enough to know when someone's trying to outsmart me? I figured some extra 'insurance' might be in order."

"So you figured you'd frame an innocent man to draw the heat off of yourself?" Heinz minced no words.

"I wouldn't put it quite that crassly, Heinz. I mean, who is a judge and jury going to believe, a twenty-year FBI agent with an impeccable record, or an oily-tongued, tassle-loafered attorney defending just one more well-heeled corporate client trying to beat the system? I think you get the picture."

"Oh yeah, only too clearly. An FBI agent who got greedy, so greedy he was willing to wallow in kidnapping and murder, for profit."

"Goodness, Mr. Ingersoll where *do* you get your imagination? If you're talking about little Natalie, any number of people could have done that, from Rowalter's top brass on down. And what possible profit motive could there be for dealing in a drug that was at least as likely as not to be banned from the marketplace? You could never prove such things, even if they were true."

"*Never* say never." The voice pierced the darkness about twenty feet away, suddenly illuminated by a flashlight. It was Jenny. *She must've seen the commotion from her car*, thought Dane. "I just have one question, Mr. Patterson. Why would you track me down and literally hand me evidence showing PZT's lethal properties, knowing that it could only jeopardize your investment?"

"That's easy. When I first was assigned to this case, I was the crusader riding the white horse, ready to shut down Rowalter for the Bureau. The other stuff came later. When I gave you the dossier that day I was squeaky clean. But a few days later the Rowalter top brass came to me with a proposition. They were worried. Get PZT approved, they said, and there was money in it for me. Lots of money...more than I ever dreamed. And if I required it, protection in South America. The kind of dollars they were talking about made my early retirement benefits look pretty silly. So I bought into it. But then something happened that really got my attention. Once word leaked out about PZT and some of its more lethal properties, Rowalter's stock value took a nose dive. And you're right about one thing: ironically, my giving you the dossier helped accelerate that nose dive. When I realized what had happened, I bought up Rowalter shares—several hundred thousand of them. I placed my bet on Mr. Ingersoll's legendary trial skills, believing that when he won the case Rowalter's sales, led by its new product, would skyrocket. It was a bet I clearly lost."

"Let me guess," Jenny's voice was tinged with sarcasm. "When Dane tried to get off the case, you started messing with Natalie."

"I may be greedy, but I'm not stupid, Miss Pemberton. There were agents guarding her around the clock, if you'll recall."

"Agents who were at your beck and call," fired back Jenny, her blood pressure rising.

"And agents who would turn me in to the United States Attorney in a heartbeat, if I did what you're suggesting."

"OK, so how'd you have it done then?" piped in Heinz.

"I'm afraid I'll have to take the fifth on that, Mr. Heinz. The point is, Ingersoll here failed us, and I want the evidence you're holding. Where is it?"

"Where is what?"

"You know precisely what I mean. The video and the photos of my house. Don't make the mistake of taking me for a fool. You just don't break into an FBI agent's house without getting footage and stills. Let me have them. Right now. Or shall I have you served with a state warrant for burglarizing my house and federal one for drug trafficking?" He motioned back to one of the agents standing in the distance as he said this.

What Dane *didn't* hear Patterson say was just as important as what he'd just heard. Dane glanced furtively at Heinz, wondering if Heinz was thinking what he was. "*He didn't mention it. "Patterson doesn't know about the hospital video!*" Heinz' and Dane's eyes locked briefly. Heinz broke the gaze first by looking downward, then broke the silence as well.

"Maybe we'll let you know what we have and maybe we won't, but first answer me just one question. Why'd you try to blow me and my partner to smithereens when we were guarding Mrs. Ingersoll?"

More than anything yet mentioned, this query appeared to cause Patterson pain, but only until he could pull himself together. "Very simple, sir. At that juncture, it looked like Mr. Ingersoll was thinking of withdrawing from representing Rowalter. That little mishap with the house explosion accomplished two things. First, it provided a strong incentive to Mr. Ingersoll to remain on the case; and second, that incident couldn't necessarily be pinned on Rowalter. But, it wasn't supposed to hurt anyone."

"How unbelievably asinine!" yelled Heinz. "Do you really expect me to believe that?"

"It doesn't really matter whether it's true or not," came a deep, gravelly voice from a place in the darkness several feet away. Startled, everyone looked around trying to place its source. That is, everyone except Jenny. She calmly stepped aside, almost as if on cue, to reveal the silhouetted figure of none other than FBI Director Henson Stockman. She smiled a bit sheepishly and whispered simply, "I thought it better to be safe than sorry." Her flashlight beam illuminated Stockman's large frame, moving slowly upward till it reached his face, where it came to rest.

"What *does* matter, Jim, is that I heard every word you said just now. I stopped counting after I figured I had enough for five federal indictments. There are other witnesses nearby who heard your statements as well. Mr. Newcombe here has given me a video recording that appears to show tampering with Natalie Ingersoll's I.V. bag at the hospital. And we've viewed another of Mr. Ingersoll's video recordings which ties a particular I.V. bag directly to bottles of PZT we found in your garage. Many more still were found in a truck to which you have the key. There's plenty enough here to support an indictment for attempted murder at the state level, not to mention federal international drug trafficking charges."

"I've got it all right here," grinned Heinz, brandishing the same smart phone that he'd had hidden in his pocket since the meeting with Newcombe. He thrust his arm out and handed the phone to Director Stockman, who nodded in return. "We also have the photographs and videos from our own investigator," said Dane, "and Mr. Newcombe here provided us with the hospital video." Newcombe nodded obligingly.

Dane surveyed the face of James Patterson. To Dane, he looked as white as a sheet, and blue at the gills, as though he was ready to puke.

Stockman turned and began barking out orders like a drill sergeant. "Agent Newcombe, please read the prisoner his rights. Patterson, get your agents back over here." Patterson meekly beckoned the four agents still standing in the shadows, who now began a steady jaunt toward the group. Dane would've paid big money for a picture of the agents' faces when they got close in, and realized just who it was who had ordered them back. Then, something surreal happened. For an eternal moment, as if all time had been suspended, Director Stockman looked at James Patterson. The other agents had just rejoined the group when Stockman broke into a strange grin and, stepping toward Patterson said, "Good work, James." In that second, Dane swore that his heart stopped beating. He watched, overcome by waves of confusion as Director Stockman took out a pair of handcuffs and pivoted on his heel to Heinz. He gestured to the agent who stood directly behind Heinz, who drew his Glock and trained it on Heinz while the Director cuffed him. All Dane could do was utter "Wh-a-a-a-t the...." Jenny was looking at him, speechless. Her jaw seemed to be dangling suspended about a yard below her chin.

"Ladies and Gentlemen," said Stockman, "I present to you the man who came within a hair's breadth of single-handedly killing Natalie Ingersoll and escaped to South America with tens of millions from the illegal sale of PZT."

"B-but, I don't understand, Mr. Stockman. Heinz has been working with us on this case ever since he left the Bureau." Dane barely got out the words.

"I don't dispute that, Mr. Ingersoll. I'm quite sure that he has. But he's also been working for Rowalter Industries, S.A., and has been funneling right back to them everything single thing you've told him. He is a very handsomely paid double agent."

Dane studied Heinz closely, who had now averted his eyes, and remained strangely silent about being arrested. "Heinz?" Silence. It was all the answer Dane needed. He grew suddenly sick at the stomach. Escorted by one agent at each elbow, his hands in cuffs, Heinz hobbled to a waiting car.

"But what about all the evidence we found in your house?" Jenny demanded of Patterson, once Heinz was out of earshot.

"Simple," said Patterson, with the look of a boy caught with his hand in the cookie jar. "Director Stockman was tipped about Heinz's planned burglary by Rick Hennings of Andrews & Hennings. Apparently, he had Rick plant some phony 'evidence' in my house to play along and see just how far this thing would go. Oh, I was fooled at first too. I thought it was an actual break-in, since I was out of town and no one could reach me to clue me in until it was over. After I returned, Director Stockman brought me up to speed. When Heinz got wind of the gold mine he thought they had found at my house, he saw his opportunity. Now that the Bureau had a high profile 'bad guy,' in its sights, it diverted attention away from him. Besides, it fit superbly with Heinz's hatred of the Bureau. I played along—all the way up to the 'confession' I gave a few minutes ago. I even made a trip to Peru to meet with the Rowalter kingpins and try to get information about Alton Dean. I figured Mr. Dean might spill the beans on Heinz while I was there, but I wasn't that lucky.

"Exactly how did you learn all of this about Heinz?" Dane wanted to know.

"Oh, several ways, but mostly through Jon Newcombe," smirked Patterson. Jon planted the camera at the hospital, which recorded the footage Heinz gave to Director Stockman just now. We isolated several visits on video from an 'orderly' who it turned out was an exact match for Heinz' body type. Also, the bottle Heinz used to fill Natalie's IV bag matched exactly the serial number on a bottle of PZT that Investigator Andrews had given to Heinz right after the break-in to my house. And the agent who seemed to be sleeping in the hospital? Well, let's just say things aren't always as they appear. Oh, and that smart phone he just gave to Director Stockman: the one with the John Newcombe meeting and my 'confession'? We sort of borrowed it one evening in an airport hotel in L.A. and had a little transmitter chip of our own placed in it. We also had a few phone taps run to Heinz' apartment, just for confirmation. He was working both sides against the middle, promising his Rowalter contact that he could deliver to them victory at trial if they paid enough cash. 'Charged 'em about twenty mil and a bunch of stock. 'Got it, too. Only one problem though: Heinz miscalculated. He really believed that once he administered the antidote to Natalie, he would become the hero. Dane would fall in line, pull out all the stops at trial, ride the White Horse and win the case for Rowalter...just like he'd been hired to do. The eggheads at the FDA approve PZT, and everyone's happy. Pretty damned naive, huh? 'Guess he'd never been a father, especially of a little girl."

It was Jenny's turn again. "I still don't get it. What about the meeting with Jon Newcombe at Elmo's today?" She fixed her eyes straight on Jon as she said the words. "You said you believed Patterson was behind Natalie's poisoning, and your tape supported it!"

"Everything I told you was gospel, except for one thing," Jon replied. I hadn't yet resolved in my own mind whether it was Mr. Patterson, or Heinz." Newcombe cast an apologetic *"I'm sorry I doubted you"* glance at Patterson as he said this. "So I observed Heinz very closely at the Elmo's meeting. He seemed just a little too happy—even relieved—about my suspicion of Mr. Patterson. But, just to be sure, I contacted Reggie Andrews and rechecked the serial numbers on the hospital tape. They matched those on a bottle of PZT that we'd planted in Mr. Patterson's garage for the break-in, the same bottle that Andrews said he gave to Heinz as part of the break-in evidence. That made it all clear.

"All right," said Dane. "So Heinz had us snowed big time. But what about the car explosion? What was that all about?"

"Oh, that," said Patterson, as though it was a bothersome, insignificant detail. "Truthfully, we had nothing to do with that. It really was executed, we believe, by Rowalter. Perhaps they were upset at the Bureau for getting involved with you and Mrs. Ingersoll. Or maybe they just wanted to signal to you how serious they were about winning the trial. Sure, it's crazy, but no one ever said they were the sanest folks around. But, if you want to know my opinion, I don't think Heinz was even dealing with Rowalter at that time. He was just trying to finish his gig with the Bureau and collect early retirement. When the explosion happened, he held the Bureau responsible. He got furious, quit, and went on a mission to teach the FBI a lesson. His motive wasn't the money at first, it was pure revenge. The money came later. But then, that's just my opinion."

"Well," said a weary Dane, "I don't know who I can trust any more. But it seems we owe you an apology. You should win an academy award for the performance you gave a minute ago."

"I'd settle for a promotion and pay raise from the Director," Patterson smiled, looking at Stockman.

"Don't push your luck," Stockman chuckled. Congress has just slashed our budget for anything that isn't directly related to Islamic State terrorism. 'Seems the world's gone crazy since nine eleven."

"Then call Jack Heinz a Radical Muslim terrorist. For my sake."

"That isn't funny. But I'll see what I can do. Good night, James. Oh...and, good work."

* * * *

Dane turned slowly and with eyes staring at the dark ground below, shuffled back to his car. Things had just come unraveled so fast, and he wasn't sure how. All he knew, and all he cared about, was that it was over. Natalie was all right, and would be home soon. Susan was safe. Rowalter would soon be history, along with their hideous drug. As he reached the car and fumbled for his key in the cold night air,

Jennie abruptly appeared. She stood no more than a foot away, her breath ascending as cloud puffs in the frigid night air.

"I just wanted you to know how happy I am about Natalie."

"Thanks. You can't even imagine how relieved I am."

"Oh, I think I can. By the way, I want you to know you were a tiger in there," she nodded her head back toward the courthouse."

"Oh, really? I felt like mush for most of it."

"No, I mean it. They don't come any better. You had the case in the bag, but you did the right thing and fell on your sword anyway. You're something else, you know?" Her hand found its way into his, and it felt soft and warm. Then, she reached up and kissed him tenderly. Too exhausted to resist, Dane let the moment linger too long. He hadn't seen it coming, and was surprised at himself. Yet, somehow it was a strange comfort at the end of the longest nightmare of his life. They exchanged good nights, slipped into their cars, and drove into the winter night.

EPILOGUE

It was 1:00 a.m. at DFW International. A week had expired since the infamous PZT trial, long enough for the Wall Street Journal, The New York and LA Times, and of course the Dallas Morning News to trumpet the rapid descent of Rowalter, S.A. into the abyss. There was talk of extradition and criminal indictments in the works against all of the top execs and, of course, the despicable FBI agent who nearly got away with infanticide. The airport was deserted at this hour, with all of the business travelers long since airborne. Only two ticket agents, a man and a woman, remained at the TransWestern Airlines counter. As the man in the brown overcoat and broad brimmed hat approached, the woman greeted him, and asked his name.

"Patterson. James Patterson," the man replied.

"And where are you flying, today, sir?"

"Buenos Aires, Argentina."

"And when will you be returning?"

"I'm not. A one-way ticket will be fine, thank you."

"That will be $969.00 one way, coach."

"I'll fly first class, please, ma'am."

"All right. That will be $1,569.00. How would you like to pay for it?"

"Cash."

The woman blinked in surprise, then regained her composure. "Very well, may I see some identification?"

The man obliged.

The lady took the cash, issued the ticket and receipt, checked two bags, and within fifteen minutes the man had cleared airport security using the TSA pre-check line. No one spotted the disassembled plastic semiautomatic pistol packed in his bag. Besides being invisible to any monitor now made, it was separated into four pieces, none of which even remotely resembled a firearm. Within fifteen minutes, Patterson was reclining in a crushed leather seat in the forward compartment of a wide body. As the jet engines roared to life, he slipped from his shirt pocket a printed confirmation from his stock brokerage. He smiled as he reviewed it:

"Short sale, January 8th, 15,000,000 shares, ROW." "Purchase, January 25th, 15,000,000 shares, ROW." "Net gain on transaction — $232,500,000.00."

A second piece of paper stapled to it showed a wire transfer for $500,000.00 to an Argentine bank, with the remaining balance transferred to a Swiss bank. Very crisp, very clean—nothing illegal. *Just doing my job, getting dangerous drugs off the market before they kill innocent people.* He smiled, sipped the wine the attractive flight attendant handed to him, and reclined as far back as the chair would go. The plane taxied, lurched into the air, and James Patterson drifted into a contented sleep.